All About
Lulu

A NOVEL

Jonathan Evison

Soft Skull Press
Brooklyn

Library of Congress Cataloging-in-Publication Data

Evison, Jonathan.
  All about Lulu : a novel / Jonathan Evison.
     p. cm.
  ISBN-13: 978-1-59376-196-7
  ISBN-10: 1-59376-196-1
  1. Teenage boys—Fiction. 2. Stepfamilies—Fiction. 3. Los Angeles (Calif.)—Fiction.
I. Title.

PS3605.V57A795 2008
813'.6—dc22

                              2007046761

Cover design by Edwin Tse
Interior design by Neuwirth & Associates, Inc.
Printed in the United States of America

Soft Skull Press
An Imprint of Counterpoint LLC
2117 Fourth Street
Suite D
Berkeley, CA 94710

www.softskull.com
www.counterpointpress.com

Distributed by Publishers Group West

10 9 8 7 6 5 4 3 2 1

For Katie

· PART ·

1

KEEPING THE PEACE

The World Is Made of Meat

First, I'm going to give you all the Copperfield crap, and I'm not going to apologize for any of it, not one paragraph, so if you're not interested in how I came to see the future, or how I came to understand that the biggest truth in my life was a lie, or, for that matter, how I parlayed my distaste for hot dogs into an '84 RX-7 and a new self-concept, do us both a favor, and just stop now.

My name is William Miller Jr., and my father is Big Bill Miller, the bodybuilder. Suffice it to say, I was never called Little Bill or even Little Big Bill. I was always called William, or Will. I bear my old man no grudge for this. Sometimes the fruit does fall far from the tree, and sometimes it rolls down the hill and into the brook, and sometimes it's washed downstream, or gets caught in an eddy.

My younger brothers, Doug and Ross, are identical twins. Moreover, they stuck close to the tree. They are the image of Big Bill: the aquiline nose, the blue eyes, the turgid smile. And, like their father, they are bodybuilders—tireless self-improvers striving for physical perfection. Not me. If I look like anybody, I look like my mother.

In spite of my status as a ninety-eight-pound weakling and my total lack of athleticism, I'm nothing short of an expert on the subject of bodybuilding. I grew up in gyms, primarily the original Gold's Gym in Venice and World Gym in Santa Monica, just minutes from the Muscle Beach of my father's youth. I know the muscle groups, the training regimens, the language, the poses. I can even tell you who won the 1979 Mr. Olympia or the 1983 Mr. Universe, because I was there. I know a great set of abs when I see them (Frank Zane), or calves (Chris Dickerson), or traps, or pecs, or deltoids. I know the acrid odor of sweat-soaked rubber mats, the iron clang of clashing weights, the tingle of sweaty back skin ripped from vinyl, the heaving and grunting and chest pounding. And none of it holds any romance for me.

My earliest memories are of meat. Enormous lamb shanks mired in beds of hardened grease. Giant carbuncled sausages, reconstituted from the vaguest of mammalian origins, glowing garish orange in the light of the refrigerator. My infant brothers were consuming meat before their teeth broke. It was not uncommon to see them padding about the house in disposable diapers, dirty-faced and slack-jawed, gnawing on drumsticks or cold hot dogs the way other kids gnawed on binkys.

I became a vegetarian in 1974, at the age of seven. My father was outraged.

"How can you not eat meat? The whole world is made of meat! Birds, cows, dogs, cats, they're all made of meat! Even fish are made of meat!"

"Well, then," my mother said. "You'll have no objection to cat for dinner."

My mother had a way with Big Bill. It's not that she outsmarted him—I could've done that—it's the *way* she outsmarted him, the way she did everything, like she was dancing with life and let life lead, doing everything life did, only backwards and in heels. Nothing seemed to disrupt her balance or upset her equilibrium. She absorbed whatever came at her.

For weeks after my avowed vegetarianism, Big Bill insisted on heaping meat on my plate.

"It's not meat, it's sausage."

He'd plop it on my mashed potatoes, park it on top of my Jell-O, but I never touched it. If I'd inherited one trait from Big Bill, it was his willfulness. And so I grew up on a steady diet of powdered mashed potatoes. Once Big Bill forgave me this eccentricity, he began to chide me about it, taunting me with pork chops, bonking me on the head with bratwurst at the dinner table.

"You are what you eat."

"I see, Bill," my mother said, with a wink for me. "You'd rather your son be a bratwurst?"

My father wasn't a bad guy, he just had a low threshold for weakness. Once, in the driveway in front of the Pico house, Big Bill and I watched a swallow with an injured wing mince and flutter in semicircles, flapping its good wing to no effect.

"What's the matter with it?"

"Hard to say. Something with the wing, I guess."

Watching the little thing labor stupidly with no possibility of success moved me for the first time to a desperation separate and distinct from my own. Couldn't it see it was condemned to futility? Couldn't it resolve itself to the cold, hard fact that it had no future, that it was doomed, grounded, finished? The answer was apparently yes. Eventually, the bird gave up, spent and bewildered.

Its little eyes went black as obsidians, as though the light no longer penetrated them.

"What happened?"

"Cutting her losses, I guess. She's beat."

"How do you know it's a she?"

"I don't."

She hardly moved at all after that. She just stood there dazed minute after minute like she was asleep standing, or she'd made up her mind never to move again. But I knew there was life beneath those shiny black eyes, because I could feel her little pulse beating inside me as if it were my own, and I could see her tiny breast beneath her keel feathers puff out convulsively now and again like she wanted to throw up. I'm telling you, I knew that bird's helplessness.

"What can we do?"

Big Bill gave the bird a little nudge with the toe of his sneaker. It didn't budge. "Not a whole lot."

The last thing that bird saw, or maybe she didn't see it coming at all, was the business end of Big Bill's shovel. There wasn't much blood. There wasn't much of anything. She was just flatter, and kind of twisted, and there was definitely no life left behind those black eyes. Big Bill scraped up the remains and tossed them to the curb. Life seemed at once fragile and inconsequential when you pulverized it with a shovel.

But cancer doesn't hit like a shovel. And while Big Bill continued to build his carcass up to world-class proportions, cancer began carving up my mother. It arrived in a terrible flash one rainy afternoon. She came home from the doctor's office and stood by the window deep into the night. Big Bill burnt frozen fried chicken for dinner.

In the night I padded down the stairs to the living room, where she was still at her post by the window. Tentatively, I approached her in the terrible silence, and she pulled me fast against her. I clutched her about the waist, and she ran her fingers through my hair as she gazed through the window into the night.

A month later she took to wearing a blue knit stocking cap.

For almost two years she fought without ever remitting. Cancer wasn't content to take her all at once; it wanted her in pieces. It took her left breast, then her right. It turned her skin to parchment. She grew so frail and reedy that I was afraid to squeeze her. And yet, if it were possible to die gracefully of cancer, my mother achieved that. It could cut her to ribbons and take her hair, but it couldn't make her ugly.

Her final months were an exercise in endurance. She spent untold hours in the fog with Barney Miller and Fred Sanford. The sandman was never more than a slow drip away. But I remember her voice in those lucid moments when the fog burned off, and how it didn't seem to come out of her body, but out of the past. And I remember a certain pride in being spoken to like an adult.

"Do you remember when you were just a baby, William?"

"Not really."

She smiled. "I suppose not. But somehow I thought you might, somehow you were different. Like you already knew something, William, like you brought something into this world with you. Do you ever feel that?"

"I don't think so. I don't know what it means."

"You never acted much like a baby. Not like Ross and Doug."

In my seven-and-three-quarter-year-old mind, there was something inherently ignoble about the condition of infancy, thus I took my mother's observation as high praise. I see it differently, now.

"You were a very serious baby. You hardly fussed. Sometimes I'd wake in the middle of the night to check on you, and I'd find you lying awake in your crib, quite content, staring up at the colored fish."

How well I remember the colored fish, and the promise of a material world moving slowly counterclockwise with no surprises.

"You were not a needy baby, William. Although I'm afraid I was a needy mother. Because I couldn't let you lie there on your back being content, I just couldn't. I had to pick you up and hold you, every time. You were so holdable, William. And you never fussed, bless you."

My jaw aches when I think what that must have felt like, to be coddled like something precious, to be absorbed finally and completely by another's affection. But for whatever reason, that feeling is not built to travel.

"Why do we forget?" I asked her.

"I don't think we ever forget, darling. I think we just have a hard time remembering."

Not me. I remember it all. Every detail has been preserved with cruel fidelity. So if there's anything I like less than gyms, anything I find more abhorrent than paining and gaining, it's hospitals, and those big colored Legos in the waiting room, and the pop-up books, and the fish tanks, and the cafeteria food, and the clipboards and the smocks and the chemical smell that hangs in the dead air. These things I carry with me always.

My mother's death was more of a coronation, really. A parade of cards and flowers and casseroles followed. The cards piled higher, the flowers wilted, and the four of us sat goggle-eyed around the kitchen table night after night, the only sound the sickly buzz of the overhead light.

"When are we going to have something besides stupid casserole?"

"Yeah, other people's food is gross. Everything's got mushroomy gunk inside. When are we going to have our own food again?"

"Shut up," I said.

"Why aren't we having juice? We used to always have juice."

"We're out," I said. "So just be quiet and drink milk."

Big Bill didn't say much during those first weeks. He was like a wounded elephant. You got the feeling he wished he could be small, but he was just too damn big, and too damn clumsy in his grief. All he could do to fight it was to make himself even bigger.

Six days a week we were all packed off to the gym, where Big Bill pained and gained until you could see the blood pumping through his ropy veins. The twins fell all over each other like puppies, lifting and flexing and posing in front of the mirrored walls, always under the watchful gaze of one hulking "uncle" or another—whoever happened to be between sets. I was less like a puppy and more like a lamp. I stuck to the corner and waited out the interminable hours, thankful on those occasions that I had homework to occupy myself.

On the seventh day, Big Bill rested. And that was the hardest day for all of us, because Big Bill's grief set him to wandering absentmindedly all over the house, looking for things until he forgot what he was looking for, turning on every television, burning toast, vacuuming in unlikely places. Then, one night, the geography of our family abruptly began to shift, and never stopped. I awoke in the middle of the night to find the twins standing in the hallway in matching footed jammies, rubbing their eyes and looking a little bewildered. All the lights were on. I could hear Big Bill bumping about in the twins' room, dragging something across the carpeted floor. Peeking in, I found him dismantling the bunk bed.

"What are you doing?"

He looked back over his shoulder, grinning like a wax statue. "Changing things up a little, Tiger. You wanna give me a hand with that corner post there?"

"Now? Can't you do it in the morning?"

"Why wait?"

Within forty minutes, Big Bill had moved out of the bedroom and into the twins' room. The twins moved into the office across the hall. And by three in the morning everybody was settled. But within a week, Big Bill relocated again, this time downstairs to the couch, where he slept in the flickering light of the television. The twins seized the opportunity to move back into their old room, vacating the office, which Big Bill soon claimed for himself, though he still spent most nights on the couch. When the twins reinhabited their original room, they switched bunks, so that Doug slept on the top bunk, and Ross slept on the bottom bunk.

As for yours truly, I stayed in the only room I'd ever stayed in, and I stayed there more than ever. And only once do I remember Big Bill coming to me there, though I know that he came more often—he must have. I was on my bed, lying on my back, watching the shadows of the lemon tree play across the foot of the bed. He came in and, not knowing what to do with his wounded-elephant self, stood at the foot of the bed, where the lemon tree shadows played across his legs.

"You all right, Tiger?"

"Yeah."

"That's good. That's real good." His gaze wandered about the room. Even his vision didn't seem to know what to do with itself anymore. He picked up a Hot Wheels car from the dresser and spun it between his fingers, then set it down again.

"You're sure?"

"Yeah."

"You don't feel like maybe you want to talk to someone?"

"We are talking."

"I mean somebody besides me. I have a friend, a counselor. She's nice. You might like talking to her."

"No, thanks."

He looked like he wanted to sit down, but couldn't make up his mind where. Finally, he squatted where he stood. "Well, if you ever change your mind . . ."

"Yeah, okay."

Now that he was squatting, he seemed more restless than ever, like he wanted to stand again.

"Are *you* okay, Dad?"

"Of course, Tiger. Don't you worry about me. I can take care of myself." Then, I swear, my father flexed his right bicep, as though the strength to endure grief actually resided somewhere in there. "Don't you worry about your old dad."

There is a family picture that was taken at Christmas, about nine months after my mother died. Big Bill bought everybody matching blue poly-fiber sweat suits with three white stripes running down the arms and legs, and little white zippers on the pant legs. He bought us matching tennis shoes, like Adidas but with four stripes. We're all wearing our new uniforms in the picture. Big Bill is doing a front double bicep pose with a twin dangling from each bicep. He's got a fake tan and he's flexing his smile, so that he looks slightly adenoidal. The twins are grinning like chimps as they swing on Big Bill's arms, impervious, it appears, to any imbalance in the universe. As for me, I'm standing off to the side; at least, I think it's me—a cheerless spectator with bad posture.

I'm not saying that Big Bill rejected me; it might have been that I rejected him. I'm just saying we didn't have much in common. He was a lamb shank, and I was fashioned of an entirely different stuff: powdered mashed potatoes. The twins, on the other hand, were carved from the very same meat as Big Bill, and in this way they managed to remain within his sphere of influence. But while Doug and Ross were playing with dumbbells and posing in their underwear in front of mirrors, I was living inside of myself; that is, my world was inside out. I had senses, but they were all on the inside. The sense that something was missing. The sense that this missing thing would forever elude me. The sense that forever as a measure of time no longer existed. The sense that I was *not* being watched, and *not* being followed. And finally, a sense that the universe had forsaken me, not out of malice, but as an oversight. And so I built my own universe, and I populated it with things remembered and things that never happened, like the smell of my mother's bathrobe, and the twin brother I didn't have.

And something strange happened to my voice. It became scratchy and frayed at the edges, like a prayer flag. I was a roaring mouse, afraid to open my mouth lest my big scratchy voice bring the world to its knees trembling. Or worse, laughing. My third grade teacher found my voice so disconcerting that she recommended to Big Bill that I have my throat looked into, to see if there was not some treatable abnormality: an obstruction, a lymphoma, a hole in the lung. Maybe I was possessed; maybe I'd swallowed Billy Barty.

And so it transpired that a swarthy man with an unpronounceable name who smelled of alfalfa and hot apple cider poked and prodded and generally violated my cranial orifices with lights and swabs and mirrors and tongue depressors, prattling on all the while about *great big trucks*, and *tractors as big as dinosaurs*, small talk fit for a boy half my age.

When the ordeal was over three days later, after the cultures were cultured and the X-rays inspected, the copper-faced doctor called us back into his office and explained to my father that he could find no abnormalities.

"The boy is unique. This is a blessing. With a little luck, he might one day grow into this big scratchy voice of his."

Big Bill wanted to know if meat would help.

"I'm not sure I understand your meaning."

"Tell him," demanded Big Bill. "Explain to my son, the eight-year-old vegetarian, that meat is good for you, that you have to eat meat to grow. How do you think cows got so big?"

The doctor explained that, while he was not a nutritionist, he himself was a vegetarian and what amounted to a weekend Hindu, and that cows, too, were vegetarians, a fact that seemed to impress Big Bill. He proceeded to enlighten my father regarding some cutting-edge research, which suggested that meat was very high in cholesterol and saturated fat, and might in fact increase the risk of thrombosis and heart disease. Big Bill was stymied. But how can that be, when the heart is made of meat?

And as ridiculous as it all sounds, Big Bill may have been right about meat. I wore the same school pants for nearly a year and a half after my mother died, and they never became high waters. Even my hair stopped growing. If my voice had changed again, I wouldn't have known it, because I kept it locked tight inside my chest. And I wouldn't have known what to say, anyway. I wanted only to grow backwards into something I used to be.

The twins' progress was unimpeded; they grew like prize zucchinis. Nearly three years my junior, they had already outsized me by my ninth birthday. They were giants, a full head taller than anyone else in kindergarten. Their brains couldn't keep up. I'm not going to say they were dull, maybe just unconcerned. They barreled through the buffet of life grabbing drumsticks and fistfuls of Jell-O, shouting and laughing and making friends without even trying to.

We commemorated my ninth birthday with a family dinner party at The Captain's Table, a queasily lit buffet of Homeric proportions across the street from the Howard Johnson's. Despite the nautical theme, there was plenty of real meat at The Captain's Table: impossibly big meat—mutant drumsticks, sausages as thick as beer cans, roasts as big as camels.

To see Big Bill carrying on in a party hat, waving a drumstick about like a ping-pong paddle, even if it was for my benefit, was an indignity to my mother's memory. Thus, I was snake-eyed and sullen on my ninth birthday, and I did my best to make the party a joyless occasion. And that's how I remember it: just the four of us and my dad's old training partner Uncle Cliff, a few months before he drove his car off an overpass. He wasn't really my uncle, of course, more of a stranger, really. According to Big Bill he'd once had the biggest chest in the world. But something was wrong with him. His cheeks were hollow. He looked small inside his hooded sweatshirt.

Cliff never went to the buffet, not even for firsts, which left the two of us alone at the table for most of my ninth birthday party—he with his empty coffee cup and me with my watermelon rinds—while Big Bill and the twins made continuous trips to the meat bar, the salad bar, and the potato bar, in addition to trips to the bathroom between feedings.

Cliff wasn't much of a talker either, which was fine by me. We were kindred spirits that way. He nodded knowingly now and again throughout the evening, as if to say: *Pfff. Birthday parties. Tell me about it. I hate buffets.* The cluster of colored balloons tied to the post nearest his seat kept hectoring him. He'd push them away, but as soon as somebody passed down the aisle, they'd drift back over and bonk him on the head, and cling to the side of his face.

"Balls," he said, at one point. And I'm pretty sure that's the last thing, and maybe the only thing, I ever heard him say.

Among the gifts I received upon the occasion of my ninth birthday were a set of dumbbells, a Joe Weider powdered vitamin supplement, an obscenely large vacuum-packed summer sausage from Vienna, and, from Uncle Cliff, a World Gym shirt with a cartoon gorilla holding the world above his head like he wanted to throw it.

Mostly About Lulu

My life began again the moment I met Louisa Trudeau. Without Lulu, I might never have existed again, might never have known the smell of a gauze bandage or felt the delicate winking of an eyelash against my cheek.

Arriving home slump-shouldered beneath the weight of my book bag one afternoon in February, I discovered her roosting in the breakfast nook in a swath of golden sunlight, as though she'd been delivered to me.

"Your dad's in the garage with my mom," she observed. There were a half dozen books spread out in front of her. "I'm Lulu. But don't call me Louisa. My grammy in Vermont calls me that, and I absolutely despise it. When's your birthday, anyway?"

I was afraid to unleash the voice. All I wanted to do was look at her. She was Mr. Potato Head beautiful. Nothing fit right. But somehow this girl in the yellow socks, with the small nose and the big ears and the gap-toothed smile, achieved a certain harmony, a beauty greater than the sum of its parts.

"It's all right," she said. "Your dad already told me. That you're shy, I mean. He said that you say about twelve words a day. Is that true?"

I nodded.

"That must be hard," she said. "I say at least twelve words every thirty seconds, I'll bet. Maybe even more. Sometimes my mom tells me, *honey, you don't* have *to say every single thing that comes into your head.* But I don't, really. I mean, say everything that comes into my head. Not even close."

She fell silent and turned her attention back to the book directly in front of her. "Don't you think unicorns are stupid?" she said.

I shrugged.

"Well, I sure do. They don't even make sense. And besides, there are so many incredibly diverse kinds of animals, why would you want to make one up?"

I could understand quite easily wanting to make things up, but I didn't say as much.

"Sandhill cranes are my favorite animal," she pursued. "Do you know about sandhill cranes?"

I shook my head.

"That's okay, not everybody does. In fact, most people don't, actually. They're very large birds with very long necks. They do beautiful dances and sing beautiful songs to each other. I might be an ornithologist when I grow up. That's a bird studier. I'm not going to get married until I'm at least thirty-two. And first I'm going to travel around the world at least three times." She went back to her book for a fleeting moment. "If you could go anywhere right now, where would you go?"

All I could think to say was "back." So I didn't say anything.

She looked at me kindly. "It's okay if you don't talk. I don't mind. Actually, I kind of like it. That's what my mom does for a job, doesn't talk. She's a grief counselor. People come to her office and talk about the horrible things that happen to them. Like when their wife dies or their daughter d—" Stopping herself, Lulu cast her eyes down and retreated into a very real silence for the first time. "I'm sorry," she said, unable to look at me. "I wasn't thinking about . . . I forgot that . . ."

"That's okay," I said. "Really, I mean it, it's okay."

When she heard my voice she looked me right in the eye, and I was frozen in the power of her gaze. "I'm sorry about what happened to your mom."

"That's okay."

"Do you want to sit down and I'll figure out your astrological chart?"

I swung my book bag onto the counter and took a seat across from her, a little jelly-legged. I stared unabashedly at her wild blue eyes as they scanned the pages, and her fast little fingers as they rifled through her astrology books. Never had I been so completely and unexpectedly disarmed by a stranger.

And soon I was talking. Talking like never before. Liberating my beastly voice without fear of humiliation, revealing my foibles without fear of judgment, and allowing this miracle of a girl to tickle the edges of my despair simply by listening to the sound of my voice, and something opened in my chest and tingled like a frostbitten hand regaining its warmth.

The more information she volunteered, the more her little singsong voice washed over me, the more I wanted to hear.

"I used to want to live above a gas station," she told me. "But not anymore. I still like the smell of gas, though. Just not on my clothes. What do you want to do?"

"I never really thought about it." And that was true, up until that very afternoon. But then it became crystal clear to me that I wanted to spend the rest of my days with her.

"Really? You never thought about it?"

"Not really. Maybe sometime I'd like to build something."

"Like what? Like a house?"

"Maybe. Or maybe just drive a car."

"You mean like a taxi cab?"

"No. More like maybe my own car."

"Like a race car driver?"

"Maybe. But maybe not so fast."

"Hmm. Well, you're a Libra like me, except that you're on the cusp. Libras make good lawyers, but I don't want to be a lawyer. We're supposed to be optimistic, too. Are you optimistic?"

"I doubt it."

"It says we can be indecisive, but I'm not indecisive. My mom says, *honey, you don't always have to know what you want right away, you can change your mind, you know.* But I don't like to change my mind. Are you indecisive?"

"I'm not sure."

"That's okay. My mom says, *Lu, sometimes it's better not to know the answer, because sometimes we're wrong when we know the answer.* But that doesn't make any sense to me, because if you know the answer that means you're right."

"Maybe she's talking about wrong answers."

"But wrong answers aren't really answers."

"I guess maybe if people *think* they're the right answers it's the same thing," I said. "My dad thinks the world is made of meat."

"Eww."

"But I don't. I'm a vegetarian. Not that I think the world is made out of celery or anything. I just think it's the world. I don't know what it's made out of. A whole bunch of stuff, I guess."

"We should find out," Lulu said, not knowing that the invitation was the single most welcome invitation I would ever receive, and that the mere gesture meant so much that the dead spot inside of me started to ache in a good way.

Over the next few months Lulu and her mother drove down from San Francisco almost every weekend, booking a room in the same hotel off Santa Monica. They hardly ever set foot in the room. Even their bags found their way to the Pico house. Lulu staged her things in my room, and Lulu's mom carved out a spot in the office across the hall.

Lulu's mom was Willow, a hatchet-faced but relentlessly kind woman who reached out to me continually, though I offered her little access. She seemed genuinely to want to engage me, which made me respect her even less. She came bearing thoughtful little gifts—gobstoppers and gliders—which I accepted begrudgingly. The twins accepted her without reservation, and I hated them for it.

Willow exhibited a strange influence over my father. He stopped shaving and grew his hair and started listening to Willie Nelson. She even persuaded him to pick up an acoustic guitar on occasion, something he apparently had not done since the year I was born, 1968. The guitar looked small and silly, like a ukulele perched on his massive leg. He didn't sing, but sometimes he moved his lips, and he always kept his eyes on the fret board, looking a little awkward and confused, as though he wasn't quite sure from which angle to approach the instrument. It seemed impossible to me that Big Bill ever knew how to play the guitar in the first place, that he ever had long hair or sat around beach fires wooing women, or that he burned his draft card, or ate LSD. But then there were a lot of things I didn't know about Big Bill.

We began to take weekend outings like a real family. And really, weren't we America's poster family for 1978? The widowed body-builder and his three motherless sons. The professional woman and her child prodigy. All of us piling into the silver-striped van with its orange-carpeted catacombs and tinted windows and Yosemite Sam mud flaps. Setting off for the tar pits, Laguna Beach, or Knott's Berry Farm. Carting coolers of Craigmont soda and enormous Tupperware vats of Big Bill's famous macaroni salad, which even the twins found inedible.

I'm not proud of my cruelty when I think of poor Willow forever craning her neck in the passenger seat, trying desperately to elicit some small familiarity or acceptance from me, with offerings like, *You know my real name isn't Willow, it's Mary Margaret*, or *When I was a girl, we used to go to Niagara Falls*. Why did I punish her with aloofness?

My favorite destination was Cabazon, out near the Morongo In-dian Reservation on the 10, where a man named Claude Bell—at the expense of a small fortune he'd amassed over the better part of a frugal lifetime—realized his dream of erecting a giant concrete bron-tosaurus in the arid flats of the San Bernardino Valley. He opened a gift shop in its belly, and immediately started amassing another small fortune to bankroll a tyrannosaurus rex.

Cabazon was my favorite not because it captured my imagination, but because it captured Lulu's. The way she put it was, "It's a lovely dream, because it's nobody else's." And that's how she saw the thing, not as a brontosaurus, but as a dream.

While the twins ran amuck in the gift shop under Willow's super-vision, Lulu, Big Bill, and I stood in the gravel lot, with a half dozen other people, gawking at Bell's brontosaurus.

"That's one big sonofabit—er, gun," observed my father, admir-ing the musculature of the beast's foreleg. "Can you imagine being eaten by one of these suckers?"

"The brontosaurus was a herbivore, Mr. Miller. That means he only ate plants."

"Plants?"

"Yes. Leaves and foliage and stuff."

My father was incredulous. "No wonder they're extinct."

"That was because of the ice age, Mr. Miller. Not because of what they ate."

Big Bill set a hand on her shoulder and bent down to eye level. "I'll let you in on a little secret, young lady: You are what you eat."

"That's just a figure of speech, Mr. Miller. If we were what we ate then we'd be cannibals."

Lulu had a way with Big Bill, and though it didn't occur to me then, her way was a lot like my mother's.

By the time Lulu became my stepsister in June, it seemed impossible that I had ever lived without her. And the closer I got to her, the more I knew that she was the only person I ever cared to know. Lulu was an entire population. You could string adjectives together like daisy chains and not describe Lulu. Verbs came closer: soaring, crashing, yearning, laughing, dreaming, kissing. But metaphors came closest: Lulu was a white-hearted starburst, a silver-crested wave. Lulu was the sound electricity makes.

With the addition of Willow and Lulu, our family geography was in flux again. The old house on Pico was a patient and tolerant host. No matter how we shuffled and displaced ourselves, whatever arrangement we wound up in, the Pico house always felt like the same old house at the end of the day. Willow and Big Bill moved into the master bedroom, while Lulu took residence directly across the hall from me, in what used to be the office. My heart thrilled watching Big Bill heft her daisy-dappled yellow footlocker out of the van and carry it up the stairs on his shoulder. The original trophy room became a storage room for everything that used to be in the master bedroom and the office. And in the spirit of migration, Doug and Ross switched bunks again.

I, of course, stayed in the same room as always. But it was different. The whole world changed. My universe was right-side-out, and my regular senses returned with a sharpness like never before. A new sense developed down in the very center of me—possibility. And, miraculously, even my voice changed. I no longer sounded like an emphysemic blackjack dealer from Sparks. The sound that came out of my throat was like velvet thunder riding on Caribbean breezes. My words came from a different place. They weren't words anymore; they were positively charged ions crackling out of my mouth like fairy dust. And I was a poet every time I spoke the name Lulu.

The Book of Lulu

At ten years and eleven months, I began the Book of Lulu, and the Book of Lulu was all about Lulu, nothing less than a catalogue of everything even remotely Lulu: what she wore, things she said, things she liked, things she hated—a Farmer's Almanac of Lulu.

August 29, 1979
  She wore her yellow socks again. She's getting a hole in one of them. I smelled her pajamas in the laundry room today, and I'm pretty sure that's weird. They smelled like frozen waffles.

September 3, 1979
  When I ask her about her dad, she says she doesn't have

one. She says it doesn't matter, but I think it does. I think everybody should have a father, even if it's just Big Bill.

September 12, 1979
   Big Bill was polishing the fender on the van today with a yellow sock. I didn't say anything.

By Thanksgiving, the Book of Lulu had grown to two volumes. I kept them rubber-banded together in the big drawer of my desk. But the truth is, Lulu's discovery of my secret would likely have come as a relief at that point, because if I got any fuller of Lulu I was sure to explode. And the only way to stand it was to grant myself the luxury of imagining that Lulu actually had a Book of William: an everything-for-and-about-me book. But I doubt it. I really don't think Lulu had the patience for a book about anybody.

Christmas of 1979 saw my new family in full blossom. It was the first holiday in three years not eclipsed by the shadow of my mother. No chestnuts, no sleigh bells, no snow, but a six-foot silver electric tree festooned with popcorn chains, a variegated mountain of wrapping paper, and enough meat to feed a small battalion: turkeys (yes, plural), hams, meatballs, shepherd's pie, mincemeat (the real deal), you name it. Three days before Christmas, even as the feast was being cured, soaked, thawed, and generally prepared, Lulu proclaimed herself a vegetarian, and for once in my life I had an ally in the meat resistance. While the Millers gorged themselves on all manner of fauna, hoofed, winged, or otherwise, Lulu and I ate baked beans and banana pudding for Christmas dinner.

As was the custom, Doug and Ross received identical gifts, but fought over them anyway. Big Bill got them football helmets in the largest size. They still didn't fit. Providence had blessed my brothers with enormous heads—one might even say presidential—though nothing to fill them but glands.

Christmas of '79 marked another milestone of sorts in that it was the first Christmas I ever looked forward to giving a gift more than receiving one—that is, the first year I understood "the true spirit of Christmas." The gift, of course, was for Lulu, and was not one gift, but two: a small, trim, leather-bound diary (which I prayed she would fill with private thoughts of me), and a new pair of yellow socks.

We did a covert exchange after breakfast in the trophy room, a small wainscoted den cluttered with little bronzed men in bronzed Speedos striking various poses. The walls were adorned with framed posters of Big Bill Miller's rippling personage in various states of contortion, but smiling, always smiling, the smile of a man rushing to deliver a painful bowel movement at the frantic behest of Turkish customs agents. And for whatever reason, the posters were autographed, though it never occurred to me then to ask *who autographs a picture to themselves?*

We sat Indian style in the middle of the room, a circle of two.

"You first," I said.

"No, you."

"Please."

She unwrapped the diary first. Her blue eyes smiled as she caressed the leather and turned the book over in her hands. "Oh, William, thank you, thank you. It's lovely. I can use it for my birds."

She leaned over and kissed me on the cheek. My face went hot in a flash. I could've given her gifts forever, could've made it my life's work, if only to look upon those smiling eyes.

"Open the other one," I said.

Deliberately, careful not to tear the already hopelessly maligned wrapping paper, she finally reached the socks, and her eyes were a circus of light.

"Yay, they have toes!" she said. "I've always wanted socks with toes!"

"I know."

"You're so sweet, William Miller." And she leaned over and gave me a second kiss, which loosed a cloud of butterflies in my chest.

"Now you," she said.

Lulu presented me with a flawlessly wrapped package the size of a Happy Meal. All I could do was look at it: the crisp folds, the carefully taped edges, the way the paper was pulled tight and shiny as a skin around the box. I felt unworthy of such fastidious wrapping, as though such delicacy were wasted on a boy made of mashed potatoes. It didn't matter what was in the box.

"Open it!"

I began to unwrap it carefully with clumsy fingers.

"Oh, just open it!"

The box said Tandy, so I knew it was from Radio Shack. I tore the flap open and liberated two squeaky Styrofoam bookends and pulled them apart to reveal a transistor radio.

"I already put the batteries in," she said. "It's AM *and* FM." Then, with a slight air of disappointment, she added: "I wanted to get you Bone Phones but they cost sixty-four dollars."

I flipped the radio on and it hissed like a theremin in hot oil.

"I like radio better than TV," she announced. "Everything's too planned out on TV. In radio, everything is floating in space and you get to choose. A radio is like a spaceship and you can land it in whatever world you want."

Navigating around the FM band, I grabbed little fits and blossoms of music and patter.

"See what I mean? On TV everything would have straight lines. On TV you don't do any work, you just watch. Radio is different."

I was soon in orbit around a voice on the low end of the AM band. I finely tuned the static out and narrowed in until the voice surrounded me with the warm deep clarity of bathwater. And the voice (which I would later learn belonged to Gary Owens), struck me as an awfully big voice to be coming out of such a little box, and awakened a possibility in me that would one day be the instrument of my destiny.

"I hope you like it," she said.

Can you fathom my fullness? Can you understand my gratitude? Can you see all that Lulu gave me?

Shortly after the main event—the general gift exchange, which saw the twins wrestling in a wilderness of wrapping paper while Big Bill continually bellowed "settle down"—we were instructed by Big Bill (who I can only assume was instructed by Willow) to select three of our own gifts to give to Friends Outside.

"Well, if they're our friends why don't we let 'em inside," said Doug. "That'll be my gift."

In the car, Doug cried at the prospect of giving up his Super Jock. He threatened to break the kicking leg so they wouldn't want it.

"Don't you dare," said Big Bill.

But within five minutes the leg was broken anyway when Ross tried to wrest the helmeted hero out of Doug's grip.

Friends Outside was not far from the airport. It was a big two-story wood house in a stucco neighborhood, with chipping paint and a sagging porch. Every three minutes or so the shutters rattled on their hinges as airliners thundered overhead. There was a sick willow tree out front, a giant, long past the weeping stage, which only served to make the house darker.

A hard little woman who looked nothing like Mother Hubbard greeted us on the porch. She led us inside through the foyer to a huge living room, where eight or nine kids of various ages and colors were lounging on ancient sofas or seated on the floor around a game of

Monopoly. A huge old television was on in the corner. The picture was squiggly. A few of the older kids looked up when we entered.

"These people have been thoughtful enough to bring gifts," the woman announced.

I'll never forget the terrible awkwardness of my new family bunched together in the middle of that living room like a wagon train, dispensing gifts. How desperately I wanted to run from that place: the sad crepe paper ornamentation, the joyless light, those old dusty couches. Everything about the place spoke of strained circumstances, of our casserole days.

Lulu surrendered every gift she received, including the yellow toe socks. I'm not proud of the fact that this gesture wounded me, that behind my lame smile I was gritting my teeth as she presented my socks to a black girl in pink barrettes roughly her own age. I knew better, but I couldn't help myself, because no conceivable circumstance, not even the threat of physical violence, could have compelled me to part with my transistor radio.

On the drive back home, Lulu pressed her face to the tinted window. She didn't say a word about it, nor should she have. I should have known how hard it was for her to give up those things. But in spite of all I'd lost in my short life, I still knew nothing of sacrifice.

Big Bill Down Under

~~~

My father was no emissary of American sophistication, a fact that became painfully clear within eight minutes of our arrival in Sydney, Australia, for the 1980 Mr. Olympia. I realize it's not a unique or unusual condition to be embarrassed by your father, but when, at every photo op, your father persists in peeling off his T-shirt and setting his hairless pectorals to dancing like a chorus line for gathering crowds, embarrassment threatens to become a lingering condition.

Big Bill was optimistic going into Sydney, and he had every reason to be. His back was ripped. His lower-body definition was better than ever, and while his proportions may have been slightly off (maybe a little top-heavy, though that's debatable), he looked better than in '79, when he finished fourth. His biggest improvement had nothing to do with musculature, but with his posing, which had come light-years under the tutelage of Willow. Having endured seven strictly enforced years of ballet growing up in Vermont, Willow managed to thoroughly transform Big Bill. In the past, he had simply lumbered onto the stage and bungled through a rapid succession of herky-jerky contortions, beaming like a jack-o'-lantern in heat. But Willow infused Big Bill with a sort of poetry, perhaps the same poetry that inspired her at seventeen to leave behind Mary Margaret and the pleated skirts of prep school in Vermont and head west for Big Sur with the wind in her hair.

I think I was more nervous than Big Bill. I knew the Olympia had become a five hundred–pound gorilla on my father's back, and I desperately wanted him to win it. Along with Mentzer, he was probably the favorite up until Arnold's controversial late entry.

After a five-year absence, with a movie deal pending, Arnold returned to Sydney in search of his seventh Olympia. His appearance made everybody uneasy, and even before the competition began there were whispers of conspiracy, fears that the Olympia might be compromised in the name of boosting the sport's popularity. But Big Bill kept his eyes on the prize. He didn't let the Arnold circus distract him.

In what I can only view as a rite of passage, my father asked me to oil him up before prejudging. I'd oiled up Big Bill before: at Mr. Southwest, Mr. Natural California, a couple of promotional appearances at Lee Dobbs Chevrolet. But this was Olympia, and even the ninety-eight-pound weakling in me was wowed by such dizzying heights.

In my hotel room, hours before weigh-in, I was presented with a blue poly-fiber sweat suit to match Big Bill's. I would be lying if I told you I was not proud of that sweat suit. That sweat suit distinguished me.

Upon our arrival at the Opera House, Big Bill and I left Willow with Lulu and the twins in the lobby, and the two of us alone padded down a long carpeted corridor in our matching sweat suits. And I knew their eyes were on my back—the twins, Willow, and especially Lulu—and I felt uncharacteristically significant carrying my father's bag down that corridor.

The green room smelled strongly of coconut and armpits. Nearly every mirror was occupied. We walked the length of the humid room, and my father nodded at familiar faces. Frank Zane, Casey Viator, Danny Padilla. Kenny Waller patted my head as we passed the pit.

My father took a place in the corner and solemnly began shedding his poly-fiber skin. When he was free of it, he stood before the mirror like a golden god, naked to the world but for a shiny blue Speedo full of giblets. And it was good. Soon he began to stretch and pump his arms and legs until the blood began to engorge the muscles. I stood close by, watching as though it were my job, ever ready with the gym bag, now and again inspecting its contents, folding my father's sweat suit, rolling up his towel.

When he was done stretching, he gravitated toward the pit, exchanging a little friendly banter with Boyer Coe and Tom Platz on his way. I followed him at a short distance and took my post, purposefully off to the side, and wore my game face as I watched Big Bill do a set of curls, and a set of bent-arm pullovers, and another set of curls. I told him *one more rep*. I reminded him *no pain, no gain*.

At last, he toweled himself off and said: "Let's do this thing."

As I began to oil him up, Big Bill set his attention to sizing up the competition. Mentzer looked impressive in his black banana hammock. Waller looked pale, but ripped. Dickerson was a monster. But Arnold cast the longest shadow. It was impossible to ignore Arnold—he wouldn't let you. He made a grand entrance and proceeded like a peacock to strut his plumage all over the green room, trying to throw everybody off of their game. As he made his rounds, mugging while the others prepared, Arnold kept his body covered with a cropped sweatshirt and sweatpants, leaving all but his patented biceps and forearms to the imagination.

"So, I see Big Bill is Bigger Bill for 1980. Zis is a lot of weight you're carrying, Bill. I hope you haff definition to match."

Big Bill looked straight ahead at the mirror as Arnold circled him, and I was proud of him for that. He acted like Arnold wasn't even there, like it was just the two of us. "Don't forget my delts, Tiger."

But Arnold was never good at invisibility. "And vut is zis I hear you haff new wife? Congratulations."

One thing I was learning about my new voice was that I didn't have much control over it. "Hey Arnold," I said, surprising myself. "Beat it."

Arnold broke into a wide grin, and set his hand atop my head. "Junior haff big voice. Maybe someday he haff—"

"Just leave!" I shouted, loud enough that Mentzer, Padilla, and a few others turned to see what the fuss was.

To my astonishment, Arnold lumbered off with a wilting smile and, for once, I didn't have sand in my face.

Big Bill couldn't suppress a grin. "Easy, Tiger."

A half minute later I heard Liam Halstead tell Arnold to *bugger off*, and I couldn't help but feel that I'd given him the strength.

"How are the lats?" asked Big Bill, spreading them like wings.

"Looking good," I said. "Remember to stay open when you make your turn. Don't close up too much, or your elbows will get in the way. And don't smile so hard. Breathe through your nose. Turn around, so I can get your abs."

He turned around.

"Flex," I said.

He flexed. His abs looked great. Six distinct pillows tapering into a perfect V at the waistline. I oiled between the furrows. "Turn," I said, with an edge of impatience. "Other way."

My father complied with a very content look on his face. He winked at me. "Who's gonna win this thing, Tiger?"

"We are," I said.

And oiling him up, tracing the horseshoe musculature of a tricep, the dimpled crown of an immense bicep, running my small hands over the impossibly hard rubber girth of his upper arms and shoulders, I thought he felt superhuman. His body was impenetrable. For the first time I could almost fathom my father's unwavering faith in meat.

I stayed backstage beside Big Bill until the moment he was announced. As the applause set in, he straightened up and drew a shallow breath.

"Here goes nothing," he said.

I patted his backside like Waller might have. "Remember. Stay within yourself."

He smiled. "Gotcha, Tiger."

The new and improved Big Bill Miller glided onto the stage as if he were skating on Vaseline. At center stage, he spun around ninety degrees, faced the audience, and stood at ease for the briefest of moments. Really at ease. Grinning like Ronald Reagan on Thai Stick. Though his skin was stretched beyond all capacity, like a mutant blood sausage, he looked comfortable in it for the first time ever.

Then the music began: something from Bach. Big Bill didn't hurry, he didn't force anything. He bowed his head and slowly exhaled, then rose up again like a sunflower to face the sea of flashbulbs. He stretched his arms out to embrace eternity, then eased them back in like he was gathering up the universe, and when he had the universe in his grasp, he closed his fists upon it and sent it crackling down his forearms to his biceps, which swelled until it seemed they would burst like supernovas. His transitions were seamless. Front double bicep melted into side chest melted into back lat spread. He made his mandatory poses look like tai chi. What's more, he invented poses, or I should say Willow invented poses, poses that didn't have names like "front double bicep" or "back lat spread," that had names like "starry bowl of night" and "valley brimming yellow with mountain lilies," and that looked just like they sounded. When Big Bill left the stage, both at the prejudging and the main event, he got a bigger ovation, more oohs and aahs than anyone, even Arnold.

Backstage, Big Bill was ramped up, couldn't sit still long enough to watch Corney or Platz follow on his heels.

"Relax. We got 'em," I said.

"You sure?"

"Sure. You heard them."

Big Bill leaned into my assurance like it was a campfire. "I think you're right, Tiger. I think we got 'em this time."

Had I been picking them, I would've picked Big Bill first, Mentzer second, Dickerson third, and Zane fourth. Arnold would've finished sixth behind Boyer Coe, maybe even seventh behind Roger Walker.

When Zane was announced at third, I quickly made the adjustments. Mentzer second, Miller first.

Big Bill gave me a wink, then held his chin up to greet the news.

I prayed that I would not hear his name next. I grabbed his hand and squeezed. It was Chris Dickerson, another surprise at second.

Big Bill gave my hand a squeeze, and looked impressed, and avoided looking at Mentzer as he rocked back and forth on his heels.

Tough luck for Mentzer, I thought. It was his last shot, and he finished out of the money. Though watching his reaction from twenty feet away, I could see, unmistakably, that he still thought he'd won it all.

But I knew differently.

There are moments when realities collide, when expectations become so real that there's no telling them apart from the future. Always in that terrible instant of contact, there's a chill that shoots through you, almost like a shiver, or a bolt of electricity, and something is lost irretrievably in that moment. For Mike Mentzer, it was his shot at ever claiming an Olympia. For Big Bill Miller, it was something else entirely. I wish I knew what. But when Arnold was announced as the winner in the Masters Division, something was inexplicably lost between my father and me. We would never again capture the intimacy we shared in those hours before the '80 Olympia.

Big Bill was irritable for the rest of our stay in Sydney, spitting vegemite into napkins, complaining about portions, refusing to walk through the Royal Botanic Gardens. Willow tried to finesse his ego-bone back into place for the next two days, but her patience had worn thin by the afternoon of our departure, and when he started grumbling about the length of the check-in line at the Sydney airport, she let him have it in front of all of us.

"Damnit, Bill, since when did you ever have any trouble moving on? Tell me that." She blew a few frizzy strands of hair out of her face, dragged her suitcase forward a foot or so, and growled in frustration. "You're so damn quick to just forge ahead at every juncture, until the minute your damn ego gets involved, and suddenly you're incapable of forward propulsion, Bill, you're spinning your wheels in the mud. And the rest of us are tired of getting spattered."

But it didn't stop. Something had burrowed its way under my father's thick skin. It soon penetrated the muscle and began to fester there. I'd always assumed it was failure in some shape. With hindsight, I see it probably had nothing to do with his disappointment at the results of the 1980 Olympia. It was probably just guilt.

Forever

∿∿∿

For all his improved posing and posturing, I don't think the discomfort of living was ever any less acute for Big Bill. Willow taught him poise, but she could not teach him finesse. Because, more than anything else, he liked short endings. Whether they were happy or sad, he liked them abrupt. He liked to avoid confusion. And nowhere was this more apparent than in his relationship with Lulu, where everything ended in yes.

"I'm asking you, because I already know what Mother will say. Can I?"

"Yes."

"Will you?"

"Yes."

"Tomorrow?"

"Yes."

"Can William?"

"Yes."

Yes, Lulu, yes. Yes, yes, yes. Not because it's a good idea, not because you earned it, but because, well, it's short. Nobody argues with
yes. In this way my father failed Lulu as a stepfather. He assumed no
jurisdiction over her beyond the word *yes*. What did he deny her by
never saying no? Suspense? Dialogue? I can't say for certain. Maybe
just the knowledge that her life was somehow conditional.

But then, maybe that's not fair. Maybe I'm not qualified to make
that judgment, having asked Big Bill for so little, and having accepted
no so readily my whole life. Probably I should be thanking him,
because if he'd been any more of a father to Lulu, she would have
only been more of a sister to me, and as it stood, she was so much
more. Without her, I may just as well have been silent, because most
people could not seem to hear my voice. Often when I spoke to the
twins, they looked at me like Saint Bernards. I'll admit there was a
genuine eagerness to connect in those big, dull eyes—a light of rec-
ognition that flashed now and again, causing them to tilt their heads
in wonder—but no matter how hard I tried, I just couldn't speak
Saint Bernard. I couldn't speak Big Bill, or even Willow. Couldn't
speak gym teacher, or math teacher either. I could only speak Lulu,
and through Lulu I could speak to the world.

I was willing to share anything with Lulu without fear of shame
or betrayal. There was no secret that I could possibly keep from her,
nor she from me. And finally, one evening in the trophy room, where
we congregated under the pretense of Scrabble, beneath the waning
light of dusk coming through the window, Lulu showed me everything without embarrassment. Lifting her blouse over her head and
deftly unclasping her bra, she revealed to me the milky-white protuberances budding beneath her blouse. She let me run my hands once

over them, let me heft the plumpness in the palm of my hand and run my thumb over the impossibly soft pink skin of her areolas until the nipples began to rise. Nothing that came before had ever prepared me for such a thrill. And more thrilling still was the promise of more—a lifetime of more.

Before I knew it, it was over, and she was fastening her bra. "You still haven't showed me yours," she said.

"It's not the same," I pleaded. For, indeed, there remained one diminutive hairless secret, which I was loathe to reveal, the same secret that inspired my tardiness to swim meets, which found me straggling into the locker room three minutes after the bell so that I could undress in solitude.

"It's easy just showing me your boobs," I observed. "It's different with mine."

"I'll show you more, then."

And so my fate was sealed. Lulu kept one eye on the doorknob as she unzipped her jeans and leaned back against the dresser. She slid the dark denim down with her underthings, over her knobby knees, until the cloth was gathered about her ankles and I could see a little spotting on her underpants, which I knew to be period blood. Numb with expectation, my eyes sought hers for approval, and when it was granted, I got down on my knees and gazed upon the downy hair of her lap. It formed a lovely letter V, cleft down the middle by a fleshy delicate thing, an exotic fruit I'd only dreamed of. I was so close to her lap that I could actually inhale the odor of it, the faint muskiness of a perfumed neck on a hot afternoon. I knew its softness without touching it. I did not even attempt to touch her, though I suspect that Lulu would have allowed me. I wanted to savor that for later. And that, my friends, is the mark of innocence. I could've kneeled there the rest of my days looking and smelling, and probably would have, had Lulu not prompted me otherwise.

"Get up," she said, pulling her pants up, her gaze still split between the door and her jeans.

And when the time came for me to hold up my end of the bargain, the blood went out of me, and I wanted for the life of me to disappear.

"You don't have to, if you don't want to," she said.

"But I do. It's just that . . ." Ever so deliberately, as though I were undressing for the gallows, I unfastened my jeans. "It's really small," I cautioned.

"So?"

"I mean, really small."

"Just show me."

When at last I exposed my willy to the cold air, I clamped my eyes shut, and when Lulu did not laugh, or gasp at my abnormality, I unclamped my lids to find her kneeling before me, gazing in wonder at my boyhood, which began to swell under the force of her gaze until it stood at attention like a link sausage. I flushed in an instant. Lulu tilted her head and inspected it from different vantages, but she didn't touch it.

"I think it's pretty," she said, with a smile.

Is it any wonder that Lulu earned my undying devotion? She had only to read my goose pimples, or the furrow of my brow, to know precisely what I was hoping or dreading. We sat side by side on the school bus, we ate lunch together, we made covert trips to the bathroom for the purpose of exchanging intelligence, and when we arrived home from school we passed the afternoons together in the trophy room, or in the backyard where the wind stirred the pampas grass. Did our friends think we were odd? We didn't have any friends. I was friendless by definition, and Lulu was friendless by choice. Don't you see? She chose me. And for that, I was forever grateful.

Even as the fabric of my new family began to show signs of wear—even as Willow and Big Bill began to fight over everything from

Reaganomics to Ragú, as the twins learned by painful degrees to covet their precious autonomy—Lulu and I grew together like two stalks into one plant. We invented our own language, in which every word was spelled out so that only we could understand it, and when spoken aloud the vowels were represented by a succession of exaggerated blinks, or squints—one blink for A, two blinks for E, and so on through I-O-U, and the consonants were symbolized by the first letter of the most beautiful words we could think to begin sentences with, sentences that sounded like spells or incantations, made up of English words and Spanish words and French words we didn't even know the meaning of, and it didn't matter, so long as they rolled off our tongues. If ever I were to summon the courage to tell Lulu I loved her, I would tell her like this: Blink squint blink, lullabies from the womb, blink squint blink squint, velvet throne of the goddess Inana, squint blink, Yoruba's black as night. Blink, squint squint blink. Blink squint blink blink blink.

The twins thought we were insane. Willow had our eyes examined, and as it turned out I was badly in need of glasses.

Big Bill wasn't surprised in the least. "Meat needs meat," he observed. "Why should the eyes be any exception?"

Soon I was outfitted with a pair of thick black safety frames—the only frames substantial enough to accommodate the telescopic lenses I required. The frames were hopelessly outdated, a relic from the mid-'60s. Not even Devo could save me. They had a fishbowl effect, so that my eyeballs looked huge, Martian-like. The sheer weight of the things caused my neck to ache.

The upside, of course, was that I could see Lulu better.

"Tell me again about sandhill cranes," I said, one gray Saturday in the pampas grass.

Lulu lay stretched out upon her back, staring up at the low sky. Moments before, she'd permitted me to cup my hands once more over her breasts through her cotton blouse, and with the blood pounding in my temples I had discovered, as per the foretelling of my vivid imagination, that they were now more than a handful. She had a dreamy cast about her now, as she did whenever she talked about birds, a faraway look, as though she herself had once tasted the thrill of flight. "Every year they gather on the banks of the North Platte River. They nest in the same spot." She plucked a foxtail and placed the stem between her teeth. "And when they meet their mate, they mate for life. And they do the most incredible mating dances. Leaping and jumping and craning their necks. And they do this thing where they stretch their wings way out like they're doing tai chi. The mates do these things called unison calls, which are different from all the other calls they make. I saw them on KCET. They're long and lovely and heartbreaking. Someday I want to go there," she said. "Before the cranes are all gone."

In time, our language evolved into a written form, and the vowels were symbolized by pictures of cumulous clouds, and planets with glowing rings like Venus, and spotted mushrooms, and fields of rippling wheat, and cows jumping over moons. There existed no word in our language for suffering, or cancer, and there was no word to symbolize the number one, although there existed a word for zero and a word for two, in fact there were a 118 words for two. And there was no word for apart, but there was a word for together, and when you saw it written down it was the most beautiful word you ever saw, and to hear it aloud was to hear a chorus of angels singing. And it didn't matter that I was motherless and forsaken and wore oversized glasses, or that nuclear holocaust seemed imminent. None of that mattered so long as there was Lulu to keep me warm through the nuclear winter.

"Even though I'm not going to get married until I'm at least thirty-two," she told me in the pampas grass, "that doesn't mean I'm not ever going to get married, you know. And it doesn't mean you can't always be my boyfriend until then, as long as you don't mind traveling around the world at least three times. My mom says that's the test. Traveling around the world with someone. She says that you can always see a person's true colors that way. But I doubt it would make any difference for us. Besides, we've already been to Australia, and that's halfway around the world. It's just a matter of whether you want to travel around the world three times. If you don't, that's okay."

"Don't worry, I do. At least three times."

"That's good. I figured you would. I think it would be better that way, with both of us. That way we'll always have four eyes."

"Six," I reminded her, tilting my glasses.

And the truth is, I doubt whether I would ever have seen much of anything if it weren't for Lulu, because, no matter how corny it sounds, she really taught me how to see. She taught me not to look past things, not to take them for granted. She taught me to look at things until I saw them differently.

"Things are changing all the time," she told me. "If you look hard enough, you can see it happening."

The Hot Dog of Despair

~~~

Lulu went to cheerleading camp in Vermont the summer after sophomore year, which was perhaps the most un-Lulu thing she ever did, and, I suppose, in that respect, the most quintessentially Lulu thing she ever did. She was going to stay with her grandparents in Burlington for the better part of the summer.

"It's not like I'm never coming back," she told me in her bedroom the afternoon she found out. "It's just summer."

"I know. But what am I supposed to do? It's not fair." I was alluding to the fact that while Willow was planning to fly out and join her for a month, I was being forced to stay behind without any good reason.

"Sit down," she said.

I sat down beside her on the bed.

"Look at me."

I looked at her.

"Quit moping and think of the adventures we'll have to talk about later."

"I don't want to have my own adventures."

"Then we can talk about mine."

"But I want to *be* there for them."

She smiled, a little sadly, I thought. She brushed my greasy bangs off my forehead and gazed into my Martian eyes. "Don't worry, you will be."

I was sentenced to six interminable weeks at the gym that summer watching Big Bill take yet another run at the Olympia. The fallout from the '80 contest had soured me forever to the charms of bodybuilding. Even if the summer of '84 had promised some form of rekindled intimacy with my father, I probably wouldn't have wanted it. I argued that at fifteen I was old enough to stay at home alone, but he made me go to the gym anyway.

A lot of the old faces had disappeared from Gold's. Waller was gone. Corney and Padilla were gone. Platz was still holding on, but something was happening to his face—it looked rubbery, like something stretched too far. Boyer Coe was still around, though I'm pretty sure he was dyeing his hair. There were a lot of new faces, young serious guys. The gym was different, too. Cleaner. Quieter. Softer around the edges. Guys weren't cranking Sammy Hagar like they used to, they weren't jumping around and hooting like sex-crazed baboons. The place even smelled different. Less like armpit.

By then the twins were already old standbys at Gold's. They'd reached puberty years prematurely, and were well on their way to muscle-bound by the summer of '84. Doug wore a mustache before his thirteenth birthday. Ross opted to shave his. Their lats were so overdeveloped that their arms would not hang at their sides—they jutted out a good foot and a half from their torsos. They walked through life like gingerbread men, trumpeting farts and grinning broadly at their own fetid bouquet. Their Adam's apples had outsized their brains. If ever I wished to turn my universe inside out again, it was that summer. But my outside senses were achingly clear. I remembered every clang and every belch and every sweaty fart that smelled like lasagna. I remembered every grunt, every wallow in sexual retardation, every pussy hair band the radio blared that summer. To this day I can hear every battle cry of *no pain, no gain* as though somebody were still shouting it in my ear.

My lone occupation during those interminable hours at Gold's was the Book of Lulu, which, in its fifth year of existence, had grown far beyond the earmarks of a healthy compulsion. It numbered seven volumes by midsummer.

July 12, 1984
Actual conversation between Doug and Ross today at the gym:

Doug: Knock it off, faggot!
Ross: You're a faggot.
Doug: No, you are.

Ross trumpets a fart.

Doug: Chew your food, ass-wipe.
Ross: You're an ass-wipe.
Doug: No, you are.

I thought life without Lulu would be like drowning. But drowning sounds peaceful. I slept in her bed again last night. Her pillow still smells like her.

It soon became apparent that something was amiss in Vermont. There were nightly phone calls from Willow, which Big Bill always took in the master bedroom, talking mostly in low tones. I eavesdropped as best I could.

"You're the one who—now, just hold on a minute, here . . . Well, that doesn't mean that—of course, I don't blame her, and I don't blame you for—let's not blow this thing out of proportion . . ."

But the proportion apparently had been blown. The calls got longer, the tones lower as the summer progressed.

"How do you know? She said that? Jesus. Yes, of course . . . of course! No, I don't think that's a good idea. I've *told* you why. This doesn't concern—well, it doesn't *have* to, then. You're the grief counselor . . ."

I grilled Big Bill for information, but he refused to disclose anything.

"It's nothing."

"Is everything all right? Is Lulu okay?"

"She's fine. Just growing pains. It'll pass."

The more I pressed him, the less patient he became.

"Everything is *fine*. Now, drop it. Pass the macaroni."

But everything wasn't fine. The calls continued, the tones remained hushed. Once, I stood outside Big Bill's room in the darkened hallway, with my ear pressed into the slight opening of the doorway.

"That's ridiculous," he said. "What makes you think the incident has anything to do with it? Of course I haven't told them. We've *already* discussed that. Well, that conversation is just going to have to wait. No . . . no, I don't expect I'll be changing my mind. Yes, of course I am, of course I do. Damnit, you were complicit too, Mary Margaret, you can't put this squarely on my shoulders. Of course I do . . . yes . . . of course . . . I understand that. Put her on."

I heard the bed creak. Big Bill heaved a heavy sigh. When he started speaking again his voice sounded weary. "Lulu, honey, I know you don't want to talk about it, but—I'm sorry about that, honey . . . Yes, I know, please don't—I understand you're angry, sweetheart. There's just so much to expl—just let me expl—I understand . . . Yes, I'd feel the same way, I don't blame you. I blame myself. But there's a lot more to this than . . . Oh, sweetheart, please try to understand. I know this sounds—I know it sounds like—I will make this up to you, but you've got to let me, honey, you've got to under—Lulu, honey, stop. Please just tell me what happened . . ."

The bed creaked again as Big Bill got to his feet. I could hear him pacing the floor. "It *is* a big deal," he said. When his pacing brought him closer to the door, I pulled back a half foot and swiveled my shoulders around to avoid detection.

"You're damn right it's a—Well, that's not what your mother said. Now, damnit, I want the straight stuff here, I wanna know just what exactly . . ." Then he closed the door, and his voice went muffled, and his pacing carried him toward the farthest corner of the room.

In the morning I confronted him again in the breakfast nook.

"Nothing's the matter. You're blowing this out of proportion. Lulu quit cheerleading camp, that's all. Just some growing pains, teenage girl stuff," he assured me.

I had no choice, really, but to toe the Miller party line—that is, to act like a traffic cop at the scene of a grizzly accident. But just because I toed the line didn't mean I believed it for a minute—not when words like blame and complicit were being whispered behind closed doors. I rounded up the usual teenage suspects—shoplifting, drugs, alcohol, sex, vandalism. But none of them quite suited Lulu. Maybe she really did quit cheerleading camp. Maybe she lied about it. Maybe she was skipping out on camp and Willow found out. Whatever it was, it would pass. Lulu would probably get grounded when she returned. Big Bill would go soft on her. Everything would return to normal. The important thing was just getting Lulu back to Santa Monica before I went out of my mind.

The longer Lulu was away, the harder it became to summon her face, her smell, her touch. At night I dreamed of her, or fell asleep trying. I pursued her down dark corridors, through vast labyrinthine cities of my own invention. But I could no sooner catch her than I could roll over and touch her.

In the waking hours I summoned her image with the help of photographs. I sat on her bed and buried my face in her bras, inhaling her scent and leaving spots of drool on the cloth. I lay belly down on her bedspread straddling her pillow with my loins on fire, caressing her breasts, sucking her nipples. And when I took my relief from the unbearable pressure of Lulu, it felt altogether different than when I thought of anyone else, and the fruit of my labors sprang from some deeper well.

July 16, 1984
    She still hasn't written. I felt so bad today that I ate a hot
    dog. Then I puked in the van. The twins called me a wuss.
    I called them faggots. They said no, you're a faggot. I said
    no, you are. Something's happening to me.

Something was indeed happening to me. After three weeks without Lulu, without so much as a phone call or a postcard, I'd lost my voice. My beautiful velvet thunder, like everything else, had forsaken me, and nobody seemed to notice. When I opened my mouth to speak, the positively charged ions did not crackle out like fairy dust. Instead, negative space streamed out of my mouth, swallowing anything in its path, and then it collapsed back inside itself and filled me with nothingness. For two weeks my hair stopped growing, my nails stopped growing.

My dream cities disappeared without a trace. No thought, no smell, no image could arouse my erotic life force. My young manhood wilted, and the seeds of my possibilities dried up before I could ever sow them.

Then the postcard came. I gazed upon its beauty without ever looking at the front of it. Every inch of the card was filled with tiny writing. Participles dangled into margins, sentences curled around stamps. It must have been five hundred words. I began reading it as I mounted the stairs.

Right away I could tell something was wrong. The tiny words ran their circuitous route down the card, forming sentences, then paragraphs, but there were no cumulus clouds, no fields of wheat, no lovely incantations. This was not our language. These were only words. Regular words.

Electives

⌇⌇⌇⌇⌇

Lulu was not the same when she returned from cheerleading camp in Vermont. She spoke without blinking and squinting, and her words were antimatter. She was distant and cheerless and she'd started smoking cigarettes.

September 1, 1984

Yesterday was the worst day of my life until today. Today Lulu acted like I was a total stranger. She wouldn't tell me about Vermont. She wouldn't tell me about anything. She won't even look at me. Maybe she knows about the bras, or about me humping her pillow. Maybe she even knows about me sucking her nipples.

I was determined not to annoy Lulu. But in the end I was weak. One evening when Lulu snuck out for a smoke, I followed her, and fell into stride with her along the shadow-dappled sidewalk in the direction of Joslyn Park.

"Do you hate me?" I said.

"Of course not. I could never hate you. I'm just not myself anymore."

"Why not?"

"It's not a matter of why. It's just a bad case of the way it is. It's nothing personal, William. It's just that if I were you, I wouldn't count on me anymore. Not like you used to."

"What do you mean?"

Lulu puffed on her cigarette. I could tell she felt my eyes staring holes into her. She looked off in the other direction. "I mean, I don't think I can be the same kind of friend to you anymore."

"And what kind of friend is that?"

"I just want to be more like, I don't know, I guess, like a sister, you know?"

I was eerily silent.

She stopped along the sidewalk. "What's so wrong with that?"

I kept walking.

Lulu hurried to catch up, and threw her cigarette into the gutter. "Well?"

"Well, what? What am I supposed to say to that? I don't even know what it means." I was practically foaming at the mouth. "You're acting all weird and distant and you won't tell me why," I growled. "It's like you're trying to give me this whole breakup speech, and you won't even tell me what I did."

"You didn't do anything."

"Then what's so wrong with me?" I picked up my pace and focused my sullen gaze straight ahead.

Lulu stopped again. "Nothing," she said softly. "Nothing's wrong with you. It's me, William."

Some dark cloud had settled on our household. There was a palpable tension between Big Bill and Willow, and Lulu and Big Bill, and Lulu and Willow. In short, between Lulu and everybody. It filled the dining room like bats. It hovered about the kitchen like a cloud of mosquitoes. Even meat could not appease it. It was a force of gravity that compacted words before they were ever uttered, a force so strong not even the twins were impervious to it. There was no farting at the dinner table. No wrestling in the stairwell.

I was so full of dread, so helpless and uninformed, that I actually looked to Big Bill for guidance. I caught him as he was packing his gym bag, a strapped canvas sausage that lay on the bed.

"Dad, what happened?"

"What do you mean, Tiger?"

"To Lulu."

He started rummaging through his sausage bag. "Oh, just girl stuff. We've been over this already at least three times. You know how they are. Probably jilted by some polo player."

"It's not that. Something's wrong."

"Look, Tiger, teenage girls are moody. I wouldn't read too much into any of this."

"What should I do?"

"Nothing," he snapped, but softened immediately. "Nothing." He set his massive hand on my shoulder. "Give her a week and she'll be back to her old self."

I think Big Bill really believed that. There was no use pushing him further. I'd only run into a short ending. I ducked his massive hand and turned to leave.

"Will?"

"What?"

"Well, son . . ."

"What already?

"Look . . . you're fifteen years old."

"Uh, yeah?"

"I'm not exactly sure how to put this, but . . . Don't you think it's time to start . . . well, you know, spreading your wings a little?"

I was determined to make this hard on my father, though it was plenty hard for him already. "My wings?"

"Well, I mean . . . socially? Don't you think that maybe you're just a little too . . . attached to your sister?"

"She's not my sister."

"Well, it amounts to the same thing. You should make some friends, branch out, join a club or something."

"A club?"

"Well, yeah, sure. An after-school thing. Chess club, or something. Debate club. Don't they have a support group for vegetarians? The point is, branch out. Give your sister a little—"

"She's not my sister."

"—give her a little space. Let her work through this stuff. How'd you like to start lifting?"

"You've got to be kidding."

"Why not?"

"*Why?*"

"Okay, then. Fair enough. Just tossing that out there." He zipped up his sausage bag. "But you better do something, Will. It's time. You need to give her some breathing room from here on out. Otherwise, you're going to suffocate her."

He slung his sausage over his shoulder and patted me on the back on his way out of the room.

Come September, Lulu and I wound up with one elective together— Sociology, with Kimball. Though there were empty seats both directly in front of and behind me, Lulu sat all the way across the room in the back corner. I must have craned my neck at least two dozen times per period to look back at her. Surely she felt my Martian eyes upon her, but she never let on. Then, craning my neck one afternoon, I caught her looking at me, just once, just for an instant, and I felt the tickle of a flame in my sternum, a dry lump in my throat.

The next day she wasn't in class. I waited for her at her locker between third and fourth periods.

"Where were you?"

"I switched to Current Events."

"Why?"

"Gaskil's easy," she said, opening her locker. "I had her for Civics last year. Besides, Mr. Kimball weirds me out."

"You're lying."

Her face was hidden in the locker, where she rummaged about mechanically.

"What's wrong with you, Lu? What did I do?"

"Just stop! You didn't do anything, okay?" She shut her locker and turned to face me, but avoided my eyes. "Excuse me," she said, pushing past me. "I need to get to Lit. Berringer's on the rag."

At home, sheer repetition managed to cut through some of the tension around the dinner table, but the dark cloud lingered. Lulu wore the same clothes three and four days in a row. She was forever locked away in her bedroom, often so quiet that Willow would tap on the door. "Lu, honey, are you in there?"

"Yeah."

Two weeks before homecoming, she quit the cheerleading squad.

"Please," she said. "Those girls are cheerful like sharks."

She showed no interest in boys, or other girls, or dancing, or flying, or learning to drive.

"Drive where?" she said. "There's nowhere to go."

Even a Sunday trip to Cabazon could not awaken her appetites. We had to coax her out of the van.

"Please, can we go now?"

And the farther Lulu drifted from all of us, the farther we all seemed to drift from each other.

Yet, through it all, her grades never slipped. She made honor roll junior year.

As for me, I may have looked studious in my twelve-pound glasses, but I couldn't bring myself to study. I'd sit on my bed, a fifteen-year-old atop Tony the Tiger sheets, surrounded by other childhood relics—action figures and View-Masters and dented cylinders of Tinkertoys—and I would gaze across the hall at the band of light leaking out from beneath Lulu's door, and I wished I could go sit closer to it, wished I could set up camp in the hallway and warm my fingers in that stripe of light.

For the first time since I'd known her, Lulu's life was a complete mystery to me, and I was a complete outsider, and the more I accepted that fact, the more all of life seemed like a cruel mystery to me. And the more I sat looking at that closed door, the more it seemed that doors were closing all around me.

When my grades started falling, the guidance counselor called me into his office for a visit. His name was Mr. Pitts, Larry Pitts. The kids called him Harry Pitts. Not everyone was assigned to Harry Pitts; there were also two other counselors. I think Lulu was assigned Ms. Huson. Harry Pitts wasn't a bad guy, really. At least he didn't try to act like an expert on teenagers, he didn't say things like awesome, or talk about when he was sixteen, back in the Bronze Age. When he talked to you, he seemed interested. Not concerned, like everything was a big deal, just sort of interested, like he'd never heard your story before, like you were a puzzle and he wanted to figure you out, even if it meant skipping lunch. He had thinning red hair, slightly wavy, which he swirled atop his bald spot like soft-serve ice cream. He wore flannel dress shirts, even when it was ninety degrees out, and those desert boots everyone else stopped wearing in the '70s. He was always kicking his desert boots up on the desk, and folding his arms, and looking at you as though the real answer to his question were written on the bridge of your nose.

"Everything okay at home?"

"Yeah. Everything's fine."

"Any changes around the house? Anything different between your folks?"

"No, nothing like that."

"Any recent transitions in your life? New house, new friends?"

"No."

"Have you got a lot of friends?"

"Some," I lied.

One of the things I liked about talking to Harry Pitts more than to most adults was that he seemed satisfied with short answers. He didn't overextend a subject. He tried to draw you out in little yes-no increments. He was interested in hard data. He wasn't one of those guys who was going to hand you a pillow and tell you to pretend it was something else.

"Why don't you tell me about your F in history."

"It's boring."

"How's that?"

"It's already over. What's the use?"

"Hmm. Okay. I guess I can see that. What about the D in gym?"

"I hate gyms."

"Yeah, me too. So then, what *do* you like?"

"Not much."

"Girls?"

"Not really. Not in general, anyway."

"A specific girl, maybe?"

"Maybe."

"Do you want to tell me about this person?"

"Not really."

"Fair enough. You're sure?"

Just how big a loser was I? The school guidance counselor became my friend. I talked with him three times a week. I ate lunch in his office sometimes. I was his favorite puzzle. He started figuring me out after a few sessions.

"Any progress with the girl?"

"No."

"Have you been giving her some space like we talked about?"

"Yeah," I lied.

"That's good."

"What about History? How's that coming?"

"The same. Maybe a little better."

"How's it working with Health instead of Gym?"

"Better."

"Good. Still thinking about the girl a lot?"

"Yeah."

"Do you think she's thinking about you?"

"How should I know?"

"Yeah, hard to know something like that, I suppose."

"Okay, yeah, I think she's thinking about me," I said. "She has to be."

"What makes you so sure?"

"I don't know, the past."

"You mean like your history?"

"Nice try, Mr. Pitts. It's not old enough to be history. It was just this summer. And besides, it isn't over."

"So, why don't you tell me how things are different now?"

"Uh, you mean, like she barely talks to me?"

"What is it you want to say to her?"

"I don't know. I mean, I guess I'd like to know what happened, but I wouldn't even ask her. I don't want to have some big talk. I just want to talk like we used to talk."

But there was nothing I could do to win Lulu's favor back. No song or dance would arouse her slightest curiosity. I invented whole systems of logic to help explain what happened to us. How can I explain my compulsion, except to say that it was the most natural thing in the world, as involuntary as an itch. I checked the mail diligently. Lulu received nothing. No phone calls, either. I followed her at school, lurking around corners, staking out her locker between periods. I watched her eat her lunch from across the cafeteria—that is, when I wasn't eating lunch with Harry Pitts.

One day I tailed Lulu from Current Events to Lit, then from the AV room to the portable behind the gym, where fifth period she T.A.'ed for Mrs. Melendez in Special Ed. I pressed my face to the narrow rectangular window and watched Lulu drift around the room in her baggy sweatshirt, dispensing charcoal pencils, passing the math ball around the circle. While I was watching, Anna Burke, the big fat retarded girl who always smelled like papier-mâché and wore one of those furry-collared coats no matter what kind of weather it was, stood up from her seat and started blubbering. There was milk all over her face, and dried boogers all around her nose, and she was really going nuts about something. Mrs. Melendez went over and tried to calm her down, but that only made her worse. She began stomping her feet and plugging her ears. She was screaming so loud that I could hear her clearly through the walls of the portable.

"Nooooo," she was yelling. "Nooooo." She was saying other stuff, but I couldn't decipher it through all the snot and the screaming and the excitement.

Then, for a second while Anna Burke was freaking out, I thought Lulu saw me at the window, because she walked right toward me, until her face was only four or five feet from my own. But all she did was turn off the light, and the room went gray, and Anna Burke calmed down immediately. Lulu went over and began stroking her big broad jacketed shoulders, and talking to her softly, so that I couldn't hear what she was saying, but whatever it was, it had a soothing effect on Anna Burke. Within fifteen seconds she was smiling. Lulu pulled Anna's handkerchief out of her coat pocket, and I remember thinking it was probably crusty. And she wiped the boogers and the milk from around Anna's face, and she kept talking softly to her the whole time. Finally, Lulu gently coaxed Anna to sit back down, and then pulled a chair up next to her. Together they looked at Anna's workbook.

I stood there for ten minutes fogging up the window, wishing I were retarded, and I sensed that the terrible day had finally arrived when Lulu could no longer feel my eyes upon her.

In the mad jumble of the corridor between classes, Lulu was always alone. She convened with no one at her locker. She ate her lunch alone. She walked to the bus alone. And I knew she was alone in her room. Clearly, it wasn't somebody else that stood between us.

The conclusion was inescapable: It was me. She had outgrown me and all of my flaws—my cowardice, my clinginess, my general lack of grace. Somehow she had managed to see past my veneer, straight through to my black little heart. The bigger world of Vermont had revealed something to Lulu. She had crossed some threshold and left childish things behind. And while she was away, she saw me for what I truly was: a toad.

"Have you ever considered that it's not you?" Harry Pitts wanted to know.

"Yeah, I have."

"And?"

"And I don't know. What else am I supposed to think?"

"Well, have you ever thought that this girl is going through some uncomfortable changes of her own, and maybe she's confused, or frightened?"

"Of course I have."

"And?"

"And, if that's the deal, I want to be there for her, because she needs me."

To this day, I can't see why Harry Pitts indulged my obsession. He must have believed me, or just been intensely curious. Or maybe he had an obsession of his own. He must have felt that there was something there to be recaptured, or rekindled, something worth saving, because he never went out of his way to discourage me, he never told me to wave any white flag.

Nothing

~~~

I'll admit that I never gave the twins much credit. I always regarded them as one person. The notion that Doug and Ross somehow shared a brain between them, or at least the better part of one, helped account for the fact that they were largely controlled by their ids. There wasn't enough brain to go around. Something had to move all that flesh. The notion that their brain was spread thin also made it easier to forgive the twins for their Neanderthal ways. Who could blame them for wrestling in stairwells and farting in libraries, when they had only half a brain?

As I saw it, not only did Doug and Ross share a brain, but they shared a will and a common destiny. I always imagined them at fifty, still living together in a one-bedroom apartment with bunk beds in Glendale or Cerritos. Maybe they'd own a gym together, or a carpet cleaning business. They'd still punch each other and call each other faggots. But they would always exist as one. Ross was no more separable from Doug, in my mind, than the holes were separable from a block of Swiss cheese, or the skin was separable from a hot dog. Even if Doug stood alone in front of me, Ross was there like a phantom appendage.

Among the 118 words Lulu and I invented for the number two, we assigned a specific word to describe the oneness that is two, or the twoness that is one—that is, the particular togetherness that characterizes identical twins and, in rare instances, lovers. Loosely translated, the word was: *it.* And Doug and Ross had *it*, which meant they were never alone. Maybe it was impossible for me to conceive of separating *it*, because I'd always wanted it, as long as I could remember, and when I found Lulu, I wanted to be absorbed by her, whether to free myself from the responsibility of being myself, or just to bask snuggly inside her Luluness. Being driven from that garden was hell. To walk away from such a state, I reasoned, would be insanity.

One afternoon I came home and found Ross in the living room, alone, just sitting. No television, no Atari, no steak sandwich.

"What are you doing home? Aren't you supposed to be at the gym?"

"I don't feel good."

"No pain, no gain," I observed dryly.

"Screw you. Why don't you go have some alone time with your notebook?"

Ross had me there. That's when I first knew there was hope for him. But I was determined to thwart him anyway.

He had quit doing his lower-body work on Tuesdays and Saturdays. "Better be careful," I warned. "If you let your legs get too skinny, you're gonna have a hard time lugging that head around."

"It's not as big as it looks. It's just those binoculars you're wearing."

Who was this guy? Certainly not Doug's better half. Doug could never have conjured something so original. Doug would have called me *ass-bait*, and left it at that. Was it possible that Ross's brain was suddenly developing after years of atrophy? By the time he cut Thursday's ab session out of his regimen, he had even resorted to reading, for lack of occupation.

"Givin' the old lips a workout, eh?"

"Very funny. Shouldn't you be jerkin' your gherkin?"

"Do you even know what a gherkin is?" I said.

"Duh."

"Well, what is it, then?"

"Screw you. I don't have to tell you crap."

Eventually, Ross abandoned the gym altogether, and in doing so cut himself off not only from Doug, but from Big Bill. The remarkable part was that neither of them chastised Ross for quitting. Doug seemed a little afraid of Ross. At the very least, he was a little suspicious.

"What's the deal with Ross, do you think?" he asked me one day in the kitchen.

"Got me."

"You don't think . . . ?"

"What?"

"You don't think he's, you know . . . ?"

"Depressed?"

"No. I mean . . . you don't think he's an ass clown, do you?"

Was I wrong to despise my brother Doug? Can you blame me? Have you any idea what it's like to look at your own flesh and blood and wonder what happened? How you awoke in the lair of your mortal enemy?

After Ross quit pumping iron completely, he moped around the house for a few weeks, a little dazedly, not really knowing which direction to turn. More often than not he parked himself on the couch and gazed at the television set, or turned toward the kitchen and the curative powers of meat, devouring entire hams in a sitting, picking at cold chickens until nothing remained but a greasy cage. And when the miracle of meat failed Ross, and he had nowhere else to turn, he turned to me.

"What are you doing?" he said, from the doorway.

"Sitting on the bed."

"Oh," he said. "You care if—?"

"Whatever."

He sat down on the foot of my bed and started gazing, like me, in the general direction of Lulu's door.

"What are we staring at?" he said.

"Nothing," I told him. "Or what's left of something."

"Oh," he said again, and kept staring at nothing.

We stared at nothing for a long time.

"Where's Doug?" I said, just to be cruel.

"At the gym."

"So, why aren't you?"

"Didn't feel like it."

There was a hard little lump inside my chest. I wanted to laugh at him. I wanted to hate Ross for walking away from Doug like Lulu had walked away from me. Nobody should ever walk away from anyone.

"Remember when we used to go to World Gym?" I said. "When Mom was still alive?"

"I remember. Of course I remember."

"You were only five."

"I know," he said defensively. "But I still remember it."

"You guys were working out even then."

"Yeah, I know."

"Big Bill was proud of you. He used to tell Kenny Waller that you guys would win the Olympia before him."

"Waller," said Ross. "Yeah, I remember."

"He used to make you pose for Arnold and Franco. 'Show them the triceps! Let's see the crab, show Uncle Arnie the crab.' And you guys would perform like little monkeys."

Ross smiled faintly, as though it were his duty to smile.

"Goddamn, I hated it," I told him. "The gym, I mean. I hated every last second of it. I would've rather been at the hospital, that's how much I hated it."

"So you quit. So what?"

"I just couldn't give two shits. Big Bill knew it, and it really bugged him. It bugged him that I sat outside in the car and read comic books. Especially because they weren't even the superhero kind. They were just Archies."

"I can't remember," said Ross.

"He never really had much to do with me."

"I don't know," he said. "Dad's weird sometimes."

"Why did you come in, anyway?" I said.

"No reason. I just saw you sitting there, so . . . I don't know."

"So, what is it?"

"It's nothing." Then, after a pause, Ross said, "You want to know something?"

"What's that?"

"Don't ever tell Doug, and especially don't tell Big Bill."

"I won't."

He still wasn't sure if he wanted to tell me.

"I promise," I said.

"I hated it, too. I've always hated it, from then until now, I've hated it. I would've been happier if Dad were a professional roller skater or a fucking dentist."

For the first time in my life I wanted to hug Ross, I suppose for having endured something I never gave him credit for. "Why did you do it?" I said.

He paused to wonder at this himself, and shrugged. "No pain, no gain, I guess. Or maybe I was just scared."

Ross stared out into the hallway. I started picking fuzz balls off my bedspread.

"I miss her," I said.

"Yeah."

A dense silence settled in, the kind that makes your ears ring.

"Well," I said, finally. "I guess I better get busy on my—"

"Yeah," said Ross, and he stood to leave.

"You okay?"

"Sure, I'm okay. But you won't tell, right?"

"Why would I?"

"That's cool." He turned to leave, but then he turned back again. "So, I'm just wondering, what do you write in all those books, anyway?"

I almost wanted to tell him. It might have been a relief. "Nothing," I said.

"Can I read some?"

"Nah. It's just stuff."

"That's cool. I draw stuff sometimes. Doug thinks it's gay."

"Screw Doug," I said.

"Yeah, I guess you're right. So, I guess I'll see you."

"Yeah."

He turned and left.

Within a few months, Ross discovered his new self, and it couldn't have been newer or more unexpected. While Doug and Big Bill spent their afternoons paining and gaining, Ross started smoking clove cigarettes and hanging out with a kid named Regan and listening to Duran Duran. Regan became his mentor: oft quoted, perpetually emulated, but always shrouded in mystery.

"Where's your imaginary friend Regan?" I'd ask.

"Why don't you look in your little notebook?"

He grew his hair out and fashioned it after the lead singer of Flock of Seagulls.

"Looks like somebody parked the Batmobile on top of your head," I observed.

"Looks like they parked it on your face and left in a hurry."

There was hope for the kid.

Much to the chagrin of Big Bill, Ross soon started wearing eyeliner.

"For Pete's sake, you look like a raccoon. Take that off! Why do you wanna go around looking like Boy Georgie?"

"You look like a dill-hole," said Doug.

We were hard on him, it was the Miller way, but I envied Ross for finding his new self. I wished I could find a new self, or even an old self, or any self that didn't require Lulu as the main ingredient. I wished I had the guts to wear eyeliner, or swagger around with overgrown muscles. I wished I had some goal, some *thing* or ideal besides Lulu to drive me forward all of my days. I wished I had the desire or passion or vision to build something, *anything*—a rippling body, a body of knowledge, a goddamn brontosaurus in the middle of the desert. Something bigger than myself. But I had only one crippling desire.

The ripples of change brought about by Ross's transformation soon set the geography of our household in motion again. Ross moved into the trophy room, and everything from the trophy room—that is, everything from our former lives—was moved into a corner of the garage, where it soon hosted black widows. Doug, haunted perhaps by a phantom top bunk, yearned for new surroundings, and soon traded rooms with Lulu, who could never resist change.

Thus deprived of my precious swath of light, I turned instead to my radio, always mindful of the fact that it had once been a gift from Lulu. The radio became my bridge to the outside world. I lay on my bed, gazing at the walls of my prison, while Ken Minyard on KABC spoke to me like a best friend about life, the universe, and

Mexican food. About history, politics, and current events. And like a best friend, I listened. That was my role in the relationship, to listen. I had other radio friends: Casey Kasem, Rick Dees, Shadoe Stevens. The radio was never about the music for me, it was always about the voices, the power of those invisible supercharged voices to lift me out of the morass, to open windows of possibility and understanding, to conjure by the force of incantation and verbal charm any image, idea, or opinion, and also their amazing power to persuade. Ken Minyard made a Bobby Kennedy liberal out of me and I didn't even know who Bobby Kennedy was. Casey Kasem taught me the fine line between sincerity and schmaltz, by dancing that line with the cascading polyrhythms of his voice. But more than anything else, it was the companionship these voices afforded me in my solitude that kept me tuning in.

While I had many friends, I had but one god, and that was Vin Scully. His voice rode crackling upon invisible wavelengths from St. Louis and Chicago and New York, arriving in Santa Monica to transform my bedroom into someplace altogether grander. And when Vin's voice streamed out of my radio, the words were no longer weightless and invisible; they expanded like paper flowers until they had form and weight and color, and they smelled like pretzels and green grass and some place far away. Vin Scully spoke to me like a father. Sometimes I wished he *were* my father. I know that sounds weird. But I'm just telling you how it was.

Everything Is a Crock

Willow in the mirror: eyes like eight balls, crow's-feet, a slackening of skin. She uses her reflection as an instrument for self-improvement, creating shadows and highlights, employing various implements. Plucking. Dusting. Applying. Sighing, stopping, looking hard at the mirror. Where? Past her reflection? Inside herself? Into the future?

Perhaps more than anyone, Willow tried to make me comfortable throughout adolescence. She reached out to me unfailingly, without ever crossing the line. She was kind and considerate. She yearned for me to confide in her, she longed to gather me up in her arms and squeeze me reassuringly, I'm sure of it. Yet, I never allowed her access. I could have made things easier on her by accepting her love unconditionally, like the twins did, and certainly she deserved as much, but I punished her instead with aloofness, and with silence.

Meanwhile, the dinner table became a nightly theater of contention between Lulu and Big Bill.

"Reagan's a senile boob," she'd say. "He's got a head full of stale jelly beans."

"You're wrong about that," Big Bill would say, with a mouthful of turkey sausage. "He's decisive. Something that peanut farmer your mother voted for wouldn't know anything about. Reagan works fast."

"So does Maalox."

One benefit of all this antagonism was that it was contagious.

"Cherry Coke sucks ass," Doug would say. "It's for butt pirates and Girl Scouts."

"Yeah, well, it's way better than Coke Classic. Coke Classic tastes like Tidy Bowl."

"Does not!"

"So then, you know what Tidy Bowl tastes like?"

Doug was powerless against such guile. He walked into every trap, he seemed to have a genius for it. And as he strained to formulate his comeback, he was like an overtaxed robot. You kept expecting to see smoke come out of his ears.

"You're the one that drinks Tidy Bowl, ass-munch."

It was nice to see the twins fighting again, even if it was a massacre now that Ross had grown a brain.

Willow rarely jumped into the fray. She ate with her eyes down, not so much like she had given up the fight, rather like she was silently nursing some grudge, letting it build up strength. You got the feeling she was a ticking time bomb at the far end of the table.

It was hard to believe that our family dinners even endured this rough period, that we all didn't take our plates and go our separate ways. It would have been so much easier than watching Willow simmer, and Big Bill bluster, and Lulu, the bright little girl who once lit up our lives, express her new disgust for the world.

"It's no wonder we have AIDS and acid rain and a giant hole in the ozone," she said. "The whole world is lying to itself. *Especially* us."

Nor was Lulu's disgust limited to the present—it extended well into the past.

"The Summer of Love was a crock."

"Now, wait a minute, here—"

"Oh, give me a break. Only two percent of the young people were actually *doing* anything. The rest of them were just posers—getting stoned and pregnant and living a complete lie."

"I was there, young lady. And let me tell you something—"

"Tell me this: Where are your hippies, now? Where are all your enlightened revolutionaries? Selling tennis shoes on television and driving Beamers, that's where!"

"I don't drive a Beamer!"

"You don't make enough money!"

And always after dinner, after the arrows had been slung and the pot roast had been whittled down to a pool of blood and gristle and some greasy string, after the vegetarian contingent had finished picking at their lemon Jell-O and baked beans, we invariably did go our separate ways, and that was the most heartbreaking part of all.

I suppose it's ironic that in a household where closed doors were rapidly becoming the standard, mine alone stayed open the last years of high school. Nobody wished more than I did to isolate himself from the supreme disappointment that lay just outside the doorway. The only reason my door stayed open was the possibility of glimpsing Lulu on her way to the bathroom, or the increasingly improbable prospect of some reconciliation between us.

Willow and Big Bill were less discreet than ever. Occasionally their discord rattled the rafters. I could hear it over the play-by-play of Vin Scully or Ross Porter, and at such times I thought of Lulu sitting in her room in her puddle of light, pondering God only knew what, and Doug, still ducking when he sat on his disjoined bunk bed out of habit, and Ross out somewhere smoking clove cigarettes and wondering how any of us fit together, wondering whether we were ever intended to be together in the first place.

One night Big Bill and Willow spilled out into the hallway. Big Bill was trying for one of his patented short endings.

"Just drop it!" he shouted.

"I'm tired of dropping it! We've been dropping it for years."

"That's enough!"

Tudor is ahead in the count one and two. Pedro singled sharply to center in the first. St. Louis playing Guerrero to pull.

"Some things you can't put behind you, Bill. That's a truth. Sometimes the best thing you can do is put them beside you."

"Don't play grief counselor with me. I'm not your client anymore."

Tudor peers in for the sign.

"It doesn't make sense not to," she said. "You admitted it yourself. There's no 'too late,' Bill."

"Well, it used to make sense! It made good goddamn sense, until you decided to—"

"I didn't decide it, my conscience decided it for me! My daughter decided it! And it's about time that—"

"Stop right there!"

Guerrero calls time, steps out of the box. LaValliere wants to have a word with Tudor.

"I'll never understand you," said Willow bitterly.

Tudor does not have his good change-up tonight, but he's been spotting his fastball well, and making good pitches when he needs to.

"Stop, right now," ordered Big Bill. "I'm dead serious about this."

"That's pretty serious, Bill. You ought to take a look at that."

"Don't psychoanalyze me, *Mary Margaret.*"

"Quit making me, then."

Denkinger out to the mound to break up the conversation. Nothing stirring in the St. Louis bullpen.

"I'm done with this," said Big Bill. "I've been done with it for years."

"You never started."

"It's done. I've moved on, damnit!"

And with that, Big Bill stormed down the hallway to the stairs.

Now Guerrero steps back in the box and LaValliere is ready with the sign.

"You moved to Santa Monica, Bill!" she called after him. "That's not the same thing!"

The Governing Laws
of Lulu

Thanks to the miracle of contact lenses, Clearasil wipes, and a growth spurt the summer of '85, my seventeenth birthday found me less ugly than my sixteenth, fifteenth, and fourteenth birthdays. I was neither toad nor prince. My nose was flat. The walls of my nostrils were too thick. I was kind of oily. But I had good teeth and cowish brown eyes (no longer three times their natural size), and my velveteen voice was dreamy to anyone who could hear it. I was in the neighborhood of happy and well adjusted for the first time since freshman year. I even stopped eating lunch with Harry Pitts. I could not put Lulu behind me, so I put her beside me.

Big Bill bought me a banana-yellow Plymouth Duster with spring-loaded seats, an ocean of black dashboard, and an AM/FM stereo. I took scrupulous care of that car, washing and waxing its yellow shell until it glistened like a mango, buffing the hubcaps, shining the nylon interior, vacuuming the black carpet, tweezing snags and loose fibers out like a surgeon. My credibility, real or imagined, depended on that car. Moreover, my psychic and emotional mobility depended on it. I drove the Duster aimlessly around the basin at night, listening to my beloved voices on KABC and KNX and KFI. Burbank, Glendale, Arcadia, it didn't matter. As long as I was moving, I was at peace.

That year, I kissed a girl for the first time. Her name was Shelly Beach, and I'm not making that up. Yes, she had an older sister, and yes, her sister's name was Sandy Beach. She had a brother named Rocky. Sometimes there's a very fine line between adoration and cruelty.

Shelly Beach was two-and-a-half years my senior. After she graduated in Yelm, Washington, the previous year, Shelly had moved to Alhambra to live with her aunt and earn resident status. She wanted to go to Cal State Northridge and study Consumer Sciences. In the meantime, she worked at a Red Lobster near Pasadena. That's where I met her, on one of my aimless sojourns into the night. Hungry from my travels, I stopped at Red Lobster and discovered Shelly Beach at the podium in front, clutching an oversized crab-shaped menu to her chest. She had poodle hair, and, arbitrary as it may seem, it was an observable fact that girls with poodle hair liked me. Especially larger ones. Shelly fit both descriptions. She was in fact quite big boned in all the wrong places, but then, look at me. I don't know why Shelly Beach decided to like me, whether her poodle hair was on too tight or she just felt sorry for me, but it wasn't the voice that attracted her, because I could feel the force of her infatuation before I even spoke. Maybe she liked oily skin. Maybe I smelled like Big Macs.

"Can I get you a Coke or something while you wait?"

"Uh, no, thanks." Had I known the Coke was free, believe me, I would have taken it in a heartbeat.

"Are you sure?"

"Uh, yeah. I'm good for now."

She smiled. "Okay, well, let me know if you change your mind. Sorry about the wait."

After that first steamy exchange, I started making Red Lobster a destination. I drove forty-five minutes across the southland to drink Cokes and coffee and order baked potatoes and side salads. I came at busy times, so that people were backed up in the foyer waiting to be seated. It didn't occur to me that the waitresses probably groaned at the sight of me: prince of the eight dollar check, the bottomless refill. The guy who tipped in silver stacks.

One night the place was crawling with Little Leaguers, and there was a line all the way to the door. I sat in the foyer, catching glimpses of Shelly Beach's ample figure as she came and went, clutching her oversized menus, seating families of five. Around minute six, Shelly Beach brought me a Coke.

"I insist," she said.

Three hours (and about fourteen Cokes) later, I kissed her in the parking lot. And it was not inexperience that bridled my passion, nor the wealth of her figure, but something else. Lulu, I guess.

"What's wrong?" Shelly wanted to know.

"There's nothing wrong. It's just that . . . something isn't right."

"Yeah," she said. "I know what you mean."

But perfection is rare, so we forged ahead anyway, going through the motions in the front seat of the Duster until our teeth hurt, and Vin Scully and Ross Porter wrapped up the post-game show. And after that, there was silence and no more pretending. We made vague plans. Nobody had a pen, but I knew where to find her. We kissed one last time before Shelly Beach drove off in her Toyota Tercel, bound for Alhambra, and I drove off in the Duster, bound for nowhere.

After fogging up the windows with Shelly Beach, it was impossible to set Lulu aside. Without her, there would be only more Shelly Beaches, a lifetime of Shelly Beaches. And there was nothing wrong with Shelly Beach, after all—poodle hair and forty pounds notwithstanding—she only shared the common flaw of all other women in that she was not Lulu. Lulu was not like anybody else; nobody else was young and weary, nobody else wore pajamas to school, nobody else inspired such fantastic speculation as Lulu. A mythology was created to explain Lulu's inaccessibility. *She dates Jose Gonzalez from the Dodgers. She only dates black guys. She's a lesbian.*

Had I myself been capable of accounting for the tantalizing and dangerous singularity known as Luluness, I would've found myself possessing large sums of social currency at Santa Monica High School, though certainly I would've hoarded such a bounty.

September 8, 1985

I saw her four times today at school. All four times her hair was down. It used to be that if I saw her four times, twice her hair would be up, and twice it would be down, or at least three times up, and one time down. I like it better up, but the point is it's like she doesn't even care anymore. It seems like she could be anything she wants, but she doesn't want to be anything.

September 12, 1985

I'm starting to like her hair down, sorta. And the really sick part is that she looks so damn pretty when she's sad, like she's smaller, or something, like this little delicate thing. That sounds totally gay, I know. But she does. Even if she were happy again, I wouldn't mind if she looked sad.

Then Lulu found somebody to confide in. Namely, Scott Copeland, the "young drama teacher" who let his students call him Scott. I watched helplessly from afar as he lured Lulu in with the promise of maturity and understanding, leaning casually in the doorway in his pink sneakers and his skinny black tie, like some new-wave refugee, not saying anything, really, just listening, nodding his head, fingering his mustache, and smiling sagely.

As a rule, I've never trusted guys named Scott. I can't say why, exactly. Scotts have done nothing personal to earn my distrust or arouse my suspicions. It's just a hunch. I've never trusted forty-year-old men in sneakers, either, so I had every reason to distrust Scott Copeland.

One day I passed him in the hallway, and he patted me on the back.

"You're Lulu's brother aren't you?"

"Stepbrother," I mumbled.

I kept walking, and he fell into stride with me, like we were old buddies.

"She's a neat girl," said Scott.

"Neat?"

"Yeah. Talented. Smart."

I was determined not to have this conversation. No way was I going to empower old Scott by letting him get chummy with me. But he just kept at it.

"She says you're the smart one. She says you've got this amazing voice. Let's hear it."

"Fat chance," I said.

"You ever think about coming out for drama?"

"Never."

"Why's that?"

I stopped in my tracks. "Well, frankly, Mr. Copeland, *Scott*, because of guys like you: old pervs with sneakers and ponytails trying to get into everyone's pants all the time."

He just smiled at me, cool as a cucumber, and nodded in appreciation. "You're funny," he said.

The guy had balls, I had to give him that.

"I'm serious, Scott. I've got my eye on you."

His mustache twitched. He may have been suppressing a laugh.

I looked him right in the bridge of the nose. "I don't know if Lulu has told you anything about our dad, *Scott*, but the guy could eat the Hulk for breakfast, okay? And you don't look much like the Hulk, get it?"

That one made him smile. The hot seat was like a butt massage for this guy. He was perfectly relaxed, calm like a cobra. And what he said in response to my veiled threat defied all explanation. In fact, I simply had to write it off as bizarre coincidence, or else the implications were just too staggering to ponder.

Patting me on the back, he said: "Easy, Tiger."

I had thoroughly underestimated Scott. His audacity flew in the face of all logic and convention. His flirtation with Lulu remained overt. He seemed almost to be taunting me: having her stay after class to work on monologues, walking her down hallways, sharing laughs, giving her books, all the while knowing that my eyes were upon him. Once, he even winked at me. To this day I don't see how he got away with it. It was like he wanted to get caught.

One afternoon he gave Lulu a ride home on his chopper. Clearly, that was crossing the line. If only Big Bill had been home. I watched Lulu dismount the bike at the curb, take her helmet off, and shake her hair out with a smile. That was the worst of it, the smile. He made her smile. When was the last time I'd inspired such a wonder?

If I'd been a bigger person, if my love for Lulu had been true and unsullied, generous, expansive, unconditional, I would've been happy for her, I would've been grateful for this sensitive Prince Charming in pink tennis shoes who managed to draw Lulu out from under her rock. But show me love without conditions. And besides, I would have been giving that dirtbag Copeland way too much credit.

I intercepted Lulu in the stairwell, and blocked her way like a sentry. The smile was long gone. "Where've you been? It's quarter to five."

"Move," she sighed.

"I wonder what Big Bill is gonna think about you getting rides home on Copeland's chopper?"

"He isn't here, so I guess we'll never know. Can I please get by?"

I stood my ground, a hand on each banister. "Maybe I should tell him," I said.

I'd be lying if I told you I wasn't drunk on power blocking her path, dangling the key to her fate in front of her like some cruel medieval jailer.

"Go ahead," she said, pushing right through my outstretched arm and up the stairs without looking back.

"Don't worry," I called after her. "I wouldn't."

September 21, 1985

Today she painted her toenails. I saw her laughing by the tennis courts, and I wanted to throw a rock at her, or a bouquet of wilted flowers. Does that sound psycho? She was talking to Kathleen Topping, only the biggest slut at Santa Monica. Popular, though. The Dodgers lost again. Valenzuela walked six. At least someone's happy.

September 27, 1985

My birthday. We went to Arby's. I had the beef and cheese with no beef. Then we went to Doug's wrestling meet. Doug pinned a kid with really bad acne. Lulu got me some headphones. I thought about hugging her, but I didn't hug anyone else. She looked beautiful eating her Big Montana. I made her laugh once.

October 1, 1985

Saw her today talking to Scott in the hallway. But it looked to me like Scott was trying to brush her off. He wasn't really looking at her. I know it makes me a jerk, but I felt really good when I saw that. I wanted Lulu to feel bad, and I know that's wrong, even though Scott's a perv and everything.

October 3, 1985

Lulu has been really bummed the last few days, and I'm sure it's because of the whole Scott thing. She hasn't been staying after class, or even practicing her lines. I know it seems like I should be happy about that, but it makes me sad at the same time, not only for Lulu, but for myself. It sorta feels like I'm giving up by not being happy.

My notebook was at my side always, a trusty old companion, a confessor, a dog to kick. It was not a body of work, it was a vessel, a heart, the place I stored all the emotions I didn't know what to do with—a gathering place for all of my unshaven affections and battle-weary defenses. I took it with me on my nightly sojourns in the Duster, up to Mulholland, or south to Redondo Beach, where I parked somewhere secluded and scribbled like a mad genius under the dome light. I filled volumes, and ferreted them away with the others under lock and key. My notebooks went to the bathroom with me, followed me from room to room. I fell asleep with them in my clutches. And I was ever scrupulous in protecting their secrets. As a rule, I never left them lying about—if they were not in my possession, they were securely locked away.

October 9, 1985

It happened. I left my notebook by the bathtub upstairs, just for a minute, and when I went back to get it, the door was locked and someone was in there. The shower was running. I knocked, and Lulu said, I'm in here. But it didn't really sound like she was in the shower. I just about shit myself. My heart was pounding like cannibals were beating it around a fire. I had that feeling of terror and delight I used to get whenever I knew I was going to get in trouble by Mom. That sounds pathetic, I know. But that's kind of the feeling I got. This flood of opposite emotions, like when a cold front hits a warm front. When Lulu came out she had a towel around her head and her big fuzzy bathrobe on, and her big fuzzy slippers with the plastic googly eyes. She smelled like the Garden of Eden. She looked pale. Beautiful, but really pale, like my love had drained all the blood out of her. There was something sort of soft about her expression, except her eyes were stiff and she couldn't look at me when she passed. She passed so close that the sweet smell of her wafted right up into my lungs, and I swear to God I just wanted to fall down on my knees and beg for something, mercy maybe, or forgiveness, or maybe just for the chance to smell her again.

The Bend of Break

The first time Lulu cut herself was two days after the discovery of my yellow notebook. It was an accident, she told everybody, a collision between the side of her face and the sharp edge of a locker door, and nobody but me had any reason to doubt her. The cut left a scar: a fleshy, pink promontory about two inches long, starting below her left earlobe and running a jagged, diagonal course toward the middle of her face. Though visible at a considerable distance, Lulu made no attempt to hide her disfigurement; in fact, she began to wear her hair pulled back behind her ears, off her face. But the scar only enhanced her beauty in my eyes. Her perfection was now held in balance by a thin pink line.

A week or so after the first incident, as the story goes, somebody launched a lit cigarette in the pool parking lot, and the cherry end struck Lulu like a missile under the right eye, so that when the burn healed it left a raised semicircle. But this deformity didn't deter me either, for now I could read the suffering and turmoil like hieroglyphs on Lulu's face, and they fascinated me, even if I couldn't make sense of them. I understood implicitly that I was the cause of Lulu's suffering, but I couldn't decipher how I'd caused it. I can't deny that I felt somewhat redeemed by her anguish, and empowered by my ability to inspire it, and I'm not proud of that. Nor am I proud of the fact that I didn't contrive some form of intervention.

It's no great wonder that Lulu's suffering managed to escape Big Bill's notice, but the fact that Willow (a grief counselor, no less) could not intuit Lulu's emotional distress, could not read it on her face and arms, or at any rate did not act upon it, still mystifies me. Or if she did see it, why didn't she react? Or was she so deep into Big Bill she couldn't see anything else?

Lulu stopped coming home at night. She spent a lot of nights at Kathleen Topping's, or Shannon Stovel's. She began hanging around with snotty Westwood kids who played tennis, friends of Kathleen's. Boys named Daryl and Troy and Chad who drove Jags and Porsches. Sons of doctors and prominent entertainment lawyers. They were known collectively as "the Benders," a self-appointed moniker bespeaking their proclivity to "party hardy," even on weeknights, for days on end, with cases of Heineken and eight balls of cocaine. I don't know how Lulu, of all people, endured their shallowness, any more than I understand how she gained their acceptance.

Lulu could have possessed any of them, could probably have possessed their fathers and their uncles, for that matter, but Troy was the one she dated, by far the ugliest Bender, and probably the richest. He was stooping and acne-riddled, but the world was his oyster and he'd probably end up eking out Cs at Princeton and driving convertibles for the rest of his life.

I met Troy one afternoon in the jaws of our downstairs hallway, where a half dozen family portraits hung in a cluster near the base of the stairs. I could hear Lulu rummaging around in the kitchen, while Troy viewed the photographs with what appeared to be something less than mild interest. He seemed perfectly comfortable, a little bored, but not impatient.

"Who are you?" I said.

"Troy," he said, extending a hand.

I left him hanging. He played it off pretty gracefully, just letting his hand wilt. "So, you must be Will."

"Must be."

"Lulu's in the kitchen packing sandwiches. We're gonna jet up to the observatory and have a picnic."

"Jet?"

"Just an expression. It means we're—"

"Yeah, I think I got it. That your car in the driveway?"

"Sort of. My dad's, actually. But he never drives it. You can jet around the block a few times if you want." He threw me the keys.

I didn't even try to catch them. They caromed off the banister and landed near the foot of the sofa. "No, thanks," I said. "The Duster might get jealous."

Once again, Troy played off my rudeness pretty well. He noted the position of the keys for future reference, but didn't go pick them up right then. Instead, he turned his attention back to the family photographs. I had to admit, for a stooping guy with acne, he was kind of a player. Lulu liked them decisive. At least he wasn't forty and wearing sneakers.

"Your sister's hot," he observed.

"Excuse me?"

"Lulu, I mean. I guess since she's your sister it probably doesn't count."

"She's not my real sister, and she looks like Mr. Potato Head."

"Yeah, she kinda does. She's got a great body, though."

Just then Doug walked in the front door, left it open, and farted to dramatic acoustical effect in the foyer. "What's up, knob-gobbler?" he said to me.

"The water level in your brain," I said.

"Good one, ass-bag. It doesn't even make sense."

"I'm Troy," said Troy, extending a hand.

Doug farted again. "So?"

Ross straggled through the open door in Doug's wake, piloting his Batmobile hair safely under the threshold. "Ach, what stinks?"

"Maybe it's your upper lip," said Doug.

"Yeah," I said. "Or your imaginary friend Regan."

"Go die," said Ross. "At least I don't talk to my radio."

Troy followed the volley around the room like a pinball. I had to wonder how it all measured up to life in Westwood.

Lulu emerged from the kitchen with a grocery bag. "Let's jet," she said, without breaking stride.

Troy scooped up the car keys on his way out.

If, by dating Troy and cavorting around west L.A. with preppy hedonists, and by mutilating herself, and by not coming home, Lulu's intention was to deter my adoration, she succeeded only in torturing and embittering me. The more unworthy her consorts, the more I esteemed her. The uglier she made herself, the more beautiful she appeared. Because the power of Lulu's beauty radiated from some unseen center, some hot, magnetic core. And that very same gravitational pull that sucked me into its orbit like a rogue meteor threatened to destroy both of us.

The day Lulu was accepted at the University of Washington marked the end of our Cold War and the beginning of my active hostility toward her. On her way out to celebrate that night, I intercepted her in the foyer.

"Boy, you look skanky."

"I am skanky. Now get out of my way."

"Where are you staying?"

"Shannon's."

"You're going to Westwood with Troy, liar."

"We live in dishonest times," she said, pushing past and slamming the front door in her wake.

"Whore," I called her. "Bitch! Cunt! Freak!"

I was at war with the world. And I was at war with myself.

I formed an alliance with Troy, to whom I was equally cruel. When Lulu's erratic ways set his head to spinning, I let him utilize me as a confidant.

"Oh, I don't know. One minute she's fine and the next it's like, I don't know, like she's off the hook or something . . ."

I listened.

"She won't open up. I know that sounds wussy, but I'd just like to know what she's thinking sometimes . . ."

And listened.

"And it's like she doesn't even really like me, you know? Like she just sort of tolerates me most of the time . . ."

Like a grief counselor, I listened, though I never went so far as to offer Troy solace. In return, I got to treat him like shit. My voice had become a formidable weapon. I launched my invective at his insecurities: his acne, his stooping, and, cruelest of all, his inability to ever truly hold the deed to Lulu's heart, to ever be anything but a well-heeled diversion, a sugar daddy, a ride somewhere, a noth-ing. But these insults were always delivered covertly and with great tact, so that Lulu couldn't help defend against them, and so that Troy was forced to expose his insecurities to Lulu, and in doing so, remain always in a position of need, and need and weakness were one and the same thing for Lulu, just as they were for Big Bill. In this manner, I ensured that Troy would always be whatever I told him he was.

The Benders' big senior blowout was a costume party at Morgan Irving's older brother's house near the UCLA campus. I wasn't invited. Lulu was going as a dead prom queen. She painted herself zombie white with dark circles under her eyes, and painted scars and lesions on her face and neck, and wore a white taffeta dress with painted bloodstains down the front.

Troy showed up at the house dressed as Julius Caesar, but he looked more like Flavius Victor or Magnus Maximus.

"You look like a total fag," I told him quietly.

"Serious?"

"Totally."

Lulu descended the stairs. "C'mon, let's go."

"See ya," Troy said.

As they walked out the door I heard Troy ask her, "Hey, so I don't look like a total fag do I?"

I went to the stoner version of the senior blowout, even though I wasn't a stoner. The fact is, I defied all classification. I was a mystery. I doubt whether anyone had an opinion of me, unless they had poodle hair.

At the party, I stood around a dirt parking lot watching kids drink keg beer and smoke pot. I probably could have scored with Rachel Kinslow (poodle hair), but she puked on my Stan Smiths while I was talking to her.

"Oh, shit," she said. "I'm so sorry, Walter."

"That's okay," I said. "It's Will."

I scraped off the vomit on a broken cinder block and, for lack of any other purpose, gravitated toward the keg. Somebody had made off with the tap. They passed the hat. Somebody went after another.

I talked for a while with a kid named Chett who didn't even go to Santa Monica. He went to Western in Anaheim.

So-and-so was his cousin, he told me.

I didn't know so-and-so, I told him. But that's cool.

That proved to be the extent of our common ground. Chett wore a yellow Spuds MacKenzie tank top, and even though it was night, he wore Oakley wraparound sunglasses.

He wanted to know if I liked NASCAR.

I told him I liked to drive more than I liked to watch other people do it.

What about Formula One, didn't I like Formula One?

Yeah, I lied. It was okay.

NASCAR, that was the shit, he said. Dale Earnhardt was his boy. Cale Yarborough was a pussy. So was Elliot. Didn't I think?

I concurred that anyone with a name like Cale Yarborough was probably a pussy. He added Foyt to the list of pussies, and Waltrip.

Other than that, the only thing Chett seemed to want to impart to me in the way of information was that he was *Chett* with *two Ts*, not one.

"It sounds the same, but it ain't."

Chett kept offering me a bong rip, and I kept saying no, and he kept reminding me about the *T* distinction at the end of his name.

"Remember—two Ts," he'd say, and offer me another bong toke. "That's how you can remember me, two Ts."

"Got it," I'd say.

I finally relented and took a toke from his green bong, which smelled more than a little like Doug's ass.

"Clear the carb, bro. Clear the freakin' carb."

I cleared the carb, and I could feel the dumbness washing over me even before I exhaled.

After that, it seemed like a bad idea to keep talking to Chett-with-two-Ts. In fact, I was ready to effect my retreat altogether, ready to go walking somewhere dark, when Troy showed up in full costume, wringing his hands like Pontius Pilate.

After Dark

⌐∼∧∧∼⌐

She'd been acting weird for weeks, Troy explained as we tore down Santa Monica in Troy's dad's convertible. The top was up. Troy was a little freaked out, and a little drunk, but more freaked out than drunk. Moreover, his concern was very genuine. I was beginning to think Troy might take the world more personally than I ever gave him credit for. But that didn't mean I had to cut him any slack. He was still a sworn enemy, so the air I projected as we hurtled toward the Bender blowout was put-upon and a little annoyed at being torn away from . . . well, Chett. But inwardly I was terrified that something might happen to Lulu, and that I would be to blame.

According to Troy, the night had gotten off to a bad start. Lulu was nasty right off the bat.

"She was doing vodka and cranberry machines. And some bumps

with Chad and Kathleen in the bathroom. Things started getting pretty wild. She and Kathleen started making out—just as a joke, for Chad's sake—but Kathleen wanted to stop and Lulu wouldn't let her. Kathleen kept trying to pull herself away, and Lulu had her by the hair. Chad got between them and tried to separate them, and Kathleen finally had to scratch Lulu's face so Lulu would let her go."

"So?"

"That's just the beginning. I spent the next hour alone in the bathroom with her, and dude, she went completely Chernobyl on my ass! You should have heard her. She told me I was a phony and a poser and I made her want to puke."

"You have that effect."

"You're a riot." The car lighter popped and Troy fished a cigarette off the dash. "You have no idea," he said. "It was like she was possessed. She just kept yelling horrible stuff at me."

"Like what?"

"I don't even want to get into it."

"C'mon, like what?"

"She told me I had no poetry in me. What does that mean, no poetry in me? She wants me to write poetry? What is that all about? I hate poetry."

"Beats me," I lied.

"She told me she could never love me, not in a million years. She says the best she could do was not hate me." Troy puffed his cigarette and sighed as he exhaled. "Your sister's a psycho."

"She's not my sister."

"Then she started going off on Kathleen and Shannon and Chad and Morgan, and Santa Monica and California and Ronald Reagan and everybody you could possibly think of. Who's Ed Meese?"

"Beats me."

"Well, she went off on him, too. And then, finally, she started to settle down a little, and I got her to sit down on the toilet. She started to cry, and I tried to comfort her and all that, and then . . . God, I don't even know exactly what happened. I turned my back, just for a second, and the next thing I know she's got one of those nail file things, and she's carving up her cheek with it, and she's bleeding pretty hard. And I go for the towel, and she runs out in the hallway, and she won't let anybody stop the bleeding. Finally, I got her to take the towel from me and hold it over the cut."

"Why didn't you take her to the hospital?"

"She wouldn't go! She wouldn't even let me get near her. She ran down the stairs and through the kitchen and locked herself in the garage."

"Is she okay?"

"I don't know, but yeah, I think. She wouldn't talk to me. Chad got her to sit down for a while, but all she kept saying was *William. I want to talk to William. Only William.* And that's when I came for you. I knew you'd be at that lame party."

"Gun it," I said, at the next yellow light.

Chad had managed to forcibly gain entrance to the garage. Having exhausted all attempts at communication, he sat silent watch over Lulu from across the garage. He was still sitting there silently when Troy and I arrived.

Lulu was balled up in the far corner, in the shadow of a storage freezer, where the sickly light of the overhead fixture could not quite reach her. She sat motionless, back to the wall, head bowed, arms wrapped around her knees. There was a bloody towel crumpled at her feet. Troy gave my shoulder a little squeeze, and Chad patted my back, and when they opened the door to take leave, the cacophony of the party flooded into the garage, but only for an instant.

Skirting a stack of boxes, two bicycles, and a surfboard, I crept carefully over to Lulu and sat beside her, not quite shoulder to shoulder. She didn't lift her head. Her body convulsed with tiny sobs. I reached out to set an awkward hand on the back of her neck, and when she didn't recoil, I began to run my fingers soothingly through her mess of hair. When she didn't object to that, I sidled closer until our shoulders were touching, just barely, and there was no sound except her muffled sobs, and the hum of the refrigerator, and the faint echoes of a party. In this manner we sat for a minute, or an hour. I could've sat there forever, grazing shoulders, touching her hair, getting drunk on her anguish. When she finally leaned into me, I felt like a giant, a benevolent God.

Eventually Lulu lifted her head just a little, and I placed two fingers beneath her chin and tilted her face up into the sickly light. I saw the gash on her face, running from her nostril to her cheekbone like a bloody zipper, and I could have kissed it.

Lulu turned her face away. "Don't."

I tried to turn her face back, but she wouldn't let me. I tried to touch her hair again.

"Stop."

But I persisted.

Lulu pulled away and slid over, so that our shoulders were no longer touching.

A cold hand gripped my heart. "I'm trying to help, you crazy bitch," I said.

She didn't say anything. Neither of us said anything for a while. She crossed and uncrossed her arms, and wouldn't look at me.

"You've got the wrong idea about me," Lulu said, at last.

"Is this about kissing Kathleen? Because if this is about kissing Kathleen, seriously, I couldn't—"

"No. It's not. It doesn't matter what it's about. That's not why I—I just wanted to see you."

I slid over, bit by infinitesimal bit, until our shoulders were grazing once more. "Are you okay?"

Lulu smiled faintly. "Am I *ever* okay?"

"You used to be okay, Lu."

"Don't," she said.

"But, what about—?"

"Stop," she said, placing a finger on my lips. "Let's not."

I knew I had to let it go or I risked losing the delicious graze of her shoulder, the ecstasy of being wanted.

"So, are you okay?"

"I've behaved badly, William. Very badly."

"It's all right."

"It's not. I was awful to Troy. I was awful to all of them. You're right, I'm a crazy bitch."

"Why do you do it to yourself, Lu?"

She turned from me. "Because I get angry."

"At yourself?"

"Yes. No. I don't know." Absently, she traced a sideways figure eight in the oily dust on the side of the cooler, and promptly obliterated it with the sleeve of her dress. "At everything, I guess. At the way everything works. At all the things I can't control, all the things I wish I could make different, all the things that are gone forever that I can't bring back."

"I know how that feels."

"Maybe you do."

But Lulu didn't believe me, and I resented it.

"You know what Harry Pitts would say?"

"Of course I know what he'd say, he'd say the same thing my mom would say. He'd say that I do it to get attention, that it's some kind of stupid cry for help."

"Well?"

"Well, it's not true. I don't want attention. I'd rather be invisible."

"I'm sure glad you're not," I said.

Lulu turned away from me again, toward the dusty cooler with her scratched-out figure eight.

"We should clean that cut up, Lu. It's probably not so bad, really."

"It's not."

I took her hand in mine, and she didn't pull it away. I gave it a little squeeze, and my blood went all bubbly like champagne.

"Thanks for coming," she said.

"Of course."

Ever so gently, with the pad of my thumb, I traced the incision on her cheek until Lulu said it tickled. Then she rested her head on my shoulder, and my heart beat triplets, and the smell of her hair filled my lungs like alder smoke and lilies and newly mown grass. When I nestled my nose into the crook of her neck and gave her a little nibble, she let go a sigh that turned into a groan, like she'd been holding it in her whole life.

"What's going to happen to me when you go away?" I said.

"Good things, William Miller. The things you deserve."

"What about you? What's going to happen to you?"

"I don't know. I guess we'll find out."

I leaned into the crook of her neck once more, but this time she pulled away, and released my hand, and rose to her feet.

"Let's go," she said.

"What're you gonna tell Big Bill and Willow?"

"The truth."

But Lulu never told Big Bill and Willow the truth about her cheek. And knowing what I know now, I don't see why she would have, or should have. She showed them the truth, again and again. She *was* the truth. That should have been enough.

The Big Fat Deal

The day Lulu left for college, we all helped her load up the old van, cramming its fuzzy orange confines full of beanbags and boxes of books, baskets of paper, Hefty bags bursting with clothing, and, of course, her yellow, daisy-dappled footlocker, a little dented but otherwise none the worse for wear than the day that Big Bill first carried it up the stairs of the Pico house.

"Watch your speed," cautioned Big Bill. "I don't know how much that old van can take."

"I will."

"Honey, call when you get there, promise?"

"I will."

"If you get tired on the road, pull over," instructed Big Bill.

"Okay, I will."

"And don't you dare drive straight through."

"I won't."

"Stop in Redding," said Big Bill.

"Okay," said Lulu.

"Redding sucks," said Doug.

"You suck," said Ross.

"Shut up, ass-face."

"You shut up, you musclehead!"

"Faggot."

"Throwback."

"You two, enough!" said Big Bill.

"We love you, Sweetie. Please be careful," said Willow.

"I love you guys, too."

And then everybody stood around a little awkwardly for a half minute or so, until Big Bill, sensing my need, it seemed, for the first time in his life, mobilized the troops.

"Well, let's let these two say their good-byes."

And so they dispersed. Ross headed straight for Santa Monica Boulevard, presumably to smoke cloves and fraternize with his invisible friend. Doug headed for the backyard, where two days prior he'd dangled a forty-pound punching bag from the limb of a lemon tree. When he hit the bag with any force, lemons rained down, bonking him on the head. But he never moved it. Willow and Big Bill made their way slowly to the house, Willow walking backward with a pout on her face. Glancing back over his shoulder on his way in, Big Bill looked a little worried. Once inside, Willow lingered before the kitchen window, as though she were doing dishes, watching our proceedings at the curb.

"Here," said Lulu, producing a Polaroid from the glove compartment and presenting me with it. "I found this going through my stuff."

It was a photograph of Lulu and me at Cabazon, standing before Dinny the brontosaurus. I could intimate the photographer, just barely, in the form of Big Bill's ghostly reflection in the gift shop window. Lulu and I were ten years old. Lulu had the red ring from a cherry popsicle around her mouth, and was wearing oversized sunglasses. I was squinting, pre–Martian glasses, but smiling ear to ear in my World Gym shirt from Uncle Cliff, the one with the gorilla holding up the world. On that particular afternoon, Ross had puked in the van on the drive out, and blamed it on Big Bill's macaroni salad. Doug had dropped a nickel down the heating vent. And Lulu had let me hold her hand in the very back seat, and patiently explained to me how sometimes Neptune's orbit, because it was shaped funny, was actually outside of Pluto's.

"I think that's about the happiest I ever was," she said, and wiped her eyes. She smiled sweetly. "Please take care of yourself, William Miller." She reached out and held my hand once more, and gave it a little squeeze.

Without another word she circled the van, climbed in, fired it up, and as she pulled away from the curb she did not recede, but only loomed larger.

An hour later I went to work at Fatburger. Lulu was gone, and I was consigned to wearing a paper visor and asking some guy with a cold sore whether he wanted fat fries or skinny fries with his Big Fat Deal. The future seemed unachievable. Willow once told me that as long as a person knew they were in despair, they weren't really in despair. I didn't see what difference it made, but it was something I kept in mind over the course of the next couple months, as I battered onion rings and bagged fistfuls of napkins. I knew I was in despair, so I must not be.

August 2, 1987

Lulu called today. She got a job already at Starbucks, wherever that is. Some café, I guess. Lulu doesn't even drink coffee. She's not going to declare a major because she can't think of anything she wants to be. I asked her if she remembered how she wanted to be an airplane pilot a long time ago, and she said no, she couldn't remember. She doubts she'll ever want to be something. Seattle's okay, she said. Babybusters (that's what she calls people our age) are moving there from all over the place. I said it sounds like the Summer of Love, and she said she hopes not.

Big Bill and Doug made a habit of coming straight from the gym into Fatburger on the days I worked. They'd lumber in wearing their ass-hugging neoprene shorts, tank tops bursting at the seams. And every single time they lumbered in, my manager, Acne Scar Joe, would size them up, and without fail he'd say:

"Hey, Miller, what happened to *you?*"

It got funnier every time.

Big Bill and Doug would order Double Fatburgers with bacon and Swiss, and fat fries and skinny fries and cheese fries. And after they'd demolished those, they'd come back up and order Baby Fats and Kingburgers and chili cups.

Doug always made a point of being a pain in my ass, just to see me sweat it out.

"This is grilled, ass-bag. I wanted charbroiled."

"These fries are skinny. I wanted fat."

"So, did you have to go to Hamburger University, or what?"

God, I hated my brother Doug. What an ass-bag.

As for Ross, we hardly saw him anymore. He and his imaginary buddy Regan had outgrown clove cigarettes and Simon Le Bon, and moved on to the greener pastures of Light 100s and black trench coats and knee-high combat boots. For no apparent reason, Ross began calling himself Alistair. He spent untold hours locked in his bedroom listening to the worst music I'd ever heard. It sounded like meat grinders and wailing infants.

"Turn that shit down, Ross!"

"It's Alistair!"

On the fronts and insides of all his school PeeChees, Alistair drafted elaborate portraits of bazooka-wielding Minotaurs with forked tongues, and gut-spewing she-devils with studded garters and impossibly large tits. It was official: Ross was weird. But not as weird as I thought, because I finally met his imaginary friend Regan one night at the promenade, outside the movie theater, and the guy actually existed. He was about four feet tall, with a cherubic face and quick little ferret eyes that I didn't quite trust. His trench coat was hopelessly big, and the hem was tattered from dragging on the ground.

"You wanna buy a half gram?" he said.

"I don't do coke, you little runt. And Ross better not, either, or I'll—"

"Noooo, of weed."

"A half gram? Do they even sell weed in half grams?"

"I do."

"He pinches," explained Ross. "He buys a gram, then he splits it in half. But not before—"

"Shut up!" said Regan.

"It's true," said Ross.

"Well, it's not like I'm making a profit," complained Regan.

"All right, what the hell, I'll buy one," I said. "How much?"

"Six bucks," said Regan.

"But I thought a gram was only ten?"

"Overhead," he said.

Six-dollar half grams became something of a mainstay. I'd steal away to my bedroom closet and smoke them in one sitting out of a 7Up can, and squeeze back out the closet door, trapping the smoke inside, and sprawl out on my bed with my headphones on and listen to the voices on the radio as I stared at the ceiling.

The only real friend I had that summer was Troy. He wasn't so bad. I didn't go in for the whole Benders affiliation, just Troy, who, having fallen well short of Princeton, had registered at Santa Monica City College for the fall. It seemed like he was the only person I had anything in common with. We'd go to Dodgers games and talk about Lulu, walk around Venice and talk about Lulu, drive up to Malibu and talk about Lulu. Troy did most of the talking. I still didn't have the courage to reveal my true feelings for Lulu to anyone else. My secret was safe with Pitts.

"I think I'm starting to get it," he said one morning at breakfast. "Lulu isn't fickle, she's just never the same person twice."

"I'm afraid you lost me."

"Like she keeps trying to reinvent herself every second so that she won't have to be who she really is."

"And who's that?"

"I don't know. I haven't figured that out."

But it wasn't for lack of effort. I had to give Troy that. He tried to get his brain and heart around Lulu like nobody other than me. Poor guy. Pining away like that with no possibility of ever reaching her. She hadn't written him, hadn't called, had barely said good-bye. The more I commiserated with Troy, the lousier I felt.

I found comfort in the voices, particularly in the voice of my god, Vin Scully. The Dodgers had a miserable season. Fernandomania hit the skids. Guerrero bounced back, but it wasn't enough to pick up Heep and Landreaux. They lost eighty-nine games. But to hear Vin Scully, it didn't matter. Vin Scully was bigger than winning; in fact, he was at his best when they were losing badly—eight–zero, twelve–two, nine–one—because he'd settle back into his psychic rocking chair and talk to me about life, and the smell of salami in the Carnegie Deli, and the weather somewhere else, and about Ebbets Field and Forbes Field and the Polo Grounds, and other places that no longer existed outside the imagination. Baseball was more than just numbers for Vin Scully. It was more than just a metaphor for life—it *was* life. It was a sensual experience, something to be smelled and tasted. Vin Scully ate baseball, drank baseball, and slept baseball. He probably fucked baseball, too.

And one fine day, of all the burger joints in all the world, the great one himself came into Fatburger unbeknownst to everybody but me.

"Hey, you're Vin Scully, the voice of the Dodgers," I observed.

"That's right," he said. "I'll have a Baby Fat with no pickles." And the way he said it sounded just like he was calling a game.

"I've probably listened to you a thousand times."

"Thanks. I'll have a side of onion rings."

"I used to wish you were my father."

He looked at me strangely, like I was speaking Lebanese, and he bobbed his eyebrows a few times. "I'll have a Diet Coke with that too, please." This time he didn't sound like he was calling a game.

And with my own two hands I made the great Vin Scully his Baby Fat without pickles, and his onion rings and his Diet Coke (which I upped from a medium to a large at no extra charge), and instead of just calling his number, I took the tray right to his table, where I paused and faltered.

And finally, I said: "Sir, have you got any advice for a guy who can't see the future?"

"Try looking harder."

"Thanks. I will."

"You're welcome."

And then he unwrapped his burger as I stood there, and was about to take a bite when he gave me a sidelong glance and hoisted a brow.

"One more thing, sir," I said.

He lowered his burger halfway. "What's that, son?"

"Well, I . . . you see . . ." But then I couldn't find my velveteen voice, my crackling words.

His Baby Fat was still poised halfway. "Well, what is it, son?"

And when I still couldn't find my voice after a moment, Vin Scully kind of squinted at me and shook his head in wonder, like I was a mirage in the desert—a juggling cactus, or a two-headed rattlesnake, maybe—until I finally came into focus, and then his upper lip curled and he raised his burger and took a bite, and he never looked back at me.

I stood there for a moment in a kind of daze. I was numb as I made my way back toward the grill. Gradually I began to regain sensations: the sensation that I was impotent, ineffectual, a loser; and the sensation that it had always been thus, and was destined to remain thus; and finally, the sensation that I didn't want Vin Scully to be my father any more than I wanted Big Bill to be my father.

"What are you looking so pale about?" Acne Scar Joe wanted to know. "Hey, flip those Baby Fats, already! Wake up, Miller."

I looked at Acne Scar Joe with his thinning hair, and I thought for a moment I might have seen my future there, and it was too bleak to contemplate. I reminded myself that so long as I knew I was in despair, I wasn't in despair.

"What?" said Joe. "What the hell are you looking at? Jesus, Miller, what gives?"

"I've gotta go," I said, untying my apron.

"What the hell does that mean?"

"It means I have to go."

"What, to the bathroom? Jesus, Miller, could you do it between orders?"

"That's not what I mean. I just have to leave."

Acne Scar Joe was starting to give me that same juggling cactus look Vin Scully gave me. "Go where, for chrisssakes? It's the middle of the lunch rush!"

"Somewhere else," I said. "I don't know."

The Day Before Thanksgiving

~~~

Willow soon set our family geography in motion once more, migrating to Lulu's vacant room. By that time, active aggression had ceased between Big Bill and Willow. They stayed for the most part in neutral corners. But it wasn't exactly an armistice—more like Willow retreated, just walked off the battlefield and put it all behind her. With Lulu out of the house, there was nothing left to fight for. Willow delivered no speeches, flew no white flag. She just turned her back and started walking, over craters and around cadavers, toward the wooded fringes.

The Pico house was growing conspicuously quiet. Even Lulu's signature was beginning to fade. Ross was running all over the basin with that little ferret Regan, peddling half grams at a twenty-percent markup. Big Bill and Doug were at the gym most evenings. This left

Willow and me alone, though our paths rarely crossed as we stole from station to station, me with my notebooks and my dark little heart, she like a soldier getting over the war.

Family dinners were a rarity those days. It got to the point where I became a bit nostalgic for those gatherings: the grunting and evading, the rank-and-file procession, the mess hall efficiency of it all. And more than anything else, I missed the repetition of it. It seemed there were no more fixed places in the universe, no reliable signposts to mark my way. All of this coming and going, all of these different directions. Where was convergence when I needed it most? The universe really was expanding. I could feel it for the first time: heavenly bodies hurtling through space, drifting farther and farther apart.

The day before Thanksgiving I found Willow seated at the dining room table with two suitcases beside her.

"What's this?" I said.

"I'm going to San Francisco."

"Does anybody know?"

"You do."

I looked again at the suitcases. They were big. "For how long?"

"For a while, anyway."

"But, what about Thanksgiving?"

"You can still have it. The turkey is soaking. Cook it at three twenty-five for about five hours. Cover it with foil—"

"Why are you—?"

"Listen to me. Then take the foil off for the last forty-five minutes or so. Are you getting this?"

"No."

"Let it sit for a half hour before you carve it. The dressing's in the casserole dish on the top—"

"Why are you doing this?"

"It's complex, William. It would be awfully hard to explain to you."

"You could at least try."

"Yes, I suppose I owe you that."

"You don't owe me anything."

She reached out and gave my hand a little squeeze. "You're a good boy, William Miller. Don't think I don't see that. Sit down," she said.

I sat down across from her.

Willow looked both younger and older at the same time as she piled her hands in her lap. "I only wish I could have been more for you," she said. "Not a mother, of course, I don't mean that. Just more. A resource, a friend. Oh, I don't know, just more."

"You tried," I said.

"Maybe I should have forced the issue a little."

"I always appreciated that you didn't. But what's this got to do with me, anyway? Why are you leaving? What is this about?"

"People change," she said.

"I thought that was a good thing."

"Some of the time," she said.

"But Big Bill's always been . . ."

"I'm not just talking about your father, I'm talking about me, too. Some people change quicker than others. Sometimes people don't change at all, but their context changes, and just by being the same they change."

It occurred to me that I'd never honestly believed people could change, I mean really change, until Lulu went away to cheerleading camp. And after that everybody started changing, and never stopped.

"So you've grown apart, is that what you're saying?"

"A great distance apart." Willow left a silence long enough to fill the great distance, or at least ponder it. She massaged the joints of her fingers like an arthritic. "Oh, so much is different, William. I was in college when I met your father."

"Big Bill went to college?"

"No. But he went to parties." A distant smile played at the corners of her mouth. "Humph," she said. "San Francisco. It seems like a lifetime ago."

"So what happened? How did things get so different?"

"I guess what's changed the most between your father and me over the years are the things that haven't changed."

"You mean like taking a backseat all the time?"

Willow shot me a searching look. "That's part of it. But only part of it."

She turned her attention back to her finger joints, which she continued to massage as she pondered the other parts. "You can't resist change," she observed. "You can effect change, I still honestly believe that. You can fight for it, you can even speed it up, but you can't resist it, because it's going to happen. It's like gravity. It doesn't matter how strong you are, or how stubborn you are, or how determined you are. The best you can do is accept it. Things happen. Bad things, good things. You have to adapt, you *have* to. It's *not* wrong to change your approach."

"Sounds a little like a political speech," I said.

That same distant smile returned to Willow's face. "I suppose it does."

I looked across the table at her, silently and unabashedly, and I felt pity for her. She'd given her best years to the Millers. She'd walked forever in the shadow of my mother, fighting for us, feeding us, trying desperately to draw us out of ourselves, to expand our horizons, and for what? What was she fighting for? The unattainable affections of her eldest stepson? A man who believed there was a necessary correlative between pain and gain? What was Willow's stake in all of this? A father figure for Lulu? Ha! A breadwinner? That's a laugh. Do you have any idea what second place in the Mr. Cal/Neva pays? A personal appearance at the Cerritos Athletic Club? Willow not only raised us, she paid more than her share of the bills. I'm guessing a lot more. And here she was, all these years later, two hundred hams and a thousand small rejections later, sitting across from me like a wilting flower. It was disgraceful.

"Willow," I said. "I've never really told you thank you for anything. I mean, you know, for everything. I'm sorry I was a pain—I mean, I still am."

"You were never a pain, William. Just distant."

"I'm sorry for that."

"It's not your fault."

There came a honk from the driveway.

"I've got to go," she said. "I'll miss my flight."

Then I knew I had to say it. I had to tell somebody before it ate me alive. "I love Lulu," I said. "And I can't imagine that ever changing."

"Of course you can't." Willow stood up and took a few steps to the window, and turned her back to me. "William, I'm going to tell you something. But first I'm going to tell you that sometimes you've just got to know when enough is enough and walk away without asking questions. And for you, this is one of those times. I may not have the right to dispense that advice, but I hope you'll take it. For Louisa's sake and your own."

"What are you going to tell me?"

"Only that your sister loves you dearly and truly, and that she is proud of you, and she looks up to you. More than you may ever know."

"She's not my sister."

Willow turned from the window. "Walk away, William."

There came another honk from the driveway.

She picked up her bags. "I've got to go." She leaned down and kissed me on the cheek. "Good-bye, William. I'll call."

Dear Will

~~~

December 27, 1987

Dear Will,

Merry x-mas (a little late), sorry I didn't come home, and sorry I didn't send gifts. Sorry I've taken so long to write. Sorry you're disillusioned, and sorry about my mom. In short, I'm sorry about a lot of things. On the bright side, congratulations on quitting Fatburger! And yes, yes, yes, I think you'd make a wonderfully stupendous radio announcer, you have a beautiful voice, and the world needs to hear it, whether or not they deserve it. I dropped out of the U, but don't tell anybody. I'm going to register again in spring, maybe. I just don't have it in me right now. I might register at SCC instead. I don't know. There are so many things I'm unsure of. I'm not even sure if life is a comedy or a tragedy, but I wish I laughed more, because I probably would make better decisions, and I probably wouldn't mind the rain so much. I quit Starbucks. I may get a job at a bookstore, or maybe not. I left the dorm (don't tell anybody that either!), and I'm renting a studio on First and Bell for $300 a month. I've still got student loan money, but it's sort of dwindling. I may get a warehouse space with my friend Dan in Georgetown.

Troy keeps writing and calling me, and I'm sorry to be cruel, but please tell him I met a boy. I know that's awful, and I know it's immature, and I know I should tell him myself, but I just don't have it in me right now, and I don't want him to suffer. Troy deserves better than me. I really did meet a boy, Will. His name is Dan and he plays the bass and works at the Comet Tavern. I don't know what I'm doing, and I don't know why anybody would ever want to be with me in the first place. I've been painting a little bit. Dan says they're good, but really they're ugly. Please don't hate me or be disappointed in me, Will. You're a better person than me. I'm sorry about all the trouble I've caused everybody with all of my drama. I'm working on it, I really am.

Probably the reason Ross is calling himself Alistair is because of Alistair Crowley, who people think was a devil worshipper, but really he was just some kind of mystic. I wouldn't worry about him being weird. It's just a phase. If you ask me, Doug is the one who could use a phase. Usually the people trying to be weird aren't the weird ones, and I have a feeling Ross is trying.

I hope that Dad is holding up okay since my mom left. Before you resent him too much, remember that he's been through a lot, and I'm not just talking about your mom. Don't forget his dad died when he was four years old, and I'm not making excuses, I just know what it's like not to have a dad, even if I call Dad Dad. I know that you're probably thinking that you didn't have a mother, and that's even worse, but some people (like you) are naturally well-adjusted, I think. I think Dad and I are young souls, and I think that you're an old soul. Dan is an old soul too. Or maybe not. Maybe he's just lazy.

So now I've come to the question that is on both of our minds. You have to believe me, William Miller Jr., that I haven't stopped thinking it. Sometimes I feel like it's thinking me. Of course I'm talking about the night in Westwood in the garage. I've been over it and over it, Will, and probably it's why it's taken me so long to write. Trust and forgive that I'm not being careful with my words here. What I mean is, I'm saying everything just as I thought it and felt it. You have to promise me you won't hate me. You just have to, Will. That night of the blowout when I came undone, you were the only person in the world I wanted to talk to. And if it happened again tomorrow, probably you'd still be the only person. And it wasn't because you are my brother, but probably that was part of it. If you weren't my brother, I couldn't possibly see you as I do, because I probably wouldn't ever have gotten close to you at all (don't take that the wrong way). I know you think it makes a difference not really being related. But the bottom line is, to me there is no difference. I can't be any more honest than that. You said things that night that nobody else in the world will ever say to me again, ever. I know that. I'll live the rest of my life knowing that. Troy could never say those things to me. Dan will never be able to say those things to me, I can see that already. I will always settle for less than you, I'm sure of it. If you mean all the things you said in your notebook, and all the things you said to me the night in Morgan's brother's garage, then you have no choice but to not hate me for feeling the way I do about this, and especially not hate me for meeting Dan, because Dan and every other boy in the world is just to try to make up for you. You have to believe that, Will. It's not fair if you don't. If I don't hear back from you in a month, I will assume you can't forgive me, and if that's the case, I guess I can't blame you, but I still think it's unfair. Or maybe not. Maybe I'm just being selfish again.

Love,

Lulu

P.S. Happy New Year! I know this is going to be a big year for you, Will! It won't be long before your voice speaks to the whole world!

.

Dear Lulu

~~~

<div align="right">January 12, 1988</div>

Dear Lulu,

I've written this letter a dozen times, so I am choosing my words carefully, every last one of them. First of all, I don't know what ever gave you the idea I was "well-adjusted." Jesus Christ, look at my handwriting! Well-adjusted people don't write like this! Well-adjusted people don't call their fathers Big Bill! Well-adjusted people don't hate their own brothers! Well-adjusted people don't fill notebooks full of fantasies about their stepsister! What you read in the bathroom was the very tip of the iceberg. So don't think you've cornered the market on not being "well-adjusted," Louisa Trudeau-Miller. And don't think you're doing me any favors by being "honest," either. It's a little late for honesty, when you've been pretending to hate me for three years, only so you could admit you loved me one night when you got drunk and carved yourself up. Your honesty hurts even worse than your lying. It really helps me a lot to know about Dan the bass-playing bartender, it helps me to picture him slack-jawed and skinny and tattooed and about to kiss you. Especially since you yourself say he's not as good as me. Thanks for the honesty! Oh, and by the way, I'm not going to break Troy's heart for you, either. Troy's about the only friend I've got. Sorry, but you'll have to tell him about Dreamy Dan the Bass Playing Man yourself! You'll have to tell Troy you think he's worthless and shallow yourself, just like you did that night in the bathroom, only this time really sock it to him, Lulu. Don't leave him any hope.

I wish Big Bill had never met Willow, and that I never met you, or touched you, or kissed you, or dreamed of kissing you, or clutched your pillow to my face and smelled you every chance I got, or jotted down every lovely thing you ever said, or every lovely thing you ever did, or wore, or didn't do, or dropped on the floor, and I wish I never cried knowing that I caused you suffering, or that I never made a deal with the devil for half my life just to be with you for a night, and I wish to God you weren't my stepsister, so you couldn't use it as an excuse to not love me back!

I hate you, Lulu, and I wish I could say it right to your scar face!

Will

P.S. Happy New Year (a little late)! Say hi to Dan!

And so after nearly three weeks of waffling and agonizing over my approach, after a dozen misfires, and a dozen restless nights, this was the letter I finally sent off to Lulu by way of a reply, and for five seconds afterward, it was exhilarating to think how deeply my words would cut her, and for five seconds I basked in the genius of my own cruelty, and congratulated myself for not having pulled any punches, and not having tempered my hatred with a single kind or conciliatory word, and for five seconds I felt that I had finally conquered Lulu.

The Modern Game

~~~

It should be noted that no member of the Miller bodybuilding contingent could ever resist a mirror, or any other reflective surface. When passing a mirror or a shop window, my father and Doug, and in earlier days Ross, would often pause for a full knee-to-shoulder inspection of their rippling personage. At the very least, they snuck a sidelong glance at their own visages as they lumbered by with their shoulders straight, their elbows back, and their Adam's apples jutting out their necks like dorsal fins. This phenomenon is not unique to the Miller men—I've observed it to some degree in nearly all bodybuilders—but in the Millers it seemed to be pronounced. The closer it got to competition time, the more time Big Bill spent before the mirror. This was especially true of the Olympia, and especially in '88. As early as February, he spent upward of an hour a day in front of the

full-length mirror in the master bedroom, polishing his poses, looking for chinks in his own fleshy armor. And that's where I found him
on Valentines Day, not three days after Willow had made it official
that she was not returning to Santa Monica.

I was never a big proponent of Hallmark holidays, but I'd be lying
if I said I wasn't a little blue that particular Valentines Day. Lulu had
been gone for six months, and I was living at home with absolutely
zero romantic prospects, zero financial prospects, and very little desire or energy to create either. School was still seven months off, Troy
was living in Venice (I scarcely saw him anymore), and Acne Scar Joe
was hounding me daily to come back to work at Fatburger. Somehow, Valentines Day just magnified all of it.

As I stood in the doorway and watched Big Bill before the mirror,
running through the very poses Willow had taught him as though it
were the most normal thing in the world, I couldn't help but wonder
what was wrong with my father. How could he move on like that?

When he registered my presence in the mirror, he winked.

"How can you act so casual about it?" I said.

He did a front lat spread, smiling as though from the inside of a
casket. "About what, Tiger?"

"What do you mean, about what? About losing Willow."

Big Bill did a quarter turn with his upper body, and eased smoothly
into a right bicep, trailing his left arm out behind him in a rooster
tail so his upper body formed a backward *S* in profile. "Who says I
lost her?"

"Dad, what is your problem? Your wife left you. How can you
just stand there flexing your muscles? Aren't you even going to fight
for her?"

"I'm through with fighting, Tiger. From here on out, I'm just rolling with the punches."

My father remained a mystery to me. Where was the wounded

elephant? Where was the guy who didn't know what to do with him-self? Had he finally arrived at a method by which grief could be converted into muscle mass like carbs? Was it as simple as consum-ing seven years of one's life at a single sitting, and then adding two sets of incline presses, and maybe some crunches? Whatever the case, Willow's departure seemed only to sharpen Big Bill's focus.

Seven years had passed since he finished as high as fourth in the Olympia. At forty, the window was closing on his career, and with or without Willow, Big Bill was determined to take a final summit run at Olympus in '88. Though he'd failed even to qualify for Gothen-burg in '87, where an impossibly ripped Lee Haney won his seventh, Big Bill remained steadfast in the belief (some might even argue de-lusion) that '88 was his year to win the Olympia.

I had no expectation or any wish for the distinction of a matching sweat suit on this occasion, nor did I harbor any secret hope that I would get the nod come oiling time. But I did watch Big Bill's '88 run from a distance, with the nagging interest of a retired coach, nursing some bitter misgivings for the modern game.

This time Big Bill altered his entire approach to conditioning. He began sculpting an entirely more subtle figure. Despite his rippling girth, and his artistry in the realm of posing, proportion had ever remained his Achilles' heel. Big Bill was top-heavy. His biceps, pecs, and shoulders were as formidable as any the IFBB had ever seen, but his legs were puny by comparison. He was shaped like a drumstick standing on end, a fact that might well have cost him a dozen bids at Mr. Olympia.

In '88 Big Bill was determined to change all of that. Sundays, formerly a domestic benchmark in our restless household deemed "at home day" (usually occasioned by Big Bill eating an entire ham in front of the television set as his children came and went), were now devoted exclusively to lower-body work at Gold's, with an emphasis on quads and calves. So, if Big Bill was suffering in the months after Willow's flight, I didn't see it, and that's the truth, because he practically lived at Gold's Gym.

Acne Scar Joe finally succeeded in luring me back to Fatburger. I was officially moving backwards.

"We need you, Miller," he told me in the parking lot one afternoon after he'd called me in to plead his case once and for all. "You may be a pussy, but nobody handles the lunch rush like you. These high school kids are always fucking up. Or their parents are calling in to say they can't come to work because they've got a fucking *track* meet, or some shit. We need somebody older, more responsible. We need *you*, Miller."

Somehow, I was unmoved by this plea.

"Look," he said. "Let's be honest here. I know what you're thinking. It's a nowhere job, right? Flipping burgers. It doesn't exactly make the world go round, right? But just remember, Miller: In the Soviet Union, college professors and aerospace engineers are quitting their jobs to work at McDonald's. Doesn't that mean *anything* to you, Miller?"

"That they don't pay professors much in the Soviet Union?"

"Besides that! Look, there's a whole goddamn world of people to feed out there—be they Russian, or Japs, or Greasers, or all these fags and yuppies right here in West Hollywood. They're all people. Even the fags. They all gotta eat. You think you can't make a difference, Miller? Let me tell you a little story. You ever hear of honey mustard dressing? Of course you have. Did you know that *this* Fatburger, *right here*, was the first restaurant on Santa Monica between Martel and Fairfax to serve honey mustard? Yeah. And you know what else? We were the first ones to serve it on the side. That's right. Now every bitch from Rodeo Drive to Los Feliz with a stick up her ass, in every yuppie bistro in town, is ordering honey mustard on the side. God-damn Salt-N-Pepa are ordering it that way. Gorbachev's ordering it that way! Fatburger needs you, Miller. Are you gonna turn your back on that?"

Acne Scar Joe should have been a recruiter. He had managed to work me up into a patriotic frenzy over hamburgers. I was practically ready to go to war for hamburgers if necessary. But mostly I needed the money, and Fatburger must have been serious about needing me, because they bumped me up to $6.15 an hour, a wage that might have afforded me a rented closet in Moscow. Ever the pragmatist, I opted to stay at home. The rent was only $150, a nominal fee, roughly enough to keep Big Bill in short supply of protein powder for about a week, but a fee nonetheless. I wasn't *living* at home, I was *renting* at home, a distinction that afforded me a shred of dignity.

The high point of spring was breaking Troy's heart. How I managed to wait that long, I don't know.

We were bumming around the beach south of Venice one foggy morning in May. Troy was already a little mopey about something, so the timing couldn't have been better.

"His name's Dan," I said. "He's a great guy from what she told me."

Troy dug some sand up with the toe of his shoe and shook it off, and looked out toward the surf, but didn't say anything.

"Lulu says he's hot," I said. "I guess he's in some band that just got signed. All I know is, she seems pretty serious about him."

For all I really knew, Lulu had dumped Dan months ago, but it was a moot point anyway, because goddamn Troy took it like a prince. I almost felt bad for rubbing it in.

"Good for her," he said, tracing a little squiggly in the sand with his toe. "That's great. I'm glad she found someone."

"You're serious? That's it? You're glad she found someone?"

"Well, yeah. I am, actually. She deserves it, don't you think?"

"I guess so. I don't know, does she?"

"Yeah, I think she does."

I drew my own squiggly in the sand with the toe of my shoe. "But what about you guys?"

Troy reached down, picked up a bottle cap, and winged it sidearm toward the surf. It caught some wind and sailed nearly straight up in a steep arc and then died in midair, and floated back to earth not fifteen feet from him. "Pfff. What about us?"

"Yeah, I guess so."

I suppose Troy was a bigger man than me for knowing when to concede, but that's not really saying much, is it? After all, what kind of measure is giving up?

Pepperoni Sticks

───∿∿───

I knew I'd reached an all-time low once I started fraternizing with Acne Scar Joe outside of Fatburger. It wasn't that Acne Scar Joe was a terrible guy, though he was. He was the kind of guy that collected beer money from high school kids in the Circle K parking lot, then bought lotto tickets with their money and told them "tough shit" when he came out empty-handed, and then bragged about it the next day at work. It wasn't that Joe was a bigot, though he was that, too. He said things like, "Hey, I got nothin' against wetbacks. Shit, my neighbor's a wetback. They're better than gooks." It wasn't that we didn't have anything in common, though we didn't. I liked to hole up in my bedroom and stare at the ceiling and listen to Ken Minyard on my headphones. Joe liked to drink a few and go to the firing range with his Glock. So, we did have one big thing in common: We were both losers.

Our initial foray into the social arena consisted of a movie at the Beverly Center one night after work. Some bad people seized an armored car. Lives were at stake. A gritty Secret Service dude kicked their asses. Pretty stirring stuff. Just the kind of human drama that roused Joe's slumbering moral imperative and sent his testosterone level through the roof. He was noticeably agitated afterward, like he was itching for the firing range. Joe's moral ceiling collapsed again within ten minutes. He bought us some beer at a convenience store near the high school, where he collected money from the usual suspects, two kids with identical *Misfits* T-shirts, driving a Honda Civic. Probably sophomores, maybe juniors.

One of the kids confronted Joe afterward outside the store. "Hey, we wanted bottles."

"Well, it just so happens that this beer ain't for you, dumbshit. It's for me and my buddy."

The kid looked to me for confirmation, and I shrugged sheepishly from the passenger seat.

"Give us the money back then."

"Pfff, right."

The kid looked more wounded than angry. "You can't do that. C'mon, dude. That's fucked."

"So, call the fucking *cops*, why don't you? Oh, wait, you're a *minor*. Ha! Nice try, Skippy."

Joe climbed into the car and handed me the beer. The kid gave me one more pleading look. C'mon, he seemed to say, isn't there something you can do? But all I could do was shrug sheepishly again.

We drank the beer by the empty pool at Joe's apartment complex, where we sat in plastic chairs. The night was warm and windless, and a gritty residue of exhaust from the nearby 10 hung in the air. Indeed, the freeway was so close that you could spot the make of the cars. Whenever the flow of traffic subsided momentarily, you could hear the buzzing of the purplish patio lights. They sounded almost like crickets. The empty pool was littered with dead palm fronds and beer cans and an old bicycle with no wheels.

Joe kept throwing rocks at his neighbor's cat every time the poor beast slunk out onto the balcony. "Climbs all over the hood of my car, the fucking rat."

We talked about work a little, about the nuances of charbroiling and the dipshit delivery driver from Rykoff.

"That dude's been at Jackoff longer than I've been at Fats," he noted.

"What's wrong with his teeth, anyway? How come he never opens his mouth?"

"It ain't pretty, dude. He's got a gnarly-ass grill. Looks like lava rocks and shit."

After about a half hour of this, Joe finally cut to the chase. "Look, Miller, there's a reason why I had you over tonight."

Terrified by the possibilities, I braced myself for the worst.

"I've got a proposition for you," he pursued.

My ass tightened.

"My girlfriend's cousin is coming to town," he said. "And I need some-body to go out with her. You know, like a double date or whatever."

"You don't have a girlfriend."

"We've gone out twice, Miller, so whaddaya call that?"

I took a long hit of my stale beer. "What does she look like?"

"She's a hottie."

"No, the cousin."

Joe didn't answer right off. He plucked a stone out of the empty planter by his lawn chair, and winged it toward the balcony. It ricocheted off the rail and narrowly missed a window. "She's okay, I guess."

"Well, that doesn't sound too promising."

"She's fine, dude. From her picture it looks like she's got big tits."

"I don't know, Joe."

"Look, dude, she'll probably suck your chode if you get her drunk enough. And believe me, we'll get them drunk."

"Let me think about it."

"Miller, what's there to think about? When's the last time you got any pussy?"

"Couple months," I lied.

"Ha! Try never. Miller, you're gonna get your knob polished. Trust me on this one."

God knows why, but I trusted Acne Scar Joe on that one. I figured a good knob polishing (or any knob polishing, for that matter) would only strengthen my resolve to forget Lulu. And so the four of us were to convene at Joe's apartment the following Friday night.

I was a wreck for three days beforehand. It took me twenty minutes to scrub the smell of Fatburger off of me after work that afternoon. I doused myself liberally with Big Bill's cologne, then promptly decided that I smelled like a freezer-burned ham. It took another twenty minutes to scrub that off, and I wasn't altogether successful. I got rid of the freezer-burned part, but the ham lingered. I wore a shirt I thought was cool.

Ironically, the prospect of failure was not the source of my anxiety that Friday night so much as the prospect of success was—that is, the possibility of revealing my little breakfast link to a perfect stranger. Though my Netherlands were no longer hairless, my willy was hardly bigger than it had been when Lulu inspected it in the trophy room at thirteen.

I arrived at Joe's casually late, having spent fifteen casual minutes in my car outside his apartment complex, gazing at my watch and listening to KMPC.

The three of them were in the kitchen when I got there, huddled around the blender, laughing. Joe was making strawberry daiquiris.

"For the ladies," he explained. "There's beer in the fridge."

I grabbed a beer from the fridge.

Joe draped a proprietary arm around his lady right off the bat, lest there be any confusion. "This is Nicole," he said, just as Nicole was wriggling out from under his arm. "And this is her cousin Cheryl."

My first thought was that there's no accounting for taste, because Cheryl, whom Joe had deemed "Okay, I guess," was pretty damn hot when you looked past the makeup and the fog of perfume. Joe's date Nicole, on the other hand, looked like an anteater in tight pants and a halter top.

One look at me and Cheryl started inhaling her daiquiri. Who could blame her? When I excused myself to take a leak in Joe's hair-encrusted toilet, I could hear that Joe wasn't exactly helping my odds.

"Yeah, Miller's kind of a wuss," I heard him say. "But he's not a fag or anything."

I might have been a solar flare for all the eye contact Cheryl bestowed upon me that evening, although she did exhibit a refreshing candor on the subject of her boyfriend back in Muskegon, a certain red-shirt freshman on the Michigan State offensive line named Bubby, who hailed from Arkansas.

"His name is Bubby?" I chortled. "C'mon, what's his real name?"

She looked me in the eye for the first time and pinched up her face. "Bubby *is* his real name."

I was the romantic equivalent of mustard gas. Where was my beautiful voice when the lights were low and the music was soft, and some lovesick middle-American girl gooned on strawberry daiquiris presented herself? My voice had forsaken me—it seemed I was incapable of saying the right thing. And as a result, Bubby seemed only to draw nearer with each daiquiri.

Joe, meanwhile, was making headway, relatively speaking. Nicole was fighting him off, but he was still managing an occasional grope. Two more daiquiris and he might've been in business.

After a covert conference in Joe's bathroom, during which Joe released a wide stream of urine in and around the toilet, it was decided that we should take the Duster, as it was roomier, and things were liable to get horizontal up at Mulholland. It was also mutually decided (by Joe) that we should switch the gals to beer.

"We just want them to lower their standards," he explained. "Not lose their motor skills and shit."

But it was too late for Cheryl. By the time we set out for Circle K for snacks and more beer, she was already a mess. And hungry. When Joe went in to fetch the beer, Cheryl joined him, wobbling on high heels.

"Is Joe always such a horn dog?" Nicole wanted to know.

"I'm not sure."

Nicole was leaning over the front seat reapplying her lipstick in the rearview mirror. Her face was about four inches from mine. I could smell the daiquiri on her breath. "He wasn't like this the first two times we went out."

"He's probably just buzzed," I assured her.

Cheryl reemerged from the brilliant light of Circle K clutching a handful of pepperoni sticks, even as she gnawed on one. She offered them around once she got in the car, but ended up eating them all herself.

Snaking our way up the canyon was a dizzying affair. Switchback after switchback, Cheryl swooned wordlessly in the passenger seat. Nicole did most of the talking, as I was intent on the spears of my headlights around each corner, and Joe was busy trying to cop a feel. For a girl who looked like an anteater, Nicole was blessed with confidence, and I admired that, although she was irritating as hell. Where did self-confidence reside in people like us—the unattractive ones, the awkward ones? Mine had only flourished in the borrowed light of Lulu, and perhaps in comparison to my idiotic brothers. But Nicole seemed to have arrived at some equation by which she was impervious to the reality that she was unattractive and profoundly aggravating.

Cheryl, who continued to sway to and fro with each corner, looked peaked by the halfway mark.

"You want me to stop the car so you can get some air?" I offered on more than one occasion.

"No—*hic*—thanks," she said. Or, "I'm all right."

By the time she uttered, "I think—*hic*—you better pull—" it was too late. Up came the daiquiris and the pepperoni sticks, all over my wide, black dashboard. Immediately the car smelled like hot daiquiris and pepperoni sticks. The windows came down in a flash. It was another quarter mile—with everyone but Cheryl hanging out the windows—before I could find a place to pull over. Cheryl spilled out of the car and staggered to the ditch. Nicole attended to her. In an act of chivalry, or more likely convenience, Joe volunteered his Husqvarna T-shirt to clean up the mess, leaving him shirtless beneath his jean vest. Were it not for the jug of water I kept in the trunk for the radiator, it's doubtful whether I could've cleaned that muck off the dashboard at all. Even as I swabbed it up, I knew I'd be finding little dried flakes in the speaker grill for months. Needless to say, Joe's T-shirt was a total loss.

We crested the hill without further incident, and parked in a little clearing off the west side of the road surrounded by long grass. After about ten minutes of this stunning vista, Joe finally wore Nicole down in the backseat. The guy was tenacious; you had to give him that. She seemed like she was pretty into it, actually. And about ten minutes later, my opportunity arrived, when Cheryl, who suddenly thought I was sweet for mopping up her vomit (I guess that's one way of developing intimacy), threw caution to the wind, forgot about Bubby, and locked onto me like a succubus. Her tongue was doing unnatural things in my mouth. She tasted of vomit. There was grit on her teeth. My eyes watered under the strain. Finally, I pulled her off of me and tried to appear as though I were not gasping for breath.

"Wh—*hic*—what's wrong?" she said.

"I just keep thinking of Bubby," I said.

That seemed to stun Cheryl into sobriety, if only for an instant. I couldn't tell what emotions were at work in her. Her eyes started lolling around in her head again almost immediately, as she did her best to stare me down. "You're—*hic*—sweet," she said at last. And then she came at me again with renewed vigor, and this time her tongue wasn't quite so unnatural, but she still tasted like rotting fruit. On this occasion, when I pried her off of me, it was my crippling fear of success that got the best of me. There I was in spades, unable and unwilling to close the deal, hiding inside my sweetness like it was a foxhole, so that I didn't have to put my ass on the line.

"But Bubby," I said. "Don't forget about Bubby."

This did not produce the desired effect. "Bubby's an asshole," she said, and forced herself upon me once again.

"I can't," I said. And this time maybe I grabbed her wrist a little too hard. When I released my grip, she pulled away and sulked in the corner, gazing drunkenly out the window.

Joe popped his head up from the backseat. "For fuck's sake, Miller, what's wrong with you? You are a fag, aren't you?"

"Just shut up," I told him.

"Whatever," he said, and popped his head back down. But this time Nicole pushed him away, and popped her own head up. "Are you all right, Cher?"

"F—*hic*—fine," she said.

Joe was giving me some heavy-duty stink eye. I could see his thoughts. Great. Nice fucking work, Miller. Not only do you screw things up for your own faggot self, you screw things up for everybody.

"Maybe we should go," said Nicole.

I was actually concerned Joe might kick my ass later. But he didn't. Nicole apparently warmed back up to him as we wended our way down the canyon. I heard some slurping and bumping in the back-seat. Later he told me he "cooter-banged" her back there.

The Incredible Shrinking Man

As the Olympia drew nearer, Big Bill began cutting and defining his physique. He tailored his sets from low reps at high weights to high reps at low weights, and in this manner molded his muscles from the inside out. He was ripped by late spring; his lats and pecs and delts were scored with fingers. He was a monster, a behemoth, the Samson of biblical lore—something Rodin might have sculpted in the feverish throes of a laudanum binge. To see him lumbering around the house in his underwear—navigating tight corners, ducking light fixtures, drinking milk straight from the carton, and crushing the empty half-gallon container effortlessly in his mighty clutches—was to witness a true freak of nature. Everything looked small next to him; a fatburger looked like a novel appetizer between his fingers, a table setting like a child's tea set. He looked better than in '80, altogether more massive and deeply pocketed. He could scarcely wink without triggering some muscular response. The mere act of chewing set his traps to rippling from his neck to his shoulders. His right pec swelled like a pig bladder every time he raised his tiny fork. I was beginning to think Big Bill might be destined for Olympus at last.

In July he started complaining of fatigue and reduced endurance during workouts. His right leg began swelling, so he worked that much harder on the left. For two weeks he forged onward in spite of the ailments. No pain, no gain. But one afternoon at Gold's in the middle of an incline press, a tightening in the chest simply could not be ignored, and Doug was forced to spot him. Big Bill was so lightheaded that he nearly tumbled getting to his feet. Doug rushed him to Cedars-Sinai.

On the phone Doug was uncharacteristically calm and serious.

"You gotta get down here," he said.

"You know I can't do that."

"You gotta."

"I can't."

He was silent on the other end. I could hear him breathing out of his mouth. "You need to grow up," he said, finally. "You need to put that shit behind you."

I insisted that Doug meet me in the parking lot at Cedars. I found him leaning on the hood of the Malibu next to a laundry truck. He was still in his neoprene short-sleeved bodysuit. The nubby protuberances in his breadbasket left very little to the imagination.

"Why don't you put some pants on?" I said.

"What for?"

"Because maybe the whole world doesn't want to look at your nut sack."

"Who cares? Anyways, I don't have any pants. They're at the gym. Now, c'mon, hurry up, we gotta see the doctor now. Then we can see Dad."

I sat down on the bumper of the laundry van.

"What're you doing? Let's go."

I gazed across the lot, away from the hospital. A Mexican guy in coveralls was pruning shrubs nearby. "Just give me a sec," I said.

Doug shifted his weight restlessly from one massive leg to the other, and gave a little tug at his breadbasket to let his nuts breathe.

Listening to the steely precision of the Mexican's shears at work, I couldn't summon the will to get up off that bumper. "I can't do it," I said.

"Oh, please," he sighed. "Get over it."

"You don't understand. You were too young. You don't remember."

"Don't fraternize me, ass-lick. Dad's in there and there's something wrong with him. He might be fucking dying, for all we know. So quit being such a baby and suck it up. Why are you always such a little wuss about everything? What are you afraid of?"

Somebody said that the things we fear the most have already happened to us. I think they were right.

When Doug saw that there were tears in my eyes, he softened a bit, and sat down beside me and rested a heavy arm on my back. I could smell his armpit. "It's not even the same hospital," he observed gently.

"I know. You're right. I'm being a baby, I know I am. It's just that . . ." But I choked on the words. My stomach tightened in an instant, and my insides set to trembling in a paroxysm of yearning like nothing I had ever felt before, not even for Lulu.

"It's okay," said Doug, squeezing my shoulder with his massive hand. "Get it out of your system."

For nearly a decade I had been in despair, really and truly in despair, not even knowing I was in despair. Of all the unlikely guides to hold my hand through the haunted halls of this darkest place, fate had chosen my brother Doug, with his overactive pituitary and his Neanderthal delicacy.

"C'mon, ass-munch," he said, giving my shoulder an impatient squeeze. "Get it together. We gotta talk to the doctor."

I walked right through those double glass doors just as naturally as if I'd been walking into Ralphs. The hospital was everything I remembered: the big colored Legos, the dead chemical air. The light made me queasy, but none of it was as bad as I anticipated.

The doctor was Asian. His name was a verb—Chew, I think. He had a facial tic that caused his left eye to wink intermittently, so that you didn't want to look him in the eye when he talked to you, because you were afraid he might think you were staring at his tic. But then when he wasn't looking at you, you wanted to look at his tic.

"Your father is experiencing what's called cardiomyopathy. That means the walls of his heart have thickened." Dr. Chew clipped an X-ray to the light box. "As a result, his cardiac functions have been significantly compromised. That's what caused the swelling and the dizziness. His blood has thickened."

"How did it happen? Is it from working out?"

His left eye twitched. "Not exactly," he said. He turned his attention toward the X-rays. "You see this shaded area around the heart, here? That's the thickening. Normally this shaded area would be considerably thinner."

"What caused it?" I said.

"It could have been a number of things." Chew fidgeted distractedly with the corner of an X-ray. His eye twitched again. "But I strongly suspect steroid use."

I was absolutely dumbstruck. I looked to Doug, with his jaw hanging agape like a steam shovel, and I knew he was as shocked as me. Big Bill juiced? How could this possibly be? Big Bill had always remained above suspicion, perhaps because his gonzo work ethic and uncompromising veneer were so easily confused with moral fortitude. Where were the indicators: the hypodermics, the tracks, the volatility, the unchecked aggression?

The very idea was unthinkable: gain without pain. Big Bill would never accept such a proposition. And yet it was true. The proof was in the massive arms and shoulders. But most of all, it was in the thickening walls of the heart.

"Is he gonna die?" said Doug.

"No. Probably not anytime soon. Your father's condition is manageable. He's going to be facing some lifestyle changes, however."

I remember looking at the X-ray and thinking it strange to see Big Bill's superhuman physique photographed from the inside out—how fragile and human it looked without all that muscle buffering it.

Big Bill was upbeat in his hospital bed, grinning less with relief, it seemed, than with forced levity. As in all varieties of clothing, Big Bill looked ridiculous in his hospital gown. The nurse had been forced to slit it up the side to get it to fit over his massive trunk.

"I smell hamburgers," he said. "I'm ready to strap on a feed bag."

"I'll bet," I said.

Doug stood at a distance, tight-lipped and sullen. I think he felt betrayed. I'd never put Big Bill on a pedestal in the first place—he'd proved himself to be unfailingly human long ago—so I was not outraged by his breach of moral conduct so much as genuinely surprised. I still couldn't see how he'd managed to hide such a big thing. But for Doug, the discovery was nothing less than a loss of innocence. I don't think he ever forgave Big Bill for the juice.

"You should have seen your little brother at the wheel," said Big Bill. "You'd have been proud. We must have run five reds, eh Champ?"

Doug grunted.

"That ice cream truck darn near T-boned us on Slauson. But your brother here just swung around him like old Steve McQueen."

"Shut up, Dad," he said. "You're not fooling anyone."

Big Bill knew a short ending when he heard one. His face colored, and he turned his attention toward the window, away from Doug and me. I felt sort of bad for him.

"You want me to bring you some books from home or anything? Magazines?"

"No thanks, Tiger. I'm sure they've got plenty of stuff here."

Big Bill stayed at Cedars for the better part of a week. Dr. Chew assigned him a strict regimen of anticoagulants and fibrinolysis and thrombolytics and lots of other voodoo intended to thin his blood. As for the thickening heart, time would tell.

When word got around about Big Bill's condition, cards arrived from Joe Wieder and the Mentzer brothers and Tom Platz and Lee Haney himself, and I can't help but think that a collective shiver ran down the spine of professional bodybuilding. How many of these guys were really juiced? When I started running through my father's rippling associates one by one, very few of them managed to elude my suspicions. The body had limits, limits to how fast it could convert protein, limits to the amount of muscle mass it could pile onto a lean frame, limits to how far one could push the conditioning envelope without allowing the body to recover. Every one of these guys tested those limits around the clock, looking for an edge, maybe even a shortcut to that ten thousand–dollar take at the Mr. Biggest Little City in the World competition at the Silver Legacy in Reno, or perhaps a share in something bigger—a Universe, or an Olympia—so you could convert those winnings into mortgage payments and hams and twelve-pound glasses for your oily-faced kid. What choice did a guy have but to look for an edge? What were the options? Squeezing yourself into a forklift? Selling women's shoes?

The days crept by through March and April and into May without any word from Lulu. My bold offensive had been a complete flop. I must have started a hundred letters begging her forgiveness, begging her to forget what I said and let me accept her terms. I'd gladly be her brother and nothing more, if only to be near her. But I could never send them, I suppose because I knew deep down that such an enterprise would only drive me crazy with frustration, and that anything short of possessing Lulu would be a profound disappointment anyway, so I was better off trying to forget her altogether. I didn't give two shits about having a sister.

Big Bill formally announced his retirement in the September issue of *Muscle* magazine, which ran a four-page spread entitled "Big Bad Bill is Sweet William Now." The article was not your standard musclehead fare. The piece was actually quite bizarre by any measure, written by somebody named Scot Menninger (note, as I did, that it was Scot with one T), who infused the tribute with a certain epic, if not gay, poetry, not unlike Big Bill's posing.

"And yet Miller, when we hold him up to the light, glistens like some Grecian god come down from Olympus . . ."

This particular line struck a chord with Doug, and threatened to become a mantra.

"And yet," he would say, philosophically, applying his deodorant in vain, "Miller, when we hold him up to the light, glistens like some caramel-coated turd coming down the pipe . . ."

There was hope even for Doug, I decided.

Health and Fitness also ran a piece on Big Bill. The author, Dale Munger, opted for a more prosaic approach in his tribute, chronicling, in twenty-five hundred words, Big Bill's harrowing chase for that ever-elusive Mr. Olympia. Munger made Big Bill sound courageous, compulsive, tireless in his pursuit, like some silver-eyed Ahab on an impossible quest.

Big Bill, of course, much preferred this second treatment. The gay poetry thing was an embarrassment. He was convinced that the gay army was taking over bodybuilding and using it as a recruiting device in their conspiracy to thwart the propagation of the species and turn everybody into vegetarians. He may have been right.

Big Bill's illness succeeded, where any attempt at reconciliation probably would have failed, in luring Willow back to the nest. Though she swore she was through with my father, Willow, who had already moved her practice back to Sausalito, closed her doors indefinitely the week of his release from Cedars and came back to Santa Monica for the end of summer, where she took up residence in the trophy room.

Just when it seemed the Millers were scattered for good, a thing of the past, here came the thickening walls of Big Bill's heart. His illness had a magnetic effect on our scattered brood. Not only was Willow drawn back into the fold, but Ross started spending more time at home during Big Bill's convalescence. He remained Alistair, and had discovered Guns N' Roses just as the rest of America's *Appetite for Destruction* began to wane. He spent a half hour in the bathroom every morning amidst a cloud of Aqua Net, teasing his scraggly hair into a rat's nest. He started tearing his T-shirts on purpose, and began pegging his pants so straight that they fit like leotards. All of this was an improvement, to my way of thinking. Even his little friend Regan made a cameo in the Miller abode on occasion, dragging the tattered hem of his trench coat up the stairs to Ross's room, though he never settled in much, and kept one eye at all times on the open door, like a cornered fox.

The Pico house was buzzing again. There were rumors that even Lulu would be home to roost before the end of summer, and this knowledge heartened me to such an extent that I actually began releasing her to a degree, or so I believed.

On Willow's fourth or fifth night back, I came home late from

Fatburger after a double and found her seated alone in the half-light of the kitchen, sipping herbal tea in her bathrobe. Immediately she noticed the disheveled gauze bandage mummifying my right wrist and palm.

"What happened?"

"Burned it on the stupid grill trying to stop a Baby Fat from falling in the grease trap. I was slammed."

She stood up and turned on the overhead light. "Let me have a look at that." She shepherded me to the sink, where she began unwrapping the gauze.

"My God, who wrapped this?"

"Acne Scar Joe did."

"Gracious, what a mess. Stay put."

She left the kitchen.

Inspecting the damage, I found that it was not so bad, really. An oval blister had burst on my wrist and palm. It was big and fleshy and pink at the edges, but it was mostly bark and not a lot of bite.

Willow returned with Neosporin and fresh gauze and some athletic tape. She cleaned and began patting dry the edges of the wound.

"This might sting," she warned, squeezing a little curlicue of ointment onto the raw oval.

"So, is this just temporary?" I said.

"We'll re-dress it tomorrow."

"No, I mean you coming back here."

"I don't know what it is. Hold this tight with your other hand," she instructed me. "Your father and I can't agree on anything, William, but it doesn't stop me from loving him." She tore off a strip of tape with her teeth, and fastened the gauze wrap tight against my wrist. "All that talk about change, I don't know anymore. I get less and less sure every day. Sometimes there are forces beyond our control. Sometimes even human forces. I'm still trying to accept these things."

She closed the fingers of my open hand and gave them a little pat. "You're ready to go, soldier."

One way or another, life makes you smaller. It whittled my mother down to nothing, and now my father was shrinking like a snowman before my eyes. He lost nearly twenty pounds in just over five weeks without the juice. His chest and arms deflated, even his head shrank. And the shrinkage was not limited to his physique. His whole manner was shrinking. He passed mirrors without pausing. His turgid smile went into hiding. The bronzed temple of his body had forsaken him, and having nowhere else to focus his self-consciousness, Big Bill turned it inward as never before. The results were disheartening. A softness was born in him, or perhaps rediscovered—a neediness, a nostalgia, an eagerness to appease.

Big Bad Bill was indeed Sweet William now. Moreover, he had a lot of time on his hands. He circled want ads, played the guitar, dusted his trophies, and pondered the future with a big thorny question mark written upon his forehead. He had spent the better part of the '80s building himself into a rippling giant, gobbling up trophies and vitamin supplements and entire hams faster than he could pay for them. Now his body was shrinking, his debt continued to mount, and he was becoming clownish.

"Sit on down with your old dad and watch some boob tube, Tiger."

"I gotta work, sorry."

"Say, why don't we all play Monopoly tonight?"

"You mean Monotony?" said Ross. "How about we all just drill a hole in our skull instead?"

"Well, maybe Scrabble, then."

"No offense, Dad, but playing Scrabble with you and Doug is like wrestling a pair of quadriplegics."

"I heard that, ass-bait!"

Sometimes Big Bill would coral Willow onto his lap and try to nibble her ears until she writhed free of his clutches, or he'd sneak up behind her and give her a bear hug while she was doing the dishes. And when that failed to yield sufficient results, he looked elsewhere for hugs. We should have got him a dog.

The most pathetic part of all may have been watching him eat. Not only had his appetite shrunk along with the rest of him, but there were also the dietary restraints placed on him by his condition. To see Big Bill with a wee slice of lean turkey breast and some blanched snow peas on his plate was painful enough. But to watch him savor those few sad bites of stringy white meat, working them between his mandibles as though it were his life's work, caressing the moisture out, puckering his lips like some French gourmand, as though the meat were unbearably succulent, was just too much to take.

Eventually he managed to arouse my outright contempt. I knew it was irrational, I knew it wasn't fair, but I just couldn't stand to see him go soft. Sensitivity fit him like a tuxedo: tight in all the wrong places. There was something unseemly about it. Big Bill was supposed to have a low threshold for weakness. He was supposed to be Darwinian in his strength. He was born to eradicate weakness, to snuff it out, to negate it with the business end of a shovel. What was his unique specialization, if not strength? If anything, the walls of his heart seemed thinner now. And every time he said please or thank you or anything else agreeable, every time he played his stupid guitar or said something gooey about Haight-Ashbury or Willow or my mother, I wanted to throttle him, because every kind gesture, every tolerant word, every mushy song sounded like a surrender.

The Prodigal Son Is a Daughter

It's safe to say that I wasn't the only one nervously anticipating Lulu's homecoming. The night before her arrival, she was the lone topic of conversation around the dinner table.

"She's an adult," said Big Bill.

"Well, she's not acting like one," said Willow.

"So, she's a little mixed up," he proceeded. "We can't push her into the right decision. Let her get her feet on the ground, she's got plenty of time to find her path. She's just a kid."

"But you just got through saying she's an adult," I observed.

"She's both," he said. "You, of all people, ought to know that."

He was right, I should have. Why else was I paying rent at home?

"Well, Jesus, Bill, we spent over—"

"It's not about money."

"Well, then, how do you propose to pay her tuition, now that—"

"We'll cross that bridge when we come to it."

I was beginning to wonder how long before Big Bill ran out of clichés.

"How is she going to pay off those loans?" said Willow. "You know, she'll have to start paying those off if she doesn't register next semester."

"She's a smart kid," said Bill. "She'll work it out."

"She'll register," I said, I have no idea why. I fully expected Lulu to quit school altogether.

"What makes you so sure she'll register?" Willow asked me.

I shrugged. "Just a hunch."

"Can I go now?" said Ross.

"Where to?" said Big Bill, who had shortened the leash on Ross in recent days.

"Out."

"Where?"

"Movies."

"With who?"

"Regan and some guys."

"Pfff," said Doug.

"You do your homework?"

"It's summer, Dad."

Big Bill grinned. Ross grinned back dutifully. It was becoming a ritual. It made me want to puke. "Be back by eleven."

"Yeah, yeah," said Ross, or Alistair, as he excused himself and took flight into the Santa Monica night, dressed like a confused vampire.

"I think we need to move her along slowly," said Big Bill. "Let her figure some things out."

"Maybe somebody should light a fire under her ass," I said.

"I don't think so," said Big Bill. "Your sister's a little combustible for that. She's going to have to do some searching, maybe a lot of searching."

"What on earth makes everyone think she's going to discover herself by dropping out of school and working at a bookstore and dating some guitar player?" Willow wanted to know.

"*Bass* player," I said.

"Bass player, then. The point is, whether or not—"

"Hey, what's wrong with guitar players?" said Big Bill.

"The point is, Bill, I'm worried about her lack of direction. She has no idea where she's headed. Ask her, and she'll tell you as much. The last time I spoke with her she spent twenty minutes talking about everything she *didn't* want to be, all the things she *didn't* want to do."

Big Bill smiled knowingly.

"Oh, no you don't," said Willow. "This is different, Bill, so you can stop grinning. Times are different. This isn't 1967. Seattle's not San Francisco."

Big Bill continued to smile knowingly.

"I may have 'dropped out,'" she said. "But only figuratively, Bill. I stayed in college. I went to class."

"What was your first major?" said Big Bill.

"Political Science."

"What about your second?"

"I don't remember. Look, I see what you're getting at. But Lulu's not me. Lulu has nothing to rebel against, not like I did. Lulu didn't endure Catholicism and ballet and charm school. Nobody tried to *mold* Lulu. Lulu's lost because . . ."

"Because she wants to be," I said.

Willow looked at me hopefully, like she was hungry for my insight.

I was trying to remember how Troy had put it. "She's never the same person twice," I explained. "She's always trying to reinvent herself so she doesn't have to be who she really is."

"Who's that?" said Willow and Big Bill simultaneously.

"Uh, well, that's where the cul-de-sac begins," I explained.

Doug ate through the entire dialogue, gobs of mashed potatoes and canned corn. His head followed the conversation like a ping-pong match, but the action was always secondary to the food on his plate. On this occasion, the hiatus in the conversation prompted him to look up from his Sloppy Joe, momentarily.

"What about this boyfriend?" said Big Bill. "What do we know about him? Wasn't he encouraging her to express herself, to paint or something? That's a start."

Doug rolled his eyes and took a bite of Sloppy Joe.

"He's a bartender, Bill. He's twenty-three."

"You sound like your mother."

Willow didn't deny it. "I just don't see how a *bass-playing bartender* makes for any sort of substantive support system, Bill, even if he is encouraging her to express herself. What else is he encouraging her to do? Have unprotected sex? Pay his rent with her student loans?"

I couldn't help but crack a smile.

Willow shot me a look.

"At least she's not working at Fatburger," I said, half ironically.

Doug guffawed and took a big gulp of milk.

"You're different," said Willow. "You've got a plan for the future, William. And I suspect you'll stick by it."

"And I think it's a great plan," said Big Bill. "I think more kids ought to take that route—take a year and do some real thinking, figure some things out."

"Yeah," said Doug. "Like how to make onion rings."

"That's enough," said Big Bill.

As much as I hate to admit it, I could feel pride coloring my cheeks. I didn't know Big Bill's approval could still do that to me.

"And if you'd just give Lulu a chance," pursued Big Bill, "I think she'll find her way."

"Oh, I don't know," sighed Willow. "I just think . . . I think we should encourage Lulu to be closer to . . . to *home.*"

"Leave her be. If she wants to come home, she'll come home. Let her figure it out herself."

Willow narrowed her gaze at Big Bill. "Hasn't she already figured enough out by herself? Jesus, Bill, you'd think you'd have learned by now."

Home

~~∿∿~~

I picked Lulu up at the airport in the Duster. The car was clean. I even waxed it. I wore jeans and a white T-shirt and my hair was falling just right. I was a little unshaven, which made me look older, wiser, maybe a little tougher, I reckoned. I was sporting a stash, too, a peach fuzzy little thing you might expect to see on a child molester.

Driving down La Tierra, I rehearsed my air of casual self-possession. I checked my hair in the mirror at every light. The stash was looking a little sad, a little wilted, but nothing a bit of attitude couldn't fix. And I had the recipe for attitude: two cups of aloof, a dash of dry wit, and a sprinkling of cruelty to taste.

Hard as I'd tried to convince myself that I'd finally escaped Lulu's gravitational pull, the minute I saw her standing at the curb next to her duffel bag, with her mess of hair piled on top of her head, and her bright lovely face, and her knees poking out of her ladybug skirt, I knew I was still hopelessly captivated by her. Just the way her little white fingers clutched a cigarette, the way her pouty little lips puffed on it. She looked bored standing at the curb, but I knew she had plenty of things occupying her. By the time she spotted the Duster, I was already grinning ear to ear. Just as I honked my greeting, a tall guy with a goatee and a plaid flannel shirt strode out of the terminal carrying a guitar case and stationed himself right beside Lulu, with a little pat on the rump.

The blood rushed out of me so fast that I was dizzy as I pulled to the curb. Before I could pop the trunk, the guy with the goatee opened the passenger door and stuffed his guitar case and bags up front with me, and he and Lulu both climbed into the backseat.

I laid some rubber pulling into traffic.

When I finally spoke, my voice came from somewhere else, down a well, or at the end of a tunnel. "So . . . this is, like, a surprise, then?"

"I invited him," said Lulu.

"My mom works for United," said the guy. "I get tickets mass cheap."

"No smoking in the car," I said.

Lulu cracked her window and tossed her cigarette. "This is Dan," she said. "And this is my brother—"

"Will," said Dan. "I've heard a lot about—"

"Stepbrother," I said. "Did you get rid of that cigarette?"

"Yes!" she said.

"I'm sorry, were you saying something, Pat?"

"*Dan*," smoldered Lulu.

I turned on the radio. Jaime Jarrin was doing play-by-play in Spanish on KWKW. Vin Scully had lost his luster for me the afternoon he'd forsaken me in Fatburger. Jaime Jarrin was my man now. I couldn't understand what the hell he was saying most of the time, but I liked the way syllables popped out of his mouth like jumping beans and his sentences built up steam until they couldn't possibly come out any faster, and old Jaime would slam on the brakes, turn on a dime, and start a new sentence, just as Griffin rounded third with a head full of steam, or Sax threw the ball into the right field bleachers. On this occasion, however, I wasn't so much listening to Jaime Jarrin as just hearing him.

"That's killer," said Dan. "Mexican radio. Dude, it's like ninety degrees here. That's so killer. Hey, check out that dude with the shopping cart."

Nobody checked out the dude with the shopping cart.

"Sweet," observed Dan. "Hey, man, thanks for picking us up."

"Yeah, it's cool," I mumbled. I snuck a peek at Lulu in the backseat, the side of her face squashed up against the window. I could only see one of her clear blue eyes, and it was looking about two feet out the window, like it couldn't see anything beyond that.

Dan saw everything. And it was all killer. I'm still not certain if he was just oblivious to the tension, or if he was painfully aware of it and trying desperately to compensate.

"Dude, check out the fat guy with the oranges! That guy's killer! How far is Santa Monica? Whoa, check out that Pontiac! Hey, so, these friends of ours from Seattle are playing at the Whiskey on Friday. They rock. We should totally check them out."

"Tacoma," mumbled Lulu.

"Same dif," said Dan. "Anyway, we should see them. They're killer. I can get us on the list, no prob."

"I'm busy," I said.

"Oh," said Lulu. "Are you working the *line* or the *register* that night?"

"Ouch," said Dan. "Roastola."

I couldn't have summed it up better.

"Neither," I said. "Actually, I'm hanging out with a friend. You remember Troy."

A glance in the rearview mirror revealed Lulu glowering at me.

I got butterflies and chills at the same time. "He'd love to see you," I said. "He never stops talking about you, and all the great times you had together."

"Who's Troy?" said Dan.

"Troy's nobody," said Lulu.

"Troy's Lulu's boyfriend," I explained. "Well, *officially* he's her boyfriend, anyway. She never actually gave him the courtesy of *breaking up.*"

Dan looked to Lulu.

Lulu looked two feet out the window. "I thought I made it pretty clear," she said. "I'm done with that."

It was an ending worthy of Big Bill. The old Big Bill, that is.

"Well, anyhow," I said, "I'll be sure and tell him you said hello, Lu."

"I'm sure you will, *Will.*"

"You guys want to stop and get a beer someplace?" said Dan. "Play some pool, or something?"

"Sure," I said.

"No," said Lulu. "You're the only one who could get in, remember?"

"Oh yeah," intoned Dan. "Bummer. But I thought nobody cards in L.A.?" he added hopefully.

"I know where we can get in," I said. "That place in Venice by Troy's new apartment. We could call him."

"Oh, shut up."

"I'm sure he'd be happy to pop down for a beer."

"Go to hell."

"Maybe you could take the opportunity to finally dump him."

"Quit it."

"*Dude*," said Dan forcefully, but diplomatically. "She doesn't want to go. Drop the whole Troy thing. Know any other places?"

"Not really."

"Forget it," said Lulu. "I'm tired. Please, let's go home."

After the initial surprise, Willow and Big Bill both seemed to relish Dan's presence, hopeful, perhaps, that Dan might lend some insight into the current state of Lulu, or maybe even offer himself up as a tool for Lulu's persuasion. He seemed malleable enough. If nothing else, Dan took some of the focus off of Lulu, a function beneficial to everyone involved.

Willow was putting out a meat and potato spread for dinner to commemorate Lulu's homecoming. Even Big Bill was to be granted a little leniency with regard to his dietary restraints. Willow wanted it to be perfect. We were already sitting around the table when the doorbell rang.

"Oh, that must be Troy," I said. "Shoot, I forgot. Can he stay for dinner? I sort of invited him."

The air was brittle. Even Doug stopped chewing.

"What?" I said, innocently. "I can't invite my best friend to dinner anymore?"

I got up and answered the door. When Troy brushed by me into the foyer, I could smell his aftershave. He was pickled in it.

Willow hurriedly set him a place.

Troy couldn't even look at Lulu when we walked into the dining room.

Willow set Troy a place strategically across from me, and between the twins. Lulu was on the other side of Ross—that is, Alistair—who was on the far side of Doug. If Troy ever did summon the moxie to venture a glance at Lulu, he'd have to lean way back or way forward in his chair.

Doug wrinkled his nose when Troy sat down. "What smells like Listerine?"

"Pipe down," said Ross. "You smell like the inside of a dead raccoon."

"Whatever, *Alistair*. Isn't that a girl's name?"

Big Bill cleared his throat. "So, how goes things, young man?" he said heartily.

"Great," said Troy. "Thanks. And thanks for dinner, too. I don't get much home cooking these days."

"He's a bachelor," I observed.

"Going to Santa Monica, are you?" inquired Big Bill.

"Yeah," he said. "Transferring to UCLA probably. Or maybe UW, I'm not sure."

"Will went to Hamburger University," said Doug.

"Yeah, well, where do you think *you're* gonna go?" said Alistair. "*Meathead* University?"

Doug didn't have a comeback for that. He started chewing harder.

"What're you studying?" inquired Willow.

"Uh, I'm not really sure as far as majoring," said Troy. "I kind of like astronomy."

"That stuff's all fake," said Doug. "Those horoscopes and all that mumbo jumbo. That stuff's made up."

"That's *astrology*, you Cro-Magnon," said Alistair.

"That's what he said, *ass-lips*!"

"He said *astronomy*!"

"Did not."

"Did too."

It was like old times again.

Poor Dan, I was thinking.

"What about you, Dan?" said Willow. "What are you up to?"

"I'm in a band," he said. "Well, I do other stuff, too. I paint some—not like Lulu or anything—just sort of fooling around, mostly. Latex on beaverboard, stuff like that. I also manage the Comet."

"The Comet?"

"It's a tavern. It's like the most famous bar in town. It's okay. But being a musician is who I *really* am. I mean, pretty much. I guess."

"Is that why you hauled your bass along, even though you're only going to be here thirty-six hours?" I inquired.

"Pretty much. It gets depressing, otherwise. I can't live without music."

"Heavy," I said.

"It just so happens that I strum a little six string myself," said Big Bill.

Suddenly, the image of Big Bill and Dan "jamming" in the living room after dinner flashed in front of me, and I wanted to puke.

"What kind of stuff?" said Dan.

"Oh, you know," said Big Bill. "Greasy kid stuff."

Dan guffawed. I wanted to puke again.

"Will plays the spatula," said Doug.

"Yeah, well, you play the sausage," said Alistair.

"Do not."

"Do too. Don't forget, I live downstairs. I can hear you shining your sausage up there."

"Hey," said Big Bill. "Cool out."

"Ass-bag," said Doug.

"Troglodyte," said Alistair.

"So, Dan," I said. "How does it feel to be in the bosom of the Miller family?"

"It's cool. You should see *my* family."

Lulu wouldn't look at anybody. She wasn't eating, just fiddling with the food on her plate like a kid, rolling a pea up a mountain of mashed potatoes.

"Glad to see that you're up and around, Mr. Miller," said Troy.

"How sweet," said Willow.

"Thanks, Tony," said Big Bill.

"It's Troy," said Lulu.

"Oh, right," said Big Bill. "Thanks, Troy. I feel great. I've been getting some much-needed rest." Then, turning his attention back to Dan: "Now, Dan, tell us about the band. Have you got a name?"

"Um, yeah."

Still chewing, Big Bill encouraged Dan to divulge said information, waving a forkful of turkey meatball around like a traffic baton. "Well? What is it? Inquiring minds want to know."

Dan desperately sought Lulu's eyes, but she was still looking down at her plate.

"Uh, Cum Dumpster," he said finally.

Willow dropped her fork.

"B-but we're changing our name," he hastened to add.

"Good move," said Big Bill. "Don't want to send the wrong message."

"We're gonna call ourselves My Mother's Machine."

"What a stupid name," said Doug.

"Shut up," said Alistair. "You don't even know what it means."

"Do too."

"Do not."

"What *does* it mean?" inquired Willow.

"Uh," said Dan. "Nothing, really."

"It means his mother's *dildo*," I said.

Doug chortled.

"Oh," said Willow. "I see. Cute."

Dan smiled sheepishly. "Brett made it up. He's the singer. I just play the bass."

"What kind of groove?" said Big Bill.

"*Groove?*" I blurted. "Did you just say *groove?*"

"Well, yeah," said Big Bill. "You know, like, what's your *thing?*" he clarified. "What's your *bag?*"

The steroids had gone to his brain. Or was it the LSD?

"Greasy kid stuff," quipped Dan.

Big Bill and Dan shared a chuckle. I almost puked.

"We're pretty much hard rock," explained Dan. "With kind of a post-punk infusion. Like Zeppelin meets the Dead Boys, but faster. Brett knows one of the guys from Sub Pop. We're talking to them about releasing an EP or something. Which would be killer."

Big Bill looked mildly impressed. "Mmm."

"Congratulations," said Willow. "Is that like an *LP*? What does the *E* stand for?"

"Uh, *extended*, I think. Like *extended play* or something like that. I'm not sure. It's like a record, but shorter. Longer than a single, but shorter than an album. Smaller, too, I think. I mean, size-wise, smaller. Like a single. Sort of like an album on a single, I think. Brett mostly handles that stuff."

"Interesting. So, when do we get to see these paintings, Lulu?" said Willow.

"They're really good," said Dan. "I mean, *really* good."

"I don't save them," sighed Lulu. "I get rid of them."

"She gives them away," explained Dan. "There's one hanging in the office at my work."

"Well, how about snapping a picture sometime?" said Big Bill.

"Yeah, okay," said Lulu. "Once I get better."

"I'll bet you're really good," said Troy, who flushed immediately. God, what a wuss.

"I *keep telling* her that," said Dan. "She did this one, you should see it. It's of these amazing cloud stacks, like all purple and silver, and it looks like the clouds are actually churning and tumbling over each other in the painting, like these big thunderheads rolling in, or something. It's like they're *really* rolling, though. And the colors are *really* ominous, *really* amazing."

"*Really*," I said.

"It's ugly," said Lulu. "It looks like dog vomit."

Doug guffawed. "You should call your band *that*."

"Well, anyway, send us a picture," I said. "I mean, if you ever get halfway decent."

"I'll bet she's great," said Troy.

"Totally," concurred Dan. "She's *really, really* good."

"*Really?*" I said. I was at the end of my rope. I suppose I could have tied it around my neck, but that wasn't my instinct. "Well, isn't that supportive," I said. "That's just killer. You rock. So, what's next for Mr. and Mrs. Going Nowhere Fast? Are you moving in together? Consolidating Lulu's assets? Any two-car garages and white picket fences on the horizon? Or is it food stamps and flannel diapers?"

Lulu dropped her fork with a clank, piloted her chair back with a squeak, stood up, and left the table without a word. We could hear her footfalls retreating up the stairs.

The air went brittle again. All eyes were on me.

"What?" I said.

The Sound Electricity Makes

—〰〰—

I found Lulu sprawled on her old bed with her face buried in a pillow. The radio was on. The Mattress Warehouse was having a liquidation sale. Kings, queens, twins. Three days only.

"Don't," she said, before I could say anything.

"You don't even know what I'm gonna say."

She bolted upright into a sitting position, and I could see she'd been crying. "Don't do *anything*, for once. Don't *say* anything, don't *write anything down*, don't even *think* anything. Just go away."

"I'm sorry, Lu. I swear, I can't help it. I just—"

"Don't ask me to forgive you. You haven't exactly been very forgiving, you know. You don't even know what you're saying anymore, you just open your mouth, and hateful things come out."

"Yeah, well, you made me this way."

"No, Will. Stop blaming me. Nobody made you this way. *You* made you this way. So you can stop punishing me now! And you can stop punishing Dan and Troy and the rest of the world."

"Okay, okay, I'm sorry." I sat beside her on the bed.

Lulu recoiled slightly and wouldn't look at me. "You're a real ass-hole, you know that?" She leaned over and cracked the window open.

"I know that."

She fished a pack of Camels and a book of matches out of her leather jacket on the back of the chair. She lit a cigarette and plopped the matchbook on the dresser. The matchbook said *Deja Vu, Show-girls, Fifty Beautiful Women and Three Ugly Ones.* I listened to her smoke for a while. I watched her. Her hands were shaking. Her mascara was running.

"I needed you, goddamnit," said Lulu. "But I *knew* you wouldn't be there. I needed you like I needed you the night in the garage, as a . . . damnit, I don't even know. I just needed you. Why can't that be enough? If you love me so goddamn much, why couldn't you be there?"

"What are you talking about?"

"Why can't I just be your sister? Why do I have to be every-thing?"

"I don't understand."

She bit at a cuticle. "I got pregnant."

My ears started ringing. I didn't know what to say.

Lulu puffed her cigarette with bloodless lips and sighed upon ex-haling. "About three months ago."

"So, you what? You had an abortion?"

"No."

"Then, you're still—"

"No." She tapped a cigarette ash into her cupped palm. "I don't want to talk about it."

Neither did I. My ears were still ringing, and there was a bitter lump in my throat. I tried to swallow it, but it wouldn't go down. "Does Dan know?"

"No. None of it."

"Jesus."

"And he won't know," she said. "There's no use in telling him, now. There never really was."

"What does that mean?"

"It doesn't mean anything."

"Wasn't it *his*?"

"Of *course* it was his. Just drop it."

The short endings, the brick walls; she was sounding more like Big Bill by the minute. The old Big Bill, that is. "I'm sorry, Lu."

She didn't say anything. She tapped another ash into her cupped palm.

"I'm sorry about the letter," I said. "I'm sorry about not being there, or whatever."

Lulu leaned over and snubbed her cigarette out on the windowsill. She scattered the ashes out the window, blew on the windowsill, and stuffed the butt and the matches in the pocket of her coat. "Whatever," she said.

"You're right. Okay? *I don't know* why you have to be my everything, Lu. You just do. You are. You always have been. And I don't know what happened. Because it used to be that I was everything to you, for a long time, and you can't tell me that I wasn't everything to you, Lu, you *can't* tell me that."

She looked toward the window. "You were," she said softly.

"Well, then, what's wrong with me? What did I do to you? Am I ugly? Am I stupid? Did I smother you? Was it my acne? Wasn't I cool enough? Wasn't I—"

"No. Stop." Exasperated, she ran her hands over her face. "It's not about you."

"You mean, it's about *you*."

"No. It's not. Goddamnit, it's *not*. What do you want me to say? I love you? Okay, I love you! Now fuck off!"

My ears were ringing again. But this time it was a good ringing. My mind was racing. I was measuring, figuring: *Okay, okay, TWO I love yous, and ONE fuck off, not bad, not bad. I can work with this.*

"Well, goddamnit, say something!" said Lulu.

"I love you, too."

"No duh, you jerk!"

"Jesus, Lu, am I supposed to thank you for loving me? Is *that* it? Because I *am* grateful, *believe* me. But don't you get it? You don't love me like you used to, you just love me because you have to. You love me because—"

"It's not true."

"Yeah, well, I just don't see it," I said, looking away. "I don't believe it for a second."

"Well, you don't see the stupid stars every night, and you still believe in them, don't you? Sometimes you have to have faith," she said.

"You should be a politician."

"What's that supposed to mean?"

"It means I can't even tell what the hell you're talking about. You're not saying anything. You object, you stall, you evade."

"I said *I love you*. That's not a filibuster."

"Everything's some fucking metaphor with you," I said. "I'm talking about *you* and *me*, and you're talking about the Milky Way! Why can't you just admit it: You either love me or you don't."

"It's not as simple as that."

"See, there you go!"

"Well, it's not. And don't start getting nasty again, either. Because I'll walk right out of this room, and this conversation will be closed. Forever."

"What kind of threat is that? This conversation never *goes* anywhere!"

"So, let's not have it," she cried. "Let's go back to the beginning. Back to the part where you came to apologize for being an asshole."

"I'm sorry."

She sniffled, and put a hand on my knee. "Apology accepted," she said. "But don't start, because you'll just find yourself apologizing again in five minutes."

Lulu took a couple swipes at her running mascara with the sleeve of her blouse. She sniffled and started to sigh, but instead a little laugh escaped her. She finally surrendered to a smile. I wasn't sure what all was written in that smile, but I thought I read an invitation. Before Lulu knew what hit her, I was smothering her with kisses, and her hair was in my fingers, and my tongue was in her mouth, and even though she was a little stiff, she wasn't pulling away from me. She tasted like hot chocolate and cold cigarettes, and it was as though I could feel electricity surging down her spine as I ran my open hand firmly down the contour of her back. And I touched her with the strongest, most delicate touch in the world—like the thumb of God running down the spine of a baby bird, and Lulu arched her back and tilted her head back and gave a breathy, achy little moan, which in all my life I'll never forget, because I could feel the force of that breath all through me like a tropical wind.

That's when Dan poked his head into the room.

Lulu pushed me away and recoiled so fast that she rapped her knuckles on the nightstand and set the lamp to wobbling with her elbow. I'm not sure what Dan actually saw, but certainly he felt the urgent discomfort of poking his head into something unexpected, because he pulled it out again instantly.

"Oh God," groaned Lulu, as Dan creaked down the stairs. "Fuck."

"Shhh," I said. "It's okay." And indeed, it was okay. Everything was okay. Because all I could feel was Lulu coursing through me, throbbing and tickling and making my heart beat like a bunch of hippies around a drum circle.

"It's not okay."

"It is."

"No," she said, turning away toward the window.

"He didn't see anything."

"It's still not okay."

"Get over it," I said.

She spun around and shot me a look. "You don't even know what you're talking about."

"I know exactly what I'm talking about. I don't care who sees. What does it matter? You're not even my—"

"Stop it," she said. "Just stop talking."

It was hard, but I stopped talking. The only problem was that about two seconds later, I was all over Lulu again, kissing and nibbling and sniffing my way closer to her mouth, which she scrunched up as she fought spiritedly to elude my advances. But I had her wrapped up so tightly that the best Lulu could do was wriggle and contort and bury her chin in her chest. Finally, she relented. At last I'd overcome her with sheer brute force. And for one miraculous, unfathomably huge, kaleidoscopic, sparkling, iridescent, rainbow-colored instant, Lulu stopped fighting me and permitted our tongues to loll around like a ball of serpents inside one another's mouths, and that was one of the great moments of my life. It ended abruptly, however. Suddenly everything flashed red and my tongue was throbbing, and Lulu broke free of my hold and stood up. She straightened her ladybug skirt and took another swipe at her mascara. "You're still an asshole," she said flatly.

And she went downstairs.

The Land of the Lost

Somewhere between calling me an asshole and sitting back down at the dinner table, Lulu reinvented herself again. There was danger in her eyes. I could see it immediately upon resuming my own seat. Troy must have seen it, too. God knows he'd had enough practice. I don't know whether Dan could see danger in Lulu's eyes or not, probably his mind was still in the bedroom upstairs.

Aside from the spark in her eyes, Lulu betrayed no outward sign of the impending storm, or the disturbance that had preceded it. The runny mascara was gone. She was a portrait of composure. She ate her cold dinner matter-of-factly, like she was filling up a gas tank. She didn't say anything.

Big Bill turned the conversation toward the Dodgers. Troy said something about the bullpen, and I said something about the

Guerrero trade, and somebody said something about Tudor's first outing as a Dodger, and Doug said that the Dodgers sucked, and how even when they were good nobody in L.A. gave a rat's ass, and for once he had a point.

Finally, Lulu said something and everybody listened.

"We should go out tonight," she said. "I mean *out*. Drive to Malibu, or Canyon Country, or the desert. Or go see a movie, or . . . oh, I don't know, do *something*."

"You can borrow the Duster," I said, so as not to look like a total asshole.

"No," said Lulu. "You *have* to come. And Troy, too."

Troy and I looked at each other uneasily.

"Can I come?" said Doug, looking up from his third helping of mashed potatoes.

"No," said Lulu and I, in unison.

"Go where?" Big Bill wanted to know.

"I don't know," said Lulu. "Somewhere."

After chewing on this offering for a moment, Big Bill rolled it around in his mouth, and ultimately swallowed it. Apparently the information sated his curiosity. "Mmm," he said.

Troy and Dan and I would gladly have consented to go anywhere Lulu decided to lead us. No matter how she tortured, abused, teased, or tormented us along the way, we would have followed her to the edge of the earth.

"So, where am I going?" I said, pulling away from the curb. Troy was consigned to the front seat with me, buckled in tightly. Lulu and Dan sat in the backseat, but they weren't exactly cuddling; they were separated by Dan's guitar case.

"Let's get a bottle of something," Lulu said, looking out the window.

"Aye, aye, Captain."

I piloted us to the Circle K parking lot, where we all fished around in our pockets for money. Dan climbed out of the Duster clutching a wad of rumpled bills, and soon returned with a half gallon of rum and a handful of change.

"Where to?" I said.

"Just drive," said Lulu.

"Drive where?"

"Just start driving."

"What, are you carjacking me? What does that mean? Where? This was your idea."

"Oh, I don't know," she sighed. "*Somewhere*. Get on the 10 and drive east."

"To where?"

"East."

I got on the 10, and started east. By the time we skirted downtown, Lulu had already hit the bottle two or three times, with Dan matching her slug for slug. I wasn't drinking, just listening to the Dodgers on KWKW. Troy wasn't drinking either, not yet. Nobody talked much, especially not Dan, who was morose in spite of a *killer* view of the skyline, though even in this state he was a bit fidgety. The Dodgers were playing Houston. It was the bottom of the fourth, one–zero Astros. Jaime Jarrin was bantering about something, I'm not sure what, something about Gibson's hands, or maybe his mother's hands, when the jumping beans came leaping out of Jarrin's mouth with the name Gibson right in the middle of them.

"What happened?" said Troy.

"Gibson homered, I think."

"You think?" he said. "Jesus, why don't we listen on KABC, so we can understand what's happening?"

"It's better this way," I said, turning the volume up.

"I agree," said Lulu, from the back, a sentiment she punctuated with yet another splash of spiced rum.

"Whatever," said Troy, folding his arms and gazing out the side window.

As per Lulu's instructions, we forged east through the basin and into the desert until the lights thinned out, and the stars burned brighter, and as far as I could decipher, Davis scored on Bell's single, or maybe it was a double, or maybe a giant carnivorous rabbit chased Davis around third, but somehow Davis scored in Houston's half of the seventh, and Lulu opened her window, and I opened mine, and hot air thundered through the car like a stampede of buffalo, and the desert seemed wild with possibilities.

The bottle pacified Lulu, or maybe it was the desert air. She no longer gave any indication that a storm was imminent. Dan, too, seemed to be coming around with each slug of rum. He popped his window open and stuck his nose out into the hot wind, and when he pulled it back in, I could see, even in the dark, that he was smiling like a kid on a roller coaster. Indeed, he *was* on a roller coaster, the only question was how long until he chose to get off.

About twenty miles west of Palm Springs, our destination revealed itself on the horizon. A half mile ahead, two rather ominous concrete giants sprouted out of the arid plain against a backdrop of mountains.

"Whoa," said Dan. "No way. Killer! Remember, from Pee Wee's—?"

"Shhh," said Lulu, as though Dan's voice might startle the giants.

"Killer," Dan repeated, in his indoor voice.

The Wheel Inn was closed, as was the gift shop in the belly of the brontosaurus. The parking lot lights, the footlights, the entire complex lay in darkness but for the beams of our headlights and a few queasy lights out back of the restaurant, illuminating a blue dumpster. When I killed the engine, the silence of the desert enveloped us. Only the distant guttural progress of a diesel truck somewhere on the interstate, and the drone of a billion chirping crickets, reached our ears. When we climbed out of the car, the stars flickered brighter and

the crickets chirped louder, and the crickets seemed to give voice to
the blinking stars.

We shuffled across the gravel parking lot toward the concrete dinosaurs. Lulu, still clutching the bottle, shuffled more than the rest
of us. We paused beneath the brontosaurus to ponder its dimen-
sions. Dan pressed his face to the glass and peered into the darkened gift shop. I surveyed the impressive length of the herbivore's
neck and gazed up into its face, which looked a bit like Michael
Dukakis.

"Whoever built these was a total genius," said Dan, with only a
hint of sarcasm. "How awesome is this?"

"He died a few months ago," said Troy. "I saw a thing on the news."

"No," said Lulu.

"Yeah," said Troy. "I guess he was planning a woolly mammoth,
too. And some other ones."

"Awesome," said Dan.

"He's dead," said Lulu, as though she couldn't quite believe it.

"Lulu and I met him when we were kids," I said. "His name was
Clyde, I think."

"Claude," said Lulu.

"That was years before the tyrannosaurus was built," I pursued.
"He was just planning it then. He had sketches and models."

"They said on the news it cost him something like a half million
dollars to build just the tyrannosaurus," observed Troy.

"What a nut job," said Dan.

"What's wrong with that?" Lulu wanted to know.

"Well, if you had a million dollars, would you build two fucking
cement dinosaurs in the middle of Bumfuck, Egypt?"

"I know *you* wouldn't," Lulu said. "You'd do something obvious. I
suppose you'd buy some *cool* car and some *cool* house."

"I'd save it," Troy chimed in.

"Of *course* you would," said Lulu. Gale warnings were officially in effect. Lulu had another slug of rum.

Dan started battening down the hatches. "I didn't say there was anything wrong with—"

But it was already too late.

"Have some respect," said Lulu. "Just because somebody builds something doesn't mean you have to tear it down. What have you ever built? Who here even *has* a woolly mammoth? Something we've charted out, worked for, something that if we died tomorrow, we couldn't finish? If we had any guts, we'd be builders, not tearer-downers."

"We all die with unfinished business," I said.

"That's *not* what I mean. That's not even *close* to what I mean! I'm not talking about *business*! I'm talking about actually *doing* something! *Building* something. Everything else is just pretending. We're all just pretenders."

"What about your painting?" said Troy.

"Pfff," said Lulu. "That's garbage. I don't even *like* to paint. I'd rather clean houseboats. My paintings are terrible. Anyone who can't see that is hopeless."

With that, Lulu stumbled off toward the tyrannosaurus, crunching gravel along the way. We followed her, as though she were towing us. Her muscular ass was amazing underneath that ladybug skirt. Her boobs had grown, so that you could almost see them from behind when they bounced. She was wearing boots that stopped just below the knee. Her legs had grown shapely. But that's not why I followed her. I followed her because she was the spark, the catalyst, the animator, the big bang. Because she was dangerous, and unpredictable, and passionate. Doubtless, Troy and Dan had their own reasons for following Lulu, and doubtless they were as compelling as my own. I suspect Dan followed her because she was brooding and mysterious and red hot, and because she looked good on his arm. I'm almost certain Troy followed Lulu because she was one of the few things in the world not within his grasp.

When Lulu reached the giant, she seated herself on its tail, which had a groove running down its length, so that if you let your butt slide back too far, you risked losing your balance. Inexplicably, there was cool jazz emanating faintly from the belly of the tyrannosaurus.

"Maybe he swallowed Kenny G," I suggested.

Lulu laughed in spite of herself. So did Dan.

"You know," I said. "It's times like these that I'm absolutely certain God exists. The stars. The crickets. This fucking cement dinosaur playing cool jazz in the middle of the desert. That's poetry."

"Right on," said Dan. "You're funny, dude."

I was starting to like Dan, just as I'd started liking Troy. That was my problem—that's why I was destined to be a loser. Because I always liked the opponent.

"Screw the news," said Lulu. "Screw anyone who thinks it's silly. It was a sweet story, and you can't ruin it." Lulu straightened her skirt over her lap and looked away from the rest of us, out into the darkened flats. "When Claude Bell was just a little boy," she said, "his father took him one Sunday to see a giant elephant statue in New Jersey. They drove halfway across the state in the rain to see the giant elephant, because the little boy wanted to see the giant elephant. You might think that's stupid, a father taking his boy to see a big concrete elephant in the rain. But you'd be wrong, because there's nothing stupid about it. And the whole time driving toward that elephant, the little boy imagined what it would be like—how big would it be compared to himself? Was it bigger than a real elephant? Was it as tall as a building? He imagined and imagined, and he built up all these expectations. And when they finally got to the elephant, it wasn't as big as little Claude imagined it might be, but it was still bigger than what he imagined a real elephant would be, or at least as big, and it was every bit as grand and exciting as all of the expectations he'd built up for it. So, in this way, little Claude built his dream before he ever started constructing it, before he'd ever realized it, in fact. He built it on expectations." Lulu swiveled still farther away from us, until she was talking out into the desert, and we were looking squarely at her shoulder blades.

"The little boy and his father circled that elephant in the rain for almost an hour. They viewed it from every angle. The boy asked questions—how did they make it? Is there a real elephant inside? The father hoisted the boy up on his shoulders so Claude could see into the eyes of the elephant. And the eyes of the elephant had little cement wrinkles around them. And the ears had little cement folds. And Claude thought it was quite an amazing and unexpected thing, that something so big should have such little details. What the little boy felt was more than just awe, it was something else; he was *inspired* by what he saw. Looking at it, he dreamed his own dream—he imagined something even bigger than that elephant. He imagined a dinosaur. He imagined it with such force that he could see it. All the tiny wrinkled details. But that wasn't enough. He needed to touch it, to climb up the neck, to peer into the belly of this thing he'd conceived. And there was only one way to do that, and that was to build it." Lulu took a slug from the rum bottle. She fished a cigarette from her pocket. When she fired it up, there was a halo of light around her head.

"But little boys don't build giant dinosaurs," Lulu observed. "At least not out of concrete and steel. So Claude had no choice but to hold on to that dream for a lot of years. He held on to it with the greatest strength of all, and that is the strength of holding on to something without being able to touch it."

Lulu fell silent and puffed her cigarette. I thought she was finished with her story. But she resumed.

"Even before Claude became a man, he realized that men didn't build giant dinosaurs either, not without a lot of money. And the young man had no money at all. So he did some figuring, and what he figured was that it would take a young fellow of his prospects an awfully long time—and maybe a little luck—to ever amass the resources to make his dream happen. And Claude was discouraged, but not disheartened. He figured he could do it in ten years. So he got a job at Knott's Berry Farm. And he saved every penny he could."

Lulu dropped her cigarette and snuffed it out with her heel. "But Claude was all wrong. After ten years he was nowhere close. Building his dream just seemed to get more expensive as time went by. He was finally disheartened. He began to think that maybe his dream was a joke. Maybe he was wasting his time. Maybe he should buy a house with all the money he'd saved. But then he remembered the thing he'd been holding on to so long, he remembered all the wrinkled details, and the awe-inspiring size. And so he went back to work, and saving, and imagining. It took him twenty more years working at Knott's Berry Farm to save the money to buy the gas station and the adjoining land. Thirty years total! And it took him five more years to build his dream out of steel and concrete. Right here, in Bumfuck, Egypt."

I remember thinking that Dan must have felt pretty stupid. I know I did. Because even the cool jazz seemed noble suddenly.

"And not only did he actually build his dream at last," pursued Lulu. "Old Claude began building another. And when he finished that one, another. And the coolest part is that after all the work Claude put into them, and all the money he spent, all the time and the energy he invested, they aren't even monuments to himself." She took a slug of rum, and passed the bottle toward Dan's outstretched hand, then fished in the pocket of her blouse for another cigarette. "It doesn't matter who thinks they're silly," she said. "Little kids love them."

God, I would've given anything to be Claude Bell at that moment—if not to watch my dream rise out of the dust, then simply to have inspired Lulu Trudeau.

Dan toasted Claude Bell and his heroic dinosaurs. We passed the bottle, mostly in silence, as we sat on the tail of the tyrannosaurus under the stars, listening to cool jazz from the belly of the beast. Lulu sat on the end and I secured the space next to her, as close as I could get to her so that on those occasions when her balance faltered, she jostled me inadvertently. Troy occupied the space next to me, though only physically. Mentally, he was somewhere far out into the ether, or maybe deep down into himself. He'd given up on Lulu, that much was clear. He looked like a big white flag sitting there.

Dan the Man was restless, never sitting, forever climbing all over the dinosaur or hanging off the scaffold, always stirring gravel with his agitated feet, or vocalizing some bass line until, finally, he surrendered to the muse and went back to the Duster to fetch his bass.

I had to touch Lulu. It was not a matter of choice. And so I tried to put my arm around her waist, but she shrank from it. I tried to rest my hand on her knee, but she brushed it off. Troy bore silent witness to my rejection, while pretending not to notice. He sucked on the bottle with a gusto I hadn't seen since his Bender days. He must have felt something coming as I persisted in my groping, because just as Lulu was about to unleash her thunder, he rose mechanically to his feet and ambled off toward the brontosaurus.

She seized my wrist fiercely and clambered to her feet. She yanked me to my feet, and began dragging me out into the desert, gouging my wrist with her painted nails. I had no idea what was going to happen to me.

After about fifty yards she stopped. She let go of my wrist, and stood at a distance of three or four feet, and looked me dead in the eye. It was the eye of the storm. She unbuttoned her blouse and tore it off and fired it into a nearby creosote bush. Unclasping her bra, she ripped it free of her arms and flung it to the ground. Then she just stood there, tall and straight as a redwood, naked from the waist up, glaring at me with X-ray eyes. I tried with all my might not to look at her full breasts and her flat tummy and the graceful curve of her hip, but I couldn't stop myself. This was no gangly-legged teen with budding breasts, but a woman.

She all but threw herself on the ground. She rolled over on her back, and hiked her skirt up. She wasn't wearing any underwear, and to my astonishment, her letter V was shorn. "Here I am," she hissed. "Fuck me! That's what you want, so just get it over with! Go on, I won't fight you. I won't scratch you, I won't bite you. Just fuck me and get it over with. Fuck me however you want to fuck me. Pretend I'm whoever you want me to be, whoever you think I am. Just get it over with."

"Get up."

"Fuck me. That's what you want."

"Get up, Lu!"

"C'mon, William. Show me how much you love me. Fuck me like I'm your sister!"

Finally, I turned and stomped away from her in the direction we'd come. I could hear Lulu scramble to her feet behind me, and for one instant I was fed up, sick of it all, Lulu, I mean, and I just wanted to climb in the Duster without her, without anyone, and keep heading east, and never look back, get a job in Albuquerque, marry a fat girl, die in the sun. But no sooner did I hear the crunch of Lulu's footsteps in my wake than I longed to feel her nails gouging me again, and her words cutting me to the bone.

Lulu stormed right past me, clutching her blouse closed in front. Up ahead I could just barely intimate the unsuspecting figure of Dan seated on the tail of the beast, plinging his bass guitar in concert with the cool jazz, as Lulu grabbed his arm and jerked him up, bass and all, and began dragging him out into the desert.

They were gone forever. Now and again I could hear the low drone of Dan's voice, but not his words, and once I heard Lulu cackle, but whatever she was cackling about didn't sound funny.

I wandered across the flat until I came upon Troy, leaning against a back leg of the brontosaurus, staring out into the firmament. He didn't acknowledge my arrival. He was drunk, and every time his weight shifted itself, he recovered with a start, like someone falling asleep at the wheel.

"What the ffffffffuck am I doing here?" he said.

I didn't venture to guess, because I felt certain that he wasn't asking me, and even if he had been, I didn't have an answer for him. I left Troy to himself and ambled over to the Duster, where I lay down on the hood and listened to the crickets, and watched the stars, and tried to keep from asking myself the same question as Troy. Time passed, but I had no measure by which to gauge it other than the timepiece my forebearers had been using for seventy thousand years or more, the stars, and I couldn't even do that. But I'm guessing an hour or more passed, maybe even two, before Dan and Lulu returned, Dan looking a little sheepish, and Lulu looking a little less determined than usual. Troy straggled in not far behind them, still toting the bottle. The bottle was empty.

We piled into the car. Only Dan buckled up. Soon the dinosaurs of Cabazon were behind us, and the mountains lay ahead of us, and no sooner did we begin our ascent than everybody passed out: Troy with his face to the window, Dan, sitting erect as though he were still awake, and Lulu with her head on Dan's shoulder. And as I guided the Duster west on the interstate toward home, I was bleary-eyed and unshaven, and the desert air, now cool, whistled through the window, and for the first time in years, I truly didn't care which way my hair fell.

· PART ·

INTO THE FRAY

Almost Twenty

⌁〰⌁

Two months into fall semester, I finally moved out of the only room I'd ever known and into the real world, a one-bedroom apartment four and a half blocks from the Pico house.

I took three classes at SMCC that fall, one in Marine Ecology and two in Philosophy. Philosophy, I learned from Gerard Smith—a slight, bespectacled fellow who owned a pair of clogs and a billowy shirt for every day of the week—was an *activity*, not a doctrine. Oftentimes class convened outdoors on a patch of brown grass punctuated by a few smog-choked palms, below a blue sky buzzing incessantly with air traffic. Here, Smith arranged his pupils in a circle and indoctrinated us with impassioned lectures on Plato's ethical solutions, Aristotle's foundations of logic, and Bacon's utopia of science. It was hard to fathom what Gerard Smith was so impassioned about, but there he was, pacing madly about in his clogs, center circle, his billowy shirtsleeves gathering wind with each grand gesture. He had hair like Richard Simmons's, which, unlike his sleeves, was impervious to wind.

As for the texts, I slogged through Plato wondering why, and limped through Aristotle asking the same question, before I caught my head in the spokes of Spinoza, which I felt was his fault, not mine, because it seemed pretty clear to me that quotidian reality had very little to do with mathematics—at least not my quotidian reality, in which one plus one didn't even equal two. Now Wittgenstein, there was a guy who made sense. Old Ludwig believed in the power of words and, paradoxically, the complete unreliability of words, or at least that's how I understood it.

It was silly and fascinating, this doctrine that was not a doctrine, these analogies about shadows and caves that sought to explain the nature of understanding. Each great thinker borrowed from the last, spinning the former's hypothesis into some new and logical conclusion, until every so often some nut like Hume came along and said, *Whoa, whoa, whoa, slow down here, let's go back to where we started.* I liked Hume. He was skeptical. He made goofy connections, then denied they were connections. He took cause and effect and bound and gagged them in a broom closet. Hume proposed that one could not assume the conformity of the future with the past, a lesson I had already learned twice, once when my mother died, and once the day I met Lulu. Just because the sun had risen every morning since the beginning of recorded time, Hume reasoned, didn't necessarily mean it would rise tomorrow or the next day.

I bluffed my way through Kant, stumbled through Hegel, and arrived senseless at the feet of Schopenhauer. According to Schopenhauer, the world was his idea. According to Schopenhauer, everybody and everything had a will of its own that enslaved intelligence.

A rock had a will of its own. A flea, a fire hydrant, a bicycle pump, they all had wills of their own. The blood had a will to flow through the veins. The veins had a will to carry the blood. The bowels had a will to empty themselves. And the will, according to Schopenhauer, was inexhaustible.

And if, like the flea, the fire hydrant, the bicycle pump, I had a will that enslaved my consciousness and my intellect, that will was only to possess the one thing that made me feel full, the one caress that set my whole being to vibrating like a tuning fork.

I kept on at Fatburger under the mentorship of Acne Scar Joe, who was once again hopelessly single. These days I was bringing in a cool eight hundred a month after taxes. The one bedroom I rented for three seventy-five was in the Tidal View apartment complex, which offered me no such view, though it did offer close proximity to several strip malls and an adult bookstore.

My apartment was directly upstairs from the laundry room. Anytime two or more washers were on spin cycle my living room rocked like Jericho; glasses vibrated off of tables, pictures fell from the wall. The vents for the dryer ducts were right below my window, and the smell was inescapable, like clean warm diapers. It penetrated the glass, leached its way through the stucco walls. The plumbing was temperamental, too. When those washers drained, they hissed and sucked and belched and rattled until you felt as though you were sleeping in the bowels of the USS *Nimitz*.

It wasn't the Ritz-Carlton, but it wasn't the Pico house, either. That four and a half blocks was a lot farther than it sounds. Freedom is all what you make of it. My emancipation consisted mainly of a fourteen-inch Toshiba, my own bathroom, a few issues of *Juggs*, some textbooks, and a lot of udon noodles. I split my evenings between Schopenhauer and *Adara's Dirty Diaries*. I bought a futon and a desk and a phone that never rang. Sometimes Troy came over with rum or a six-pack. I didn't drink much, though I did buy my share of six-dollar half grams. Troy and I would sit at my kitchen table and smoke herb out of a tinfoil pipe. We'd talk about the Dodgers or school or Lulu, but more often than not, we'd end up talking about how we could get rid of that diaper smell.

I soon discovered that the apartment was haunted by a cat. I saw its shining eyes a couple of times in the dark, glimpsed its gray form slinking across the room in my peripheral vision, heard it gagging on hairballs and padding across counters. It seemed to go about its business just like a regular cat, except you didn't have to feed it. I called the cat Frank. It never came when I called it. Maybe it was a girl.

My apartment manager was a little potato of a guy named Eugene Gobernecki, with a gold tooth and a Super Mario Bros. mustache. Eugene was a Soviet defector, once an Olympic hopeful in Greco-Roman wrestling. Eugene jumped ship in '84 at the summer games, whereupon he soon discovered the job market for Roman-Greco wrestlers to be even smaller in the United States than it was in the Soviet Union. So he started mowing lawns, washing windows, stealing grapefruit. He rented a one bedroom at the Tidal View. Within six months he was the manager.

For whatever reason, Eugene Gobernecki wanted desperately to be my friend, which probably said more about Eugene Gobernecki than about me.

"Come to my house," he'd say. "We cook a duck."

Thus he propositioned me for weeks every time I came upon him sweeping the parking lot, pruning the hedges, or cleaning the gutters. And it was always the same, always "we cook a duck." Never "we watch a game," or "we drink vodka." The duck was always part of the deal, as if the act were somehow symbolic. Eugene wanted to cook a duck with me—nay, he was determined to cook a duck with me, and I had no idea what that meant.

Eventually he began to extrapolate on the evening's events as he envisioned them.

"I buy vodka. You bring chicks. Friends, whoever you want. You come to my house. We cook a duck."

The truth is, whenever I encountered Eugene, I always wanted to say something about the cat haunting my apartment—file an official complaint, so to speak. But I didn't want to encourage Eugene. And besides, Frank was kind of growing on me.

"Sure, sure, one of these nights," I'd say. "After midterms, maybe. Or maybe after the holidays or something."

"Okay, fine. You have girlfriend? You have sister? You bring sister. Maybe she have friends. I buy vodka. We play music. Footloose. All zat shit. Make sure you bring friends and chicks. We make a party. I even cook two ducks, maybe. And I know a bar—maybe later we go out."

"Sure, sounds good. Let's plan something. Yeah, listen, so I gotta run, I've got an ecology lab, let's talk."

Finally, one evening, Eugene cornered me in the laundry room. "How come all the time you saying, okay, sure, we cook a duck, we make a party, zen you never make party. This Friday, we make party. You bring friends, chicks, whoever. Already I buy vodka. I rent pornographic movie. I rent other movie, too. You know who is Rowdy Roddy Piper? Okay, so I take care of everything, you take care of chicks and friends."

I took care of the chicks and friends. That is, I brought the only person I could get, which was Acne Scar Joe. Troy was in Malibu, and even Ross (Alistair, that is) didn't want to come. Eugene met us at the door in his apron.

"Will! How you doing, Will? All day I been cooking ducks. Hello, yes, Joe, glad to be meeting you, come, come, sit down. We drink vodka, wait for others to come."

We sat on plastic chairs around a Formica table. Eugene had the immigrant's love of plastic. We drank vodka. Eugene's pad was extravagantly furnished in early flea market. The couch looked like something Leif Eriksen might have rowed over in. The floor lamp belonged in a brothel. The coffee table was a wagon wheel. A Rowdy Roddy Piper poster hung slightly askew next to a Mexican beer poster depicting four balloon-breasted brunettes in a red sports car. We drank from plastic tumblers.

"Yes, okay, finally now we make a party."

We waited for the others to show up. And waited. And drank vodka. Eugene continued his preparations restlessly between shots of vodka. He changed the cat litter. He kept changing the music. He played John Cougar Mellencamp and Wang Chung and Andrew Lloyd Webber and Glenn Campbell and something with a zither and a trumpet.

"So, who else is coming?" he said. "Who else you are inviting to our party?"

I shrugged. "Uh, you know, a few people. What about you?"

"Not so many," he said. "I invite Derrick from 309, but he say he's working."

"Cleaning pools at night?"

"Crazy, I know, zat's what I say. What about you, Joe? You have sister, friends, you know chicks?"

"Some," lied Joe.

"You call up on phone, invite. Friends, chicks, no problem, we make big party at my house."

"They're out of town," said Joe.

"Shit motherfuck. Oh, well, we drink vodka. Eat a duck. I know Russian hooker maybe I call. You ever been with Russian woman? Oh shit. Zey fuck like forty-foot Amazon woman."

"Let's just eat some duck," I said.

The ducks were kind of small for ducks. They looked more like pigeons to me. They were greasy as hell and threatened to squirt off the cutting board every time Eugene tried to carve them. He'd also prepared a beet salad, and tuna fish on crackers. While I had no intention whatsoever of eating duck, I didn't want to risk offending Eugene, and so I did a serviceable job of pretending to eat duck, aided by sleight of hand and a half dozen felines mulling about under the table. We talked about chicks and money and hot cars. All the things we didn't know squat about. Then we talked about cleaning gutters and making French fries and drinking vodka, and all the things we did know about.

Here, at last, was my suburban Bohemia, all the parlor talk and camaraderie I'd always yearned for without knowing it. Within the murky confines of this shag-carpeted apartment reeking of cool menthols, cats, and vodka, eight long blocks from the Pacific Ocean and two short blocks from Thrifty, home of the ten-cent ice cream cone, I, William Miller Jr., bore witness to a summit meeting between two of the great minds of my generation: Eugene Gobernecki, a poultry-obsessed Russian free-market capitalist, and Acne Scar Joe, a rabid patriot and confirmed homophobe somewhere to the right of Jerry Falwell.

"Chinese, Japanese, whatever. They're all a bunch of kung fu fighting commies. We should've blown their slant-eyed asses up in Vietnam."

"Joe, you cannot stop democracy. These people are dying for democracy, Joe. They yearn for free-market system. Think of the hamburgers you will sell."

"Dude, they don't eat hamburgers. They eat cats."

"Look, Joe, all I am saying is, Joe, communism doesn't work."

"No shit, Sherlock."

"Yes, but what you are suggesting is not making sense. Zen why let the world's biggest market toil in rice bogs, when you could be selling zem hamburgers!"

"They don't *eat* burgers, dude. Don't talk to me about markets. I sell thousands of burgers a month and I don't sell more than a dozen to Orientals. And we're talking about the ones living right here in friggin' hamburger heaven. They've never even seen a hamburger over there! They don't know a hamburger from a goddamn Frisbee!"

"You sell one in one thousand, you sell two million hamburgers. Zat's what I'm talking about. You'll see. Just you wait. I've seen zis all before in Soviet Union. If you smart, you see differently. Do you want to know what is great thing about capitalism? I will tell you great thing. Opportunity. *Zat* is great thing. You see opportunity, you make opportunity. Opportunity plus hard work equals big bucks, big success."

In my lone contribution to the proceedings, I humbly pointed out the necessity of capital in such an equation.

"Yes, there is that. This one I am working on. Free rent, you see, zat's a start. Apartment manager gets free rent. Soon I get other job painting houses, or maybe Joe, you get me job at Fatburger, where I learn business. One day I build hamburger house in China, and I hire you Will, and you Joe, to run Chinese hamburger house. I give you benefits, stock options, big bucks."

"You're dreaming," said Joe.

"Zat's right, Joe. I am dreaming."

Twenty-Nothing

Dear Will,

It doesn't feel like spring in Seattle, doesn't smell like lilacs or rosebuds, although my days do seem longer. I'm not in love with Dan—at least not the crocus and nightingale kind of love, but maybe a different kind. I was never really big on spring, anyway. We're autumn people, you and I. I'm not sure if Seattle is the center of the universe, or the bottom of the vortex. Dan just joined a different band—one you may have heard of. He seems to think Seattle's the center. It's like our Summer of Love, he says. I fucking hope not. To be honest I don't really care if it's the center or the bottom, it's the middle I'm afraid of, and if my life doesn't begin soon, I fear I'll wind up there. Yet, I can't seem to get started. What's holding me back? Who am I?

What am I afraid of? Why do I feel that I'm all these different things to all these different people, and yet at the end of the day I feel I'm nobody, nothing.

Is it because we spend every night in the same five taverns, talking, talking, talking? Because we wear our angst like badges? Because we regret things we haven't even done yet? Because we're afraid of building a new world out of the same crappy materials? It's not fair of me to say "we," because Dan is actually doing something, or believes he is, which may or may not amount to the same thing. This is really about me, whoever that is.

Enough about whoever I am. How are you? Dad says he doesn't hear much from you. He talks in a way he didn't used to. I'm proud of him, and scared for him, and trying to forgive him for his shortcomings. We should all forgive each other, don't you think? I understand him now more than I used to, maybe. And I understand that people deal with their shit in their own way.

Dan is on tour for five weeks and will be in L.A. the second week of May. I told him he should call you. He likes you, though you got off to a rough start. I know you probably think he's stupid, but really he's just honest. There's a difference.

I do miss you, Will, I hope you believe that, and again I'm sorry about the night in Cabazon. I was drunk, but also I was crazy for a number of reasons, which someday maybe I can explain, or begin to. I'm proud of you, William Miller, you're one of the smartest people I know. Please say hello to Troy. I'll try to write again soon.

Love,

Lulu

Dan called the second week of May, from the Sky Bar, no less, where he was drinking with an A&R guy from Geffen. I was not in the least surprised to learn that Dan was doing killer. Lulu was also doing killer, in Dan's estimation. The Chateau Marmont, the band, the tour, life in Seattle, they were all killer. I told him I might show up at the Whiskey, where his band was headlining.

"That would be killer," he said.

He put me on the list. I didn't go. I think I watched *Alf* instead, or maybe *The Wizard of Ass*.

On the Soul, the Self, the Mind, and God

‿‿⌒⌒‿‿

Hume: An Overview
By Will Miller
(with a ton of help from Albert Hakim)

David Hume was born in Edinburgh in 1711 (arguably the effect of his mother's pregnancy). He formed syllables, learned to walk, talk, dress himself, say please and thank you, mastered his changing voice, and matriculated. His family wanted him to be a lawyer. He tried halfheartedly, gave up, and began a program of "private study" in literature and philosophy.

Impressions and Ideas

Hume believed that experience provides the first access to knowledge. Whatever came to us via direct experience, Hume called "perception." He divided perceptions into two categories: "impressions" and "ideas." Impressions were the immediate data of experience: sensations, passions, emotions. Ideas were "faint copies," mere abstractions of our impressions.

Hume said: "Every simple idea has a simple impression which resembles it." A sensation, an emotion, a direct and immediate response. Not so with complex ideas, which were extrapolations. If, therefore, impressions are the direct consequence of experience, they are the main vehicle for our knowledge of objects. The more closely our ideas correspond to our impressions, the more reliable they are.

On the Supposed Necessity of Causality

Hume noted that there was no correlating sensation for the idea of cause and effect. We merely associated in our minds those objects that are constantly associated outside them, as we merely associated flame with heat, and without further ceremony we call one cause and the other effect. Since there was no impression for cause, since we could not "know it," only "believe it," to believe in effect was little more than a leap of faith.

On the Self, and God

Hume observed that there is no sensation, no single experience in which the unity of the self is perceived. The self is merely a collection of qualities, perceptions, conjunctions, and beliefs: "When I turn my reflection on 'myself,' I can never perceive this 'self' without some one or more perceptions; nor can I ever perceive anything but the perceptions."

As for God, he was just another cause, the ultimate cause, another perceptual conglomeration that had no specific corollary in the realm of sensations. God wasn't demonstrable.

Hume died in Edinburgh in 1776.

Nice job, Will! Clearly stated. You seem to have a firm grasp on Hume's brand of skepticism. Interestingly, toward the end of his life, Hume granted God a few concessions.

—G.S.

Why Anyone Would Want to Live Here

⌁⌁⌁

In June of 1990, two weeks shy of the twins' high school graduation, I got a call from Big Bill. He said he was driving out to Lucerne Valley to some old turkey ranch on the following Saturday and wanted to know if I'd like to come along. I wanted to know why. He didn't know why, exactly. He thought it might be fun. I doubted it, but I didn't tell him so.

My first thought was that Big Bill, under mounting financial pressure and the further duress of a severe identity crisis, was about to do something rash—that he was contemplating or possibly even intent upon buying a turkey ranch in the middle of the Mojave, and that it was my duty and responsibility to persuade him at all costs against undertaking such an enterprise.

Things were worse than I thought. Big Bill was driving a minivan.

It was the color of Carlo Rossi sangria, the only alcoholic beverage I can remember Big Bill condescending to drink upon occasion, usually with ice cubes and a splash of 7Up, frequently gulped in concert with a beef burrito the size of a football.

The van still smelled of new vinyl. Even in his present state of shrunkenness, Big Bill looked hulking and ridiculous at the wheel.

"Where did this come from?" I said, dumping my book bag between the seats and settling in.

"Willow bought it up north," he said.

"How's the mileage?"

"So far so good. Better than the old Dodge."

Through Hollywood and Sherman Oaks and Burbank we engaged in small talk. News from the gym (where Big Bill was still relegated to spectating), some talk about baseball, and a little talk about my upcoming finals—but not much. I couldn't see discussing Spinoza with Big Bill any more than I could see discussing the French Enlightenment with Yogi Bear. Thus, we opted for the greener pastures of chitchat until, somewhere around Newhall, Big Bill switched gears.

"Lot of changes coming, Will. Lot of changes. Especially for your brothers. Have you talked to them lately?"

"Not like *lately* lately, a couple months."

"Well, Ross is getting an apartment with that friend of his, the one with the red leather pants, Regis, Regan, Reagan, you know the one. He's lined Ross—er, uh, I mean *Alistair* up with a job selling women's shoes downtown somewhere, one of the department stores. Apparently the commissions are pretty good."

"That's cool," I said.

"Of course, he'll have to stop dressing like Ronald McDonald," said Big Bill. "And comb that hair of his. I can't even light a match in that upstairs bathroom anymore. I'm afraid I'll blow up the house with all those hairspray fumes."

I couldn't help but grin. Big Bill grinned back.

"He's something else, isn't he? He and Lulu. Every time you turn around there's something new. A cape, a nose ring, a crazy haircut. Have you seen the T-shirts he's wearing lately? They hang like ribbons on him. But darnit, I've got a good feeling about him. He's going to grow into himself one of these days. It's his brother I'm worried about."

"Doug?"

"Of course, Doug. I never worried about you, Will. Never had to. Somehow, I always knew you'd be okay."

I felt a twinge of resentment.

"You're made of strong stuff," he pursued. "Your mother was made of strong stuff, you know. She was a fighter. You've got her determination."

"Hopefully not her endurance," I said.

"You'd have made a hell of a bodybuilder, you know that? All that determination and compact musculature."

"Thanks, but no thanks."

"Oh well. To each his own, I guess. You'll find a way to use it. There's a big market for determination."

Whatever gave Big Bill the idea that I was strong and determined? Was it my tireless and unyielding pursuit of . . . nothing? Why were people forever overestimating me? I almost said something to that effect, but Big Bill, in his silence, had begun to furrow his brow, like something was weighing upon him.

"What's wrong?" I said.

"Doug's got it in his head to join the air force." He shook his head and frowned. "I should have seen this coming. He watched that darn *Top Gun* every day for two years."

"Why don't you stop him?"

"There's no talking him out of it."

"You could say no."

"He's eighteen," observed Big Bill. "And even if he weren't, I can't see the advantage of forbidding things. Everybody has a will of their own, everybody makes the same mistakes in different ways. You can't stand in anyone's way."

"Well, at least they'll pay his way through college, right? It's not like he'll be marching off to war. He'll be vacuuming cockpits in Arkansas, or something."

"I suppose you're right. But something about it still troubles me."

We rolled down Soledad Pass and into the high desert. I could smell deep-fried fat on the desert wind. Victorville was no longer a quaint desert outpost, it was a sprawl of low-density development, gray modular homes, fast food joints, gas stations.

"It wasn't always like this," observed Big Bill. "Heck, I remember when there was nothing here. It's sad." Indeed, he was wistful for a moment, but then he wrinkled his nose a little. "You hungry?"

"No."

"Me neither."

The development spread through Hesperia into Apple Valley, an undeterred rash of deli-marts and affordable housing. It didn't matter that the landscape was Venutian, that there wasn't a museum for a hundred miles. There existed no place too inhospitable for a Gulf station or an Arby's. Build it and they will come. Lucerne Valley would be next, maybe a year, maybe five, but eventually Colonel Sanders would come knocking.

By the time Big Bill and I hit Highway 247, we'd finally left the development behind us, and soon there existed hardly a trace of anything at all—an occasional homestead, a crooked row of fence posts, a blown-out retread.

Big Bill guided us off the highway and down a dirt road that headed east into a wasteland of greasewood and sand.

"Maybe we'll run into Moses out here," I said, but I don't think Big Bill got the joke.

The road got worse the farther we bumped along. Two or three miles in, Big Bill veered off down a second unmarked dirt road, this one heading southeast into obscurity. Here and there a rusty barrel or an engine block jutted out of the earth. After a quarter mile, the road ended abruptly in a pile of railroad ties. Big Bill stopped the van and killed the motor. He unbuckled his seat belt and climbed out of the car. I got out, too. We trudged a ways out into the desert, stopped in our tracks, and just stood there. The air was dry and heavy with the smell of sage.

"Well," said Big Bill. "Here we are."

Here: scorched earth as far as the eye could see, a few crumbling foundations, a giant ditch with a bunch of old tires piled up in it.

"Where are the turkeys?" I said.

"Oh, they're long gone. Haven't been any turkeys here for at least fifty years, I'd guess."

It wasn't hard to believe. In fact, it was somewhat more difficult to comprehend why there were ever turkeys here in the first place, why there was ever anything in this place.

"Why are we here?" I said.

Big Bill didn't answer right off. I wasn't even sure he heard me. He stood perfectly still in a sort of reverie. "I dreamed it," he said.

"Dreamed what?"

"Dreamed this place." Big Bill squatted down and sifted some sand through his fingers like he was panning for gold. When all the sand had slipped through, he scooped up another handful and began sifting again, this time without looking.

"Your mother wanted to buy this land. She wanted to start a commune before it was too late."

"Too late for what?"

"Too late for such a thing to work." All my father's sifting had yielded a tiny rusting hinge. He turned the relic over in his hand before lobbing it back out into the sand. "It was already too late by the Summer of Love," he said. "Haight-Ashbury was nothing. Squatters, dope fiends, dropouts. The dream was over. All that flower power smelled rotten by the Summer of Love. There was just enough time for the ad stooges and the soda companies to cash in on it. Your mother wanted to start something out here, preserve something, away from all that. She wrote a charter, drew up plans. Housing. Irrigation. A Garden of Eden right here in the Mojave." Absently, Big Bill drew shapes in the sand with his index finger. "Humph," he said, scratching them out. "By God, we almost did it."

"And what? The Manson Family beat you to the punch?"

I don't think Big Bill heard me. He was far away—in 1967, I guess. He surveyed the landscape, west from the San Bernardino Mountains, north across the dusty flats, and east to the Bullions. Finally his eyes settled on the ditch with the pile of tires. "That used to be an irrigation pond," he said.

"So, what happened?"

"It dried up."

"No, with the commune, what happened?"

"You happened," he said, sifting some more sand through his fingers. "Your mother got pregnant. That changed her thinking. She finished school. We moved to Santa Monica." He sounded a little disappointed by it all. He tossed his handful of sand out into the void before he'd finished sifting it. "I dreamed it all again last week," he said.

I scanned the horizon. Here and there a little compound sprouted up out of the desert: a house, a few aluminum outbuildings, the rusting carcass of an old Chevy. Other than that, nothing. I tried to envision Big Bill and my mother and a dozen half-naked hippies making a go of it out here in the middle of nowhere. All I could think was *why*? Why here? There wasn't any shade. What the hell would they eat? Where would they go to the bathroom?

"Why would anyone ever want to live here?" I wondered aloud.

He looked genuinely surprised. "You don't like it?"

"What's to like? Some sand, a few rocks."

"Shhh," he said. "Listen."

I listened. I heard the faint but incessant buzzing of a single-prop aircraft on the horizon, but I think I was supposed to be listening to the silence. And the more I tried to hear the silence, the more I heard the buzzing.

That's when the inconceivable came to pass. Squatting there, Big Bill reached in his shirt pocket and fished out what appeared to be a crooked joint, then a book of matches. He was very matter-of-fact about it all. He never even looked at me. He just straightened the joint out between expert fingers, popped it in his mouth, lit it, hit it, and passed it up my way, a tendril of smoke curling between us. I tried to be equally matter-of-fact.

We smoked. We stopped talking. We stared out into the nothing.

Pretty soon I heard the silence, and it occurred to me that the desert landscape all around me was just visual silence, and I thought that was a pretty cool idea, because it made me see emptiness in a whole new light. The beauty of emptiness wasn't in the emptiness itself, it was in the fact that you could make emptiness into whatever you wanted. You could build absolutely anything—a turkey ranch, a commune, a cement brontosaurus—and it would define the emptiness. Now I envisioned the commune through my mother's eyes, and it made a little more sense: the garden, the pond, the rows of vegetables, the kids running around in moccasins with stardust blowing through their hair, the half-naked hippies dancing around a drum circle, the light of the campfire reflected in their eyes. All of it made sense except the taking-a-shit part. There wasn't any plumbing for miles. Suddenly, I had to take a dump. I remembered my backpack.

I left Big Bill squatting there and walked a couple hundred yards to the west, where I dug a hole behind a creosote bush and did some squatting of my own, utilizing several pages of Schopenhauer's great anthology of woe to a purpose that would have surely pleased its critics.

When I rejoined Big Bill, he was lying on his back with his eyes closed, and for a moment I watched the slow, steady rise and fall of his breathing. I lay down beside him. He opened his eyes for an instant, smiled, and shut his eyes again. The smile stayed there for a few minutes. The sand was warm through my T-shirt. The breeze all but disappeared that close to the earth. I rested my head in the butterfly wings of my arms, like a guy in love lying in the grass watching clouds roll by. Except there was no grass, and no clouds, and the love was unrequited, and something was poking me in the small of my back, which my probing hand soon discovered to be the rusty hinge Big Bill had cast off.

I tried reading a little Schopenhauer, but I had no use for the world of ideas at that moment. So I closed my eyes, and emptied my mind, until nothing was left but images of Lulu and me alone in the desert, with our very own pond and our very own vegetable garden, and the light of our very own campfire reflected in our eyes.

And it didn't occur to me then to guess what Big Bill was imagining as he lay there on his back with a smile stuck to his face.

A Normal Life

~~~~~

<div align="right">September 27, 1990</div>

Dear Will,

Today is your birthday, so this is late. I usually begin with an apology of some sort, so here goes . . . I'm sorry . . . And I'm sorry I couldn't make it down for the twins' graduation, or this summer, like I'd planned to. My life here is chaos. Summer is a blur already. I've tried everything, Will: I've tried acid, I've tried poetry, I've tried drinking, I've tried AA, the Bible, skydiving. I've tried being a waitress, a messenger, a stripper. I've tried being cool, I've even contemplated lesbianism, which I was accused of on more than one occasion by Dan, but I've yet to feel satisfied. So I'm putting the search on hold, at least for a while.

I'm digging a trench. I'm putting my shoulder to the wheel. I'm back in school, this time in earnest. I'm declaring a major once and for all. I haven't decided what, yet. Maybe accounting. Numbers are manageable. Or maybe even sociology. I'm starting therapy. I want a normal life, or at least I think I need a normal life. And so I'm equipping myself with normal things—a normal education, and a normal lifestyle—and willfully ignoring my responsibility to try and define my culture by drinking microbrews and wearing lumberjack shirts and puking my inner turmoil out onto canvas and selling it as art (not that anyone was ever buying). I've decided to let other people build biospheres and write anthems and protest the inequities of the world. I don't want to change the world, or conquer it, or seize the day, or skydive, or snowboard, or hang glide, or climb Mt. Everest. I don't want all that thrill of victory and agony of defeat. My goal is no longer to find a goal, but to pursue the standard goals that have been set before me. Maybe I'll start calling myself Louisa. Maybe I'll join a sorority.

I wonder whether I'm making sense, or if I sound like I'm whining? You once said that dreams, or maybe it was aspirations, were the car keys of life, and that they were easily misplaced, and hard to find. That may be bullshit, I'm not sure. But I do know that the finding part is hard. And frankly, I'm sick of looking under dressers and couch cushions and every pocket of every pair of pants I ever owned.

I broke up with Dan. We got back together for one night, but then we broke up for good. He took it kind of hard. Dan was sweet, or I should say, he is sweet. He'll find a new girl. He'll find a whole string of them. In clubs. In Portland or Chicago or Minneapolis. Dan is eager and optimistic and dreamy and idealistic, and all the things I'm not. Most of all, Dan is spreading his wings, and he doesn't need a lead weight around his neck, and I would always be pulling him back to earth. I don't want that responsibility. I have a hard

enough time living with myself already. Sooner or later he'll understand that. I'm getting better at breaking people's hearts cleanly.

I hope you are well. I'm sorry I'm so flaky about returning calls.
Dad says that you've got some radio classes—or communications
classes or whatever—this fall. I hope you'll tell me all about them
sometime. Call me! I'm out a lot, but keep trying. Can you believe
Doug joined the air force? What a blockhead. Then again, who am
I to talk?

Well, I've got a biology lab and I'm working tonight. Take care of
yourself, brother. I hope you know where your car keys are . . .

Love, as always,
Lulu (or maybe Louisa)

P.S. Remember how I used to want to live above a gas station? I'm
getting closer. My new apartment on 45th is a half block from an
Exxon station.

Kierkegaard: Now You See Him, Now You Don't

Soren Kierkegaard: An Overview
By Will Miller

Kierkegaard was the son of a gloomy religious zealot. It stuck. His commitment to Christianity was undying, though he proposed that group congregations were meaningless, and that in the hands of "the crowd," Christianity became an empty religion.

As I understand it, Kierkegaard believed that philosophers ought to be judged by the sum of their lives, rather than the sum of their intellectual artifacts. So he distanced himself from his own works by all manner of subversive techniques, such as employing multiple (and quite often contradictory) pseudonyms in the same text, appending authorship, sometimes editorship, publishing two ideologically opposed books at the same time, all in a grand design to undermine his own credibility. At first I thought this made him a loser. But now I see that he was forcing readers to take responsibility for their own beliefs, instead of trumpeting his own. Only then could the individual arrive at truth.

It may be overstating the case to say that what old Søren was proposing (in opposition to his nemesis Hegel) was that what we call objectivity is not objective at all, that it is, in fact, totally subjective. This is consistent with his belief that the individual must take responsibility for his own existential choices. The individual must question the very impetus of his existence. Doubt, he supposed, was a fundamental tenet of faith. Without doubt, one could not possibly know Enlightenment.

Good work, Will! Kierkegaard's approach seems to suggest that his audience suffered from too much knowledge, rather than not enough. I read somewhere that he was considered something of a gadfly by his contemporaries.

—G.S.

Where the Alamo Was

—∿∾—

December ? 21st or 22nd, I think, 1990

Dear Everybody,

Sorry, not too much time to write. I have fire watch tonight from 22:00 to 04:00 which is 3:00 in the morning until 4:00 in the morning and its 21:30 now. Im using a flashlight to see what Im writing, and all I could find was a pencil and the tip sucks, so sorry if this is sloppy, but I dont think it really is. I hope you all have a merry Christmas and a happy new year, and I wish I could be there, but oh well. I got issued my rifle today, an M-16 three shot burst. We start ground combat training soon, which sounds weird, I know, with this being the AIR-force and all. The food is good at Lackland, and the drill sergeants arent that bad, really. Ive only been dropped once. Lackland is near San Antonio where the Alamo was but you wouldnt know it. Its its own world. Theres a lot of talk about Kuwait. The armys deploying VII corps to Saudi Arabia, and theyve already doubled ground forces there. Some of the guys here are gung-ho for active duty. Im not so sure how I feel. I wasnt expecting this to be an issue, oh well. Im staying in good shape, but losing weight. My biceps arent as big. Some of these guys are in crappy shape, I feel bad for them, but oh well. I have to go, but Ill write again soon and let you know how things are.

Doug

Monument Valley

~~~

The only time I ever saw Big Bill cry was January 15, 1991, the UN deadline for Iraqi withdrawal in Kuwait, also the day Doug left Lackland Air Force Base for tech school in Illinois, as well as the day escrow closed on the Pico house. Big Bill had been purging the old house for weeks, with little help from anybody—hauling furniture to the curb, driving rented vanloads up the coast to Sausalito, where he was set to join Willow in her empty nest. But in spite of his efforts, he'd hardly managed to dent the accumulated mass that twenty years of family life had created.

When I dropped by late in the evening to pick up a beanbag and some other relics, I discovered that I no longer recognized the geography of the Miller household. I discovered curio cabinets and nightstands and dressers I hadn't seen in over a decade, staged in the foyer at the foot of the stairs, draped with moving blankets. I discovered an empty living room with shaggy geometric patches that didn't match the rest of the piebald carpet. And I discovered Big Bill sitting at the dining room table, surrounded by cardboard boxes fit to burst with every conceivable form of printed matter, from dental receipts to vacuum cleaner instruction manuals to muscle magazines. The boxes were stacked to precarious heights, and out of the uppermost boxes poked picture frames and trophy tops, so that the overall effect was a Monument Valley of boxes, constructed over decades by the collective forces of our family. And there was Big Bill, sitting alone in the middle of it, with mounds of photographs covering the tabletop in front of him, and a few empty boxes. Some of the photos were black-and-white, some of them color, some of them Polaroids.

"Hey, kiddo," he said hoarsely.

"What's up?" I said.

Big Bill laid the picture of my mother on one of the mounds and straightened his posture a bit.

"You all right?" I said.

"Yeah, I'm okay. Sit down."

He didn't look okay. He looked haggard and drawn and a little bit gray.

"What're you doing?"

"I was just sorting through some old stuff," he said. "A *lot* of old stuff, actually."

I felt bad for him. All that history there in front of him—and all that unfinished business surrounding him—none of it was conducive to a short ending.

"Funny," he said. "How it takes the future sometimes to look at the past. I guess I'm the kind of guy that needs to see it all in boxes before it starts to sink in. Humph. What a mess." Looking around at the valley of boxes, he sighed. "The truck will be here tomorrow."

"What time? I can get Joe to cover me in the afternoon and skip my—"

"No, no," he said. "I've got hired hands. Thanks, though. Ross and that little Regis are helping, as well."

"You mean *Alistair* and *Regan*."

"Yes, *Regan*, that's right. Ross is back to Ross, though, or Alistair is back to Ross, however you look at it. He cut that swifter off the top of his head, too, thank heavens. Do you know, he pulled down nearly two grand in extra commissions over the holidays?"

"Oh," I said, and started thumbing through a mound of photos.

"Sangria?" he said.

"No thanks," I said.

"That's Quicksilver Messenger Service," he said of the photo I was holding, which pictured a vast and colorful throng of young people in various stages of dishevelment strewn around an outdoor stage. "One of the free concerts. I knew the drummer."

I wanted to indulge him, but I couldn't, somehow. "Mmm," I said, flipping to the next photo.

Big Bill piloted his chair around the corner of the table and hunched over my shoulder. "That was taken in Park Merced, out front of your mother's apartment."

"Nice hair," I said.

"Thanks," he said.

"You look skinny."

"I quit pumping iron in those days," he explained. "Up until you came along."

I supposed that bodybuilding must have been square, unmellow—an act of aggression. Brute strength was hard to reconcile with flower power. Big Bill may not have been training, but he was still posing, decked out in full hippie regalia bordering on cartoonish: barefoot in bell-bottom jeans, a billowy shirt with leather drawstrings worthy of

Gerard Smith, a mustache like Wild Bill Hickok's mantling a defiant grin, flying a peace sign in the face of *them, the enemy, the establishment*, whoever or whatever they were, a guitar at his side for strumming out anthems, *teaching the world how to sing in perfect harmony*, whatever that was.

"That's more like it," I said, flipping to a photo of Big Bill shirtless on the beach somewhere, striking a front double bicep, grimacing like a man with a hot curling iron up his ass.

"I wasn't exactly cut yet," he observed. "But the arms and chest were starting to look decent, especially the pecs. The lats don't look half bad, but the abs are weak, that's for sure. I still had legs like a chicken, too. That must have been '71 or '72."

I wondered if it were ever possible for Big Bill to turn this critical eye for self-improvement inward, and if so, what was the scouting report on his patience, his tolerance, or his honesty? How would he appraise his stubbornness, or his refusal to have certain conversations? In all those years of building muscle mass, all those years of crafting lines and curves and finely fingered muscles, had it ever occurred to him to build up his insides? To define his temperament, his faith, his emotions?

"Who's this?" I said, indicating a black-and-white portrait of a guy with dark circles under his eyes, who I was guessing was the grandfather I never met—the guy who was married to the grandmother I never met. He looked like an encyclopedia salesman, gimlet-eyed and determined, wearing a crisp gray fedora. He wasn't smiling. In fact, he looked rather determined not to smile, as though nobody had told him the war was over, that America was enjoying unprecedented wealth and abundance. Despite his rigidity, he was a little rumpled about the lapels. He looked like a guy who might conceal a flask in his coat pocket.

"That was my father. He died the next year." The personage bore no resemblance to Big Bill, less, in fact, than I bore any resemblance to Big Bill.

"Do you remember him?"

"Sometimes, but I'm not sure. Sometimes I think I'm just remembering pictures."

"I know what you mean," I said.

"Do you remember this?" said Big Bill, fishing another photo off the pile. "This was at Big Bear Lake, just before your mother died. Ross had a terrible fever. Remember? Your mother ran the twins back to Redlands and they took Ross to the doctor and stayed in a hotel. You and I camped. Don't you remember? A black bear ran right through our campsite in the middle of the night. He was splashing around in the lake after something. Hey, what about this one?"

A quick glance at the photo in question revealed the story of my life after my mother and before Lulu. There were the matching blue sweat suits, the twins dangling from Big Bill's biceps, and me standing off to the side.

"Who took this picture?" I said.

"Nobody. Don't you remember? You set the timer, but you could hardly reach the top of the tripod, so you stood on the coffee table. You thought you didn't get back in frame for the picture. That's probably why you're sulking. Ha! Look at this one!" It was a Polaroid of my mother, very pregnant in a blue bathrobe, shielding her face as though from the paparazzi. "Right before we bought this house, your mother and I lived in a one bedroom on Centinela, by the municipal airport. She was pregnant with you. There was a teenage kid a few doors down. His name was Tony, I think. He was . . . I guess you'd say he was retarded. Downs, maybe. He was a great big kid, and good-natured. Someone bought him an Instamatic camera and he'd knock on your door at six in the morning, and when you answered the door, he'd snap your picture, which of course was always terrible. Then he'd sell you the picture for fifty cents. Sort of like blackmail. Your mother refused to pay it the first half dozen times."

"Why did you leave San Francisco?" I said.

"It was over. I was done with it. We were starting a family, we had to get out."

"Why Santa Monica?"

"Because it was home. For me, at least. I've spent all but three and a half years of my life here."

"Think you'll ever come back? I mean, to live?"

"No, I think it's over, Will. It could never be the same, it never *was* the same after your mother died. Different place. Different time." Big Bill looked at the clock face and his wistfulness wore off instantly. He straightened up and patted the tabletop with both hands. "Well, better get moving on this mess." And he stood up.

When I left Big Bill that night he was packing and stacking like a madman in the open garage. As I loaded up the Duster, he paused in his duties momentarily at the head of the driveway, under cover of the garage door, bathed in a rectangle of stale light.

"Still running, eh?" he said, indicating the car he'd bought me the summer of my junior year of high school.

"Still running," I said.

"I'll be darned."

"Yep."

"I wouldn't take her too far."

"Me neither," I lied.

I told him goodbye, and left him to his work.

Among the relics I hauled back to the apartment with me that evening were my old radio, a leaky beanbag, and the cardboard box my fourteen-inch Toshiba black-and-white television came in, the television itself having long since given up the ghost when Doug, during the course of borrowing it, dropped it down the stairs. The box now contained eight and a half unmarked volumes of The Book of Lulu, rubber-banded in stacks of three.

Res Cogitans Rehashed Zoroastrian

———~~~———

Cartesian Dualism: A Short Overview
By Will Miller

Descartes was distinct among his peers and predecessors in being the first one to distinguish the mind from the brain as the center of mental activity. This may seem like a no-brainer now, but consider that in 1630 Galileo still hadn't figured out that the earth moves. They couldn't even make ice, for godsakes. Barbers were treating gangrene. Frankly, I'm surprised they even knew what a brain was.

But it was the mind, not the brain, Descartes reasoned, that was the *res cogitans*, the thinking thing. The mind was the essence of self: the doubter and the believer, the hoper, and the dreamer. The brain was just a place to sit. So convinced was Descartes of the noncorporeal properties of the mind that, among his considerable inventory of doubts (indeed, he built a whole methodology on the basis of doubt), he discovered that he could easily doubt whether he really had a body—after all, he might well be imagining his body, dreaming it, hallucinating it—and yet he could not doubt for a single instant whether he had a mind. The mind was inescapable. Ponder that one too long over some doobage, and I guarantee you'll start feeling a little cagey. I did.

It could be that Descartes never really overcame his doubt of the body being a distinct substance, because even his mustache looked a little dubious to me. At any rate, he stuck to the dualism model, staking his very reputation on it. Mind and body—two ontologically distinct substances, one of them immaterial. Where things got sticky was the causal interaction between the two. How can an immaterial mind cause anything in a material body? Beats the hell out of me. Descartes never had an answer, either. Poor guy.

Maybe what I like best about Descartes is that in Franz Hals's famous portrait, he looks like one of the villains from Scooby Doo. Something about the black robe and tousled hair—as though he'd just been unmasked in the linen closet. You can almost see Velma, just out of frame. Her glasses are fogged up. Fred, Daphne, the whole gang's there.

And there's old Descartes—with his doubting mustache and tousled hair—unmasked, exposed.

"And if it weren't for you meddling Newtonians," Descartes seems to be saying, "I would've got away with it."

Sounds like you've gleaned a basic understanding of the mind/body distinction, Will, although I think this one bears further investigation on your part. Also, I must say that I'm a little dubious about the Scooby Doo reenactment. Not sure Descartes would've approved of this type of grandstanding. You should really watch your reefer intake.

—G.S

The Pitts

Near the end of February, I found myself browsing in the adult bookstore around the corner when I spotted Mr. Pitts in the used aisle. He didn't see me—or at least if he did, he didn't let on. He was a little scruffy, still wearing a flannel dress shirt, still wearing those desert boots. His ice cream hair had melted, and his bald patch was visible. He had a bag of donuts by his feet.

Had I spotted just about anybody else, I would have ducked out before he made me, but somehow it wasn't that big of a deal running into Mr. Pitts. After all, I'd already laid my heart bare for the guy at least ten times over the course of a half-million lunch-hour Cheetos junior year. What did I care if he read *Barely Legal*?

"Hey, Mr. Pitts."

He recognized me instantly, and didn't look embarrassed. In fact, he hardly looked up from his magazine.

"How goes it, Miller?"

I thought he smelled a little like gin. But it could've been his aftershave.

"Good, Mr. Pitts, real good."

"Call me Larry. Christ, even Harry, I don't care. Anything but Mr. Pitts."

"So are you still a counselor at Santa Monica, or what?"

"Yep, still at it, for better or worse. A thankless racket, but it pays the bills." He tapped his *Barely Legal*. "And of course it keeps me in a good supply of smut. What's your poison, Miller? Let me guess, older women?"

Old Pitts hadn't lost a step. "How'd you know?"

"Just a hunch. Twenty years ago, that was my thing, too. Funny how that works. And I'll bet you like big natural gazongas, too, with a little bit of hang time." He demonstrated as per size and hang time. "Am I right, Miller?"

"You're good, Mr. Pitts. Maybe not that big, though."

"Larry, call me Larry. Let me ask you something, Miller. You ever get over that girl?"

"No."

"Good for you."

"I never got her back. How is that good?"

"Maybe you never got her back, Miller, but you had her once. And if you had her once, you can have her always. Even if it does drive you bonkers. Nothing wrong with a healthy obsession, Miller. Madness is always worth it. Trust me."

I must say, I was a bit surprised. I'd never pegged Pitts for an agent of chaos. But looking at him now, with his melted ice cream hair and his issue of *Barely Legal*, I wasn't sure what to think. There was a glimmer in his eye that I didn't recognize from our former noontime association in his cramped office. I wasn't sure I trusted his logic. I was even less sure just what course of action he was recommending I take, indeed, if he was recommending I take one at all. I guess I just wasn't quite sure about Mr. Pitts in general, anymore, but I still liked him.

He put his issue of *Barely Legal* back on the rack and started leafing through another. "I know a thing or two about wanting, Miller. Do you know where she lives? Have you kept in touch with her? Or is she just a little hole in your heart, forever sixteen, that kind of thing? Which is it?"

"We keep in touch a little. She lives in Seattle."

"Any restraining orders?"

"Oh, no, nothing like that."

"Well, you've got that going for you. I was married once, Miller. Very much in love."

"I didn't know."

"She died in a roller coaster accident in Orlando. Eight years ago. Struck by lightning."

I thought he was joking.

"On our anniversary," he said.

He had to be joking.

"The universe is a perverse place, Miller."

"You're serious?"

"As a heart attack."

"Geez, Mr. Pitts, I'm sorry. Nobody ever told me."

"Shit happens," he said. "Nobody knew. We were living in Chevy Chase then. I moved out west a year and a half after it happened. I never told a soul here, not even my colleagues know. So keep that one under your hat, eh Miller? That gets out and I'm forever stamped as the guy whose wife got struck by lightning on a roller coaster on their fifth anniversary. And I'm not sure I could handle that."

Poor Pitts. How do you even attempt to order the universe in the wake of such a thing? And on top of all that, how do you keep it a secret?

"My mom died when I was little," I told him. "Cancer."

"I know. It was in your file."

"So, then, if you knew, how come we never talked about it?"

He shrugged, and turned the page. "You never brought it up."

"I guess I didn't know any better."

"Apparently I didn't either. Sorry, kid."

"No big deal."

"I figure everybody has a few secrets," he said.

"Yeah, I guess so."

"Say, Miller, you ever get yourself into anything like this?" He tilted his magazine to reveal the visage of a young, doe-eyed brunette woman in a prom queen tiara performing fellatio on a hairy fat guy.

"Not yet," I said.

"Me neither."

That was the last time I saw Pitts. I kept an eye out for him whenever I went to the bookstore, but he never resurfaced. I should have got a phone number. I should've dropped by the high school and paid him a visit. Maybe I could have comforted the guy, as he once comforted me. I guess I'll just add that to my list of should haves.

Years later, I heard Pitts offed himself with a rifle one morning in his apartment. Poor guy. Maybe his secret finally caught up with him.

The Biggest Reason

―⌒∿⌒―

March 6, 1991

Dear Will,

I feel better since I gave up being a flighty soul-searcher and gave in to life. The highs are not as high, but the lows aren't as low, and I think that's a healthy trade-off for me. I don't really miss flying high. Being a bird isn't all sunshine and shitting from high places.

I work at a florist now after school and weekends. I like the flowers. They're beautiful. They don't have to mean anything. I wrote a story in English Comp about a girl who works at a florist, and she's very lonely, and all day long she takes FTD orders from boyfriends to their girlfriends, and sells flowers to husbands, and talks to women about bridal bouquets, and at night she goes home and eats chicken pot pies and watches the news, and practically cries herself to sleep wishing she had somebody to watch the news and eat chicken pot pies with, and fall asleep with. She can't even have a dog in her apartment. The story wasn't about me, though. Because in the story, a lonely guy starts bringing her flowers picked from his own garden, which he arranges himself, and the girl and the guy fall in love, and they live happily ever after. If the story were about me, the girl wouldn't accept the flowers, or she'd throw them away. Anyway, I got an A for the happy ending.

I haven't seen Dan, and I hardly ever go to the Saloon anymore, or the Frontier Room or the Vogue, and never the Comet, because Dan still hangs out there sometimes. That whole scene is done with, anyway. It's all hype now. A lot of the kids are just bored rich kids and European tourist kids looking for the heart of "the Seattle scene," hoping to catch a glimpse of Mark Arm or Chris Cornell, hoping to touch the hem of Kurt Cobain's flannel shirt. The rest of them are just drinking beer.

I hardly drink anymore. I stopped drinking coffee. It makes me restless. I drink this herbal tea that smells like poop, I forget what it's called. It looks like homegrown pot. I buy it in big bags at Tenzing Momo. It has a calming effect.

Mom said something about you working at a radio station? Is that true? Why didn't you tell me that? Why are you always so modest? What are you doing there? Are you a DJ or something? I hope! I hope someday you have your own show where all you do is talk. Or I hope you call the Dodgers games like Vin Scully, like you did when we were kids. Whatever you do, I know it will be special, it will be good. I hope you get everything you ever wanted.

So does this mean you quit Fatburger again? If so, good for you. If not, oh well. A job's a job, right? Did Troy decide where he's going to transfer? Am I asking too many questions? It's just that I DO miss you, and your sad funny insights, which makes it even harder to tell you what I have to tell you:

I don't think it's a good idea that you visit me spring break, for a number of reasons. And hear me out, before you get mad. For one, I'll be extremely busy with work, also I'm starting an internship around then, so I wouldn't get to see you hardly, anyway. And the biggest reason is, even though my life is starting to have the appearance of a normal life, I'm still not on terra firma. I'm not sure I could handle all the feelings your visit would stir up. And when I say I'm not sure, I'm even less sure what the consequences of not being able to handle it might be. So, let's plan something for summer. I'll come down. Or better yet, we can meet in San Francisco.

Love,

Lulu

P.S. It's called valerian tea.

The Second Loneliest Number

It was drizzling, and my duffel bag was heavy, and I was tired, and full of bad coffee, and my eyes were playing tricks on me, and my ass was asleep, and the daisies I'd bought twenty-two hours earlier were already wilting by the time I reached Lulu's doorstep. But nothing could deter my giddiness as I anticipated the sight of her.

She answered the door in baggy pants and a gray T-shirt. She wasn't wearing any makeup, and her crazy hair was tamed into an uneven bun atop her head. Her heart was not singing, that much was clear, and she wasn't even smiling; in fact, she was frowning, but she was still more beautiful than Helen of Troy.

"Oh, William, William, William, *why*? How could you just *show up* like this? How could you not tell me? You promised."

"Great to see you, too," I said. "Here, I brought you these."

I handed her the daisies, and stepped around her into the apartment. I hadn't even set my bag down when I heard the toilet flush down the hall. A moment later, Troy emerged. All the spring went out of his step the instant he saw me.

"*Oh*, hey," he said.

I didn't say anything. I didn't need to. So, here we were, the familiar crowd of three. Someone had some explaining to do. Troy must have been thinking the same thing.

"I'm maybe transferring here for fall," he explained. "I just came to—"

"I invited him," said Lulu.

"I thought you were busy."

She was still frowning. "I am," she said.

Disoriented, and stupid with surprise, all I could do was look at them for a moment. "Why the hell didn't you tell me?" I demanded of Troy.

"Why didn't *you* tell me?" was his reply.

"Well, one of you ought to have told *me*," said Lulu. "*Somebody* ought to have."

"I wanted to surprise you," I said. "I'm sorry."

"Well, you've done that," she said. Then she looked at me, disheveled, miserable, and a little wet, still clutching my duffel bag, which was getting heavy. She softened. "Here," she said, taking the bag. "Sit down. And don't be sorry, *I'm* sorry, that was awful of me, I'm awful. You came all this way, and all I can do to welcome you is—I'm sorry. Make yourself cozy."

As Lulu turned her back to me, setting my bag in a corner, I gave Troy the stink eye. He looked a little hurt and confused, but mostly guilty.

Lulu's apartment was sparse. There was very little to define the space: a pair of straw mats, a paper lantern, some white walls. The wood floors were warped, gouged, and painted gray. Her old yellow foot-locker was draped with a black silk scarf and served as a coffee table. Beyond that, the lone piece of furniture was a queen-size futon, an amorphous blob with a gray slipcover, coaxed and cajoled onto a wooden frame, where it perpetrated a sofa, upon which Troy and I presently sat, shoulder to shoulder. There were two plants, one on either side of the Blob; they could not have been farther from the window nor could their placement have made them any less accessible to the eye from our vantage. As for Lulu's bedroom, I could not see into its darkness through the partially opened door.

Lulu stood in the adjoining kitchen clutching a freezer bag of valerian tea as she watched the kettle, which had uttered its first groans of expansion atop the glowing burner.

"It kind of stinks like poop," she said, unsealing the ziplock and taking a whiff of its contents. "But it's incredibly relaxing."

Indeed, the stink was inescapable, as though a Great Dane had parked his Alpo on the coffee table. While Lulu fidgeted with the tea preparations, I began to notice something else about her apartment. For all its straw-mat simplicity, the space could not belie a certain clutter. Papers were wedged beneath the Blob in stacks, candlesticks and umbrellas were stuffed inside baskets along with magazines and books. Everything was tucked away, compartmentalized, hidden from view, but if a big enough wind were to blow through the apartment, it might look like her old room.

A white cat emerged from the bedroom, unfurling its tail and licking its chops. It had green eyes and spots of brown and orange on its face, and one spot of brown at the end of its tail.

"That's Esmeralda," Lulu said. "Esmeralda's my absolute darling, the answer to all of my prayers."

The cat vaulted onto the kitchen counter and sniffed around a bit before it began the business of circling and circling, finally settling into the shape of a cinnamon roll upon the countertop, where it closed its eyes.

"Since when did you start praying?" I said.

"Since a long time ago," she said. "Anyway, I just adore Esmeralda. I aspire to be like her. She teaches me absolutely everything."

"How long before you're shitting in a box?" I said.

"Very funny," she said, but she wasn't laughing, she wasn't anything, really. "Go ahead, you guys can tease me all you want."

"*I'm* not teasing," said Troy.

"*I'm* not teasing," I mimicked in a whiny falsetto.

"Well, it's true," said Lulu. "Esmeralda is my best friend. She's patient, she's sweet, and most of all, she never lies. I know what to expect from her. She's straightforward and true."

"Animals can't lie," said Troy. "That's what the Garden of Eden was all about. The forbidden fruit was self-knowledge, you know, like self-consciousness. That's the original sin."

"Thank you, Joseph Campbell," I said. "And what the hell's a snake? A fucking vegetable?"

"It's a *myth*," said Troy. "I'm just saying—"

"You're just *talking*," I said.

He stopped talking. He shifted slightly away from me atop the Blob.

"Oh, let's not talk about religion," said Lulu. "I've tried just about all of them, and they're none of them worth arguing over."

"I'm not arguing," said Troy.

When the tea was finished, Lulu brought it steaming on a tray and set it on the coffee table. It stunk like a bedpan. Lulu sat on her knees on the wood floor across from Troy and me. As the tea steeped, Lulu spoke at length on the subject of Esmeralda and her many charms and fascinating idiosyncrasies. Troy and I listened and listened. We watched Esmeralda, though there was really nothing to see—she was conked out on the counter, inert as a paving stone, probably dreaming of tuna fish or a clean litter box.

Lulu stood up at one point and put on some New Agey music that I didn't recognize: a potpourri of cellos and chimes and didgeridoos, the musical equivalent of frankincense. Then she sat back down on her knees across from us, and she poured the tea into three cups.

Lulu raised her cup to her lips and blew softly upon it, so that a ghostly curl of steam crawled upward over her face, and when she sipped, she looked at Esmeralda on the counter, and her eyes smiled lovingly over the rim of her cup. I used to know that smile, and what it was to have those crinkly eyes bestow their unreserved approval upon me.

"Here kittykittykitty," I said.

Esmeralda opened her eyes and unfurled her tail. I encouraged her further with little smooching sounds, and the cat waved her tail about playfully by way of reply. I held out my fingers as though I were dangling a herring, and Esmeralda hopped off the counter and padded toward me across the wooden floor. But before she got to me, Troy scooped her up and set her in his lap, whereupon she circled, circled, and settled to rest.

"She likes you," said Lulu.

"Troy always had a knack for pussy," I said.

"Oh, stop it," she said. "Why do you always have to be so disgusting?"

"It was a compliment," I said.

"You're just jealous," she said.

I could feel my face color.

"She's soft," said Troy, petting her.

Lulu leaned over and they both pet her. "She's the softest. The softest and the sweetest and the wisest."

Oh brother, I thought.

"Isn't this tea nice?" she said.

"I really like it," I lied.

"Me too," said Troy. "It makes you feel . . . in the moment."

I nearly choked. *In the moment.* Please. Ha! The tea tasted like boiled shit, which of course I would eagerly have partaken of, had Lulu set it in front of me. "I see what you mean about the calming effect," I said.

"Yeah, it's really nice," she said. "It's one of my simple pleasures. I'm finally starting to enjoy the little things. I'm tired of thinking big. It gives me a headache. I'm tired of being smart." Then she turned her attention back to Esmeralda. "Ith wittow kitty gittin watts of wuv from mummy and Twoy? Duth wittow kitty wike wuv? Mummy wuvs wittow kitty thooo much. Wittow kitty make mummy thooo happy."

I never thought I'd want to kill a cat. I love animals. Or maybe it was Troy I wanted to kill. I wanted to kill something, or stop something, or communicate something, before Lulu lost her mind completely. But maybe Lulu was right. Maybe I was just jealous. Maybe Lulu was truly content in her little daily things, maybe normalcy was the answer: cats and nowhere jobs and sparsely furnished apartments. Maybe valerian tea was the doorway to enlightenment. Maybe stable, reliable Troy was the man to carry her across that threshold, but I doubted it. It seemed to me that Lulu was even, too even. Like she didn't even know she was in despair. I longed for that strong wind to blow through the room and scatter Lulu everywhere in all her swirling, eddying complexity, and though I knew that it was within my power to stir those winds, the very rules of engagement had changed. To win Lulu, I had to disarm her. And the best way to do that, I reasoned, was to stop talking. And so I did.

We spent the remainder of the evening sipping tea and engaging in normal conversation, a ritual of mediocrity at which Troy proved proficient and quite eloquent. He talked about job markets and IPOs and 401(k)s and wouldn't stop talking about the World Wide Web.

Now and again the phone rang, but Lulu never answered it. She kept listening to Troy paint a picture of a world that could be quite easily finessed and persuaded and in most cases predicted (I wished Hume were there to set him straight on that account), a world where morality and fiscal responsibility could coexist, a world where every fruit you ever wished for was ripe for the picking, where free will was its own kind of destiny. Opportunity and capital were the tools to achieve whatever end you could possibly wish for. It was really quite simple: Ask for little, and little you shall receive; expect opulence, and the universe would surrender its bounty. By this measure, gratitude seemed like a dangerous proposition.

As Troy painted this picture of reality, I realized for the first time that I was raised by peasants. I recognized that the world in which Troy lived was the world into which wealthy people brought their children—a world that engendered possibilities and was easily navigable given a philosophy that instilled confidence, a mythology in which destiny was a ladder and all you had to do was climb it, a world where morality was simply a matter of good taste. I, however, was taught (and so, mind you, was Lulu) that the world was made of meat, that everything had a short ending, that without pain, one could not possibly expect gain. All the opportunity and capital in the world didn't matter, damnit, it had to hurt! And I was supposed to be well-adjusted?

Not only was I *raised* by peasants, but I was a peasant, too, because Troy's ideal seemed colorless to me—safe, predictable, virtually without struggle. And that's why Lulu nodded and nodded and smiled occasionally, but not like she smiled for Esmeralda, not like she smiled for me in the pampas grass, when we spoke in blinks and squints and lovely incantations. When Lulu smiled at Troy, she smiled like a straw mat, or a paper lantern, or a black scarf draped over a yellow footlocker.

Normal conversation lasted until about midnight, at which point Lulu decided it was time for bed. She gathered up Esmeralda, and they retreated to the bedroom. She reemerged moments later in a nightgown with blankets and pillows for Troy and me, which she set in a big pile next to the Blob.

"Goodnight," she cooed.

"Goodnight," said Troy.

Lulu pulled the string for the overhead light, and the room went dark, but you could still see the Chinese lantern bobbing in the darkness as she disappeared into the bedroom. Lulu shut the door behind her, and when she did, most of the universe went dark, leaving only a puddle of bleak light, which filtered through the hedges and into the window from the street. In this bleak light, Troy and I groped and wrestled the Blob until it was almost flat. In silence, we kicked our shoes off and lay down side by side on our backs, and dispersed the blankets and pillows equitably. We stared at the ceiling for a few minutes without comment before turning our backs to one another.

As I lay there with my best friend, I looked out the window and over the hedges and tried to forget him completely, and hoped that the sun would not rise on one of us—preferably him.

Alternate States
of Formlessness

~~~

When I awoke, I was alone on the Blob, and daylight spilled dull gray over the hedges into the living room. It was spitting rain and the windows were fogged up around the edges. It could've been 5:30 AM, or it could've been noon. It could have been fall, it could have been winter. The clock on the stove read 10:09. At some point during the night Troy had found his way to Lulu's bedroom, for that's where I discovered him, on his back, under the covers, gazing out the window.

"Morning," he said.

"Hadn't noticed," I said, looking around. "Where's Lulu?"

"Work, until five-thirty. Then she's got something downtown."

The inner sanctum of Lulu's bedroom was more chaotic than the rest of the apartment. Keys and bracelets and pocket change gathered on flat surfaces everywhere. The dresser top was littered with miscellany. Panties lay strewn about. A wicker chair in the corner lay buried beneath an avalanche of sweaters and coats and jeans. Photographs were affixed willy-nilly to the edges of her vanity. I noted with satisfaction that no less than three of the pictures featured myself, and only one featured Troy, and even in that one his face was partially obscured by somebody's shoulder.

Troy climbed out from under the covers, naked from the waist up. He scratched his ass and ambled across the hallway to the bathroom. The shower nozzle sputtered to life. I continued my appraisal of Lulu's room, particularly the chaos atop her dresser, where I found ticket stubs and bus transfers and an old paycheck and a pack of American Spirits and two books of matches and some Nag Champa incense, and I'm guessing about eight bucks in change.

I sat on the edge of the bed, on the opposite side where Troy had lain. I picked up Lulu's pillow and buried my face in it and smelled it, I mean really smelled it, like I'd been under water for eleven minutes and it was my first breath of air, and it smelled like that song "Back Home in Indiana," like hay and candles and the Wabash River, and something else, maybe Lulu's scalp, or my mother's bathrobe, or sweaty feet soaked in rose water. Whatever it was, it was good.

In a Mexican cigar box on the nightstand, among the aspirin bottles and Carmex and hair clips, I discovered the cause of Lulu's evenness, or at least one of its harbingers, in the form of a prescription bottle of Prozac. I pocketed the Prozac so swiftly and without reservation that I can't honestly say what impulse prompted me. But in my heart I felt that Lulu's wilderness must never be tamed.

The shower nozzle stopped sputtering, and I heard the little rings clink together as Troy drew back the shower curtain. I retreated to the living room and began folding blankets and wrestling the Blob back into its alternate state of formlessness.

Later, Troy and I walked down the hill through the rain and ate breakfast at Stella's. We agreed it was overpriced, and Troy insisted on paying. Then we saw a matinee, a celluloid disaster called *Problem Child 2*. We walked out midway, and poked around record stores on the Ave for a few hours, all the while scrupulously avoiding the subject of Lulu. Troy bought a CD, a T-shirt, and a smoked-glass Jimi Hendrix mirror. He also bought a hat that said *Loser*, which I thought suited him perfectly. I bought Lulu a record for a buck called *Take Another Lap for Jesus*, with an old guy on the cover in the most vivid yellow poly-fiber sweat suit I'd ever laid eyes on. He looked just like Jimmy Johnson, the Dallas Cowboys coach, and he was jogging down the street, presumably for Jesus, with a smile on his face like something Big Bill might've crafted midway through a front double bicep. The artist's name was Norman something, and not only could he croon, according to the liner notes, *like David, the sweet singer of Israel*, he was also an evangelist for something called the Overseas Crusade Ministry, whose stated endeavor was something to the effect of *stimulating and mobilizing the Body of Christ to continuous, effective evangelism and church multiplication on a nationwide basis, so millions will be transformed into victorious Christians.*

Troy wanted to walk around campus, so we walked around campus. The place was deserted. As we crossed Red Square past Meany Hall, Troy finally broached the subject of Lulu.

"I wasn't trying to be sneaky, you know. I mean, by not telling you."

"Weren't you?"

"No. That's what I'm trying to explain. I would've told you, I wanted to tell you, it's just Lulu was worried that—"

"It's none of my business," I said. "You don't owe me an explanation. And I don't want one. What happens between you and Lulu is between you and Lulu. What do I care? I'm her brother."

"Stepbrother," he said.

"Whatever."

"There's a big difference."

"Not to her way of thinking," I said.

"Maybe not," he conceded. "But . . ." He waved it off.

"But what?"

"Well . . . sometimes it seems like, I don't know, like . . . do you remember when Lulu and I were going out, and she wasn't always very nice to me?"

"You mean, like always?"

"Okay, sure, like always. I always felt like that was because of you, because I wasn't you. I wasn't funny like you, I didn't make weird analogies like you, I didn't describe things the way you described them."

"Whatever gave you that idea?"

"Because all those nights in Ventura, we ended up talking about you."

"Don't blame me."

"I'm not blaming. I just don't know what I *am* to Lulu, that's all. I never did know."

"So welcome to the club."

"You used to tell me that I was nothing to her, and I believed you."

"That was wrong of me. I was just jealous."

"But now I think maybe I am something to her, but I don't know what. It's different now, a lot different, except really, when it comes down to it, maybe it's the same. Maybe it will always be the same."

"I wouldn't bank on it."

"All I know is, is that she genuinely cares about me now. She *begged* me to come, Will. And believe me, after that night at Cabazon, I needed some convincing. She made me feel like I was never born that night."

"That one was my fault," I said. "I'm sorry. It was a dirty trick. I should've never—"

"Forget it. She was crazy that night, and we were drunk." Troy stopped at the ledge in front of a sculpture that looked something like a rusty pencil poised vertically atop a rusty pyramid. He turned his back to it and leaned against the ledge, and I did the same. Together we gazed out across the empty square, which wasn't square.

"But then the first night I got here, Will, she almost convinced me. She said things about the future, and I've never known Lulu to be a forward thinker, at least not where she and I are concerned. I'm telling you, she was different, Will. She was calm, and focused, and she seemed to know who she was, or who she wanted to be. Then yesterday you got here, and . . . I wasn't convinced anymore. This morning, she tried to convince me again. She apologized over and over, but she never said for what." He threw his arms up. "I don't even know what I'm trying to say. Convince me of what? That I'm *what*?"

"Ask her."

"I can't."

"Why?"

"Because even if she does have an answer, I'm afraid I won't like it."

The statement had the ring of truth. The kind you don't want to ponder. "Well," I said. "Then just ask her *again* in five minutes."

Somehow this truth was less unsettling, I suppose because it afforded us both a degree of hope. Troy and I shared a little grin. Troy pushed off from the ledge and started slowly back across the square. After about five steps, he broke into a sprint toward the center of the square, then slammed on the brakes and skated across the wet bricks in his tennis shoes for about ten feet, and waved me on.

When we returned to Lulu's apartment, I put the Prozac back in the cigar box. The first step in disarming Lulu, I reasoned, was to quit exerting my will, to quit pushing and pulling at her fate and let it decide itself. I would concede victory to Troy and the rest of the normal world. Then, under the guise of normalcy, I'd infiltrate this world. I'd woo Lulu with my evenness. And so when Troy and Lulu wanted Chinese food, I acquiesced. When they wanted to see a movie, I acquiesced. Every time Troy wanted to sit next to Lulu, I acquiesced. I said only positive things, and thus I hardly spoke. And bit by bit, as the week wore on, Lulu began to let her defenses down. On occasion, she even went out of her way, circling the table at The Moon Temple, or stepping over Troy's knees at the Guild, to sit next to me. One night she clutched my hand while we were walking down the Ave toward Dante's, where Dan and Lulu used to get drunk with the guy who played Mike Brady on TV. And not only did she hold my hand, but on our way up the stairs she even spanked my bottom.

And once Lulu was defenseless, I began to speak again, and I spoke in lovely metaphors and similes about sparrows and sandbags and hulking brute machine works rusting behind trapezoidal chain-link fences. I spun metaphors about snowflakes and wormwood and just about everything you could think of that wasn't the thing itself, because Lulu, like myself, understood the world only as metaphor.

But Not Forgotten

—⁓⁓—

Troy flew out on a Friday morning while Lulu was at work. I gave him a lift to the airport. The day was glorious, brimming with brilliant light. The colors were popping, especially the blues and yellows. Everything looked crisp and defined, separate from everything else.

Troy kept thanking me for the ride.

"Really, man. Thanks for the ride. I owe you big time."

"You don't owe me anything," I said.

"You're a pal, Will. You always pull through."

I felt a little pang of guilt. "It's cool," I said.

"Seriously, I appreciate it."

"Okay, okay, I know you do."

After the third such outpouring, I distinctly began to feel as though Troy were thanking me for something other than the ride.

Like maybe he was apologizing for something. Something like fucking Lulu four nights in a row while I lay pining on the Blob. Or possibly he was entreating me to undertake some course of action on his
behalf, like giving up on Lulu.

"Well, cool man, thanks again, really. So, I'll see you in a couple
days, right?"

"Right," I said.

"Remind Lulu to call me tomorrow."

"Will do."

"About the apartments."

"Yeah."

"Thanks," he said. "And tell her good-bye for me. And thank her."

"Right."

The moment I dropped Troy at the curb in front of the United
terminal, I began planning a celebration for that very evening: a
grand feast for two, designed to thrill the ten-year-old heart of
Lulu, because *that*, I decided, was the key to possessing her. That
was where her will lay, unencumbered by the intellect. For five
years I'd been trying to get Lulu back in that Westwood garage,
when all the time I should've been aiming at her ten-year-old heart,
simple and true.

I bought canned cranberries at Food Giant, the jellied kind, and
I bought marshmallows and lemon Jell-O and baked beans and
powdered mashed potatoes. I bought mac and cheese and ice cream
and Fritos and old-fashioned rolls, like the kind that came with our
school lunches, and bread stuffing, and pudding—in short, every
high-fructose, artificially colored, culinary comfort that ever nour-
ished us in our youth. I almost bought wine, but thought better of
it, and bought chocolate milk instead. And I bought two bunches of
gerbera daisies—one pink and one yellow.

Like a mad scientist, I ransacked the cupboards for skillets and pots and casserole plates, and for two hours I mixed and stirred and whipped, and heated and covered and cooled, and washed the dishes and cleaned the kitchen, and spread it all out banquet-style on the table, until it looked like an Appalachian wedding reception, with garish mounds of food, red and orange and yellow food. I made a Matterhorn of mashed potatoes, a caldron of baked beans, a quivering brick of lemon Jell-O. It was beautiful and horrendous.

When Lulu came home from work and gazed upon the Technicolor feast spread out before her, she was awed, and I could almost hear her ten-year-old heart singing.

"Nooo way," she said. "*This* is amazing. Oh, this is *perfectly* amazing. I can't believe you did this. Of course you did this! An authentic Miller buffet."

"Minus the lamb shanks," I noted. "Everything here requires silverware."

"Oh, Will. This is so perfect. This is everything we ever—"

"I know. All for twenty-three bucks."

She gave me a big hug, and her hair smelled like the flower shop, like lilacs and roses, and hugging her, I felt for once that I, William Miller Jr., weak-eyed vegetarian, might actually be nice to come home to.

When Lulu sat down at the table, she tucked her napkin in her lap like a big girl, and held her knife like a lady as she dissected her lemon Jell-O into even squares. She dug a deep crater in her mashed potatoes and filled it with baked beans until they were bubbling out like lava. She sliced off even rounds of jellied cranberries and halved them and cut open her roll, and placed a wedge of jellied fruit inside, and parked the roll on her plate. Then she took a handful of Fritos and did a most amazing thing. She set them end to end and fashioned a roller coaster around the perimeter of her plate, until her dinner looked like an amusement park, and she smiled. Then she moved her mouth in ten different directions at once, and she said, almost like a ventriloquist:

"Rook! Itsa Gord-zira!" Then she began to trample the amusement park beneath her walking fingers like Godzilla. The roller coaster buckled and the Jell-O squares quivered as Godzilla marched right up the side of the mountain and into the bubbling caldera, where he sank with a chorus of agonized wails into the steaming beans. Then Lulu wiped her hands off and ate a bite of lemon Jell-O and smiled.

"This is lovely," she said.

"I'm glad."

We ate together mostly in silence. Once Lulu giggled with her mouth full of beans, and once, while her mouth was full of lemon Jell-O, she smiled, and a little yellow blob squirted out of her mouth and stuck to the table. That started her laughing. And soon she couldn't stop herself from laughing, until she actually shot a little blob of Jell-O out her nose onto my plate, and that made her laugh so hard that she started gagging, but even while she was gagging she was laughing. Finally, she managed to put the brakes on her laughing, and after a few staggering breaths she swallowed and heaved a sigh, and tears filled her eyes, and just as she was catching her breath, she began to sob, and she was out of breath again. After she stopped sobbing, she giggled a few times, and some yellow phlegm oozed out of her left nostril, and that stopped her from giggling. She blew her nose into her napkin and smiled. "So much for mood stabilizers," she said.

"Mood stabilizers? You mean, you're—"

"Was," she sniffled. Then suddenly she brightened. "But things are so much clearer now. Tonight I feel normal again, not *normal* normal, but *for me* normal, I mean. Tonight is really lovely, William.

I'm glad there's tonight." She wiped the leftover tears from her eyes. "Pass the stuffing," she said.

And after we stuffed ourselves, we sprawled out gurgling on the Blob and drank valerian tea, and watched *Murder, She Wrote* with the sound off, and made up our own dialogue for Angela Lansbury. Then we played Crazy Eights atop the yellow footlocker, and Lulu won every time, and I was glad. I petted Esmeralda, and she purred and circled and finally curled up in my lap, and Lulu said, "Duth wittow kitty wuv William? Duth wittow kitty sweep in William's wap?" And I continued to pet Esmeralda until she purred like an air compressor, and I said, "William wuvs wittow kitty thooo much."

Lulu leaned in and kissed Esmeralda behind her ear. "Sometimes I think I'd like to be a mother."

"I know what you mean."

"I'm not saying I think it would be easy, but I think it would make the rest of life easier. Family dinners, all that stuff. The ritualism. I guess that's what home is. How can you have that without kids?"

"Pets, I guess."

"It's not the same. Pets don't grow up, they just get older. Sometimes I wish Dad didn't sell the house, you know? Because even with everyone gone it was—oh, but let's not talk about that," she sighed.

So I told her about Eugene Gobernecki, instead, and his obsession with cooking ducks, and I aped his dialect to comic effect: *Come to my house, we cook a duck, we make party!* Lulu nearly peed her pants laughing, and I told her about Eugene's dream of building an American hot dog house in China, and how I was starting to believe that he would someday make it happen, because he was already managing a Fatburger *and* an apartment complex. Lulu told me that in high school Shannon Stovel said she wanted to either be surgeon general or the wife of somebody very rich, and how she'd heard from Troy that Shannon had married the son of the CEO of some big pharmaceutical company, and she told me how Kathleen Topping, who always wanted to start her own cosmetics line, was married too, except she hadn't married anybody rich, she married a tattoo artist from Long Beach, and she was a junkie. I told Lulu I'd probably never get married, and Lulu told me she wouldn't either.

"Oh, but let's talk about something nice," she said.

And so we talked about Bigfoot and cherry Popsicles and Saint Thomas Aquinas. We talked about heirloom tomatoes and morphic resonance, about lemurs and glaciers and strange lights in the night sky. We talked about everything that happened before the big bang, and everything that happened after we closed our eyes at night. When I talked to Lulu, she listened, and when I knew she was listening with her heart, I said:

"*Blink squint.* Logarithmically speaking, *squint.* We are not exponents, nor even real numbers, *squint. Blink.* You are a stop sign, and I am a dog chasing its tail, *squint.* Suppose you and I were to invent a new math? *Squint.*"

"Do it again, slower," she said.

I said it again, slower. And I watched Lulu's face as she figured the blinks and the vowels and the consonants and the periods according to our ancient custom, and like a kiss, the word began to take shape on her lips.

And the word was *always*, because *always* is the shortest way to say I love you, and also the longest.

And after that, a kiss. Just one. Like just one Temple of Artemis, or just one moon, or just one dying moment. And when our lips separated, our phantom kiss remained, and Lulu took me by the hand, and we rose to our feet. And Lulu pulled the overhead string, and the Chinese lantern bobbed in the dark behind us as we headed for the crack of light that signaled Lulu's bedroom door.

Everything had a supernatural glow about it. The room was illuminated by strings of soft blue Christmas lights festooned between ledges and windowsills and door frames. It was not the same room. Everything in it had been transformed, everything had a new significance. If ever old Hume rang true, it was this night. The future simply wasn't conforming to the past. At one point I was completely outside my body and I observed myself belly down on the bed with my face in Lulu's lap. But even as I was outside my body, I was still inside my senses, because I could smell her, and the smell of her lap was the fertile smell of wet earth.

Ever so softly, as softly as if I'd been whispering a prayer, I blew on the lovely folds of her blossom, until goose flesh began to rise along her inner thigh, and Lulu writhed and groaned and arched her back until she could no longer contain herself, and forcefully she took hold of me behind the ears and pulled my face into her, and I began to kiss and nibble her there, and soon her breathing was frayed at the edges, and when I came up for air, she pulled me right back into her before I could draw a breath, and I submitted. The taste of her was like mushrooms and cucumbers and sweat. And the slickness of her was like nothing I'd ever known, or even imagined.

As she received me, as I sunk into her, it felt as though she were trying to suck me up inside of her, all of me, and when I boiled over and exploded inside of her, after five minutes or an hour, I saw white light, inside and out, then I saw spots, and bursting bubbles full of something orange and effervescent.

Afterward, Lulu cried into my armpit, and told me not to take it personally. And I stroked her hair and told her I wouldn't.

Nothing Like Gold's

～～～～

April 30, 1991

Dear Tiger,

I thought of you on Sunday when the Dodgers beat the Giants. Gross pitched a helluva ballgame. I didn't think I'd miss Santa Monica but I do. I miss the old house sometimes like an old pair of slippers. I miss you kids (now that you're gone). And I miss Gold's. Sausalito is nice, though. The health spa I'm working at is nothing like Gold's. But even Gold's is nothing like Gold's, anymore. Nothing's the way it used to be.

Doug is being transferred to Travis to work as a jet engine mechanic. Ross is still selling shoes and started taking night classes to get his real estate license. He's also working out again, at a spa downtown. He looks good. A little scrawny still, but good muscle tone. I don't hear much from Lulu or you. Are you a big radio star yet? I hope you won't forget the little people (actually, I'm back up to 190 with about four percent body fat). Got any girlfriends I should know about? I'll bet you do now that you're a big time disc jockey. I'm proud of you, kiddo. Maybe you could record one of your shows for me. Sometime maybe I could call in and make a request. Maybe I could drive down and we could catch an afternoon game out at Chavez Ravine. I never could stand the Stick, too windy. Imagine the numbers McCovey could have put up without that wind! Let me know (Saturdays and Sundays work good for me).

I've been trying new things (like last week I rode a skateboard, if you can believe it. The kids at the end of the street have a ramp. I skinned my hands up pretty good, but oh well, you know what they say, "no pain, no gain."). I've been learning to play the mandolin also. Different from the guitar. But the same. I'm getting calluses on my fingers for the first time in years. I'm eyeing a couple of competitions for this fall sanctioned by the NANB (National Association of Natural Bodybuilders), which means they're steroid-free contests. They've asked me for an endorsement, but I'd rather compete than endorse. Maybe I'm not as washed-up as I thought.

The pictures were taken in Sacramento. The girl is Willow's niece, Sarah (you met her when you were little). She goes to UC Davis. Pretty cute, huh? She's single! Well, I love you, kiddo. Let me know about the ballgame. I'm home in the evenings if you ever get the urge to call. Willow sends her love.

Dad

The first thing I noticed about the pictures was that Sarah was not cute. She looked like a guppy. And why was Big Bill trying to set me up, anyway? Why did he keep mentioning girlfriends? Did he think I was gay? Lonely? Did he know I was in love with Lulu? Did he mind?

The second thing I noticed about the photographs was Big Bill's new look. He was wearing a ponytail and a soft leather hat, a wilted, wide-brim thing that would've looked right at home on Duane Allman, or the father from *Hillbilly Bears*. But nothing personified the sad state of Big Bill's nostalgia quite as vividly as his blue and orange tie-dyed T-shirt that probably came from the Gap. As for Willow, she must have been the photographer, because she didn't appear in any of the pictures.

The image that sticks with me more than any of the photographs is the image of Big Bill on a skateboard. More specifically, that very instant in which Big Bill *ceases to be* on the skateboard, the instant in which the skateboard is shooting off down the street, and Big Bill, all two hundred rippling pounds of him, is about to fall on his ass, which is tightly packed into neoprene shorts. Most vivid of all are the expressions on the skater kids' faces as they stand around in a group watching in their baggy shirts, baked out of their minds, with their braces glistening in the sun, as they laugh their asses off at Big Bill's folly.

Hot Dog Heaven

⌁

One Sunday morning in late May, 1991, when I hadn't heard from Lulu in two weeks, and I was flat broke, Eugene Gobernecki knocked on the door of my apartment. My blinds were closed. I was still in my bathrobe.

He was wearing coveralls and holding a wrench. "Will, how you doing, Will! Can I come in?" He pushed past me through the door. He was nervous and excited, a little twitchy. He sat down at the kitchen table. "Sit down," he said. "You have cup of coffee?"

"No."

"Shit motherfuck. Oh, well. Sit down anyway."

I sat down.

Eugene smiled. A slant of light through the blinds caught his gold tooth just right. "Now that you big radio guy, I have business proposition," he said.

"Eugene, I produce overnights at the college station. Do you know what that means? I'm not even on the *air*. I answer telephones. I stack pastries. I don't even get paid! So if this is about venture capital or something, I—"

"Okay, okay," he said, fashioning a yield gesture. He rubbed his Super Mario mustache thoughtfully for a moment and furrowed his brow. "Okay, okay. You know what is sweat equity?"

"Uhhh, sort of. I think."

"It means you work for ownership of somesing."

"Of what?"

"Zat's what I'm getting to. But first I say *zis* before I offer you great business opportunity: When I do wrestling, I always win. When I do business, the same. So. Now you know. You know where is Venice Beach?"

"Of course."

"You know where is hot dog stand?"

"Maybe."

"I have opportunity. Lease to own. No start-up cost. Steam table, cash box, coolers, napkin dispenser, all zose things it has already. Permits, credit accounts, all zat. Some money we need to buy inventory, but not so much. I have money. Maybe not enough, maybe I sell bronze medal, or maybe Joe have money. Somehow we get. We start in June, second week. Tomorrow I quit Fatburger, Tuesday I sign lease."

"So what are you asking me?"

"You work. Me, you, Joe, we work. We sell hot dogs, lease to own. No down payment, no loan, low overhead. Zis makes great opportunity, Will! We make Hot Dog Heaven in Venice Beach! Some profits we split sree ways. You buy new car, not piece of shit Plymouth the color of old man's pants. Other profit we pay toward principal, until we own free and clear. You still have radio show, maybe you say,

Come on down young people, come to Venice Beach and eat hot dog at Hot Dog Heaven!"

"I told you, I don't talk."

He waved it off. "Bah. Radio advertising is not so good, anyway. Nobody really listening. Word of mouth is best. All day long in summer, we get walks-ins, tourist, young people. We have markup of five hundred percent! You know what is zat? Zat five dollar for one dollar. Big margin. We keep simple, no bells, no whistles. Create cash flow, that is the key, generate revenue stream, branch out, you understand?"

"Yeah," I lied, but if nothing else, the river-of-money metaphor was coming through loud and clear.

Having given voice to his excitement, Eugene settled back in his chair and kicked his feet up on the table.

"Zis is gonna be good, Will. You wait and see."

He clasped his arms behind his head as though he were fashioning an abs-and-thighs pose and reclined even further. But before Eugene could meditate too long on Hot Dog Heaven, he lurched suddenly forward in his chair.

"Shit motherfuck. I forget to turn water on in 219!"

He was out the door in a matter of seconds.

Consummate professionals to the bitter end, Eugene and Acne Scar Joe issued Fatburger their two weeks' notice the following day. I, in true Miller fashion, opted for the short ending. I didn't show up for my Monday afternoon shift, leaving hamburgers behind forever. My destiny lay in hot dogs.

Still, there remained the question of short-term sustenance. And the matter of capital. I couldn't bear to see Eugene sell his bronze medal, which, for the record, I'd never actually seen. So I wrote Big Bill and put the touch on him for five hundred bucks. He sent a thousand. In the letter that came with the check, he said that he was *proud of my initiative* and took the opportunity to remind me that not only was I *a radio star*, I was soon to be *a restaurateur. By the way, had I heard anything from Lulu?*

I had not. A half dozen times I had phoned Lulu in Seattle, but she never answered the phone. I left messages on her machine.

"What's the deal, Lu? What happened? I know you're there, pick up. What's wrong? Are you all right? Is this about what happened? Is this about Troy? Talk to me, Lu."

But she never called. And so I called Troy and left messages.

"What's up? Have you heard from Lulu? What's the deal, why won't you call me back?"

And when Troy never called me back either, I cursed them both as conspirators. My vexation was such that it threatened to become an affliction. I conjured a thousand scenarios, ranging from the improbably hopeful to the infinitely bleak, that might account for Lulu's silence, and I believed every last one of them. I was lost. It was as though Lulu had gone to cheerleading camp all over again.

Mercifully, as the weeks progressed, the whirlwind of activity surrounding me kept Lulu off my mind, at least some of the time. Mornings I went to classes.

None of my other instructors could match the billowy sleeves of Gerard Smith for pure passion, but some of it was pretty interesting. I read Swift and Fielding, and they were both funny, but not as funny as that crazy Frog Rabelais, and not as funny as Voltaire. Nobody was as funny as Voltaire. In anthropology, I learned such useful methodological concepts as *cultural relativism,* an idea I liked because it was all about context, it was wide open, it made all the other ideas it came into contact with more complex. I also learned that every female anthropology major in Santa Monica in 1991 had the same hair—lusterless brown, awkward in length, willful, confused, neglected, didn't know whether it wanted to be long or short. I thought of it as *anthro hair*—and like its distant cousin poodle hair, the women who wore it were inexplicably attracted to me. This was definitely the case with Elaine Niemeyer. Though Elaine was an anthropology major, I met her in a sociology class. Her hair was completely conflicted. One side of it would be tucked neatly behind an ear, while the other side would be hanging in frazzled disarray over her face. Sometimes she pulled the back up, and the front back. Other times she wore uneven ponytails. Her hair seemed to set the tone for her whole personality.

Elaine never engaged in class discussions directly, but she always reacted to them—usually by furrowing her brow, or muttering *bullshit* under her breath. Sometimes she laughed out loud like a crazy person at nothing discernible, then, an instant later, retreated into frowning silence. There was something hard about Elaine Niemeyer, that much was clear—not hard in a cold way, but in a world-weary way—or at least that's what her scowling manner projected. I caught Elaine stealing glances at me one afternoon during a lecture on symbolic interaction. The first time I registered her gaze, I was certain she was looking at someone behind me, but soon realized I was sitting in a corner. After about twenty minutes, there ceased to be anything furtive about her glances. She was staring at me. There was nothing come-hither in her gaze—curious, perhaps, maybe even slightly annoyed. It was the gaze of an anthropologist—an unstable one. And I suppose it was this instability that I found attractive about Elaine Niemeyer. Between her instability, and her confused hair, and her gently sloping forehead with the little pockmark scars, there was just enough about Elaine Niemeyer to remind me dimly of Lulu Trudeau.

I started stealing glances back at Elaine. But I did nothing to actively pursue her. I was still stifled by the awkward silence of my waning moments with Shelly Beach, still trying to get the daiquiri and pepperoni taste of Cheryl off my tongue—and, not least, still terrified of exposing my wee soldier to the theater of battle.

One day as we filed out of class, she fell into stride with me.

"What a load of bullshit," she said. "I'm so fucking sick of the bullshit. Everywhere I look is bullshit. Every stinking text I read is just oozing the stuff. Don't you just hate it?"

"Yeah."

"Bullshit. You love it. I watch your face during lectures, you're all lit up. You're like the rest of them. But whatever—I don't care. If that's what floats your boat, more power to you." Elaine swept one side of her hair back, and released the other. "I guess I just have a low bullshit threshold, that's all. You wanna hang out sometime? You could buy me dinner or something."

How could I refuse such an offer? I'd be lying if I said that ions didn't prickle on the back of my neck, that a few slumbering possibilities weren't awakened by Elaine's invitation. But those stolen glances before we ever exchanged a word were as close as Elaine and I would ever come to romance. It wasn't long before I was back on familiar turf. I can't say whether Elaine's erratic disposition was to blame, or whether my own bullshit quotient simply proved beyond her threshold. Whatever the case, Elaine got drunk at TGIF's and started yelling about Catholics, espousing a theory of religious codependency between bitter exclamations of "bullshit!" I didn't mind so much, I wasn't Catholic, and my own bullshit threshold was apparently relatively high. At least she wasn't dull. In fact, things seemed to be moving in the right direction. Elaine invited me back to her apartment, where she fumbled with her CD collection, and started making some gin and tonics. After about five minutes, she forgot about the drinks and stretched out on the sofa with her bare feet in my lap. Her big toes were misshapen by knobby yellow calluses. Had they been Lulu's toes, I would have loved them. Instead, I didn't know what to do with them. What kind of girl put her sweaty feet in your lap? Was I supposed to touch them? Before I could formulate any kind of conclusion, Elaine passed out with her face pressed against the arm of the sofa. She was soon sawing logs. What was it about me that inspired drunkenness in women? Not bubbly, effervescent drunkenness, or even sloppy, willing drunkenness, but the kind of drunkenness that drove women to vomit on dashboards, or lose consciousness.

I sat pinned to the sofa beneath the dead weight of Elaine's feet for a while. I don't know why I lingered. I guess because it made me feel like a stranger to myself, being in someone else's space, and there was a certain comfort in such an estrangement. But also there was desolation and sadness—for her, for me, for all but the fortunate in love. When I finally excavated myself from beneath Elaine's feet, she did not awaken. I covered her with a dusty afghan, and still she did not stir. In spite of her snoring, Elaine looked softer and sweeter lying there than I'd ever seen her. Gravity had arranged her hair into some semblance of order. There was no scowl on her face, or any sign of the word *bullshit* on her lips. I wished that I could be whatever it was Elaine Niemeyer needed me to be, but at the same time knew that I could never be that thing. If only I had pursued that line of thought a little further—and seen that nobody could ever be that thing for anybody—I might have spared Lulu a lot of suffering.

After that night, Elaine and I stopped exchanging glances in class. There was no unpleasantness between us—only a slight lingering discomfort born of embarrassment. Elaine cut her hair off and changed majors at the end of the semester. But I doubt that had anything to do with me.

The Nature of Illusion

⌇

In Radio Programming and Management, I learned about focus groups and groupthink and leadership skills and the whole cluster-fuck of middle management. I learned about money demos and TSL and cume. I learned about market research. Units. Trends. Quarterlies. Above all, I learned to abhor the entire concept of management. Didn't they know that no amount of formulating could ever create the magic of Vin Scully or Jaime Jarrin or Bill Balance? Didn't they see the futility of all their research and marketing? Were they *trying* to kill the poetry? Were they trying to silence the beautiful voices? You couldn't teach radio any more than you could teach philosophy. It wasn't a doctrine, it was an act. Thank heavens for Gerard Smith for understanding that. Gerard didn't teach philosophy, he inspired it. His clogs walked on air, high above the vagaries of day-to-day life. Even Sartre could not deflate his billowy sleeves. Never mind that humanity was condemned to futility, that life was irrational, and being absurd. Never mind that suicide was the only question. To hear Gerard Smith contemplate the tenets of existentialism, to see him spinning circles in the dead grass under a slate-gray sky, waving his arms about like semaphore flags, you'd have thought he was contemplating the *Nutcracker*, not suicide. To Gerard Smith, the turgid prose of Bergson rang like a boys' choir. Croce's *Filosofia dello Spirito* was to be sucked on like a Lifesaver until the tongue cleaved it into two even crescents and it disintegrated in the heat of your mouth. Philosophy really floated his boat. And why not? Why not occupy your mind every waking moment with loftier questions than *Which way is the bathroom?* and *What the hell's buried in Al Capone's vault?* Why not celebrate the fact that we're not condemned to the mental life of a saltine cracker? Gerard Smith made a philosopher out of me.

In the afternoons, as Eugene and Joe served out the last of their tenure at Fatburger, I prepared for the grand opening of Hot Dog Heaven: I scrubbed and shined and organized. I phoned distributors, hung junk-store prints of Coney Island behind the counter for atmosphere, painted a sandwich board, repainted the menu board. And this work was altogether different from my toils at Fatburger. I was building something in the emptiness, defining it, giving it context. In the evenings I came home tired, but deliciously so. I ate udon noodles. I slept. If I dreamt at all, it was only in those moments right before sleep, when I willfully dreamt of Lulu. I woke up shortly before midnight, drove groggily to the station, and worked as the overnight producer until 6:00 AM, where I answered phones, screened requests, drank coffee with nondairy creamer, catalogued music, organized the refrigerator, and tended to all the other glamorous enterprises that populate the life of a radio producer. Sometimes I studied Anthropology or English Lit. Sometimes I fell asleep with my face in a book in my wainscoted cubicle, which, being in the basement with the rest of the station, was really more of a catacomb, windowless to the outside world.

A shaggy-haired kid named Nate Obergottsberger was the overnight host to whom my production expertise was assigned. I spent countless hours at my post by the board, watching Nate through the glass. His head was gigantic, like the moais of Easter Island. He could barely get his cans on, distending the headset so far beyond capacity that the phones never sat flush on his ears. His forehead was greasy, greasier than mine. You could almost see your reflection in it. Night after night I watched him in his little terrarium, punching carts and leafing through stacks of CDs and records.

Four times an hour Nate did spot sets and station IDs. This he managed, just barely. But once every hour he was forced to read the events calendar, an endeavor that accounted in large part for his greasy forehead. The task was a source of great anxiety to him—the very thought of it set him to pacing in his terrarium. It was unsettling to behold. And even if he read the calendar every hour for the rest of his life, it seemed the chore would never get easier. He had no gift for gab. Worse, he seemed to have no aptitude. He lacked radio instincts almost as much as he lacked good pipes. His voice neither resonated nor cut. It was wholly without texture. His cadence varied between faltering and spasmodic; at times words tripped out of his mouth and tumbled down stairwells, while at others they didn't come out at all—they just froze trembling at the top of the stairs. His chair was always squeaking in the background.

Nate constantly repeated himself, ending sentences with the same word or phrase with which he began them.

"Sub Pop Records released the EP last November on Sub Pop Records."

"Thursday marks the third consecutive week of our tribute Thursday."

"We began our set with a release from The Melvins, who began our set."

Nate's saving graces were two: One, his speech impediment, a slighty lazy *S*, lent him a degree of pathos (or as he himself would say, *pathoth*), and two, he loved the music—he had an encyclopedic knowledge of it, and a genuine appreciation for those who created it. Nate simply didn't understand the concept of projection. He lacked the ability or desire to voice his enthusiasm, assuming, perhaps, that the music would do it for him. More importantly, he did not grasp the concept of illusion, the ability to generate enthusiasm about anything at will—music, carpet cleaner, boiled eggs. Creating this illusion was an indispensable skill to the broadcaster, whose livelihood demanded that he make *Grunt Truck* sound like *Stravinsky*, and the campus blood drive sound like Mardi Gras. Nate made *Grunt Truck* sound like *Grunt Truck*. He made the campus blood drive sound like the campus blood drive.

Lastly, there remained the problem of Nate's brand. The brand was all-important. A catchy handle went a long way. Nobody named Kemal Amin Kasem ever hosted *American Top 40*. And Shadoe Stevens commanded a whole lot more attention than Ted Pritchard. For months, as his friend and producer, I beseeched Nate to change his last name.

"Obergottsberger doesn't exactly roll off the tongue," I observed. "It sounds like a neurological disorder. Obergottsberger's Disease. What about Nate Mars, or Nate at Night? Something sexy, something mysterious."

But Nate wouldn't budge. Obergottsberger was the name God gave him. And besides, with a name like Obergottsberger, he'd never have to worry about making a big name for himself.

A Solid Mass of Probabilities

⌁∿∿⌁

A one-celled organism changed my life. Lulu would say that was a metaphor. I'd say it was an accident. But it happened. It was presumably a one-celled dinoflagellate that infected the habitat of the razor clams Nate Obergottsberger ate at a restaurant in Pismo Beach on a Monday afternoon in early June, 1991, that changed my life irrevocably. By the time Nate arrived at the studio, minutes before airtime, he was feverish, sweating, clutching his gut. He went straight for the altar and spent the better part of his shift there—passing clams out one end or the other. Goggle-eyed, pea-green, and stammering, with puke on his shirttail and toilet paper stuck to his shoe, Nate managed to plod and falter his way through all of his spot sets. It was a heroic performance. He didn't sound any worse than usual. But the top of the five o'clock hour caught him off his guard.

"You gotta do the calendar, man, you gotta. I'm gonna bust, man, I'm gonna bust," he groaned. His forehead was filmy, even by Nate standards. Sweat was beading on the end of his nose. His eyes were like squashed beetles.

"Okay, I've got it," I said.

Fifteen seconds to airtime. A cold hand gripped my heart. I'd spoken once before on the air. Once! Nate had asked me during the calendar to confirm a date, and over the talk-back from the control booth, I'd said: "Yeah, April 10th." That was it, the sum total of my on-air experience, *Yeah, April 10th.*

Five seconds to airtime. I wanted to disappear. But something happened when I sat behind the mic: My fear went away. My throat opened up like it had a will of its own, and my voice streamed out like the Blue Danube Waltz. My diction was flawless, my cadence was harmonic perfection, and the words danced and pirouetted off my tongue and into the mic. And it didn't even matter that *Tad* was playing at *The Cat Club*, or *The Roxy* was giving a benefit show on May 23rd—I might as well have been talking about the flight of the albatross, or the splendor of the Leonids—because it was all about the voice, the dazzling, hypnotic voice.

When it was over, the last item recited, I punched a cart and sat back in my squeaky chair—which hadn't squeaked once during my performance. I relived the experience three times over. With a welling of blood in my chest, I reveled in the potency of this miracle. It wasn't pride thumping like a herd of elephants in my chest, but gratitude, as though I'd been granted a gift. Maybe it was my destiny to speak to the disenfranchised masses—all the hopeless ineffectual dweebs like me, sitting alone in their darkened rooms, pining for a fate grander than acne—maybe I'd pull them together by the force of my hypnotic mint-smelling rhetoric, inspire them from my electric pulpit, like some secular Elmer Gantry for the new millennium. Or maybe it was just my destiny to do overnights at a college radio station. Either way, I was grateful.

When I played the air-check the next day for Eugene Gobernecki, he was in awe of my radio persona.

"Shit motherfuck. How come all the time zey not having you talk? Zey have guy talking he sound like Donald Duck! But *you*, you good. You sound like pro. Zey gonna get rid of him, give talking job to you."

When Nate heard the air-check, he said, "That wuth good, man, really, that wuth good, but . . ." Then he mopped his greasy forehead with a shirtsleeve and mumbled a few halfhearted suggestions about *hitting the post on the muthic bed* and *thlowing down a bit* before suggesting that I do the calendar every night.

The next night I did the calendar every hour, and by the third hour I started adding little flourishes and personal touches, and once I even made a joke. And the morning after I made the joke, Eugene Gobernecki knocked on my door in his coveralls again, this time clutching a manila folder, and he walked past me into the kitchen like it was his own kitchen and sat down at the table and flashed his gold tooth.

"Oh shit. Zat was funny what you say about band from Milwaukee. And when you screw up the date and you make choking sound, zat's good stuff."

"What were you doing awake at four in the morning?"

"Zis," he said, slapping the folder down on the table. He opened it to reveal a stack of clumsily handwritten pages.

"What's this?"

"Business plan for Hot Dog Heaven," he announced.

"Wow. Geez, Eugene, I . . ."

"What?"

"Well, I don't know if I'm ready to commit the next three—"

"I know, I know," he said. "You big radio star now. Not to worry. You give me three months. After that, I buy you out anytime. We set fair price."

"Deal."

"Good. Now I fix sink in 117." Eugene closed the folder, swept it up, and hopped to his feet in one fluid motion. He was gone in a flash.

After a week, the events calendar served only as a rough guide, like directions scrawled hastily on a cocktail napkin. I began spinning my own verbiage, and it was good: fast, funny, succinct. The words simply aligned themselves on my tongue in endless streams. My inflection improved daily. My voice got smarter, it knew instinctively just how to wrap around syllables—just which syllables to wrap tightest about, which ones to let glide, and which ones to balance precariously on the tip of my tongue for the briefest of moments before releasing them like tiny dirigibles into the atmosphere. And interestingly, I found that when I flexed my voice, I always smiled, so that the words sounded happy. And I don't mean that *Feelin'-Groovy-Hello-Lamppost-Whatcha-Knowin* smile, but a *Beaming-Like-Big-Bill-in-the-Middle-of-a-Front-Double-Bicep* smile. A turgid smile. The smile of a pro. The smile of a champion. Smiling from the outside in, not because I was happy—though certainly I was happy—but smiling because it was impossible to create the illusion that I was happy without smiling. Smiling because it was impossible to sound enthusiastic with a straight face. And people don't listen to radio to hear straight faces. I never hurried. I was cool. I was suddenly infused—as though by magic—with the confidence of a Chad or a Daryl or a Troy. And for once in my life I had reason to be confident, because on the radio I looked like Matt Dillon. I sounded like Casey Kasem. I pulled words out of thin air like David Copperfield.

Nate did not object to my progress. Good old Nate. It wasn't in his nature to feel threatened. If anything, he was relieved, content to punch carts, leaf through records, sweat through spot sets, content to leave all that yakking to me. And maybe it was just my imagination, but his own performance seemed to be improving as the days progressed, as if by osmosis, or perhaps by scholarship. His pauses were becoming measured, he was breathing, I could see his teeth more when he spoke. He was still terrible, but at least now he was self-conscious about it.

I soon found that I had influence. Eugene Gobernecki was not the only lonesome schlub in the greater Los Angeles night who found fellowship in my voice as it surfed the crest of those twenty-thousand-watt radio waves. The very Saturday that Hot Dog Heaven was set to open its doors (or its hatch, as it were), just two scant weeks after the debut of "the voice," Phil Spencer, the program director himself—apparently an insomniac or a baker—called me personally at five-thirty in the morning and told me that he'd been *tuning in* and that he *really liked what he was hearing.*

"That choking thing was a gas. Did you plan that?"

"Why would I do that?"

"I guess not. So you write the jokes? Like the one about Tad eating the left side of the menu at Barney's?"

"I just open my mouth and they come out."

"Yeah? What about the cat haunting your house? Frank the cat? That's yours? You made that up?"

I was tempted to tell him it was true, but somehow that seemed like the wrong thing to do. "Yeah, I just made it up."

"It sounds true. Funny stuff."

"Thanks."

"Have you got any prior on-air experience?"

"No."

"So, you're just a natural?"

"Yeah, I guess so."

"Big family?"

"Kind of, I guess." I had wanted to ask him how he knew, but before I could get the first word on my tongue, he was on to the next question. He was sort of like old Pitts that way, always one step ahead.

"You the baby?"

"The oldest."

"Humph. I'm surprised."

"Why?"

"Just surprised. Had you pegged as the baby. So, off the record, what do you think of Nate?"

"Well, I think Nate really loves the music." Of course that was like putting a sunbonnet and perfume on a gorilla.

"How would you like his shift?"

I paused. "His *shift*? Well, what do you mean? Is he leaving or something?"

"Depends. I'm just asking you how you'd like his shift."

"I just think . . . well, Nate really loves the music."

"You afraid of success?"

I knew why he asked, because once again I'd formed an attachment to the competition. I'd come out shaking hands after the bell had rung. I hadn't the strength to capitalize on anyone's weakness unless the stakes were personal.

Waxing philosophical, as had become my habit anytime I didn't know the answer, I told Phil in so many words that I wasn't sure whether I was afraid of success, or if I just didn't believe in success, having no *correlating impression* of success. Lacking any *immediate data* from experience, the idea of success was patently not demonstrable in my case.

Phil laughed at that, and there was something about the way he laughed—benevolent, but patronizing—that suggested he understood everything about me; that my psyche, my will, and possibly even my future were visible to him.

"Okay, I see," he said. "Well then, how does weekend overnights sound?"

"Uh, yeah, sure, I guess. I mean, of course, Mr. Spencer."

"Spence. Call me Spence. And just one thing."

"What?"

"Keep doing what you're doing, but don't get too personal. Familiar, yes, but not personal, not self-indulgent. Keep the reins on the personal stuff."

"Got it."

"You wanna get better, listen to Balance, listen to Owens, the guys with substance. Don't try to be Rick Dees, don't try to be Mark and Brian, be yourself, but don't rely too much on one part of yourself. Be a whole person. If you want to be persuasive, listen to your callers. Don't get wrapped up in what you want to say before they've spoken."

"Yeah, okay."

"And always, *always* listen to your air-checks. Sit down with them and take notes. See what works, where there's room for improvement—and trust me, there's always room for improvement—read books, educate yourself, books about everything, practice framing your thoughts and subjects, practice seeing all sides of an issue, hearing all aspects of a song, and laugh with yourself, don't depend on the listener. You're a good talker. Spin words like Nate spins records."

That was, and remains, the longest one thing anyone had ever told me. And the moment Spence bestowed those confidences upon me, something happened. I ceased being William Miller Jr., a blob of mashed potatoes, and I became somebody bigger and brasher and altogether grander. I became Will "The Thrill" Miller, a solid mass of probabilities.

Blueprint for Heaven

～⌒⌒～

Mission Statement for Hot Dog Heaven

Selling hot dogs of highest quality making perfect for consuming on Venice Beach boardwalk for young people and others. Also tourists consuming with families. Offer good deal for setting price and making good customer relations for return customer. Friendly service for wanting to come and eat best hot dog. Building franchise for serving hot dog using same idea for success everywhere. Spreading hot dog throughout China and other free markets once they are free from communism and other non free market systems.

Description for Company of Hot Dog Heaven

Company will have three equal partners that are Will Miller and Joe Tuttle and me Eugene Gobernecki. Maybe we incorporate for tax purpose. For gross revenue we split in half and put first half for over-head and for paying principal for leasing to ownership. Part of over-head equals hourly wage of six dollars in one hour. Net revenue we split equal three times for Will and Joe and Eugene. For Will he pay part extra from profit or have sweat equity by subtracting for hours at six dollars for one hour. All decisions about Hot Dog Heaven made like democracy for making fair.

Strategy for Growing Hot Dog Heaven

First comes high quality and friendly service and from here we grow. Not to overextend when coming time for franchise. Making choices prudent with questions of expansion of Hot Dog Heaven. But also taking risk which is calculated. Always making sure for friendly employee. Not to make expanded menu but keep simple with hot dogs and chili. Also extras for making it your way like from Burger King. Also promoting healthy hot dog of highest all natural quality for consuming. Makes good not only for health but for business also. Hot dog with chili is balanced meal for feeding nations. Having strong brand for global franchise to boost im-age. Making same everywhere. Hot dog is international language.

Cost Analysis for Hot Dog Heaven

For startup cost needing approximately one thousand dollars for im-provements to current Hot Dog Heaven now called Hanks Hot Diggity. With this we make new sign and menu and buy uniforms and make promotion for new Hot Dog Heaven with balloons and free soda. Also for startup cost needing $402 toward vending license and some money extra for buns mustard relish chili and cleaning supplies.

Sales projections for first year Hot Dog Heaven

We selling maybe one hundred hot dogs in one day. Bottom line for operating costs equals one day and thirty to forty hot dogs depending on extras making for sixty to seventy hot dog profit for one day or three hundred to three hundred fifty dollars. At seven days makes for seven times. For whole year makes for one hundred nine thousand to one hundred forty thousand depending on extras.

Out of This World

—◦◦◦—

Opening day at Hot Dog Heaven began at 8:00 AM in a blaze of expectation, with Eugene, Joe, and I dicing onions, loading napkin dispensers, and filling relish and ketchup tubs as though our lives depended on it. At any moment the flash flood of revenue was sure to crash upon us. By ten o'clock we were prepped and poised in starchy white aprons, tongs and buns at the ready. Eugene insisted on caps. White mesh adjustable baseball caps. Hot Dog Heaven, Out of This World emblazoned upon them in a red and yellow script suggestive of ketchup and mustard. Joe wore his cap backwards. I wore mine tilted rakishly off-center. Eugene wore his straight ahead.

For two and a half hours we stood expectantly behind the counter, monitoring the steam table, turning the onions occasionally, giving the relish a stir. We clicked our tongs and scratched ourselves and peered miserably out from beneath our wooden hatch into a thick fog. The boardwalk was deserted; even the seagulls weren't interested.

"It look like fucking Bering Sea in middle of winter," observed Eugene bleakly. "Maybe we need foghorn or some bullshit. Motherfuck." Indeed, a foghorn might have come in handy—you could barely see the surf. Not hot dog weather. But the optimism of Eugene Gobernecki was indefatigable. "Oh well. Zis probably burn off."

At one o'clock we were still socked in. A few people were walking their dogs. A speeding bicyclist passed now and again; twice it was the same guy. Somebody was bouncing a basketball somewhere in the distance. Occasionally the rim thrummed, and the chain net rattled. A guy in a fleece Patagonia stopped at the counter and asked for directions to Windward Plaza. He didn't order anything. But Eugene's faith was unwavering.

"Sings starting to pick up," he said. "Put on cassette of Springteen with 'Born Running.'"

Around one-thirty the fog finally burned off. The basketball courts began brimming with chatter. The foot traffic began flowing in broken streams, and Venice began to swell with color. And though it was a far cry from the Muscle Beach of the early '50s—a Muscle Beach buzzing with acrobats and strongmen and human towers and teen spirit that wasn't canned but rather trumpeted by the wholesome likes of Joe Gold and Bill Trumbo and Jack LaLanne and Big Bill Miller—though it was a far cry from all that, still, if I listened carefully, I could intimate the clanging and grunting of Muscle Beach in its modern incarnation from my post in Hot Dog Heaven. I could envision the new generation of bodies assembled there, rippling personages in neoprene shorts and torn T-shirts, heaving and pounding their chests, paining and gaining, paining and gaining, until their hearts beat in their biceps and their jaws hung agape. Nike swoops everywhere. Bottled water. Women with fourteen-inch biceps. A different kind of prosperity.

By two o'clock boom boxes were competing up and down the boardwalk. The current had started to eddy in places. The henna tattoo lady was out. The qigong massage guy, even the shaved ice guy was out. A few tentative souls began contemplating hot dogs, but only at a distance. Finally, a homeless guy with dreads and a shopping cart purchased an all-beef dog. Eugene waited patiently as the full balance was paid in nickels and dimes. The dready guy heaped inordinate amounts of sauerkraut and relish on his dog, and though Eugene smiled politely through the ordeal, he could not belie a wince when the guy went back for his third helping of relish.

Fifteen minutes passed before a few Korean gang members bought foot-longs, and a few teenage girls lined up, along with a black guy in a cowboy hat. And suddenly, we were slammed. The torrent of revenue crashed upon us at last, the steam table lid rang like a cymbal, and the ketchup bottles splurted and belched. Orders arrived three and four at a time. An hour elapsed in an instant, then two. America was alive and well. The beleaguered masses were ravenous for hot dogs, and Hot Dog Heaven provided them. By four o'clock we were exhausted, disheveled, spattered with ketchup. The coolers were empty. The garbage can was heaping with soiled napkins and foil wrappers. And Hot Dog Heaven grossed three hundred and eighty bucks.

We rang four hundred and sixty the following day. The third day we broke five hundred, which soon became the standard. Within three weeks Eugene had his bronze medal out of hock. Success was empowering. One afternoon a sun-kissed goddess arrived on roller blades, with pale blue eyes and a cleft chin and a chest that may or may not have been real—I didn't care. She ordered a foot-long and ate it at the counter. She talked with her mouth full. She said she was

an actress. I said, *Aren't they just calling everyone "actors" now?* She said
that she still preferred actress. Then she dribbled mustard down her
cleavage, and I boldly wiped it off with a napkin, and gazing down
into the golden valley, I felt a lump in my throat and a slight ar-
rhythmia in my chest, and for a few precious moments there existed
another woman in the world besides Lulu. The actress didn't object
to any of it. In fact, it seemed to amuse her. When I recovered suf-
ficiently, I told her that being a restaurateur was just one of my business ventures (this, as orders were backing up and Joe was shouting
C'mon, ass-munch). I explained to her that I was a radio personality
(*C'mon, man, who's got my back? I need three foot-longs and a medium
Coke!*), in fact, I told her, she could tune in that very night and
hear my voice surfing the radio waves anywhere in the L.A. basin, a
fact that seemed to impress her somewhat, but not enough to make
me good-looking. I didn't get a number, or even a name. But I was
making progress. I'd had a chance with her. There was a palpable
moment, a brief window of opportunity when it could've gone the
other way, when the future might have ceased conforming with the
past. Perhaps if I'd let my radio voice do the talking.

My whole orientation to American culture was changing. I was
assigning myself a new caste. I finally learned the difference between
coveting success and simply pining for it. The difference resided in
action.

To watch Eugene Gobernecki handle a hot dog was truly inspiring. The way he nestled each sausage lovingly into its bun, wrapped
it fastidiously in gold foil (*Gold!* he insisted. *Everybody doing silver!*),
the way he tucked it snuggly into its paperboard cradle and passed
it over the counter like a newborn, like every hot dog was his god-
daughter. Hot dog vending was Eugene's love story. He handled the
money just as lovingly as he handled the sausage, smoothing out the
wrinkles, scrupulously laying all the bills in the cash box face up in

the same direction, wincing every time Joe and I refused to do the same. Eugene did it all with panache. He didn't serve customers, he seduced them. The guy just looked good with a hot dog in his hand. Some guys were born to hold a hot dog, I guess. Eugene knew how to woo the hungry masses. Like a siren, he crooned to would-be customers as they passed.

"Come, join us at Hot Dog Heaven. See what is our secret sauce." His gold tooth glinted in the sunlight, his hat brim pointed straight at the world.

Strangely, the longer Eugene spoke English, the more problems he encountered with idioms. But he made it work. People loved it. He was a poet when he talked about Hot Dog Heaven. "Come, fresh yourself at Hot Dog Heaven. We have secret sauce for making perfect. Hot Dog Heaven make you out of this world." Eugene made hot dogs sound like a transcendental experience. That's conviction. And you can't fake it.

"First time I'm having hot dog, I say, *Shit motherfuck, why I'm eating cabbage and beets all my life?*"

Over and over he shared this sentiment with patrons, and over and over they ate it up.

Hot dogs were not, however, a transcendental experience for Acne Scar Joe, who was a klutz when it came to hot dogs because he didn't much care for them. He was still a hamburger man. Hot dogs were tubular; they had a way of getting away from you. They were messy. The buns were always blowing out at the seam. But what Joe lacked in grace, he made up for with effort. He worked hard because he liked the money. Joe was flashy with his hundred bucks a day. The first week alone he bought a red suede jacket, two pairs of Air Jordans, and four new rims for his purple Honda. He wasn't thrilled with the whole paying-off-the-principal arrangement. He didn't seem to care about equity, he wanted a spoiler, and a subwoofer, and some fuzzy dice.

Plenty of Room
in Heaven

On the afternoon of June 11, 1991, shortly after I graduated from
Santa Monica City College two years behind schedule, I ran into
my old mentor Gerard Smith on the promenade, and I couldn't
help but notice that his sleeves had lost some of their billow. His
clogs were mired at last in the vagaries of day-to-day life. He'd lost
his teaching job, I soon learned. His partner of ten years, Randall,
had left him for a surfing Buddhist. His dog died of pancreatic
cancer. His glasses were fastened together with tape. I hated to see
him that way.

I spotted him a bagel and a cup of coffee and we wandered in the
direction of the pier, where we leaned against the rail. Gerard was
schlumpy. Even in a stiff breeze, the best his sleeves could do was flap
around like wind socks.

"I *feel* like a bagel," he said. "Like there's a hole in the center of me."

I lived that feeling for most of my life, but I didn't say so. There were times when I felt like the hole and not the bagel, but I didn't tell him that either. "Well, you know what old Locke would say. He'd say that just because your bagel has a hole in it doesn't mean it will always have a hole in it. Observe."

Using my index fingers as a putty knife, I mortared over the hole in my open-faced bagel with cream cheese, until the surface was smooth and seamless.

"Voilà!"

"It's not the same," he intoned.

Gerard proceeded to explain that upon losing his post, he'd turned to his old pal Aristotle for comfort, ransacking *The Organon* at length for some logical solution to the hole, trying to devise a syllogism that concluded in happiness, and when that failed, he turned to the rigid determinism of Hobbes and the haughty empiricism of Locke for answers, and when all else failed, to his old friends Kierkegaard and Nietzsche, but neither the Lutheran piety of Kierkegaard, nor the syphilitic rantings of Nietzsche, could fill the hole.

Finally, Gerard said, he turned to hedonism. For two full months he loafed around his apartment trying to fill his hole with pinot noir and donuts, neglecting his existential anxiety altogether, surrendering completely to his Epicurean appetites without guilt or moderation. He completely redefined success by developing a whole new paradigm for it. He took money out of the equation (though it probably cost him Randall), he cut bait on the adoration of his fellow man, awards dinners, professorships, reliable cars, you name it. He managed to whittle success down pretty good. He even went so far as to devise what he called the Sweats to Pants Ratio (SPR), by which success was measured relative to the number of days a week he spent in casual versus formal attire, formal being anything with pockets. By this measure, seven days a week in sweats was the pinnacle of success. Gerard managed to achieve a ratio of four to three within a month of losing his job. He was at six-to-one when Randall left him. Pretty damn successful.

Gerard tossed the remainder of his bagel to a frenzy of gulls, and talked about the future, specifically his own murky future. There might be an adjunct position up north in San Mateo in the fall, he explained, but nothing for sure. He confessed that he was uncertain whether or not he still believed in the future. The idea was elusive. What did I think?

I told him I already saw my future (which was a lie), and it *wasn't all sunshine and shitting from high places* (which was probably the truth).

"But all in all," I concluded, "it looks better than the inside of a coffin."

I decided at that point that what Gerard Smith needed was not knowledge, or allegory, or even a rope, but inspiration, pure unmitigated old-fashioned American inspiration. So I told him about Hot Dog Heaven, in particular about my poultry-obsessed Greco-Roman wrestler slash Soviet-defector free-market-capitalist business partner from Rostov, and the formidable body of knowledge he'd amassed regarding all things hot dog. Gerard listened with a furrowed brow until I finished, whereupon I asked him whether he thought hot dogs could ever be a transcendental experience for him.

"I doubt it."

"What about a hundred bucks a day?"

"I doubt that, too. But it would put me in some new clogs and some new glasses."

So, without conferring with my business partners, I offered my old mentor a job at Hot Dog Heaven right on the spot. We drove down to Venice that very afternoon in my Bondo-dappled '84 RX-7, which I bought from an ex-cop in Riverside, whose satisfied patronage of Hot Dog Heaven had in fact helped pay for it, and which Eugene had promptly christened "Za Srill Mobile." It was a little rough around the edges, but it wasn't gutless, and the driver's side was pretty clean. It had a decent stereo and sheepskin seat covers. I always sat real low in the seat. I didn't have a choice—it was stuck in the back position. My feet barely reached the pedals. I had some cop glasses I found in the glove box, the reflective kind with the wire frames, which I usually wore when piloting *Za Srill Mobile*.

Cruising our way down Ocean Boulevard toward Hot Dog Heaven, I missed as many lights as possible for the purpose of revving the twin turbos, even though the timing was off and the fan belt was slipping. I sat really low in my seat, like a guy with so much self-confidence he didn't need to sit up straight. I was a city-college graduate, a restaurateur, my hair was falling just right. I tingled with a sense of my own nobility.

Gerard (who didn't seem to notice he was in an RX-7, or that it growled like a mythological beast) looked like a big white flag in the passenger seat. He turned the crosshairs of his anxiety outward, aiming his uneasiness at the state of the civilized world, at Rodney King and Jack Kevorkian and the Church of the Creator. The world had gone mad, he concluded. We were building *smart* bombs and *stupid* people! Electroshock was back! The drug war was a fraud! Ronald Reagan was a confirmed rapist! All signs pointed toward the end: *Tornados* in Kansas! *Cyclones* in Bangladesh! A guy was killed by *lightning* at the US Open!

But what about Lithuanian independence, the end of apartheid, the nuclear nonproliferation treaty, I beseeched him, to which Gerard countered with cholera in South America and the death of Frank Capra.

Poor Gerard. It didn't matter which way he turned, his disillusion was complete.

I reminded him, in the rare spirit of Danish optimism, that as long as he knew he was in despair, he wasn't actually in despair, and giving the twin turbos a rev, I observed that a hundred bucks a day could buy a lot more than clogs and new glasses. This seemed to comfort him somewhat. By the time we reached Speedway, Gerard had rolled his window down and rested his arm out the window, and his sleeve began to billow slightly.

We arrived at Hot Dog Heaven shortly before closing. There were no customers about, though a wealth of evidence pointed to a late-afternoon rush: overflowing garbage, disheveled napkin dispensers, swampy sauerkraut.

Acne Scar Joe was red and blotchy. He had a black eye.

"What happened?" I said.

"Fucking high school punks."

Eugene was whistling as he wiped down the nozzle of a mustard dispenser—not in itself a trustworthy indicator—but whistling Rampal, which invariably meant a twelve hundred–dollar day.

Leaning tentatively against the steam table, Gerard Smith appraised Hot Dog Heaven through broken glasses, and in greeting his deliverance, seemed somewhat less than awed. His handshake was as limp as his sleeves when I made the introductions.

But Eugene soon wooed him. "*Zis* is *great* honor meeting *professor*," he said, flashing his gold tooth.

Gerard blushed. "Well, actually, I'm not a—"

"*I* have philosophy for selling *hot dog* in China. *Business* plan. Maybe sometime I show you, and you help me expand. You come to my house, we cook a duck."

Gerard consented to this arrangement with a nod. His glasses were starting to fog up. "Of course, business isn't technically my area of scholarship, you understand. But I do like duck."

Acne Scar Joe, for his part, was skeptical. He was always skeptical, in particular where business arrangements were concerned. Joe thought my old mentor was a fag, I could see it in his eyes, which made *me* a fag by association. But deep down Joe was an egalitarian.

"I don't give a shit," he told me later. "As long as he shows up on time and he can find his way around a hot dog."

Gerard quickly proved that he not only *knew* his way around a hot dog, he handled them expertly and passionately. In the heat of the lunch rush, he was Baryshnikov in clogs, spinning like a whirligig, with a hot dog in one hand and five bucks in the other. His billowy sleeves grazed the relish boat without ever getting soiled. Moreover, he brought a philosophical flair to Hot Dog Heaven. "A hot dog," he mused, "is the noblest of all dogs, for, is it *not true* that it *feeds* the hand that bites it?" He likened Oscar Mayer to an alchemist, turning lips and assholes into delicacies, like base metals into gold. The hot dog was not only an American treasure, according to Gerard Smith, it was practically a tenet of democracy!

"For the hot dog, like the great democracy out of which it was born, owes its unique flavor and hearty spirit to the diversity of its origins! A tube of the finest steak does not a hot dog make!"

But Joe Tuttle was still a hamburger man. "The hot dog was invented in *Germany*, dumb ass! In *Frank*furter, Germany. Same as the hamburger was invented in *Ham*burger, Germany!"

"Oh, Gerry, do not listen to Joe. Hot dog is not frankfurter. *Zat* was *genius*. Zat was pledge of allegiance for Hot Dog Heaven, Gerry! Zat was marvelous. You write *for me* book about hot dog philosophy, I make for you *big* seller!"

"Well, I suppose I could . . ."

"Zat would be book for *everybody*. Everybody like hot dog, Gerry. In former Soviet Republic, too, they liking hot dog. You think they having coup if hot dog was invented in Russia? I sink, Gerry, zis is brilliant idea you have."

And with each gust of admiration from Eugene Gobernecki, Gerard's sleeves billowed anew, and his clogs took flight like rockets into the ether. And it was official—I, *Will Za Srill*, had saved my first soul in the name of Hot Dog Heaven. And it was good. At least for a while, it was good. Gerard wound up taking that adjunct position up north in the fall. And from there, I heard he got a teaching gig at De Anza.

He sent me a postcard once when he was living in Los Gatos. It was a picture of a mummy from the Rosicrucian museum in San Jose.

> Dear Will,
>
> Philosophical traffic report: Still stuck in the intersection of free will and determinism, but I've put eternal recurrence in the rearview mirror, at least this time around. I've been trying to reduce life to arithmetic, but the equations are too often illogical. I find myself adding and subtracting and multiplying, but I never get to the sum. The one thing I know for sure, and you showed me this truth, is that anything, even hot dogs, can be a transcendental experience. Say hello to Eugene and the crew!
>
> Semper experimentum,
>
> G.S.

But that was the last I heard of my old mentor Gerard. People just slip away if you're not careful. Big people. Everything is smaller in the end.

Brothers Against Brothers

‹‹‹‹‹∿∿∼›

One Friday morning when I was in the bathtub reading *Forum* (a little yarn about a sorority initiation involving dog collars and sodomy), I thought I heard a knock on the door, but I couldn't be sure because there were at least three washers in spin cycle downstairs, and the apartment was quaking at a seven-point clip.

As the knock persisted, my manhood wilted, and I finally wrapped myself in a towel and went for the door, certain that I would discover Eugene on the other side in coveralls and a Hot Dog Heaven hat, holding a pipe wrench or a rake, or a new brand of mustard from the former Czech Republic that was forty percent cheaper even with shipping. He would be impatient about something. Something would need to be done. Something would need fixing, or preparing, or replacing. Or just moving around. Whether here or in Venice, something would need to happen, somewhere, as soon as possible. Making dreams happen is not about sitting around on your ass, it's about the tireless pursuit that never drains you.

"Zis is what make American world go around."

Eugene was undrainable. He was Ragged Dick on steroids.

A week earlier Eugene had caught me in a similar towel-clad, semi-erect disposition when he came to my door before work to tell me that Frank was haunting, among other people, the Ramirez family in 214.

"You need keep an eye on for that cat. Now he bugging people in other building, even. Miss Boswell saying she hearing bumping in her closet at night. I telling her maybe mice. But I know zis is Frank bumping around."

"What am I supposed to do?"

"Maybe you not let him out so much at night."

"He's a ghost, Eugene."

"Zis is no matter. He your cat. You better keep an eye on for."

My last thought before I opened the door was that I hoped Frank wasn't in trouble again. Instead, when I swung the door open, I discovered my brother Doug standing in the causeway in clean pressed military attire, hefting a giant green duffel bag.

Before I could ask him what he was doing there, he was bear-hugging me, even though I was wet and practically naked. He didn't smell like armpit. He smelled like lavender and leather. I felt tiny in his embrace.

"What's happening, big brother?" he said, releasing me.

"What are you doing here?"

"I'm on leave. Four days. Got the hell out of Dodge."

"So you came here?"

"Where else would I go?"

I had about five answers off the top of my head, but the more I thought about each one, the more sense his answer made. "Well, come on in," I said, stepping aside. "Let me throw some clothes on."

Doug stepped in with his duffel bag and took a long look around my dark hovel. The apartment had stopped shaking for the time being, but the dryer vents under the window were working overtime. There were dishes in the sink, laundry scattered on the floor. Frank had knocked over a lamp during the night.

"Not bad," he observed.

I must admit that Doug cut a handsome figure standing there in the living room. He was all grown up—and I don't mean in terms of size, but overall carriage. He stood straight. His mouth wasn't hanging open. His skin was unblemished. But I was most impressed by the fit he'd managed to achieve with his military wardrobe, in spite of his hulkish build. Big Bill could never have pulled such a thing off. He would have looked clownish—the cuff of his pant legs would have been halfway up his shin, the material would have been stretched tight over his massive quads, the shoulders of the coat would've been cinched up around his neck. But Doug's uniform hung like it was tailored. His hair was cropped short and neat, but not too short. He looked pretty sharp.

"What smells like diapers?" he said.

As if on cue, the washers began their gurgling drainage.

"It's the laundry room," I explained.

"Jesus. How can you stand it?"

"Somebody has to."

I retired to the bedroom to put some boxers on, and when I came out, Doug was sitting on the sofa, an ancient kelly green castoff from the Pico house, perusing Hegel's *Phenomenology of Spirit*. His lips weren't moving. The book looked small in his clutches.

"I gotta hand it to you, Will. You're a pretty smart cookie if you can make any sense out of this crap."

"I can't."

"You hungry? Sizzler's got an all-you-can-eat buffet going for $6.99. I saw it on TV."

"It's 9:00 AM. You wanna eat at Sizzler?"

"Why not? You gotta work or something?"

"Actually, no, but I don't even think Sizzler is open for breakfast, are they?"

"Yeah, maybe not. Hey, let's call Ross and go play some pickup down in Venice. Like old times."

"What old times? When did we ever play pickup at Venice?"

"Well, I did a few times, anyway."

The thing about sports was that I listened to them, I knew the language, I could talk about them fluently, from baseball to bodybuilding. But the stars were never Magic Johnson or Kirk Gibson, the stars were always Vin Scully and Chick Hearn, the beautiful storytelling voices. I deplored basketball, begrudged it, actually, for being, like everything in the athletic realm, so far removed from my skill sets. Yet, Doug's plan sounded agreeable to me, if only because it would allow me to demonstrate my prosperity and financial independence. And besides, I had a case of napkins and three gallons of sweet relish from the commissary in the back of the RX-7 that Joe and Eugene would be needing for the lunch rush.

Ross called in sick at the shoe store. He met us at the apartment. Knocking once, he walked through the door with his black gym bag and was immediately tackled by Doug. They crashed to the floor like a couple of elephants, and wrestled around madly, scrambling for leverage, upending the coffee table, huffing and grunting and trailing strings of saliva in their wake.

They were evenly matched. Surprisingly, Ross had a slight size advantage in terms of muscle mass, but Doug was more agile.

In the end, it was Ross who gasped "Uncle."

Doug lent him a hand up, and they both brushed themselves off. It was all rather gentlemanly in its way. No one farted, or called each other "ass-clown" or "knuckle-dragger."

"You got me when my weight was up high."

"Yeah," said Doug. "But it wasn't really fair. I caught you napping. Plus I had you pinned in a defensive posture up against the couch. I think you might have had me, otherwise."

"Yeah, maybe," said Ross, untangling his long wavy hair.

Doug looked him up and down. "Dad said you were training again, but I wasn't expecting this. What are you benching?"

"Two ninety."

"Ten reps?"

"Sometimes twelve."

"Wow, not bad."

"What about you?"

"About the same. But never twelve reps, usually eight to ten. And I usually need a spot near the end."

After a little catch-up—talk of jet engines and women's shoes and more iron pumping—we outfitted ourselves for Venice. Doug wore some military cargo shorts, an olive drab T-shirt, and lace-up boots. Ross wore a Slayer shirt cut into a muscle tee and some neoprene shorts worthy of . . . well, Doug. A dearth of athletic wear left me in Levi's, Docs, and a white T-shirt.

The three of us squeezed into the RX-7. Doug, upon his own insistence, wound up crammed in back with the napkins and the relish, his chin wedged firmly between his knees. But unlike the Doug of even the most recent past, he was not whining about it. Ross kept asking him if he had enough leg room. Doug kept saying he was okay, but thanks for asking. Maybe it's true that we grow more cautious with age, but we also grow more considerate.

I'm proud to say that the Thrill Mobile was roaring like a tiger that morning. I'd just had her lubed, plugged, and timed. Even Doug was moved to comment, and being a jet-engine mechanic for the United States Air Force, he ought to know.

"Rings sound tight," he said. "I'm starving."

The hatch was open and Eugene was prepping onions when we got there with the napkins and the relish. I always tingled with the pride of a father when I approached Hot Dog Heaven. Just as I had hoped, Doug was impressed by my heavenly domain.

"Great location," he said, casting a vague look around. "But somehow I don't see you selling hot dogs your whole life. Let's eat."

The twins each devoured a cold foot-long while I tended to some unfinished business with Eugene—namely, trying in vain to resolve the ongoing debate about lemonade.

"I can get concentrate for next to nothing at the commissary," I insisted.

"Lemons cost nothing, too. I get almost two cases from tree behind complex. You give fresh for same price."

"I'm telling you, there's the labor to consider."

He waved it off. "Bah! Cheaper not always better. Most times, yes, I admit. But not for freshness. You not worry about squeezing lemon. I squeeze lemon."

The pride that Eugene must have tingled with made me sad for the rest of us.

They were running full court five on five on the near court. A father and toddler were taking up one of the back courts, rolling a Nerf football around in wobbly circles. Back in the far corner, three black guys were playing twenty-one.

They didn't seem to notice our approach, but after a while, the fat one pulled a rebound, wheeled around to clear it, and happened to notice two muscle-bound behemoths and a little dweeb in dress shoes standing on the sideline. He nodded at us.

"You guys up for some threes?" said Doug.

"That's cool," said the tallest guy. He was wearing a Payton jersey.

"Mind if we shoot around a little first?"

"Go for it," said the fat one, delivering Doug a firm chest pass.

Doug dribbled twice and threw up a knuckleball that left the chain net ringing for a few seconds after it hit the rim. The ball careened off the rim right to me.

Here began phase one of the awkward dance. The sizing-up phase, in which Will the Thrill distinguished himself as a complete athletic poser—though not without a certain sprightly grace—hoisting a pair of scissor-legged air balls, and a confused layup attempt. The big dude tried to dunk my put-back, missed, and hung on the rim long enough for me to scurry out from under him like a hamster.

To my surprise, Ross had a pretty decent stroke. But he navigated the court like that big red Kool-Aid pitcher who crashes through walls. At one point, he went for his own rebound and came over the back of the short guy with the big shorts.

"Chill, homey. We just shootin' around. Damn."

After a few minutes, the fat guy suggested we shoot for teams.

"Eleven by ones. Winners after three."

The fat guy passed the ball to Ross. "Shoot for outs."

Ross missed.

The other guys jumped off to an early three–nothing lead before Ross lumbered into the lane with a hippity-hop dribble and nailed an awkward running jumper to put us on the board.

They called the tall guy "Big Smooth," but it was his rotund teammate, the obligatory "Tiny," who accounted for all three of their early points. Tiny was light on his toes for a guy the size of a hippopotamus.

His footwork was precise. And he was a monster in the low post. Even Ross, of the 290 bench press, was no match for Tiny down low. Once Doug was pressed into double-teaming him, Tiny would kick the rock out to Big Smooth on the perimeter. Pretty soon they had a six–one lead.

I was assigned to the little guy who jabbered a lot and by all rights should've been wearing the Payton jersey. He was quick, and invariably eluded my coverage, but he couldn't finish for squat.

Doug grabbed an offensive board at six–one and muscled it back up over Big Smooth for six–two.

The little guy clunked a wide-open jumper on their next possession. Ross cleared the rebound to me, and by some divine intervention, I slung one from the hip like Bob Cousy and sunk it from the top of the key.

"Pfff. Happy birthday," said the little guy, tossing me the rock.

"Thanks, but my birthday's in September."

Just after I checked the ball, Doug rolled off a Ross pick, and I hit him in the lane for an easy layup, which brought us to within two. We high-fived, midcircle.

"That's what I'm talkin' about," said Doug. "That's some chemistry."

"That's some ugly," said the little guy.

"Four–six," I said, checking it in.

Ross missed a jumper, but Doug hauled in the board and cleared it to me in the corner, where I was essentially hiding.

"That's you!" he yelled.

"Shoot!" said Ross, muscling for position on Tiny.

I let one fly from the hip again. It hit the corner of the backboard but ricocheted right to Doug, who banked it in over Big Smooth, for five–six.

"Pfff. Nice pass," said the little guy.

This time Ross rolled off a Doug pick on the baseline, and a crisp feed from Will the Thrill completed the patented Miller pick-and-roll. All of a sudden we were tied—a fact that was not lost on the other guys, who began to bicker amongst themselves.

"C'mon, Tiny, you gotta stuff that weak shit!"

"That's *your* man, Smooth! I got Captain America to deal with!"

Ross checked it to Tiny, and with a quick first step rumbled right past him into the lane for a scoop shot that bounced around the rim and fell in. Seven–six Millers.

"Shit," said the little guy. "This ain't happening."

I'm almost embarrassed to admit it, but all of that sweating, ass-slapping, high-fiving camaraderie felt damn good to me. I felt connected, as though I were speaking Saint Bernard at long last. I felt like a Miller. I felt like an American. I was engaging the world with my appetite for victory, body first, charging through the buffet of life like my brethren, with my chin stuck out, grabbing fistfuls of meat. We were outmatched to the man; they were quicker, more adept in almost every way, better shooters, better passers, better ball handlers, but we were connected, we were Millers. As corny as it sounds, I wished Big Bill were there to see us, or Lulu, or my mother. I wished they were all there to see it.

"Let's see what you got, Poindexter," the little guy said, facing me off at the in line.

I looked him up and down, all four foot six of him, waiting to produce the definitive comeback to Poindexter. I couldn't bench press 290, I couldn't eat four game hens in a single sitting—technically, I couldn't even play basketball. But I could spin comebacks.

"Whatchutalkinabout?" I said.

The little guy let his guard down. "Say what?"

I drove right past him into the open lane, and I'm telling you, I was grace incarnate. The ball was cooperating; it felt tiny in my clutches. There was nothing between me and the basket. I could already see the ball nestling into the net, already hear the chain sing-ing, already feel the sting of Doug's high five in my fingers when I lifted off like Air Jordan from the top of the key. Eight–six Millers, I could already see it in lights.

Suddenly, a shadow descended. The earth rocked. The sky opened up, and I saw stars. I heard a voice from above, and even in my dis-oriented state, I was pretty sure it wasn't the voice of God.

"Not in my house," the voice said.

Apparently they tied it at sevens. I heard the chain ringing.

"You good to go?" Tiny wanted to know.

"Yeah," I said.

He offered me a fat hand up.

"Shake it off," said Doug.

I was face-to-face at the in line with the little guy again.

"Okay, Ricky Schroder," he said. "This is lights-out time."

He threw a crossover, and I bit. Ross and Doug collapsed on him in the paint, but he managed to kick the ball out to Tiny on the base-line. Tiny rose like a brick shithouse on butterfly wings and nestled the ball home. Eight–seven them.

My bell was still ringing. I shook off the cobwebs and faced up with the little guy again. I still felt in my bones that we had them.

"You ready to throw the towel in yet, Donnie Wahlberg?"

I smiled.

Nine times out of ten, victory happens quietly, just like defeat. More often than not, momentum shifts in some unremarkable way. It's not always a turnover, a fumble, a botched coverage. Sometimes it's just a little face-up jumper from fifteen feet, without so much as a hand in the face, like the one the little guy hit while I was trying to think of a clever comeback for Donnie Wahlberg.

"My bad," I said.

"Pick it up," said Ross.

I had every intention of picking it up. In fact, I was right in his face this time, like a mirror image, toe-to-toe, twitch for twitch, head fake for head fake. He couldn't see the light of day to pass or dribble.

Then he threw that damn crossover again and I bit, and he flew by me like a bat out of hell and dished it to Big Smooth for a layup, and all of a sudden it was game time.

"My bad," I said.

"Pick it up," said Ross.

Ross intercepted the inbound pass, and cleared it to Doug for an open J.

Nothing but net.

Eight–ten, and we had the rock.

"Win by two?" said Doug.

"That's right," said Smooth.

"Don't get ahead of yourself there, General Schwarzkopf," said the little guy.

"Is that a mosquito I hear?" said Ross.

We were in our element. We still had a chance.

I'm not usually competitive. This wasn't personal. But somehow there was a lot riding on this game. Not pride exactly, not redemption, none of the usual spoils of victory. Something strange and unexpected was at stake in this pickup game—forgiveness, maybe, or acceptance.

For a split second, the world was my idea. It was as though I willed Doug to cut across the baseline and into the open lane, where my pass was already waiting for him.

High fives all around.

"Ten–nine," I said.

"Nine–ten," said the little guy.

Don't ever assume the conformity of the future with the past. But if you see the same window open twice, there's no reason you shouldn't go through it again. Doug broke baseline and met my pass in almost the identical spot.

Tens.

If the window opens three times, you might want to rethink things. I should have. Big Smooth closed the lane and picked off my inbound pass. Without breaking stride, he cleared it, swung around, and fired a bullet to Tiny in the low post. Ten–eleven.

"Point," said the little guy.

Just about everything short of a natural catastrophe comes down to a decision if you unravel it to the source. In a perfect world, you weigh the odds, consider the scenarios, try and figure the probabilities, and make an informed choice. Like whether or not to slacken up on the perimeter and guard against the penetration by a guy who's way quicker than you, has a wicked crossover, and is one for seven from the field. Sometimes the right decisions are the wrong ones. I gave him the open look from twenty feet.

The minute he let it go, I knew he nailed it. The chain sang like the Mormon Tabernacle Choir.

"Don't nobody call Daryl's bluff," said the little guy. "Daryl sting you like a scorpion."

But the loss didn't really sting after all. It wasn't as bad as I thought it would be. The stakes weren't as high as I thought. Despite the spoils of victory, maybe sometimes we gain more by losing. If you believe that, then I've got news for you: You're an even bigger loser than me.

"Good game," said Tiny.

We shook hands all around, even the little guy and me.

"Good game," he said.

"Good game."

Then the Millers took our ball and went home. Well, almost home. We went to Sizzler.

Sizzler

〜〰〜

Let me tell you about the $6.99 all-you-can-eat buffet, the one they were running at the Sizzler on Highland in June of 1991. For sheer breadth and gastronomic complexity, it was no match for The Captain's Table, but it was tough to beat the Hollywood Sizzler for atmosphere: the platinum-blonde hookers and blue-haired waitresses, the toothless crazies. These are the things I think of when I think of Hollywood. Not Brad Pitt. Not Army Archerd. Not Mann's Chinese Theater. I think of a guy in a filthy coat stuffing a lamb chop in his pocket, some sixty-year-old hooker with six-inch heels hoisting her ancient fun bags up in the reflection of the window, some guy with a bad rug and a checkered coat and a broken sewing machine by his feet. In short, when I think of Hollywood, I think of the Sizzler on Highland.

But even the Hollywood Sizzler had never seen anything the likes of my twin brothers lumbering in after a hard-fought battle. Had the management seen them coming, I'm certain they would have shut their doors and run for the hills, or at the very least, slapped an asterisk after "all-you-can-eat" and called the legal team.

The host looked uneasy right from the start when he learned we wouldn't be needing menus. He didn't pay me any notice, but he sized up the twins over his shoulder as he escorted us to the booth, and he looked nervous. As we were rounding up our trays and platters, I saw him whispering earnestly with a few of the kitchen staff. His brow was deeply furrowed. He kept checking his watch. He must have been trained to profile for such things. Maybe he was mulling over protocol for buffet disasters.

The twins hit like the atom bomb. They decimated the buffet. Sirloin tips and T-bone and skirt steak and jumbo shrimp, and baked potatoes and coleslaw, and three different kinds of corn. Big fat doughy rolls, and little skinny short ribs, farfalle with grilled zucchini, and meatballs the size of casaba melons. The twins were a two-headed hydra eating everything in their path. The beleaguered busboy couldn't keep up. The cook staff was frantic. Somebody called the manager at home. By the time the second round was over, there was only smoldering rubble—a smattering of grease, a lone shriveled baked potato. There was a brief gurgling interlude, during which the harried cook staff ran about madly restocking the steam tables and bread bar.

"My ass opens like a trapdoor every time I eat here," Ross said. "It's like there's a bypass right past my intesti—"

"Okay, I get it," I said. "Go."

Ross lumbered off toward the bathroom, patting his six-pack.

"So, basically," I said to Doug. "It's not that I don't have opportunities, I just haven't really met anyone."

"Do you get laid at all?"

"Some," I lied.

He cocked a brow.

"Well, okay, once," I conceded.

"Once?"

"Yeah, once, so what? It's not a numbers game. At least it was fucking amazing."

"Who with?"

"Just a girl from school."

"Just a girl from school? And it was fucking amazing? C'mon, who with?"

"Nobody."

"Do I know her?"

I began to blush.

"What?" he said. "I know her? C'mon, who is it?"

"It's nobody!"

"C'mon!"

Then I saw the realization creep into his face, and he almost looked a little frightened by it, but I never felt that he was judging me, and I've got to say that I love him for that.

"Whoa," he said, shaking his head. "That's . . . whoa, that's a trip."

I always thought "that's a trip" was letting me off easy, and I guess that speaks to my own guilt more than anything else. But then, how could Doug know the unnatural depths of my longing, or guess at the torture I caused Lulu? The simple fact that she was my stepsister was nothing beside that. Still, I can't tell you my profound gratitude and relief at having confessed my knobby old secret and not suffered for it. It made me want to shout it to the world.

"So, what about you?" I said, spearing a cold new potato. "It's not like you've ever had a girlfriend. What's your excuse?"

Doug burped, but not like he used to burp; he didn't broadcast it, he just let it die on his lips and blew it out the side of his mouth. "I'm gay," he said.

I dropped my new potato. For a second I thought he was joking. But after a long hard look in his silver eyes, I knew that he wasn't. And when *he* knew that *I* knew that he wasn't joking, he smiled.

"*You?*" I said.

"Yup."

How was it possible that people eluded my expectations without fail? Ross I would've believed, I'd had suspicions all along, but Doug? Never.

"And Ross too?"

Doug waved it off. "Nah. He's not gay. Believe me, I'd know. Ross is just . . . free-spirited. A little insecure."

Ross soon returned, a confirmed heterosexual, patting his belly and smiling.

"Wow," he said, plopping down in the booth. "Can anyone say *mudslide*? Lordy. You guys ready to load up again?" When nobody answered, Ross knew something was wrong. "What's up?"

Doug and I exchanged blank looks.

"Not much," I said. "Doug's gay and I had sex with Lulu."

Ross looked at us both in disbelief. We looked back at him, eager for acceptance. He began to shake his head.

"Duh," he said finally. "Was I born yesterday, or something?"

"You knew?" said Doug.

"How could you know?" I demanded.

"I'm not fucking stupid," he said.

Doug was suddenly tense. It didn't occur to me that it was a very different thing for him to divulge his secret to me than it was to divulge it to Ross. I see now that by blurting it out like that, I stole something from him, but I can't say what.

"Does Dad know?" said Doug.

"Hell no. He's clueless."

"What about me? Does he know about Lu?"

"I don't know. I doubt it. It's not that big of a deal, right? It's not like it's incest or anything. She may as well be anybody, as far as that goes."

"Does Willow know about me?" Doug wanted to know.

"Doug, the cable guy knows, okay? You weren't fooling anyone with all that homophobic bullshit. Well, apparently you were fooling *somebody*." He looked at me like I was a knucklehead. I never had a twin look at me that way before. "I mean, c'mon, Doug," he pursued. "That kinda stuff is just as obvious as walking around in a feather boa and humming show tunes."

Poor Doug must have felt pretty transparent. I know, because Ross turned his gaze on me, and I felt like a fishbowl.

"And what about you?" he said. "Following Lulu around like a puppy dog, worshipping the ground she walked on. All your little talks, and spats, and lovers' quarrels. I don't know why you guys couldn't just figure that stuff out. You might have had something good."

At what point did my nineteen-year-old brother surpass me in wisdom? He, who so recently, it seemed, had been padding around in diapers gnawing on frozen corn dogs, whose hair had measured a staggering twenty-one inches in height his junior year. He, who had not studied philosophy but real estate, and women's footwear. At what point in time did he fill that gigantic melon of his with wisdom and insight?

"So, are you guys ready to load up again, or what?" he wanted to know.

Doug and I looked at each other.

"Yeah, I guess," I said.

"Yeah, sure," said Doug.

And that was the last anyone said on either subject. Everyone had bigger things on their plates.

The Past, the Present,
the Future
(in no particular order)

Troy finally called me near the end of June. He was apologetic and a little nervous, like he'd been putting me off as long as possible, and we both knew it. He'd been busy preparing for his move to Seattle, he explained, *tying up loose ends, making arrangements up north*, and so forth. He sounded rather unsure about it all. I wondered whether I was a loose end. And if I was, did I even deserve that much?

We met for breakfast at Norm's on a Sunday morning after my show. I was eight minutes early. I took a window booth by myself and waited, sipping burnt coffee and watching the lights change on La Cienega. Troy was twenty minutes late. I ordered without him. I was already at work on my omelet by the time he arrived, listless and a little blotchy about the face.

"Sorry," I said, indicating my plate. "I thought you spaced."

He plopped down on the bench with a poof of forced air. "My bad," he said. "My alarm didn't go off." He flagged the waitress. "Better late than never, I guess. Good to see you. I keep meaning to listen to your show. Lulu told me you're on the air now, in the middle of the night or something. I quit drinking, so I hit the sack pretty early these days."

It looked to me like he hadn't been hitting the sack much at all in recent days. He looked drawn. There were dark circles under his eyes. But maybe it was just early.

"That's overnights for you," I said.

"Yeah, I guess so. Oh well, you gotta start somewhere." Then he turned to the passing waitress. "Whatever he's having, and coffee, thanks." He turned back. "So how's the hot dog biz?"

"Really good, actually. I'm clearing over a hundred a day."

"Hmm," he said. He didn't hoist an eyebrow, didn't even flinch. "How many days?"

"Six, sometimes seven."

"Ooof. Ouch."

I felt my face color. First my beautiful show had been dismissed as a starting point, now my hundred bucks a day had been disregarded completely, as though it were fifty a day, or thirty-eight. I was a peasant all over again: still working too hard, still greasing the wheel, still eight minutes early. And here was Troy, princely in spite of his blotchy complexion, twenty minutes late, unconcerned, tying up loose ends before moving on to something bigger and better. Something bitter began rising in my throat.

"You look terrible," I said.

"Do I?"

"Yeah."

He slouched a little in his orange seat and issued a sigh. "I feel terrible, Will. Awful." The edges of his voice were ragged. He was trying hard to elicit my sympathy. He wanted to talk about it, wanted me to commiserate like always. But how could I commiserate when we weren't in the same boat? His boat was destined for Seattle, and the most exotic locale of all, Lulu's embrace.

"When are you leaving?" I said.

He diverted his attention to the empty creamer. "Tomorrow morning, I guess." It was almost an apology.

"Good for you. Wow." I couldn't look at him. I gazed instead across the dining room past the register toward the waitress station, where a line cook snatched an order off the chrome carousel.

"It's not what you think," he said plaintively. "Really. I wish it were. God, I wish it were."

"I don't think anything," I said. At the register, our waitress was scratching the small of her fat back.

"I don't believe it," he said.

"Believe what?"

"That you don't have the wrong idea about—"

"Believe it." I pinched the phrase into a sharp little bullet. I don't know what I wanted from Troy. An unconditional surrender, I suppose. In the deepest part of my heart, in the pampas grass and mashed potatoes part, I knew that Troy had no claim to Lulu's heart, and therefore nothing to forfeit. Still, he was one more obstacle between us. What was my friendship with Troy in proportion to Lulu?

"I suppose you'll be fucking my sister some more," I said.

"She's not your sister."

"Whatever."

"Anyway, I doubt we'll be sleeping together."

"Fuck her. See what I care."

"Doubtful."

"Doubtful that I won't care? Or that you'll fuck her?"

"Both." Troy produced a folded letter from his jean jacket and passed it to me. "Go ahead, read it."

I tried to pass it back.

He wouldn't take it. "I'm asking you, read it for yourself, Will. What does it mean? Help me understand. I'm so fucking tired of secrets, so tired of trying to fit life together like a puzzle when there's all these missing pieces. Why do I bother? Why do you?"

"Okay, okay, spare me the soliloquy. I'll read it."

The letter was indeed well-worn with Troy's anxiety.

June 25, 1991

Troy,

Sorry I hung up on you last night, I was confused and exasperated. Forgive me for being such an arbitrary and ungrateful excuse for a friend. You don't deserve me, and I certainly don't deserve you. I know I must seem like a complete basket case most of the time. I feel like one. I'd tell you all of this over the phone, but I'd only start not making sense again or hang up. I've been acting erratic for years, as you well know, but lately more than usual. Sorry about all the crying and the shouting. As for the crying after sex, you must not take it personally. Certain things happened to me. If I were made of stronger stuff, if I were a better healer, if I were someone else, if I were who I wish I was, these things would probably be resolved already. I'm not angry, exactly. Sad, maybe. Regretful. Maybe even a little guilty.

Also, there are other unresolved things I can't explain, which aren't your fault either. They are complex and unfair and hopelessly entangled with other people's lives and decisions. They are lies, and I hate them, but there's nothing I can do to change anything. These lies are part of my very fabric, like scabs that have grown through the cloth. Don't ask me to pick them, or explain them, because I won't—not now, maybe not ever. Just know that I've been conflicted about a number of very basic things since the time I was fifteen, and that I've struggled every single day to do what I was led to believe was the right thing, suspecting all along that it was the wrong thing. And trust me when I tell you that there's no chance for my redemption.

What's done is done. That's what my dad would say. But like my mom always said to my dad, there are some things you can't put behind you, the best you can do is to put them beside you. And with these things beside me, I find that I can't take comfort in nostalgia, I can't seize the moment. Whatever consolation the future might offer, it will only be that, a consolation.

So here I am: the daughter of a grief counselor and a muscleman, unequipped to move forward, and too weak to carry my own burden. I'm not sure which one I want to run from most: the past, the present, or the future. Maybe the present, as I'm facing some of the toughest decisions of my life, and I can't run from them, they're too fast. I've been running a long time and you've been trying to catch me, and I'm very tired. I don't mean to sound hunted. I don't mean to discourage you. I know you're excited about this move. I know you have a picture in your head of what the future is going to look like—in fact I know you have many pictures of the future—and I know I'm probably in all of them, and that's a lot of pressure. Please don't count on me, Troy. I can't be counted on. Please, let's take things one day at a time. The apartment is a bad idea. I need space. It wouldn't be fair to you. I'm sorry. I can still give you the money if you need it, the deposit and first and last and the rest of it, and I promise we'll see each other and go out to dinner and hang out like always. But that's all I can promise, and I'm not even sure how good my word is.

I know you feel a need for definition. I don't blame you. You've asked me time and again what you are to me, and what you are to me is somebody I've loved. Somebody I still love. There's continuity there. I know that's not enough. Maybe my heart is missing some specialized faculty to arrange or categorize, but I can't define you any better than that. I'm sorry. I hope someday you're okay with that. Call me about the money when you get to town, or if you need help moving into your apartment.

Love,
Louisa

I folded the letter and handed it back to Troy, who was straining to read my thoughts. I was poker-faced, though behind my facade a riot of fragmentary thoughts were at work, spinning and refracting and fanning out in kaleidoscopic fashion.

"What is she talking about?" pleaded Troy. "What happened?"

"It's none of my business," I said.

"She was raped or something?"

"It's none of my business."

"What's all this unresolved stuff? What are these lies? What is she talking about? *What* is part of her fabric? Is she dumping me?"

"Really, it's none of my business."

"I'm worried about her."

"Maybe you should worry about yourself."

"Jesus, what's wrong with you? This is Lulu we're talking about."

I took a bite of my omelet, though I could feel the rest of it wanting to creep back up my throat. "Exactly," I said. "I'm done with all of it."

Troy slumped. He looked miserably out the window. I felt his anguish. It was my anguish. After Vermont, once I could no longer inhabit Lulu, or even gain access to her, I built my life like a scaffold around her and circled her endlessly, peering through her windows into darkened rooms. And yet at the end of the day I knew nothing about her—nothing of the immutable events that shaped her past, her present, and ultimately determined her future in a single terrible flash of inspiration. Had I even guessed at Lulu's immediate future, had I possessed the slightest intimation of how sudden that future would play out, you can bet I would've done something differently. But how could I, when I knew nothing of her fabric, or of the forces that caused it to wear so thin?

Independence Day

⌁⌁⌁⌁

On the Fourth of July, 1991, Lulu broke Troy's heart one more time. He phoned me the following evening, not two hours after Willow had called with the news about Lulu.

"Just calm down," I told him. "Start from the beginning."

According to Troy, his tireless will to understand Lulu had finally overexerted itself. It happened over a late dinner in Lulu's kitchen—a menu that included frozen raviolis, bagged salad, and cheap merlot—as Troy pressed her for answers regarding her enigmatic past.

"She just kept evading me," he explained. "She started growing impatient, and finally she stopped responding at all. But I kept pushing her, Will. I kept pushing and pushing her! I was just so sick of all the mystery—sick of feeling like there was all this stuff going on that I didn't know about, all this stuff she wouldn't tell me. Jesus, Will, this is all my fault."

"It's not your fault," I said.

"It *is*. I know it is. I promised I'd let it go. And I meant to, I swear. But I just kept pushing her. It's like it all welled up in me for so long that I finally just burst."

"And what happened?"

"Nothing. She just sort of glazed over. It was like she no longer saw me. Like I'd completely disappeared off the face of the earth. She cleared the table, and talked to the cat, and just went about doing stuff like I wasn't even there. I'm telling you, I actually started to feel invisible."

Finally, without so much as a word, a gesture, or a glance in his general direction, Lulu scooped up Esmeralda and retired to the bedroom with an *Utne Reader* and an issue of *Cosmo*. Troy heard the box spring protest as she plopped down on the bed and clicked on the lamp.

Troy sat at the table for half an hour listening to Lulu's fingers leaf through the pages. Eventually, the flow of his thoughts slowed to a trickle. He felt his heart beating in his brain. Around ten o'clock he began to hear the distant mortar blasts of fireworks from Lake Union. When he finally summoned the will to leave, he found that his legs had fallen asleep. He left gradually, like a sunset, pausing one final instant before closing the door. Troy returned to his desolate new apartment on Eastlake where, surrounded by cardboard boxes and disembodied dresser drawers, he spent the remainder of the night on his back in the living room, searching for answers in the nubby constellations of his plaster ceiling. He dreamt of empty boxes and disembodied drawers.

In the morning, Troy returned to Lulu's place, determined to re-write their ending. This time there would be no dialogue, only action. Clutching two vanilla lattes, he knocked on the door, but Lulu didn't answer. He knocked some more. Nothing. He rang the bell. It gave a death rattle. He rang it again. Still, she didn't answer. Troy set the coffees down and checked the door. It was locked, but he knew she was in there, avoiding him. He leaned out over the handrail and peered between the slats of the Levolors, where, through his own ghostly reflection, he spotted Lulu instantly. She was balled up in the mouth of the hallway in a slant of dusty light. She wasn't moving. He could see little paw prints all around her, like they'd been stamped in ink upon the gray wood floor. The cat was nowhere to be seen. Troy said he got a sinking feeling right away. Pressing his face still closer to the pane, he tapped on it, but she didn't stir. He rapped his knuckles on it to no effect. He hollered. His appeals only fogged up the glass.

"When I jumped off the porch, I kicked over one of the lattes," he said.

Troy twisted his ankle on a rut and skinned his hand on the walkway. He scrambled to his feet and circled the duplex. He fought his way through the hedges and wedged his fingers under the bedroom window, prying the bloated wood frame open as far as it would allow. He wiggled his way through the window onto the unmade bed, and darted down the hallway. What he remembered best later—indeed, what he would never forget—was the prostrate figure of Lulu illuminated in a shaft of light, naked and coiled like a fetus in her own bloody slough. Her mouth was agape. Her eyes were closed. There was vomit in her hair.

"It was all so fucking unreal," Troy recalled. He began to sob into the receiver. "There wasn't any fucking dignity in her lying there like that, Will." His grief picked up momentum until his voice gave out. And when he spoke again, he choked on the words. "She just tossed herself aside like garbage."

"Shhh," I said. "What happened next?"

As far as Troy could tell, Lulu was unconscious, but still breathing. He said he was afraid to touch her and he didn't know why.

He remembered making the call, and how his voice sounded as though it came from outside himself when he spoke to the dispatcher.

"And after I hung up, I wanted to say something to Lulu as she was lying there. I wanted to go over to her and hold her hand, and tell her everything was going to be all right. But I was frozen. My teeth were clattering together like hell."

Though Lulu had carved both arms lengthwise from the wrist halfway to the elbow, leaving no hesitation marks, she had missed the arteries. The blood had stopped flowing to her extremities. And so Lulu was condemned to another day.

Troy was as devastated as if he'd lost her. "It's my fault," he kept saying.

"*How? How* is it your fault?"

He began to choke on his grief again. "I didn't know, Will. I swear, I didn't know. Not until the doctor asked me if I knew anything about it, and I told him I didn't."

"What? You didn't know what?"

"About Lulu being pregnant."

"Jesus," I said. And I actually had to sit down.

Troy groaned. "It's all my fault," he said miserably.

I knew I'd been there for that child's conception, just as sure as I'd emptied myself into Lulu amidst the supernatural light of her bedroom, and just as sure as Lulu had cried into my armpit afterward. And yet I let Troy suffer the belief—then and always—that it was his own loss, that he was the complicit party in pushing Lulu to the edge of the precipice.

I'm not proud of that.

Willow and Big Bill flew immediately to Seattle, where Troy picked them up at the airport. Nobody blamed Troy for getting Lulu pregnant, but it had to be uncomfortable. For three weeks Willow and my father roosted in Lulu's apartment with Esmeralda. I was gently persuaded, overtly discouraged, and finally forbidden to make the trip to Seattle.

"You've done enough," Big Bill reassured me.

Remanded to a clinic near the university, Lulu remained for two weeks under supervision, undergoing psychiatric evaluation and counseling. There she sat in circles, clutching a bear with button eyes to her chest. There she drew pictures of her emotions—trees like skeletons wrapped in barbed wire, faces without mouths.

Powerless during Lulu's convalescence, restlessness moved me about in the world without purpose. All that was formerly meaningful and right in my world had been mysteriously altered. Hot dogs ceased to be a transcendental experience. Nothing, in fact, was transcendental. I was distracted behind the mic, never more than a few words ahead of the voice. My beloved events calendar, once the springboard for my wry witticisms and clever asides, was no longer imbued with a magical significance. My jokes weren't funny. The blood drive sounded like a blood drive. The voice did not belong to me; it was alien and disembodied, floating unheeded through the Los Angeles basin, touching no one. And like the amateur I had become overnight, I could not even bear to listen to my air-checks.

The all-knowing Phil Spencer was quick to note the turnabout in my performance, and was even moved to pay me an unexpected visit at Hot Dog Heaven one afternoon during the tail end of the lunch rush. Spence ordered a chili-cheese foot-long, mounded it with onions and relish, and asked me if I could take a break.

I appealed to Joe with a glance. He nodded his assent, then grabbed his nuts when he thought my back was turned.

Even though it was my hot dog stand, Phil led me to the farthest plastic table, the one that always wobbled because of a lip in the concrete.

"Take a load off," he said.

I should have taken my apron off, is what I should've done. A pro would have taken his apron off. Look at Phil. Even though it was a Saturday, Phil was still dressed for the office. He was always dressed for the office. That's because Phil was a pro. Although, I must say, he had one chink in his armor in this respect. He always wore the same suit. And I think he just refastened the same tie knot over and over. Every Monday Phil was pressed and clean; he cut the buttoned-down figure of a hale and hearty radio exec. On Tuesday, he was still pretty sharp—good crisp lines and sharp pleats. By Wednesday, the fabric started to wilt a bit, and his tie knot started to go a little catawampus. Thursday lunch, maybe he got a spot of mustard on the lapel, and his pockets began to sag. By the end of the week, Phil looked like he'd just rolled off a couch and washed three aspirin down with some warm club soda. And by Saturday, all bets were off. Life wears you down, I guess. What I never figured out was—*when* did he dry-clean the suit? *How* was it possible?

It was Saturday when Phil sat me down at Hot Dog Heaven, so he was pretty rumpled. We sat quietly. A cloud of seagulls caused a fuss nearby. The tide was receding and the wind was kicking up, and you could really smell the ocean in the air, even over the myriad scents of Venice Beach: patchouli and sunscreen, hot dog gristle and barbecue smoke—the smell of my wayward adolescence. There was a steady flow of foot traffic along the boardwalk.

I kept expecting Spence to launch into one of his sage radio lectures, but he didn't say anything for a while. He set to work on his foot-long, a little distractedly, I thought.

"You're getting mental," he said finally. "Losing your focus."

"But I—"

"*Tut tut*," he said, raising a finger. "Hear me out. See, what happens is you're not distilling anything—you're just opening your mouth and—"

"But, Phil, that's all I ever did in the—"

He silenced me with the finger. "Listen."

I listened.

"You hear that?"

"What, the seagulls?"

"No, your thoughts. Shush."

"Whaddaya mean?"

"I mean, when you sit still and shut your mouth, can you hear your thoughts?"

"Well, yeah, of course."

"That's your problem." He nodded, as if to say, *yep, just as I expected*, and took a big bite of his foot-long, which he seemed to enjoy for the first time. "Ev fif fing feef?" he asked.

"Huh?"

He rolled the big bite over into one cheek so that he looked like Sparky Lyle. "Is this thing beef?"

"It's everything," I said, not realizing the philosophical implications of the statement.

He chewed a little more, nodding his head, and finally swallowed. "Hmm. Not bad. See, now, your thoughts should be quiet, Miller— as quiet when you open your mouth as when you close it. The brain is not so good at distilling—fucking thing spins in circles. You wind up with more in the end, not less." He tore into his foot-long again. He was really beginning to like it. "Vif fing if big," he observed, wide-eyed and masticating contentedly.

He then raised the finger to buy a few chews. When he finally choked down the bite, he wiped his mouth with the sleeve of his jacket and looked me in the eye.

"It doesn't come from up here," he said, aiming the finger at his head. "It comes from in here."

I'm still not exactly sure if he meant to say it comes from the heart or the gut, or even the rumpled shirtfront, because Spence was point-ing just a hair below his solar plexus, but I definitely caught his drift.

"So how do I turn my thoughts off?"

"Beats me. How did you do it before?"

"I don't know."

Phil went thoughtfully back to work on his foot-long. He turned it around in his hands, inspecting it between bites. "Let me tell you a story, Miller," he said, with his mouth full.

A momentary calm washed over me. Finally, I thought, the an-swer. Straight from the oracle. I leaned forward attentively in my plastic chair.

But he waved the idea off. "On second thought, forget about it."

I was a bit crestfallen, and I'm sure Spence could see it, because I could see real empathy in the folds of his crow's feet. "Look, Miller, I'm just guessing here, but I'd say you're having doubts. I've seen this kind of thing before—and understand, it doesn't matter the nature of the doubt—maybe you think you've got genital warts, maybe you think the world is poised on the brink of nuclear holocaust, hell, maybe you've fallen out of love with radio."

"No," I assured him.

He gave me a searching look. Spence was the master of pause. He understood pause like Gary Owens understood pause, like Balance understood pause, like Billy Graham understood pause; he under-stood that the effective pause was not all about the pause itself, or even the act of pausing, but about where you left the pause, what kind of English you put on it. In its rudimentary form, pause was punctuation, slightly evolved it became a question, but suspended just right, left out there long enough, it became a turning point for the listener. I'll bet you that back in the day Spence could give his listeners a searching look right through the radio dial—he'd done it to me on the telephone.

"You just gotta look doubt in the eye, Miller. On second thought, don't look at it at all. Just lower your head and charge at it. You need to find your center again, that's all I know. That, or discover a new one."

"How am I supposed to—"

"Shh." He stopped me in my tracks with the finger. "Whaddaya hear?"

"Nothing."

"Bullshit."

I listened distractedly. "Questions, all right, I hear questions. A lot of them. And, yeah, okay, doubts. Nagging ones."

Spence nodded gravely. "Miller, you're depressed, okay. It's pretty simple. Here's what I want you to do. Here's what you *need* to do."

"I'm not depressed, I'm just . . ."

"I want you to take some time off."

"But I don't think I need to take—"

"*Tut tut.* Shh. I insist. Just a week or two—however long it takes for you to stop thinking." Phil set the last three inches of his foot-long down and patted his belly. I noticed a little chunk of pickled relish poised on the lip of his shirt pocket.

"We don't think our way out of corners, kid. We act."

Upon Lulu's discharge at the beginning of August, she accompanied Willow and Big Bill back to Sausalito, where she agreed to remain indefinitely—or at least until the beginning of fall semester. According to Willow and Big Bill (only one of whom I had reason to doubt), a critical bargaining point in negotiating Lulu's extradition was her stipulation that she receive no contact from either Troy or myself during her convalescence. Not until she was ready to initiate the interaction herself.

"She's healing," Willow explained over the phone. "Women *feel* their way through grief, Will. You have to respect that."

"But when can I see her?"

"That's not for me to say. Whenever she's felt her way to that point."

Thus, Willow and Big Bill withheld my letters and disregarded my Trojan horses, all for the sake of defending the sanctity of Lulu's grief. I could forgive them a lot of things—their judgment, their hypocrisy, their deceit—but I couldn't forgive them for shutting me out when I scratched on the door.

Ch-ch-ch-changes

⸺〰〰⸺

I suppose before all of this is over, you're going to want some type of accounting for my decision to drop everything—including what was shaping up to be a burgeoning, if not vaguely dissatisfying, future for Will the Thrill—and set out for Sausalito. You'll probably want to know what I expected to gain by any of it, and if I don't tell you, then you'll probably just assume the answer is Lulu. But you'd be wrong, because I can't honestly say that I allowed myself to believe for even one minute that I was actually going to claim Lulu's heart. I was simply driven as a moth to flame. I could no more resist seeing Lulu than I could operate a hydraulic scissor lift blindfolded, or cure Klinefelter's syndrome with a croquet mallet. In my heart, I knew that the real question was not what did I expect to gain by going to Sausalito, but rather what did I stand to lose by not going to Sausalito. And the answer, of course—though I didn't know it yet—was clarity.

Joe wasn't too thrilled about the idea of covering my ass indefinitely, especially on such short notice. The very evening of my departure he was scheduled to party with a chick in Cerritos who worked at Stereo Lab.

"Dude, she looks like Kim Basinger. Except she's got braces."

Indeed, it was a big night for Joe—preparations were in order. And I was really gumming up the works. He wanted to polish his rims first. He had to square off his sideburns and gel his thinning hair. He wanted to stop by Sam Goody and pick up the new Whitney Houston.

"Chicks dig Whitney Houston, dude. I'm gonna bang this chick, for sure. No way, I'm closing."

"I tell you what, guys," Eugene interjected, stocking the napkin dispenser. "I close." He clicked the chrome cover shut. "Joe, you go have party wis chick, and Will, it's not to worry about. Is no problem. It freshes me to stay late. I am winding down when I am closing." He gave the chrome surface one final wipe for good measure, checked his reflection in it, and replaced it on the counter. "I cover for you tomorrow, too. As many days as you need. Sree Muskateers stick together. You want also I feed your cat?"

"He's dead, Eugene. He doesn't eat."

"I leave bowl of milk, anyway."

"Look, Eugene, the thing is, I don't know how long I'll be gone. I mean, I don't know what's going to happen, I don't even know why I'm going, really, or how long I'm staying. I guess what I'm trying to say is, I may need a lot of covering for a while. I just don't know."

He waved it off. "Bah! For however long you are talking, is no problem. We build Hot Dog Heaven so we can make for this kind of freedom."

Good old Eugene. I think he knew all along I was in love with my stepsister. All those hours he spent listening to me as we diced onions side by side, all that talk about Lulu, surely he intuited it. Somewhere in his Russian soul, he understood the complexities without knowing them, I'm almost sure of it. I really loved that guy. I loved it when he called me *Will Za Srill*. It was never the least bit ironic—it was always genuine. It made me feel like somebody. I'm not sure that anyone ever believed in me more, or ever expected more of me, than Eugene Gobernecki. So how do you thank a person like that? How do you thank a person who never asks for anything more than a little solidarity in return, a little companionship, a guy who would walk to the end of the earth for you—and then cook you a duck once he got there? Maybe you never thank him, maybe you just mean to. That's all I ever did. And I'm just guessing, but I'll bet at the end of the road, when I'm cashing in my regrets, I'm going to wish I thanked Eugene Gobernecki for being the first real friend I ever had.

"And whatever you do," he shouted from behind the counter as I was leaving, "don't crash za Srill Mobile."

Maybe I should have stuck by Eugene, maybe I owed him that. Maybe together we could've taken China by storm, or maybe just gone bankrupt trying, like he did. But that was not my destiny. I've always suspected that Eugene had an inkling my journey north was the first step in my incremental disassociation with Hot Dog Heaven. I can't really say that I had an inkling myself. Certainly I had no inkling that I would allow Eugene Gobernecki to slip away for good—not by design, or by any act of agency, but simply by the force of changing winds.

Last I heard, in the wake of the Chinese hot dog debacle, Eugene had moved up near Torrance and started a hugely successful lawn maintenance service with none other than Joe Tuttle. Two musketeers. I saw a TV commercial for Heavenly Gardens late one night during a Clippers rebroadcast. It was one of those shoestring budget commercials, where the colors are all blown out, and the audio sucks, and the graphics leave ghostly tracers in their wake. Despite his thinning hair and some new wrinkles, he was the same little potato of a guy; his gold tooth was still gleaming, the light of optimism still showing in his silvery eyes. And, by God, he still knew how to sell it—whether it was hot dogs or hedge trimming—that is to say, Eugene knew how to believe.

"So, why you waiting for, then?" he asked. "Why you not calling Heavenly Gardens right now? Heavenly Gardens making *your* garden out of this world!"

At the end of the commercial, they left the camera trained on Eugene at least two beats too long. But his smile never wilted. His tooth kept gleaming.

Revisionist History

‑‑‑∿∿‑‑‑

On that Wednesday in August when I left Hot Dog Heaven, I was inside of myself, knowing and forgetful at the same time. I shot like a gray bullet through the basin and over the grapevine and right up the gut of the Central Valley with the hot gritty wind in my face. The Dodgers were in Cincinnati, I remember, still three and a half games up on Atlanta in the West. I lost Jaime Jarrin in the third somewhere north of Bakersfield, and I was forced to listen to Vin Scully, my old god, on KNBC. I had to admit it was comforting to hear his voice again, warm and steady with a touch of the nasal. A voice to lean into, whose calm authority and unwavering confidence called down out of the ether, inspiring a sense of well-being in an increasingly chaotic universe.

The Dodgers were up two–zip when I lost Scully around Kettleman City. After that I just listened to my thoughts and the riotous wind rocketing past my ears. And crossing the Golden Gate into Sausalito I tried harder than ever to see the future. All I saw was a tollbooth.

The sun had already set when I reached Willow's condo, which looked identical to the condo next to it, with the lone exception of a lighted walkway.

Big Bill's girth soon filled the doorway, a nimbus of light from the foyer wrapped around his head. He wore a beard, with little flecks of gray. The ponytail was gone. His hair was lopped off in an even line in back, like he cut it with a buck knife. He wore his bangs like Ray Conniff. My people are shape-shifters, I guess. You never really get used to it. I could hear the television in the living room, and something smelled like onions.

He looked down at me and shook his head grimly. "Darnit, Tiger, you driving up here doesn't change a thing."

"I want to see Lu."

"She needs rest. We've been through this for weeks. Now I'm sorry, I really am. I wish I—look, let me give you some money for a ho—better yet, let's go to dinner first, you and me."

"I'm not hungry. Let me in, Dad, I have to see her. You have to let me see her."

"I can't do that, Will. I promised your sister. C'mon, we'll talk about it at dinner."

I tried to push my way past him into the house, but he blocked my way, clutching one of my wrists. Breaking free of his grip, I took a step back, and no sooner did I step back than I rushed him again. But he caught my head under his arm and held it there in a rather gentle headlock, as if my head were an Egyptian vase, until I stopped squirming. He released me slowly and stood me up straight, holding me at arm's length. He smiled sympathetically.

"Not now," he said. "Give it some time, Tiger. Give your sister a couple of weeks to recover. You're not helping her by being here. I know that may sound harsh, but that's the truth."

"You can't do this."

"I've got no choice. Now c'mon, we'll grab a bite and get you a hotel."

I tried to rush past him again, and he restrained me in a bear hug. He lifted me, effortlessly, it seemed, and carried me kicking and squirming outside to the driveway, where he set me down like a mannequin. His patience was wearing thin.

"It's over," he said. His shortest ending yet.

I darted past him for the door. He clotheslined me from behind and tackled me. We tumbled across the walkway, flattening the low hedges on our way to the grass, where the sprinkler was making its rounds. I was no match for Big Bill. Despite his girth, he was quick. I tried to roll away through the soggy grass, but he had me covered. He sat on my stomach and pinned my arms to the ground and looked down into my face. I struggled halfheartedly to free myself. We were both breathing heavily. I could smell his aftershave. He had onions on his breath.

"We need to talk," he said.

We crossed the bridge silently until about midspan. After a year, the minivan still smelled new. Big Bill looked more hulking than ever behind the wheel. My back was wet, my pride smarted. I was an incorrigible prisoner, beaten but not defeated.

"Where are we going?"

"The city," he said.

"Where in the city?"

"I don't know. I haven't got that far. The Haight, I guess."

"Goodie. What for?"

"To talk."

"Why do we have to go to Haight-Ashbury to talk? Why not the living room?"

What did it say about the Millers that we were forever driving off somewhere to talk? Anxiety drove us to the open road. At the first sign of crisis we were off and running, over bridges, into deserts, always into our past.

No sooner had I asked than Big Bill provided the answer.

"I don't know. Just because."

I gazed sullenly out the passenger window, away from the twinkling city and out over the mutinous Pacific toward the horizon.

Big Bill released the breath he'd been holding. "Will . . . sometimes life comes at you pretty fast. Things happen. Sometimes a lot of things at once. You've got to manage it all somehow so that you don't lose everything. You try to do the right thing, but sometimes there's not a right thing. Sometimes just a less-wrong thing." He cast a sidelong glance at me. There was something hopeful in it.

"Keep talking," I said.

"Okay. Good," he said. "Good." He was gripping the wheel tightly. His knuckles looked old. There were blue spots on his hand. The muscles of his forearm had grown sinewy. "I just need you to understand that . . . I thought I was . . . I didn't know that— Oh, Christ, Will, all of this is my fault. It was a big mistake, all of it. Not telling you, letting things go on so long like they did."

"What are you talking about?"

"I'm talking about Lulu. I'm talking about . . ."

"What about her?"

"Oh, Will, damnit, all about her," he groaned.

"Such as what?"

"Such as . . ." He broke off to sigh, and when he did his throat rattled. "Such as you've got to let go of her, son. You've just got to. It's just not healthy. It's not . . . right."

"What's not right?"

"The letters, the notebooks, the rest of it. Yes, I've read them, Will. I know. I've known. I should've put a stop to it years ago."

"*Years?* You've known for years?"

"I thought it would pass. It didn't. Now it has to. You've got to stop loving your sister the way you do."

"She's not my sister."

"She's your *half* sister."

"So what?"

"No, Will," he said, leveling a meaningful gaze at me. "Listen to me: *half* sister." He gave the statement a moment to sink in. His eyes were drooping like a bloodhound. "I'm her father."

Abruptly, the green of the Presidio closed in on both sides of us. My ears started ringing. You really can't assume the conformity of the future with the past. Sometimes there's an invisible line between cause and effect.

"I did it to protect your mother," he said. "She never knew."

"What are you saying? You did what?"

"I was going to . . . I intended . . . we intended, Willow and I, as soon as you were old enough, to . . . explain it all."

"So what happened to that plan?"

"You've got to understand, Tiger, when your mother died . . . you lost so much. I couldn't see depriving you of something you never knew you had in the first place. What good would it have done? All this explaining about the past? It would only create more confusion. And there was confusion, Will. Chaos. And if it hadn't been for Willow—"

"And what's her excuse?"

"She doesn't need one. She wanted you to know all along, ever since Annie died, anyway. She wanted Lulu to know."

"So she told her."

"No. Yes. It was Vanessa, Grammy. She let something slip. Lulu started asking questions."

"Vermont."

"Yes."

"Jesus. Well, what—how come—at that point, why the hell—"

"You were your mother's son, Will. You were her pride and joy. Her little man."

"Forget about me! Forget about Mom! What about Lulu? She didn't deserve to know who her father was?"

"It was the only way."

"How? How was it the only way? How was it that I got the honor of having you as a father, while Lulu got to find out when she was fifteen years old that the guy she thought was her new stepdad is the father who never claimed her in the first place! How is that the only way?"

"There's more to it than you understand. It was more complex. I just didn't ever want you to think . . ." He trailed off into a dense silence.

We hit the tunnel in a rush of sickly light. Everything I never understood about Lulu was illuminated in an instant—her eternal ambivalence and her maddening evasion, all of it had a context at last. The little girl in the yellow socks had died in Vermont, and poor Lulu had been changing ever since. People really do change. Don't let anyone tell you differently. That the future does not conform to the past is not the exception, but the rule.

By the time we emerged at the far end of the tunnel, I understood for the first time, with excruciating clarity, everything that Lulu endured, all that she owned in the name of illusion. I understood why she mutilated herself and disfigured herself, and why she ultimately tried to destroy herself. She did it all to push me away. To make herself ugly so I wouldn't want her. That's how much she loved me.

And I thanked her by never relenting, no matter how hard she tried to repel me.

Neither Big Bill nor I ventured to speak again until we were skirting the park on Fulton.

"To think what?" I said. "What didn't you want us to think?"

"That I was unfaithful to your mother. That I ever loved anyone else, that I ever loved any of you less than completely."

"*Were* you unfaithful?"

He didn't answer right off. He swung a right on Stanyan and continued down the hill. "No," he said. "Yes. Technically, once. It was . . . there was more to it than—it was an ending with Willow. It wasn't a fling."

"What does that mean?"

"It means I dated Willow before your mother. It means she introduced me to your mother at a party on Oak Street, not four blocks from here. They were good friends, best friends at the time. That was 1967, the beginning of the end. It was awkward, Will. We were all friends for a while, and . . . damnit, I don't know, it's all so complex, and so far in the past." Big Bill squinted, as though trying to intimate the past. "You've just got to understand," he continued. "Willow and I were on different paths at the time. We were broken up. It just . . . happened one night. It shouldn't have. I loved your mother so much, and Willow knew that, she loved her too. She was okay with raising Lulu by herself. She was. She told me that. She wanted a child, not a husband."

He hung a left at the golden arches. "I always sent support for Lulu, every month for ten years. Your mother never knew that, either."

"If you loved Mom so much, why didn't you tell her anything?"

"I couldn't tell her."

"Why not? Why couldn't you tell her?"

"She was pregnant with you, and we were getting married, and it just seemed . . ."

I turned away, looked out the window. "It wasn't fair to Lulu. It was a dirty trick."

"I only meant to . . . I thought I was doing the right thing, Will. I thought it would work."

"Work? What does that mean, work? That you'd get away with it?"

"No. Not . . . I don't know. I didn't want to muddle things. I loved your mother more than I ever—look, I didn't want to screw it up."

"If you didn't want to *muddle* things, you should have kept your dick in your pants in the first place!"

He stopped the car in the middle of Haight Street and looked out his side window at nothing. "Okay," he said calmly. "I deserved that."

"Of course you did! And why didn't you tell me Lulu was pregnant? Why did I have to hear it from Troy?"

Big Bill piloted the van slowly forward, then stopped again and looked me dead in the eye. "Because that was *Lulu* and *Troy's* business, now, wasn't it?"

And what could I say to that without laying bare my own shameful secret?

We parked on Cole Street and sat in the darkened car without speaking. Silence is the sound that gravity makes. I was comfortably numb, strangely peaceful and accepting, like a guy who's fallen off a cliff and broken his neck and lies in the dust watching the buzzards pinwheel above him. I was outside myself again in the silence.

After a moment Big Bill started drumming incessant little rhythms on the steering wheel with his fingers.

"Stop," I said.

He stopped. But the silence had fled.

"I'm sorry," he said.

Of course he was sorry. What else could he be but sorry? I was ready to give short endings a try. Why not? What the hell did long endings ever do for anybody? Big Bill was right. I felt his giant hand on my shoulder. I wouldn't look at him. I looked instead at the sloping black dashboard, the tape deck, the missing cigarette lighter.

"I know you are," I said. "It's over. Now drop it."

"You're okay with this? You understand?"

"No and no. Of course not. It's just too much, right now, all of it. It's stupid. I should've known it all already, whether or not you ever explained it. Somewhere in me I did know, and just didn't want to."

"I should have told you," he said.

"Yes, you should have. But you didn't, and it doesn't matter anymore. So now what?" I said.

"Let's walk."

We walked down Cole, then west on Haight with a gentle breeze at our backs. Big Bill remained silent for the first half block, but then he began making little peace offerings along the way.

"That used to be the Straight Theater . . . That used to be the Trib . . . That used to be I/Thou."

To these offerings I only grunted, which was encouragement enough for Big Bill. "Jesus, the way times change. I still can't believe there's a McDonald's right here. Boy, I should've seen that one coming a mile away. It's a damn shame. Humph. You hungry? I'm kind of hungry."

If crises drove the Millers to the open road, resolution made us hungry. And food always inspired in my family a spirit of philosophic inquiry, as was the case with Big Bill at the McDonald's on Haight and Stanyan.

"Is it my imagination," he wondered aloud, midway through his third Big Mac, "or have Big Macs shrunk? It seems to me they're smaller. I can hold two in one hand—see, look at that. I didn't used to be able to do that. Also, is it just me, or does everything taste like French fries now? Everything. The milkshakes, the pies, even the ice water tastes like French fries. Have you noticed that? So, do you guys have a special sauce? I mean, for your hot dogs? How does that work?"

After McDonald's we went across the street to the grocery, where Big Bill bought a jug of Carlo Rossi sangria. We crossed Stanyan into the park and walked up Hippie Hill. At the top of the slope we sat in the grass and Big Bill unscrewed the jug and immediately took a long pull and passed it my way.

"Good stuff," he said.

"I'll take your word for it."

"Suit yourself," he said, and took another slug.

"Oh, okay. Give it here." I took the jug and drew a small sip. It tasted like diabetic grape candy.

"See? What'd I tell you? Annie and I used to drink this stuff back in '67."

He patted me on the back, and scratched the scruff of my neck, and finally mussed up my hair. "You're a good man, Tiger. I'm proud of you. I'm really glad we're doing this."

"Yeah, this is great, Dad. The park, the wine. Maybe we can hop a freight afterward."

Big Bill smiled. "You got that from your mother, too. The quick wit. Annie had a nimble mind. She was funny right up until the end."

"I guess I missed that part."

He kept calling her Annie, which I'd never known him to call her in life; it was always Ann, but then, that was 1967, Starship was Airplane, and the moon was still the final frontier.

I listened without comment as my father began meandering somewhere between regret and nostalgia, recalling his Lower Haight days some more—before the fall of love, before Grace Slick was giving drunken blowjobs to microphones and puking onstage, before the Hells Angels were working security, before the junkies were epidemic, before the ad moguls cashed in with their VW buses and Coca-Cola, and suddenly love was not free anymore, and hippies were a demographic. He explained how Willow met Annie, and how Annie met *Not-So-Big* Bill, and how soon everything was a little more complex. Annie got pregnant with William, and Willow got pregnant with Lulu. Yet in spite of all its complexities, life was simple because it seemed you had forever to sort it out, or a while, anyway. And even as darkness set in, and the whole world—from Vietnam to Buena Vista Park—seemed like a great big *maybe*, and the word *we* suddenly meant a lot of different things, and the word *me* started popping up a lot more in everybody's vocabulary, even then Annie and Willow perused maternity magazines together, exchanged paint swatches and childcare books. And when the babies were born there were outings to zoos and planetariums and Half Moon Bay, afternoons of peanut butter sandwiches cut into tiny squares, plastic bags of green beans, sticky strollers, baggy dresses, skinned knees, throwup, hard-to-find public restrooms, Kodak moments involving carousels and duck ponds and Pier 39.

But nothing lasts. Indecision is not a fate in itself. Just ask the Prince of Denmark. Eventually you choose. You act. You define your life. You, Big Bill, touched down in Santa Monica with Annie (or was she Ann by the time of your departure?) and eighteen-month-old William (destined never to be Little Big Bill), and in doing so, turned your back on Lulu. You chose to call Santa Monica home, 436 miles from Willow and Lulu, because, you reasoned, it had been home all along. You know how distance is, you know how jealousy works, you know how time erodes everything in this world, including memory, which is not made of meat, though it may as well be. Everything may as well be. And you learned, finally, that it doesn't matter how big you build yourself up, what you mold yourself into, how strong you think you've made yourself, love will kick your ass anyway if you give it the chance.

You made a great big mess of love, Big Bill, but who didn't?

Big Bill had forgotten short endings altogether. He'd found his voice, at last, and the more he used it, the better he seemed to feel. That's the power of voices. I let his words wash over me, listened without listening, and thought about how the biggest truth in my life was a lie, but that didn't make it any less real, especially not for Lulu, who'd been forced to live it all these years.

At some point I noticed Big Bill was slurring, and chutes and eddies began wending their way through his longer phrases, and his voice was starting to carry, but in a warm, gregarious kind of way, somewhere between the don't-you-feel-good-about-7Up guy and Yogi Bear. And how do you not forgive that guy? It's impossible not to forgive that guy. Finally, Big Bill wobbled to his feet and brushed off his ass. He took a deep breath and held it in, and when he let it out, he seemed to watch it rise invisibly into the ether.

"Good talk," he said. "Good talk."

With that he stumbled off toward the tree line, presumably to take a leak. About halfway there he lost his footing on the sloping grass and fell on his ass. He laughed as he bumbled to his feet, and I heard keys and change rattling in his sweatpants pockets. Resuming his journey, he began to sing, at least I think it was singing. After a minute or so, I'm pretty sure he fell into the bushes, because I heard him thrashing around in the brush and then the don't-you-feel-good-about-7Up-guy laugh.

Upon returning from his adventure, Big Bill took one last epic pull on the Carlo Rossi, managed to swallow most of it, smacked his lips, and looked thoughtful.

"You know," he said, wiping his mouth with a bare wrist. "It's funny the distance between looking forward and looking back."

That was his closer. I'm not sure what all he meant by it, but it must have been a good summation as far as he was concerned, because it was the last thing he said. He lay on his back with his arms behind his head and looked up at the sky. He had a smile on his face. There were twigs in his hair. He was humming under his breath. Thank God he didn't have a guitar.

My mind sought corners for refuge. I sat there beside him for a while, percolating, knowing I was poised on the edge of decisive action, but not rushing it.

Eventually Big Bill stopped humming, and within fifteen minutes he started mumbling inaudibly. Soon he was snoring in apneic fits. Looking down on him, I forgave him all over again. He seemed kind of childlike there in the grass. He had a red ring around his mouth from the Carlo Rossi jug. His Ray Conniff bangs were pasted crookedly to his forehead. I had to forgive him, because the truth is, I wouldn't have had it any other way. Without the lie, the whole balance might have been disrupted. Lulu might never have been Lulu, I might never have been Will, and without all that pain, all the grunting, gas-inducing anguish of love and loss, what was left to gain?

It was a little nippy on the hill. If I'd had a coat, I would've covered Big Bill with it. But I didn't have a coat. Besides, with all that rippling girth, he had to be warm. If I'd had a pen and paper, I might have left a note. Or if I'd had anything smaller than a twenty, I might have left him some extra cash. But I didn't have any of that, and who was I kidding, anyway? Of course Big Bill would be okay. He'd navigated himself that far, he'd find his way back to Sausalito. He might get a little cold, but nobody would fuck with him. Who was gonna fuck with the Incredible Hulk, even if he was sleeping? I did what I had to, and I'd do it again. I fished the keys from the pocket of Big Bill's sweats and left him sprawled in the grass on Hippie Hill in the middle of the night. I could hear him snoring halfway to Stanyan. I'll bet he had good dreams that night.

The World's Longest Short Ending

⸺〰⸺

This time I didn't knock. I stole quietly through the unlocked door. Lulu was asleep on the hide-a-bed in the living room, bathed in the flickering blue light of the muted television. I kneeled beside her and watched the rise and fall of her breathing. I reached out to touch her hair when suddenly her eyes popped open.

"Shhh," I said.

"What are you doing here?"

"Shhh."

She sat up on her elbows. "You're drunk."

"Not so much. Shhh."

But it was too late. Footsteps padded down the stairs. The light in the foyer snapped on. Willow walked in. She was in a robe, still in the process of wrapping it about herself.

"William, what on earth—where's your father? What are you do-ing here at this hour?"

"It's okay, Mom," said Lulu. "Go."

Poor Willow looked helpless and bewildered standing there in her bathrobe. "But what—where's your—William, I—"

"It's okay," I said. "Everything's okay."

"But, darling, I—"

"*Mom*," said Lulu. "Go. Please."

Willow retreated, but not without hesitation, through the foyer and up the stairs.

I never took my eyes off Lulu. I kneeled there watching her glow in the blue light. I was looking for changes, looking to see her as though for the first time in my life, expecting something or some-body new to be revealed in her place. I'm sad to report that Lulu was just as beautiful as ever, and that underneath her nightgown sleeves her scars were beautiful, too. These things I know to be true, because I longed for Lulu Trudeau, Lulu *Miller*, as achingly as ever. And the force that drew me toward Lulu, whatever you chose to call it, was the same force that moved planets.

"He told you," she said groggily.

"Yeah."

She searched me for answers. "Everything?"

"More than enough. Why didn't you just tell me, Lu—about the baby—about all of it? Why did you let me torture you?"

She turned her face away so that I could see the little raised half circle on her cheekbone, faded pink and smooth with age. "I didn't want you to have to lose what I lost," she said. "Believe me, Will, it was better not to have known."

"Either way, I lost you, Lu."

"But you never lost hope."

"I never had any," I said.

Lulu cast her eyes down and faced the blue glow of the television screen. She looked so sad and beautiful with that light on her face that I couldn't help but reach out and touch her. I ran my thumb gently across her scarred cheek, and I swept the dark hair out of her face so I could look down into those bottomless blue eyes—the only other eyes through which I ever saw the world.

"So now you see," she said.

I cast my own eyes down, and they were burning. I closed them and they burned a hole straight to my heart. "Yes," I said. "Now I see."

And what I saw on the back of my burning eyelids was a future stretching out before me, and Lulu wasn't in it, and quite suddenly the future seemed vaster than ever before.

P.S.

And what about now? After all of this talk about the future and the past, what can I tell you now, with the benefit of hindsight, that could possibly illuminate anything? What can I tell you about the nature of love, the thickness of blood, or the delicate shades of truth? I could tell you that my father hums to himself now as he walks around Sausalito in a sweat suit, with a shock of grey hair atop his narrowing shoulders. But what would that tell you? I could tell you that Willow treasures the cards I buy her on Mother's Day each year, but then, she's had those coming for a long time. I could tell you that Lulu is the mother of two children, and that one of them is named William, but that might be giving you the wrong idea. I could tell you that I'm very successful and very happy, but then I'd be lying about one of those things.

So which among all of these philosophies, among all of those platitudes, is the one kernel of truth that has left its signature on my life?

That we are all a mystery to each other at the end of the day?

That you should never assume the conformity of the future with the past?

That despair does not know it is despair?

That the world is your idea?

Sorry, but I've got to go with the meatheads on this one:

No pain, no gain.

Acknowledgments

Thanks to my patient, loving, and endlessly supportive wife, Lauren; my friends and tireless advocates, Mollie Glick and Jessica Regal; my wise and witty editor, Richard Nash, along with everybody at Soft Skull, top to bottom; my entire family (whom I love very much and to whom I apologize for any small similarities to the Miller clan); my friend and trusty reader, Michael Meachen; some of my favorite writers, who consented to reading my little opus and even went further in praising it: Keith Dixon, Brad Listi, Adam Langer, Josh Emmons, Greg Downs, and Natalia Rachel Singer; my writers' group (Carol, Dennis, Suzanne) for supporting and believing in me; my old friend and fountain of book knowledge, Jan Healy (and everybody at Eagle Harbor Books); my friend and editing mentor, Mary Ribeski, at University of Washington Press; Harriet Wasserman for always reminding me that the word comes first; my best friend, Tup; Carl and Lydia, Matt Comito, Paul Miller at Crossroads Films, Roxy Aliaga at Counterpoint, Bryan Tomasovich and all my friends and kindred spirits in the fiction files (you know who you are!).